I0760483

Wine, Women, & Song

Wine, Women, & Song

Bubba the Monster Hunter, Season 3

John G. Hartness

Falstaff Books
Charlotte, North Carolina

Also by John G. Hartness

The Black Knight Chronicles - Omnibus Edition
Paint it Black
In the Still of the Knight
Man in Black

Scattered, Smothered, & Chunked - Bubba the Monster Hunter Season One
Grits, Guns, & Glory - Bubba the Monster Hunter Season Two

Year One: A Quincy Harker, Demon Hunter Collection
Heaven Sent - a Quincy Harker, Demon Hunter novella
Heaven's Door - a Quincy Harker, Demon Hunter novella
Heaven Help Us - a Quincy Harker, Demon Hunter Novella

Queen of Kats Book I - Betrayal
Queen of Kats Book II - Survival

From the Stone
The Chosen

Cover Design by John G. Hartness

Formatting by Susan H. Roddey
www.shroddey.com

ISBN-13: 978-1543049794
ISBN-10: 1543049796

Published by Falstaff Media
Charlotte, North Carolina
Printed in U.S.A

Contents

Acknowledgements

Thanks as always to Melissa Gilbert for all her help, and for trying in vain to teach me where the commas go.

The following people help me bring this work to you by their Patreon-age. You can join them at Patreon.com/johnhartness.

Sean Fitzpatrick
Sharon Moore
Sarah Ashburn
Wendy Taylor
Sheelagh Semper
Charlotte Babb
Carol Baker
Noah Sturdevant
Leonard Rosenthol
Lisa Kochurina
Patrick Dugan
Melinda Hammy
Jeremy Snyder
Emilia Agrafojo
Brian Tate
Michelle E. Botwinick
Candice Carpenter
Theresa Glover
Salem Macknee
Trey Alexander
Jim Ryan
Word of the Nerd
Tracy Syrstad
Russell Ventimeglia
Elizabeth Donald
Samantha Dunaway Bryant
Shael Hawman
Bill Schlichting
Steven R. Yanacsek
Scott Furman
Rebecca Ledford
Ray Spitz

Moon Over Bourbon Street

Chapter One

We were walking down Bourbon Street when my phone rang. I looked around. Everybody I thought had my number was walking next to me or near enough. After healing up from my little brother's attempted Apocalypse, we'd hit the road to New Orleans without leaving word with anybody where we were heading. So I was wading through a sea of inebriated humanity with Amy, Skeeter, and Uncle Father Joe, staring at boobs and drinking beer when Katy Perry starts singing "Roar" out of my right butt cheek. Now I like Katy Perry as much as any red-blooded man with a love for breasts and pop music, but I did not expect to hear her voice emanating from my nether regions.

I looked at Skeeter. "You reprogrammed my ringtones again, didn't you?"

He tried to look innocent, but he was three Hurricanes into the night, and that was a lot of alcohol for his skinny ass, so all he really did was smirk and giggle. I pulled the phone out of my pocket and dropped it into a nearby storm drain.

"Aren't you going to look and see who it is?" Amy asked.

I looked down at the gorgeous federal agent walking with my arm on her shoulders. "Nope. Ain't nobody I want to talk to that can't reach out and poke me if they want to say something."

"Nobody?" she asked.

"Amy, my daddy's dead, my brother's dead, I ain't got nothing to say to the woman that birthed me, and Uncle Erskine can't see to dial the phone no more. So nope, ain't nobody I want to talk to outside of y'all tonight."

"Awwww, ain't that sweeeeeet. The big stupid one loves everybody!" The voice came from the sidewalk right in front of me. I looked down at four college kids, athletes from the look of them, blocking my path and generally making a nuisance out of themselves.

"Son," I started, but Amy took my arm and moved me along the sidewalk.

"No point," she said. "If you don't kill it, it won't ever shut up, and if you kill it, you'll probably go to jail."

"Only probably?" I asked.

"Well, your girlfriend does work for the government, so no telling what kind of strings she can pull for you. But let's try not to find out, okay?"

"Okay," I said, pulled her a little tighter, and we all moved across the street away from the JV asshole team. I was mentally patting myself on the back for my improved impulse control when Skeeter's phone rang.

"Is that your daddy, Skeet?" I asked.

"No, it's—" I didn't let him finish, or answer. I just took the phone out of his hand and threw it high into the air. It made a beautiful arc, catching the last rays of the setting sun as it flew ten, twenty, thirty, forty feet into the air over the French Quarter, then came crashing down onto the roof of a bar without a discernible name. I heard the tinny strains of RuPaul fade into nothing as we kept walking.

"You don't change your ringtone near as often as you change Bubba's," Uncle Father Joe said, right before Handel's *Messiah* chorus blared from his shirt pocket. I snatched the phone out before he could even move his hand, much less put down the yard of beer he was drinking, to answer. The display said, "Archbishop," but the area code was New York, so I figured the caller couldn't be too important. I took the battery out of the phone, threw it down an alley we were passing, and shoved the phone in the cleavage of a girl working a pole outside of Big Daddy's Topless & Bottomless.

Joe looked at me and just sputtered for a second, like Sylvester the cat in a priest's collar. "Bu-bu-bu…y-y-you sh-sh-sh-sh-shoved—ow!"

I might have thumped him on top of his head to get him to quit stuttering.

"You shoved my phone in that woman's breasts!"

"That's right."

"Why would you do something like that?!?"

"I was out of dollar bills." Seemed like a perfectly reasonable response to me. Joe didn't seem to agree, but he also didn't look like he wanted to pick a fight over it, either.

"Did you at least see who was calling?"

"Yeah, I looked. It didn't say 'Vatican,' or 'Pope,' or even 'Jesus.' Just said 'Archbishop,' so I dumped it."

Joe's face took on a peculiar green shade, and he whirled around to bury his head in a nearby trashcan. "Skeeter, hold his beer," I said. Skeeter jumped to like a pro, keeping Joe's priorities straight and his beer safe. I stood there watching for a minute until I realized Amy wasn't standing next to me anymore. I found her leaning up against a building, cell phone pressed to her ear. She was nodding and generally not paying me any attention, so I walked over to her. She gave me the "hold on" finger, and I nodded. Then I leaned against the building next to her. After the third "uh-huh, yessir," in a row, I reached down and pinched her on the ass. When she jumped, I snatched the phone out of her hand, said, "Vacation, bye!" into the device, and dropped it into the beer of a passing tourist.

"Hey!" Amy and the tourist said at the same time. "That's my phone/beer!" They kept on shouting at me in unison. I was pretty impressed, until the tourist turned out to be one of the college kids from earlier, and he decided that would be the right time to throw a punch. He nailed me pretty good on the jaw and clipped his buddy's shoulder in the process. His buddy's beer went flying, and he turned to see the cause of all the ruckus.

All of a sudden I had four college-aged jocks and one very pissed off government agent glaring at me in the middle of downtown New Orleans. I knew which one I was more afraid of, but the jocks didn't seem to understand the severity of the situation. I turned to address the most serious threat first—always important in times of extreme danger.

"Amy, I'm sorry, but you know he ain't gonna fire you, and you're the one that said—"

The punk who punched me cut off my brilliant repetition of Amy's reasons we needed a vacation. "Look, you old fuck, you owe me a beer!"

I turned and looked down at him. He had the look of a rugby player, a little under six feet, squat build, thick chest, nose that's been broken enough times to have its own identity, and a rugby shirt. His buddies all looked pretty tough, too, for kids who've never gone ten rounds with a werewolf or had to punch Bigfoot in the dick to survive. In contrast, I had a gorgeous woman who looked like a blonde Angie Harmon on my arm, a black gay tech super genius who weighed a buck-fifty soaking wet, and a forty-year old man in a priest's collar. I wouldn't have been afraid of us, either, if I wasn't the size of an average door and had more tattoos than the crew of a Navy destroyer. As it was, I decided that in the name of vacation, I'd give the kid one more shot to keep all his blood on the inside of his body.

"Junior, I don't reckon you realize this yet, but I've done give you two strikes for free. I moved on instead of beating your ass when you got in my way the first time. Then I didn't break your arm when you punched me because I'm on vacation and going to jail wasn't in my plans for tonight. But if you don't shut the hell up and get out of my face right the hell now, I'm going to hurt you. Then I'm going to hurt you some more. Then, if you ain't done being stupid, I'm going to move on to the 'hurt you very much' part of my evening. Now what's the plan, little man? We gonna move on with our drinking, or am I gonna have to beat your ass for you?"

One of his buddies, the oldest one by the looks of it, grabbed Dumbass's arm. "Come on, Cody. We don't need to get in a fight out here on the street."

"You're right," Dumbass agreed. "I'm going down this alley. If you want me to leave you alone, come back here and do something about it." With that, he turned and walked off down an alley between two bars.

I watched him go, then looked at his friend. "So you're the smart one, huh?"

"I've seen eyes like that in the sandbox, sir. You've been in the shit once or twice."

"Good call, soldier. I'm going to let your friend go down that alley, and I got no need to follow him. I ain't got shit to prove."

"Yes, sir. I didn't much like the idea of getting my ass kicked on his account tonight, anyway." I held out a hand to young soldier, and we shook, sharing that look that men have when they've, as he put it, "been in the shit once or twice."

I took one step back toward The Famous Door, one of my favorite music clubs in the Quarter, when Skeeter grabbed my arm.

"I think we've got a problem, Bubba," Skeeter said, pointing down the alley.

I looked to where he was pointing and said, "Shit. Amy, call the local office. Tell 'em you're on the clock."

"I can't. You killed my phone."

I looked at the soldier. "What's your name, kid?"

"Davis, sir."

"Davis, my very attractive government secret agent girlfriend needs to borrow your phone to call a branch of the government that doesn't exist and tell them that we're going into that alley to beat the shit out of something that isn't real, so if they hear about us getting arrested, they can come make sure we were never here. Got that?"

"I was Marine Force Recon, sir. Sounds like every weekday to me." Force Recon? Hell, I might not have been able to whoop his ass after all. "Sir?" he went on. "What's down that alley? I don't see anything."

"That's the problem, son. It's a straight alley and a dead end. Where's your friend?" I asked.

"Son of a…" He started toward the shadows, but I put a hand on his chest. His friends were looking distinctly uneasy at our conversation.

"No," I said. "Leave this one to the pros. Take your boys, go to Pat O's, we'll send your buddy along when we get him back."

"Will you? Get him back, I mean."

Joe stepped forward. I let him. This part was more his bailiwick anyhow, the whole dealing with worried people thing. I was usually what people were worried about. "We'll find your friend. What was his name? Cody?" The boy nodded. "We'll find Cody, and whatever is in that alley, we'll take care of it. This is what we do."

Amy hung up and handed the phone back to Davis. "There've been reports of a vampire hunting the Quarter the past few nights, but the local office has nothing to confirm."

"I'm pretty sure we're about to give them confirmation," I said. "Who's packing?" I pulled a Glock 19 from an ankle holster. "I've only got lead, no silver."

"I've got silver," Amy said, checking the chamber of her Sig Sauer.

"I didn't bring anything," Skeeter said.

"I feel safer already," I said with a grin. My best friend since middle school gave me the finger.

"I have holy water-tipper hollow points," Joe said, holding up a little Ruger LC9 with a fixed laser.

"Okay, I'll take point. Joe, you're in the middle. Amy, you've got the rear," I said. "Skeeter, stay near the mouth of the alley and keep a line open to the local field office."

"You threw my phone away," Skeeter protested.

"Use your spare," I replied.

"How did you know I have a spare?"

"You didn't cry when I broke the other one, and I know if you go more than twenty minutes without checking Facebook, your eye starts to twitch. Now let's go hunt a bad thing." I turned and headed down the alley with my Glock in front of me and a bad feeling in the pit of my stomach.

Chapter Two

WE GOT ABOUT THIRTY FEET DOWN THE ALLEY BEFORE THERE was any hint of bad things happening. I kept my eyes to the ground, scanning for clues and counting on Joe to watch the rooftops and windows. Our first clue that something was out of order was the flip-flop on the ground. All the chumps that hassled me had worn the universal uniform of the Southern Douchebag—striped dress shirt rolled up to the elbow, khakis or khaki shorts, college baseball caps, and Rainbow brand flip-flops. And here was a Rainbow flip-flop laying in the alley at the base of a wall. I looked up and saw nothing, but a flicker of movement a little to my left caught my eye.

"I got an open window, third floor," I said, pointing up for Joe to see.

"I think your drainpipe-shimmying days are behind you, Bubba. How do you think you're getting up there?" Joe asked.

"He's not," Amy said from behind him. "I am."

I saw her holster her pistol and take off her belt. She started to unbraid the paracord belt and put one end of the line between her teeth. She stepped into my hand, and I put everything I had into the most important caber toss of my life. I flung her upward and outward, aiming for the wall across the narrow alley. My girlfriend flew up and landed perfectly with both feet on the second-floor windowsill across the alley, then used her momentum to spring off the narrow ledge upward and back across the alley to catch the open window with her fingertips. There was a heart-pounding moment as she scrabbled for a grip, but then one foot found purchase and she hauled her cute butt up and into the open window.

I looked at Joe, held my hands out, and said, "You next."

His eyes got saucer-sized, and I almost peed my pants laughing at him. "I'm kidding, Joe," I said, trying to keep my voice low. "She'll drop the paracord in a sec and you can climb up." Sure enough, right as the words came out of my mouth, a narrow line of black rope descended from the window to dangle in front of Joe's face. He wiped his hands on his pants, white-knuckled the thin line, and scampered up faster than I expected for a man whose daily exercise most days is hunting the right Bible verse.

Once Joe vanished through the window, I took a wrap around one fist with the paracord and hauled my gigantic butt up three stories and heaved my sweating carcass through the window into an empty apartment. I sat on the floor for a second rubbing the blood back into my fingers and catching my breath.

"There's nothing here," I said. Or panted, really. I'm not what anybody in their right mind would call a small guy, and climbing up the side of that building like old-school Batman was pretty rough. They call that stuff 550 cord for a reason. Good thing I only weigh 350.

"I wouldn't say nothing, Bubba," Amy whispered from across the room. I looked at the floor where she had her flashlight pointed and saw a still-wet drop of red on the floor.

"Whatever grabbed that idiot doesn't have much of a lead on us," I said, heaving myself to my feet and drawing my pistol again. "Let's play follow the blood spatter."

The drops led us to a room three doors down and across the hall, where a bloody handprint on the doorjamb gave the surprise away. Joe and Amy took up positions on either side of the door, and I stood square in front of it. We weren't going to bother with announcing ourselves. I figured the guns would do a good enough job of letting everyone know we had arrived. I lifted my right foot and rammed it into the door just beside the deadbolt. The door behaved as you would expect a door to when a giant man slams a size sixteen combat boot into it. It splintered at the lock, two hinges popped off, the top part of the doorjamb came clattering down, and a semicircle of drywall and plaster stove in beside the doorknob. I gave the beleaguered door a shove and it gave up the ghost, falling completely out of its frame and crashing to the floor.

Also on the floor was one skinny vampire with greasy blond hair and a velour frock coat. The vampire/Robert Smith cosplayer writhed on the ground clutching his head. I leaned down and said, "You were looking through the peephole when I kicked the door, weren't you?"

He glared up at me with his one good eye and snarled. His fangs dropped and I put three rounds from my Glock through his forehead. He fell to the floor, true-dead. "Look on the bright side," I said. "Now your head doesn't hurt anymore."

I held up my gun and spread my focus to the room. "I'm looking for a human. One of you idiots snatched him out of the alley a few minutes ago. His friends want him back."

"Why should we care what a bunch of humans want?" A short vampire with thinning hair walked up to me and bumped me with his chest.

"Did you just chest-bump me, Mighty Mouse?" I looked down at the top of his head, honestly baffled.

He stepped back a couple of feet and looked up. "What did you call me, human?"

"Where's the kid?" I asked.

"Don't know anything about a kid. Don't care. What are you doing in our lair? And why shouldn't I eat you just on principle?"

"First off, the blood trail led to your door, so I don't believe you don't know anything about the missing kid. Second of all, littlest Lannister, I'm in your lair on a rescue mission for a federal agency and the Holy Roman Catholic Church, so I've got God *and* the government on my side for once, and thirdly, Short Round, this is way more than you can order off the kiddie menu, so if you want some, come get some. But you'd better bring a damn army if you're planning to kick this ass," I said.

"Actually, Bubba, I kinda don't have any jurisdiction in Louisiana…" Joe said behind me.

"And I'm on vacation, so I don't really have any authority, either," added Amy.

"So you got no Church backup, and you got no government backup, you got nothing but three little pea-shooters and a shitload of attitude and now you bring that crap into *my* house?" The short dude's voice made it all the way to full-grown by the time he was done yelling at me, but he was still only about five-seven.

I took a deep breath, then let it out, centering myself.

"You gonna do something, you overgrown jackass, or you just gonna stand there panting at me?" Mighty Mouse said.

I stepped forward, planting one heavy foot on the little bastard's toes. He yelped and tried to pull back, but I had him pretty well nailed to the floor. Then I caught him on the chin with a roundhouse right that I threw from about three blocks away. He flopped back onto the floor, bending at the knees 'cause I was still standing on his toes. His head cracked into the floor with enough force to kill a human, or to knock a vampire out for a good five minutes. I didn't plan on needing any more than that.

I stepped past the knocked-out Napoleon and surveyed the room. There were five vampires and three humans. Two of the vamps looked pissed and two looked confused, like they'd never seen a human fight back before. The last one was sitting on a couch sipping blood through a straw and trying to suppress a laugh. I decided she was probably the one to make it out of the room alive, so to speak.

The two pissed-off vampires rushed me, but 9mm rounds to their legs dropped them before they got close. I heard shots ring out from Joe and Amy behind me, and another pair of vampires dropped. None of these guys were true-dead except for the one I killed when we first walked in. Seems if you do enough damage to the brain, it'll kill pretty much anything. I stepped forward into the apartment, grabbed a cheap wooden chair, and swung it into the face of the last vampire standing. He spun around once, then stopped and grinned at me.

"You think that's going to stop me?"

"Nope," I said. Then I slammed the chair into the floor, breaking it into a million pieces and jamming one of the longest chunks through his chest. He looked down at my impromptu stake protruding from his chest and fell to his knees. I kicked him in the face, and he fell backwards, dead for good.

I made stakes out of the rest of the chair legs and back and tossed a couple to Amy and Joe. I walked back over to where Napoleon was trying to get to his feet and reared back with a stake.

"STOP." The voice resonated with power, even without yelling. I turned to the window and saw a female vampire standing there, glass tinkling to the floor around her. She hadn't bothered coming in through the open part; she just took out wood, glass, and anything in her way. I stopped. So did Amy and Joe. I don't think I could have ignored that voice in the middle of a rock concert, or an avalanche.

She was a whiter shade of pale than anyone I'd ever seen, living or dead. Her hair was a muted auburn and fell down her back in loose curls. Her green eyes flashed with power, and her strong jaw and razored cheekbones spoke of a woman who put up with absolutely zero shit in her life. She walked past Joe and Amy and strode across the room to me, her long legs wrapped in black leather tight enough to be her real skin. A tight black sweater left very few of her curves to the imagination, and it looked like a road that was meant to be traveled. She stepped up to me and took the stake out of my hand, then took the pistol from my other hand, popped the magazine, ejected the round from the chamber, slid it into the magazine, and put the mag back in the gun.

She leaned into me, grabbed my belt just above my Not-So-Little-Bubba, pulled my pants forward, and shoved the pistol into my jeans.

"We won't be needing to shoot anyone tonight, will we?" she purred, taking a few steps back and shifting so she could see Amy and Joe in her peripheral vision.

"I might agree with that if I knew who you are and what you did with a certain stupid college kid that I climbed all this way to find."

"My name is Catherine, and I am the Master of the Crescent City. All the vampires in this town are under my protection. Even these. And you have killed several of my people. That must be answered, human." She gave me a glare.

I gave her a shrug back. "Sorry about your idiots," I said. "Now you wanna fight some more about the idiots I killed, or you want to count your blessings that you got here in time to save the few you got left? Then you can help us find our idiot, and we can return the very important drinking we were engaging in until a few minutes ago."

She looked at me for a long moment, then threw her head back and laughed. I laughed with her because, in my experience, when somebody is laughing with you, or even at you, they are way less likely to try to kill you than other times.

After a good belly laugh, Catherine sobered up and looked at me. "You all will come with me, and we will talk about your idiot friend. I will forgive the killing of my idiot children, and we shall be, how do you say it, square?" Her accent got heavier and her eyes got smokier the more she talked, and I decided that going anywhere with this woman was probably a terrible idea.

"Let's go," I said, proving once again that I am a man with poor judgment and worse impulse control.

Chapter Three

WE WALKED ACROSS THE HALL, AND CATHERINE OPENED THE door into a well-appointed parlor, complete with two small couches, several armchairs, and a chaise lounge. I stood behind an armchair facing the door and watched everybody take up positions roughly aligned to the points of the compass. Except Napoleon. The little vampire sycophant stood two steps to the left and behind Catherine with his heels together and hands clasped in back like a parody of a guard.

"Are you supposed to be guarding anybody, Mighty Mouse?" I asked. "'Cause if you are, you oughta think about keeping your feet shoulder width apart and your hands loose at your sides. It'll help your balance."

"My balance is fine, human," the short vampire said, but I noticed out of the corner of my eye as he spread his feet apart and took a more balanced stance.

"So what are we doing over here that we couldn't do across the hall?" I asked once Napoleon closed the door.

"We are talking, Bubba. Is that so strange between your people and mine?" Catherine replied.

"Well, in my experience, there are only a couple of outcomes of a run-in between 'your people' and 'my people,' and that's my people getting eaten, or your people getting dead. And I'll admit to being the cause of a lot of that getting dead over the years, so yeah, if we're just gonna talk, I'm a little surprised."

"We are just going to talk, Bubba, unless you have something else in mind, perhaps?" She stepped toward me and ran her fingers along my arm. Her very long, delicate fingers, tipped in nails the color of arterial blood, the same color as her lips, standing out against her alabaster skin like something from a painting.

"Nope," I said, taking her wrist and removing her hand from my bicep. "Not only do I not have anything in mind, if I did have anything in mind, I have faith in my girlfriend, the beautiful and lethal federal agent standing ten feet away from us, to correct that shortcoming."

Catherine laughed again, and I didn't have to look over at Amy to know she wasn't laughing. "I'm sorry, Bubba, and my apologies to you as well, Agent Hall. I mean no offense. I am simply a very old woman who occasionally likes to tease young men." I stiffened at her words, not at the flirty bits, but at the part where she knew Amy's name. This woman had a bad habit of knowing more than she was supposed to, and while I understood that master vampires had their fingers in a lot of pies, I didn't have to like it.

I glanced over at my girlfriend and knew from the set of her shoulders that she picked up on it, too. We needed to watch our step with this woman or we could end up permanent residents of The Big Easy. "Well, you've got us here, Catherine, what are we here to talk about?"

"I need your help." She said it simply, and it almost sounded like she was asking, but I could tell from her tone this was a woman who didn't like asking from help, especially not from a man. And a human one, even worse.

"I'm listening," I said. "But understand that we need to get to Cody before the vamp that took him turns him or kills him."

"I apologize for that," Catherine said, "but you are too late for him. You were too late for him before you ever started down the alley."

"What are you saying?" Joe asked.

"I'm saying that we found his body on the roof of the building across the alley, took steps to make sure he will not rise, and he will be returned to the authorities by sunup."

"So everything we did hauling ass up here, following a blood trail…" Joe looked confused.

"The blood was mine. I needed to speak with you. About the very vampire that took young Cody, as a matter of fact."

"You tricked us into coming here!" Joe was slow to catch on, but he'd made it to full-on pissed now. I held up a hand.

"Chill, Joe. She wanted to talk, and that was the safest way to lure us away from the street. Besides, if the kid was already dead, then no harm, no foul. If we find out later that she had something to do with it…"

"Then what, Bubba?" Catherine's voice was cold.

"Then I put you down like a dog," I said in a voice equally as frosty. "But until then, go ahead and pitch me your case. What can a set of Church and government monster hunters do for you, outside our jurisdiction, without our tech guru and with no real money or weapons to speak of?"

"Well, you aren't without your technical wizard. We brought him to you." She snapped her fingers and a vampire came in carrying Skeeter over one shoulder like a very pissed-off bag of profane dog food.

"Good lord, Skeeter, do you kiss…never mind, I don't want to know who you kiss with that mouth. Okay, lady, you found Skeeter. Good job, you found the one black gay dude in the middle of the whitest street in America while it's saluting heterosexuality on every corner."

"Don't worry, Bubba," Skeeter said. "I found my fair share of street corners, too."

I didn't want to think too much on that, so I turned my attention back to Catherine. "So you've got a rogue. What's the big deal? It's your city, just hunt it down or hire a freelancer. No need to trick us into helping."

"The problem is that this is no ordinary rogue. He is much more powerful than he rightfully should be, powerful enough to take out one of my four-man enforcer teams that went to collect his weekly corkage fee."

"His what?" Amy asked.

"Just like a restaurant charges a corkage fee if you bring your own wine, master vampires charge a fee to visiting vamps to hunt their territory," Catherine explained.

"So the rogue didn't pay and kicked the shit out of your guys," I said.

"That is an accurate, if unfortunate, summation of events," Catherine agreed.

"Well, excuse me if I'm fresh out of shits to give, but that seems a whole lot like an internal vampire issue, not a hire a monster hunter issue," I said.

"I need your help," Catherine said, a slightly frantic note entering her voice.

"I'm on vacation," I replied.

"If you walk out that door, there will be war between your people and mine," she said.

"Do you think we care?" Amy asked. "First of all, we just came out of a war and we're still standing. Second of all, if you threaten my people again, I will call in a drone strike and nuke every hidey-hole you've gotten straight to glass."

"What about money? I can pay for help."

"We're not mercenaries," Joe said. "We work for the Vatican. You know, the city so rich it's also a country. If you want our help, you're going to have to come up with something better than that."

"Please, I don't know what else to do. This bastard has killed a quarter, maybe more, of my people, and I'm at a loss. I can't find him using my typical means, and I don't want any more of my people to die."

"Okay," I said.

"Okay?"

"Okay," I repeated.

"You mean you'll help me?" she asked, her eyebrows knit.

"Yeah, of course. It's kinda the job. We just wanted you to ask nicely."

The vampire matron's eyes got big, and judging from the look on her face, she couldn't decide whether to crap herself or go blind, but after a few seconds of apoplexy, she got herself under control and stuck out her hand. "So you'll help me find and dispose of this rogue vampire?"

I shook her hand. "We'll help you find the rogue, and if it's the threat you claim it is, we'll help you put it down. But you gotta play straight with us on everything about this rogue and his activities, starting with the idiot tourist we were looking for."

"Deal," she said. "As I said, he will be found by the authorities before sunrise. By the rising star of the New Orleans Police Department Homicide Squad, Detective Louis Ponté."

"And how will Detective Ponté know where to look?" Amy asked.

"I am very good at my job, Agent Hall," came a voice from the hallway. A good-looking man in his early thirties stepped into the room, all relaxed lean muscle and perfect teeth. Louis Ponté was the kind of guy that made guys like me grab our women tighter. His wavy blond hair was styled with some kind of gel that kept it in place even in the Louisiana humidity, and his smile made his blue eyes crinkle at the corners. He wore a light gray wool suit, black loafers, and a black belt. Everything on him either matched or coordinated, and I felt very much like the redneck who blows shit up for a living. Which is pretty damn accurate, of course.

Ponté stepped into the room and shook hands all around, finishing with Skeeter. I was a little surprised by that—usually dudes want to introduce themselves to Amy last, so they can linger over her hand long enough for me to growl like a Wookie.

"So where will I find young Cody's body?" Ponté asked. Catherine handed him a folded piece of paper, he looked at it, nodded, then tossed the paper into the cold fireplace. Catherine stared at the paper for a second, then it burst into flames. I jumped a little.

"I'm not your ordinary vampire, Mr. Bubba," she said with a smile.

"I'm not your ordinary incredibly well-armed dashing hero with a tendency to shoot first and ask questions later, Ms. Vampire." I gave her my best "piss me off and I'll floss with your intestines" smile. She took half a step back before she caught herself, and it was all I could do to keep from laughing out loud.

"So what's the plan? We don't know the lay of the land, so a police escort couldn't hurt," Amy said. I growled low in my throat, and Ponté looked up at me, like he'd just realized that Doberman wasn't asleep after all.

"I'll be happy to help however I'm needed," he drawled, his eyes barely flickering over to Amy. "But first, I believe introductions are in order?"

"Sorry about that, I've been downright remiss," I said, earning a raised eyebrow from Amy, who probably didn't think I knew what "remiss" meant. And honestly, I wasn't exactly sure. "I'm Bubba Brabham, Southeastern Regional Monster Hunter for the Holy Roman Catholic church. This here's my girlfriend, Agent Amy Hall. She works for DEMON, a government agency that don't exist. This is Uncle Father Joe. He's my handler, a Catholic priest, and Skeeter's uncle, thus the whole 'Uncle Father' thing. This over here—"

"I'm Skeeter," he said, stretching out a hand to the newcomer. "Technical wizard, surveillance specialist, whatever you need, tech-wise, I can handle it." Damn, Skeeter almost *swooned* over this dude.

And the dude at least had the good grace to blush, but he grabbed Skeeter's hand and shook it for a little longer than I thought was absolutely necessary and stared in his eyes the whole time. "Thank you, Skeeter. If I need any other resources, I'll be sure to come to you. First, I mean."

Amy and I exchanged glances, and I grinned. Seemed like Skeeter's crush on the pretty detective might be returned. "What's the plan, Detective?" I asked before the two of them went off picking out china patterns.

"I need to scout the crime scene, both the alley and the rooftop. Then I'll get back to you with my findings," he said.

"Fair enough," I said. "I'm gonna go tell his buddies that they're down a wingman, then I'm gonna gear up and start looking for clues, Bubba-style."

"I'll handle the notifications, if you don't mind," Ponté said. "It needs to come down through official channels, and I am those channels. And what exactly does 'Bubba-style' mean?"

"It means that he and I go lurk around cemeteries, voodoo shops, swamps, and other places where supernatural creatures are most likely to be found, then he punches them until they give us the information we're looking for. You'd be surprised how effective it is," Amy said.

"I think I'll stay with Detective Ponté and see what we can dig up from the crime scenes. I bet he can get me into their CSI lab as a visiting expert of some sort, and that'll give me a back door into the police department's computer system and all their records. That's about the best I can do working from my laptop," Skeeter said.

"I suppose that sends me to the Archbishop's office to coordinate with our people there. I don't know who the Hunter is for this part of the country, but I know it is customary to stop in for a visit whenever we're passing through."

"And what will you be doing, Ms. Master of the City?" I asked Catherine.

"Oh, the usual," she replied with a breezy tone. "Drinking the blood of tourists, overseeing my vast criminal enterprises, and trying to make sure that this goddamned interloper doesn't destroy the fragile peace I've built between the supernatural entities in this city before the sun comes up." Her eyes flashed and I was suddenly a lot more willing to accept her as the head vampire for all of New Orleans and the surrounding areas.

Chapter Four

"I HATE CEMETERIES," I MUTTERED AS AMY SLID BETWEEN THE GATES of St. Roch Cemetery #1. The rusted chain holding the gate closed left plenty of room for her slender form to fit between the bars, but there was no way the Bubba belly was getting through that tiny space. It was well after midnight, and the nearest streetlight was half a block away, so we were in pitch black, with just a couple of red-lensed flashlights to help us find our footing, or any bad guys.

"How can you hate cemeteries? Half of your working life is spent in cemeteries," Amy whispered, looking at me through the nine-foot gate leading into one of New Orleans' oldest cemeteries.

"Yeah, well, I'd rather be fishing," I replied, trying to no avail to jam myself through the gate. "That ain't happening. Got any other bright ideas?" I tried to keep my voice down and the gate noise to a minimum, but I've never been accused of excess subtlety.

"Sure, what about this?" She reached into her pocket and pulled out a small key ring.

"What's that?"

"Master keys for every U.S. manufacturer of padlocks." She spun the ring around, selected a key, and seconds later we were both inside.

"Why didn't you do that in the first place?"

"Sometimes, Bubba, it's worth it just to hear you gripe." She shot me a grin bright enough to see in a deserted cemetery in the middle of the night, and I gave her a quick kiss before getting down to business.

"Now what is it about St. Roch #1 that makes you think we'll find something here?" I asked.

"Honestly, it was just the closest of the old cemeteries to the latest attack. I figured if we're going to spend all night roaming through the halls of the dead, we might as well start with the nearest one."

"Huh," I said. "That's almost poetical. Halls of the dead. That's a lot prettier-sounding than graveyards or zombie farms."

Amy stopped walking and held up her hand. I froze, then looked down at her. She pointed at her eyes, then off ahead at her two o'clock. I followed were she pointed and saw a faint green glow in that direction. We stepped between the tombstones single-file, heel-toe in a slow crossover walk that kept sound to a minimum and left my right hand free to draw Bertha from my shoulder holster. I couldn't see what we were walking into, but usually if it was glowing in a graveyard in the middle of the night, it was bad enough that I was gonna be glad we went back to the hotel and got our medium-sized guns before we went out hunting.

Yeah, a Desert Eagle is my medium-sized gun. I know, I've got issues. Amy tells me that shit all the time, too.

I stepped left and waved Amy to the right as we broke forward into the same line of headstones as the light. I stretched my thumb forward and flipped the red lens cap off my flashlight, directing the xenon beam on whatever nasty thing was glowing in front of me.

Like a glow stick. A green glow stick laying on the ground in front of a skinny twenty-something kid who just about jumped out of his skin when me and Amy suddenly appeared out of the darkness with flashlights in his face and pistols pointed at his head.

"Whatthehell!" he screeched as he half-jumped up, then ducked back down, then turned to Amy, then spun back to me, then decided to just curl up in a little ball. "Please don't shoot me! I've only got like forty bucks, but you can have it if you just don't kill me!"

I looked at Amy, who stared at me with what I figured was probably a mirror to my dumbass expression, then I holstered Bertha and reached down to pat the kid on his trembling shoulder. "We ain't gonna kill you, kid. I promise. Just…stop with the yelling for a second."

He stopped hollering about getting killed, and Amy put her gun away. She kept her best federal agent voice, though, when she asked the kid, "Who are you and what the hell are you doing here?"

"My name is Jacob Wylie. I'm doing research for a school project."

"In the middle of the night?" Amy asked.

"I work until midnight at the casino to help pay for school. This is the only time I can come out to the cemetery and get my research done."

"What kind of research?"

"I'm doing grave rubbings," he said. I motioned for him to go on because I didn't have any damn idea what he was talking about. "It's a way to get information off of headstones when the writing has faded. I take a sheet of butcher paper and I tape it to the headstone. Then I rub the paper with charcoal to highlight the carving on the stone. When I take the paper down, the parts that are white are the parts where there was carving, and I can read it a lot easier than by the naked eye. I'm researching my family tree. They came to New Orleans back in the early nineteenth century, but a lot of our family records were lost. What wasn't lost was destroyed by Katrina, so I'm trying to rebuild my history back to the first ancestors that came here."

"Kid, it's not that I necessarily believe you, it's just that I think that story is too damned boring to be made up! I mean, damn, who in the world would come up with all that to justify being in a graveyard after dark?" I said.

"But if y'all ain't here to kill me, what are *you* doing in a graveyard in the middle of the night?" the kid asked.

"Hunting vampires," I said, and waited for the laugh, or whatever was coming. The last reaction I expected was the one I got: indifference.

"Oh, okay."

"You say that like it's something people do all the time," Amy said.

"Ma'am, I don't mean to sound rude, but we're in *New Orleans*. Hunting vampires down here is no stranger than hunting gators. I mean, Anne Rice does live here, you know. And a fair number of her fans have moved here, too. And they all gotta make a living. Vampire tours are second only to voodoo tours in New Orleans. Now, if you're really not gonna kill me, I've only got a couple hours left before I have to go get some sleep, so I need to get back to work. And y'all only have about four hours of night left, so if you're chasing vampires, you'd best get on it."

"Sounds good," I said. "Good luck, kid."

"Y'all too," he replied. "Try not to get dead."

"Always the goal," I said. Amy and I slipped the red lens covers back onto our flashlights and moved off toward the center of the graveyard. I figured any chance we had to sneak up on anything went out the window with all the yelling, but we might as well check out the rest of the cemetery before we moved on to the next one on the list.

And I was right. We saw nothing else out of the ordinary in St. Roch #1, or St. Roch #2, or St. Louis Cemetery #1. It was less than two hours before dawn when Amy opened the gate of Lafayette Cemetery #1 and we stepped foot into our last graveyard of the night.

"Something's different," I said, drawing Bertha and checking that I had silver ammunition in the gun and cold iron in my spare magazine.

"I feel it, too," Amy said. "Can you hear or see anything?"

"Nothing, but this place just feels wrong. Let's see what we can find." I started down a main aisle of the cemetery, the ubiquitous above-ground tombs pressing in on me from all sides. The light from my flashlight penetrated just a few feet in front of me, and the dark was almost palpable. I felt Amy's hand on the small of my back, using touch to guide her when her sight failed.

We'd wandered through the cramped graveyard for a good fifteen minutes before I stopped in mid-stride. Amy froze behind me, then dropped as I went down to one knee.

"You hear that?" I turned back to Amy and whispered.

"Barely," she replied. I listened harder, trying to pick words out of the air. It was a faint chanting, like at a great distance, but it was there underneath the car noise, the far-off party sounds of the Quarter and the chirp of cicadas in the weeds. I crept forward, trying to pinpoint a direction, and the chanting got louder. I turned left, deeper into the cemetery and toward the noise. I could discern voices now and pick out the occasional word.

"Sounds like some kind of ritual," I said, creeping forward.

We broke into a clearing, and it was indeed a ritual, but not one I'd ever wanted to see. Half a dozen people stood around an empty grave, with an open casket resting on a pile of dirt next to the very recently created hole from which the casket had emerged. Lying on the ground at the feet of what I assumed to be the high priest was the most recent occupant of the casket.

The high priest was a powerfully muscled black man, over six feet tall and a good two-twenty if he was an ounce. He stood over the body and chanted, wearing nothing but a necklace of bones and feathers.

Amy let out a low whistle, and I waved her to silence, but it was too late. Every eye in the voodoo circle turned to face us.

"Oops," she said. Then, recovering from the shock of finding a naked man making a zombie in the middle of the night, she stepped forward. "Hi there," she said. "I'm Agent Amy Hall with DEMON, the Department of Extra-Dimensional, Magical and Occult Nuisances. This is my partner, Bubba, and we're looking for a rogue vampire. Anybody seen him?"

Chapter Five

HAVE YOU EVER NOTICED HOW GRUMPY PEOPLE GET WHEN YOU interrupt their black magic zombie-making rituals to ask an innocent and completely unrelated question? Maybe this just isn't something that happens to normal people, but I have found that at no time in my life have I stumbled across a man butt-naked in a cemetery in the middle of the night that had much of a sense of humor intact. Well, there was that one time with a high school football coach in Newberry, South Carolina, but that had a lot to do with a bachelor party.

Well, this situation was not a bit different from all those other times I'd stumbled across naked men with bodies chiseled out of obsidian raising the dead in a graveyard late at night. You know, I think this was the first time I'd ever run into a good-looking man performing necromancy naked in the wee hours of the morning. Usually necromancy was kinda like community theatre—the people willing to get naked at the drop of a hat are not the people you want to see naked in the first place. I had run across my fair share of knobby-kneed basement-dwellers trying to bring Aunt Sadie back from the dead, but this dude looked like he could handle himself in a fight. And he probably could handle me in a fair fight, too.

With unpleasant memories of naked Sasquatch grappling running through my head, I drew Bertha and pointed it at the High Priest's most valued member of his congregation. "I don't want to fight, but if I have to start shooting, you can see where my first target is."

The priest nodded and waved his fellow zombie-makers back. "What can we do for you this evening?" He looked at me with steady eyes, and I made it a point to look him right in the eyes as well. For one thing, I didn't need any more insecurity in my life.

"We're chasing a vampire. A bad one, not one of Catherine's crew." At the mention of the Queen Vamp of New Orleans, the priest spat in the dirt. "You're not a fan?" I asked.

"I am the High Priest Edgar of the Holy Church of the Afterlife. I am a man of God, and I do not answer to some undead bitch with fangs and fetish wear." A chorus of amens met his declaration, and I gave my first look to Edgar's half dozen followers. They were a cross-section of mid-thirties and forties New Orleans citizenry, two white, three black, and one Asian dude. Four men, all in relatively good shape, one skinny woman and a white woman in her thirties who looked like she approached every buffet table the same way I do: like a challenge to be conquered. Their clothing was varied in style and budget, from work boots and jeans to a designer dress. They were apparently only brought together by their desire to see this dead dude come back to life.

"So, what's going on here?" I asked. "Y'all making a zombie, or having a séance, or did I stumble on something really freaky?"

"This man, James Artile, was a member of our flock who was killed in an automobile crash several days ago. It was his greatest desire to serve as a member of our congregation even in death, so we are calling upon the spirits to return him to us."

"Yeah, because nothing ever goes wrong with that idea," Amy muttered beside me, then spoke up. "Look, I'm going to ask very nicely, once, that you return the nice dead man to his casket and then put him back in the vault and fill in the hole. While you do that, we're going to look around for a vampire. How does that sound?"

I never heard how that sounded, because right about then was when the zombies attacked. Not Edgar's zombie, who he hadn't ever actually turned into a zombie, but a pack of half a dozen zombies, all armed and way more nimble than I was used to out of dead dudes. They came at us silently, a fringe benefit of not having to breathe, and wielding machetes and metal pipes. Two of Edgar's followers hit the dirt in the first few seconds, one bleeding out from a neck wound and the other unconscious from a shot to the head with a pipe. The other four worshippers ran off into the night, the whole raising of the dead thing now a lot more immediate and painful than it had been mere moments before.

With the innocent bystanders out of the way, I drew Bertha again and dropped a pair of zombies in quick succession. Amy put three in the face of two more walking dead, then we turned to see Edgar hand to hand with one of the remaining zombies. The last zombie raised its arm to cave in Edgar's skull, and I shot it in the back of the head with Bertha. Brains splattered all over the big man, who shot me a grateful grin. Then he dropped his arms, taking the last zombie off-balance, and twisted its head until we hard a sharp *crack*.

"I'm guessing those weren't yours?" I asked Edgar.

"No, not at all. They were not members of my flock, and I recognized none of these men." That's when I realized that all our assailants were men.

"What does that mean?" I asked Edgar.

"It could mean nothing," he admitted. "There are many practitioners in the Quarter, and not all of them like to share the cemeteries. It could just be a random attack from someone who doesn't want me playing in their sandbox."

"Or it could be someone trying to interfere with us," Amy said.

"Which, given our normal tendency for sticking our nose in where it doesn't belong—" I started.

"And the number of times people have offered to remove that nose for us—" Amy continued.

"Makes it a strong possibility that they were here for us," I finished.

"Yeah, the fact that there's another dozen coming through the headstones right now certainly makes me think this might be our problem," Amy said, then turned to Edgar. "As much as we appreciate the assist, you might want to get out of here now. These zombies are moving faster and better than the last set, and you've got an awful lot of exposed flesh to get bitten."

"If they are resurrected zombies, that should not be a problem. I would only be in danger if they were zombies created by disease, and therefore capable of transmitting the disease. But I will, in fact, take my leave of you at this time. Mother and Father spirits, please consign our unfortunate friend and brother back to your loving arms to serve you in death as he did in life. Let him know he would have been welcome as part of our undead flock, but circumstances did not permit it." Edgar reached down, flipped the dead body back into the vault, and slid the concrete lid back on. Then he picked up a backpack lying in the shadow of a headstone and ran off into the night, neatly dodging zombies as he did so.

"Did you see that?" I asked.

"I did indeed," Amy replied with a little bit of a dreamy look on her face.

"Not *that*," I growled. I'd seen more than enough of his *that* myself, but that wasn't the point. "He moved that vault lid all by himself, without a crane or nothing."

"Is that good?" Amy asked,

"Good? That slab of concrete must have weighed five hundred pounds if it was an ounce. He could have been some real help with this mess." I spun and fired twice, dropping two zombies in their tracks. I ejected the spent magazine and slapped a new one home.

"Duck," Amy said, her voice smooth as a lake at sunrise.

I dropped to one knee and looked behind me as another zombie's head exploded. I stood up and got back to back with Amy, and we made short work of the zombies. They weren't all that fast, and they weren't particularly well-armed, so it didn't take too much of a stretch to take them out.

After they were dead, we sat on a couple of headstones reloading our weapons and checking the bodies for clues. Okay, I was reloading Bertha while Amy checked the bodies for clues. I'm not much of the investigative type; I'm more the blow shit up and ask questions later type.

"Find anything?" I asked.

"Other than a couple of empty wallets and a condom, which is disturbing on so many levels, no." Amy sat on the ground by my feet and I leaned down to stroke her hair.

"Well, what do we know?" I asked. "Let's start from there."

"We know there's a rogue vampire in town. We know that he has the capacity to raise zombies, and we know that we haven't seen a vampire do that before, so I don't like it."

"I don't think we know that the vampire raised these zombies. Maybe it was an accomplice," I said.

"So we either have a vampire that can raise zombies, or a vampire with a friend that can raise zombies," Amy said. "I like neither of these things."

"You'll like this even less," Skeeter's voice crackled in both our ears.

"What the hell, Skeeter! I though you woulda figured out what team Detective Big Easy is on by now and be working your way through three hurricanes trying to find the courage to ask him out. Instead you're firing up the comm without telling anybody and scaring the shit out of me!"

"For one thing, I know exactly what team Detective Ponté plays for and am heading back to the hotel to get a shower and a quick shave before I meet that lovely bit of gator-bait for sunrise beignets at Cafe du Monde. For another, our corpse was gone."

"Gone?" I asked.

"Gone," Skeeter confirmed. "But not only was our corpse missing, so were the heads of the two vampires Catherine sent to dispose of the body. But the body snatcher was kind enough to leave a note telling us to get the hell out of New Orleans before dawn or there was gonna be hell to pay."

I chuckled. "I don't think whoever left that note understands the trouble they've opened themselves up for. Hell to pay? Shit, if that was all I had to pay, I'd call that a tiny bill. Did Detective Hair Gel get anything off the note?"

"He let the forensics people do their job. I'll ask him at breakfast. When are you two heading back? It's almost dawn."

"Yeah, but nobody told these guys," Amy said, pointing back into the cemetery where dozens of new zombies were making their slow but steady way toward us.

"Shit, Skeeter, I gotta go. We got more zombies to kill."

Chapter Six

I TURNED TO AMY. "HOW ARE YOU FOR AMMO?"

"I've got fifteen in the mag, one in the pipe, and one spare mag that's half-full from earlier. My backup piece carries six. What about you?"

"Pretty low," I said. "One full mag for Bertha, a couple rounds in another, the Judge loaded with buckshot, and a couple of knives, but those aren't real good against zombies." I looked around and picked up a shovel lying next to the emptied grave. "And this," I said, snapping the handle off behind the head and twirling the impromptu quarter staff around like a demented majorette.

I leaned the shovel handle against a nearby tomb and drew Bertha. The nearest zombie twitched at the sound of my holster snapping open and picked up speed in his approach. A couple of the other shambling corpses seemed to be shambling a little faster, too.

"Hey, Amy?"

"Yeah?"

"Do these guys seem to be moving faster to you?"

"Yeah, maybe a little, but—holy shit!" She squeezed off five shots in rapid succession as the four zombies nearest to her suddenly went turbo, all at the same time. Mine did the same thing, going from regular, staggering slow zombies to holy shit these guys are on meth or something zombies in the blink of an eye. In a couple of seconds, I went from having ten feet clear around me with a few zombies in my line of sight to three right on top of me with jaws gaping and teeth snapping and a solid wall of twenty of the undead bastards coming my way.

"Get back to back!" I yelled to Amy and felt her slam her shoulder blades up against the middle of my back. I crushed one zombie's head with Bertha's butt, then emptied the magazine in a half-circle of fifty-caliber death, dropping ten zombies with head shots. I ejected my magazine and slammed the spare home, squeezing off three more shots before it was spent. I holstered Bertha and drew the Judge, but its buckshot load wasn't gonna be nearly as effective the big Desert Eagle slugs.

I heard a pause in the shooting behind me and turned to talk to Amy over my shoulder. "You empty?"

"Yeah, just my backup left." That didn't stop her from reaching back to pull the Buck hunting knife off my belt and jab it through some shambler's eye socket.

"Climb up on the tomb," I said.

"I can't reach."

"Get on my shoulders," I said, turning around and grabbing her belt with my off hand. I put a face full of buckshot into the nearest zombie, but it didn't go down. I swung the shovel handle up under its chin hard enough to decapitate the monster, and it fell back onto its compadres, giving me a little breathing room. Amy scrambled up me, then pulled herself onto the roof of the tomb.

"Now what?" she asked.

"Now you stay on the roof while I go all Bruce Lee on a shitload of zombies." I reversed my grip on the Judge pistol and crushed the skull of a zombie climbing over the one I'd just shot. It went down like a sack of dead, smelly potatoes, and another one took its place. I lowered a shoulder and shoved it back like an old tackling dummy, then shoved off to create some distance and snatched up my new shovel/quarterstaff.

Now I've never trained in any martial arts, but I spent my whole childhood watching Kung Fu Theatre after church every Sunday, and me and Jason used to practice everything we saw on TV, which usually ended up with him not able to move very much on Mondays. So I've swung a stick around my head once or twice, just never when my life depended on it.

This time it definitely felt like my life depended on it. I couldn't tell if these were magical zombies like High Chief Edgar had talked about, or plague zombies like *The Walking Dead*, but I figured if they wanted to eat my kidneys, it didn't much matter. I still needed my kidneys, so we had a problem.

The first zombie took a hard shot right across the forehead and went down, brains obviously scrambled from the impact. Then I swung the staff back and forth crushing skulls as the zombies got within range. I heard a *crack* from above and felt, rather than saw, the body of a zombie collapse to the dirt behind me.

"Keep your back to the tomb," Amy barked. "I've only got five rounds left."

"Can you see an end to the walking corpses? My arms are getting tired," I said, then promptly proved my statement by getting my stick caught under the arm of the next zombie I swung into. I lost my grip and found myself on one knee, surrounded by what was probably four, but felt like a dozen snapping mouths and tearing fingers. The only thing keeping me alive was the notoriously bad fine motor skills of zombies—as long as they couldn't get their mouths on me, they couldn't quite figure out how to make their hands work enough to rip me apart.

I shoved one nasty dead face away and pushed it into the mouth of another zombie, who bit down on the first one long enough to let me stand and shoulder a couple more back. Amy emptied her magazine into the mass of death writhing on top of me and took out four zombies with five shots, but she couldn't go for the really close ones without hitting me. I felt my shoulders press against the concrete of the tomb behind me and went back down to one knee, pulling a zombie over my head and backwards as I went. This smashed his forehead into the concrete hard enough to make him perma-dead and give me a little cover as the other zombies couldn't figure out how to get through my once-human shield. But the sheer number and weight of them was starting to be a problem because it was almost impossible to draw a good breath without getting a face full of grave funk and wanting to puke all over my clothes. Of course, given what was smeared all over my clothes, a little puke might have been an improvement.

I was contemplating which smelled worse—Bourbon Street puke, which has a special air of cheap beer and frat boy horniness, or zombies—when one of the monsters at my right shoulder jerked backward, then forward, then dropped. Half a second later, the flat crack of a rifle shot reached my ears just as another zombie dropped off the pile.

"You still under there?" Father Joe's voice came across the comm, and I swear in that moment I found a little religion. I mean, I've always known that God exists, I just never thought he had a whole lot of use for his front-line employees, as it were. But in that moment, when Joe appeared from out of nowhere to save my ass, I *believed*.

"I'm here, and I am glad to see you," I gasped under the weight and stink of the zombies.

Two more fell before Joe replied. "Well, let's see if this old Remington has enough juice in her to take out a dozen or so zombies."

"A dozen? Is that all that's left?" I asked.

"Yeah, that's it. There's a good fifty wandering through the cemetery, but only about a dozen in your immediate area." Another zombie fell off the pile, and I could see a sliver of predawn sky through the animated corpses.

One more *crack*, one more zombie hit the dirt, then all at once, everything stopped. The moaning fell silent, the scrabbling at my zombie shield went preternaturally still, and the snapping and biting at my fingers ceased. Even the female zombie, who had latched onto my shin and was persistently trying to chew her way through my calf, stopped, all at the same time. Then, with an almost audible sigh, like a great escaping of breath, every zombie in the graveyard went still at the same time.

The ones on top of me collapsed, momentarily redoubling the weight on top of me, but then just *sliding* off to the dewy ground at my feet. I knelt there, surrounded by recently mobile dead people, holding one over my head as a human shield, but once I was relatively sure they weren't getting back up, I dropped the zombie I was holding, now just another corpse, and stood up.

Amy jumped down as I was taking inventory of my injuries. I had a bunch of bites and scrapes on my hands and wrists—those were going to need to be soaked in Neosporin and rubbing alcohol before I got infected. One ear was bitten pretty bad and might need stitches, but for the most part, I was in good shape. My Carharrt jacket and Duluth Trading Company firehose work pants proved to be fashionable and zombie-bite-proof options, as that chick zombie left some serious grave slobber on the back of my leg but never managed to get through.

"What the hell happened?" Amy asked, throwing her arms around me.

"Well, your incredibly chivalrous boyfriend sacrificed himself on the altar of true love by letting you climb onto the tomb and live while he fought off a ravening horde of flesh-starved monsters, only to be saved at the last minute by his faithful sidekick and something else that nobody understood."

"Sunrise," Joe said over the comm.

"What?" I asked.

"Sunrise," Joe repeated, and his voice was a lot closer this time. He came around a bend in the cemetery carrying a hunting rifle with a scope and wearing a grin. I hugged him, not only expressing my gratitude at him saving my life, but also making sure that he smelled as bad as the rest of us. I wanted him to really feel like part of the team. And in this case, smell like part of it, too.

"What's that about sunrise?" Amy asked.

"I don't know," Joe admitted. "I just know that the second the first beam of sunshine split the horizon, zombies started dropping in their tracks, and now they're turning to dust all over the graveyard. See?" He pointed at the piles of dead guys all around me, and sure enough, they were burning away like the morning mist.

Chapter Seven

"AND THAT'S WHEN I DECIDED THAT SOME OF NEW ORLEANS' world-famous beignets would be the perfect finish to our long and pretty disgusting night," I said to the table. We were at a far corner outside under the world famous green and white striped awning, and there was a conspicuous lack of seating at the tables nearest me. That might have had something to do with the fact that I hadn't bathed before coming to breakfast and was still covered in cemetery mud and zombie bits.

I expected the smell to put my much cleaner companions off their feed, but as soon as the waitress that drew the short straw, and I actually saw two of them play rock-paper-scissors for who had to wait on me, came over with a tray piled high with enough sugar-covered delicacies to fuel a regiment and enough coffee to float a tank, my companions dug in like a bunch of folks that just survived an all-night fistfight with the walking dead. As the only one who actually *had* been in a fistfight with the walking dead, I took two beignets before I passed the plate and started mainlining coffee right out of the pot. It's not my fault that a coffeepot in my hand looks like a demitasse cup in a normal person's.

"So you decided to join us for breakfast. How thoughtful." Skeeter's ironic tone was the driest thing to ever be found in the soggy Crescent City, and I didn't much blame him. After all, Detective Ponté was looking very dapper in khakis and a pastel green polo, with sunglasses that probably cost more than my boots. Skeeter looked pretty good for Skeeter, which meant he'd put on clean cargo pants and someone had run an iron over his short-sleeved dress shirt. At least he'd left the pocket protector at the hotel, so he didn't look like the complete stereotype of a computer nerd.

"What can I say, Skeet? Your call made me hungry."

"And my call didn't make you want to bathe?"

"Priorities, buddy, priorities. What have y'all found out about the rogue while we were busy fighting our way through all of *Z Nation's* season two extras?"

Detective Ponté leaned forward, taking a handkerchief out of his pocket and pressing it over his nose. I snorted a little, I couldn't help myself. "Our forensics people found nothing on the bodies, which were deteriorating rapidly. As you know, once a vampire is killed, the aging process asserts itself on the remaining tissues, so the older a vampire is, the more quickly the body deteriorates. These were relatively young vampires, only twenty or thirty years dead, but that's still a long time for a corpse to wander around, so when the laws of physics reasserted themselves on the flesh, it turned to goop within the hour. There were no tool marks on the bones, so we assumed that the heads were severed manually."

"Wait a second," I said, holding up a hand as he drew breath to continue. "By manually, do you mean with a hand tool like a knife or saw, or do you mean—"

"I mean manually as in by hand, yes." Detective Ponté nodded. "These heads were ripped from the bodies and left as a message for us."

"Well, that's evidence right there," I said. "There can't be that many critters that can rip a vampire's head clean off, can there?"

"That's a good point," Amy said, sipping her coffee. She had an adorable little trail of powdered sugar running down her chin and onto her shirt, and I was having some distracting thoughts about trying to make sure she was as clean as possible when she caught my eye and gave me her patented "work now, think dirty things later" glare. No matter how good I am at multi-tasking, I'll never convince my girlfriend that I can stare at her boobs and fight monsters at the same time.

She turned to Skeeter. "How many things can rip the head off a vampire and still function in an urban environment? I think we can safely rule out trolls and ogres; those would stand out even in New Orleans."

"Well, a strong enough lycanthrope could do it, depending on its were-shape and if it had the control to partially shift. An older vampire could do it, some species of Fae could manage it, and still look relatively humanoid. What else?" Skeeter mused.

"A golem," I added. "That thing the kid made last year outta rocks was strong as hell. A Sasquatch, and they blend in better than you'd think. A rakshasa *could* do it, but would be more likely to use swords or claws."

"The right type of zombie could manage such a thing," came a voice from over my shoulder. "And you stink to high heaven, white man." I turned and saw Edgar leaning on the wrought-iron railing surrounding the cafe's patio. He straightened up, stepped over the railing, and pulled out one of the empty chairs. "May I join you?"

"Please," Amy said, giving him a warm smile that made me growl a little in the back of my throat.

"Down, boy," my girlfriend muttered while still grinning at the voodoo priest who we'd last seen butt-naked in the middle of the cemetery where we'd been attacked moments after his departure.

"Fear not, large white man, I have no interest in your woman," Edgar said with an accent thick and slow as molasses.

"Oh cut the shit, Eddie, and tell us why you're here." Detective Ponté's posture had gone rigid the second Edgar appeared on the scene, and his voice was cold enough to freeze my coffee. Obviously the two men knew each other, and just as obviously it wasn't pleasant.

"I am here to help, Detective, whether you believe that or not. This is my city, too, and whatever affects her, affects me. And these new *houngans*, they affect me more than most."

"Because they make it harder for you to get girls to work in your clubs, Eddie?" Ponté's voice dripped with sarcasm.

Eddie picked up a beignet with the posture of a man who gave absolutely zero shits what the world thought about him. "I run a number of high-end gentlemen's clubs throughout the Quarter and New Orleans. Detective Ponté has been investigating me for years to make sure that all my business dealings are scrupulously honest, which they are, and that my girls are not being abused, which they are not. He has never found anything to arrest me, so he remains perpetually irritated with me."

"You're a sex trafficker, Eddie, and one day I'm going to put you away," Ponté said from behind a coffee cup and a glare.

"Perhaps, Detective, but today is not that day. Today is the day I wish to help you find these *houngans* who are upsetting the balance of my city,"

I leaned over to Skeeter. "I thought a *houngan* was a witch doctor, or a voodoo priest, kinda like Eddie." Skeeter elbowed me to be quiet, but it was too late.

"You are partially correct, Bubba," Eddie said. "But these false *houngans* are calling upon bad *loa* to give them power and wealth. Real voodoo is not about the gathering of money or the comforts of the flesh. We are about honoring our ancestors and making sure all souls have an easy passage through to the next life."

"So we've got rogue vampires, good vampires, bad voodoo priests, and good voodoo priests. How am I supposed to know which is which?" I asked.

"I'd start with the ones that aren't trying to kill you. They'd be what I'd call the 'good' ones," Ponté said. "Now what were you saying about zombies that can rip a man's head off, Eddie?"

"Some *houngan* will imbue their living strength, and even the strength of their followers, into the bodies they raise. This allows their zombies to be stronger and faster than the normal dead and accomplish feats like fighting vampires and decapitating them. But the *houngan* would have to be very close to control a zombie so precisely, or give something of himself to the zombie to tie them together. Otherwise a zombie would not have the speed or dexterity for a fight with a vampire."

"Yeah, that makes sense," I agreed. "The ones I fought last night weren't any stronger than a human and were pretty clumsy. No way they could handle a full-grown vamp."

"So how do we find these *houngan*?" Amy asked. "I doubt they have a sign hanging out on their front porch that says, 'Evil witch doctor here'."

"Don't be so sure," I said. "Tourist dollars being what they are and all."

"Bubba raises a good point," Eddie said.

"I do?" I asked.

"He does?" Amy's eyebrows went sky-high.

"First time for everything," Skeeter muttered simultaneously.

I glared at my friends, then turned to Joe. "Thank you for showing what must have been truly herculean restraint there, buddy."

He just grinned at me. "I figured as far as smartass goes, those two had us covered, so I'd just wait my turn."

"Screw every single one of you guys," I said with a half-grin. We'd been through a hellacious year, and if we were still tight enough to give each other shit in the middle of a zombie investigation, we were gonna be fine. Maladjusted and pretty much unfit for polite society, but fine.

"What I mean is that many of the *houngan* around town do advertise their services, and we may be able to find out a great deal about them through a simple internet search. Then a little in-person investigation would give us a great deal more information."

"That's my cue," Skeeter said, standing up to a distressed look from Detective Jawline. "You can come with me," Skeeter said to his disappointed beau. "The searches will go faster with some navigation from a local."

"I wish I could, *chere*, but I'm due at the station in an hour to fill out a mountain of paperwork about a missing tourist. I'll meet up with you after my shift and we'll grab dinner."

"If I'm not in the middle of killing vampires or zombies," Skeeter said. He leaned down and brush-kissed the detective's cheek, then headed up the street toward our hotel and his three travel computers.

"What's our plan?" Joe asked me.

"I'm planning on a shower, then a few hours of sleep. This coffee has enough juice to get me back to the hotel, but just barely. Then we see what Skeeter's dug up and go bang on doors."

"Sounds like a plan. What will you be doing?" Amy asked Eddie.

"I also need sleep, then I will ask my congregation if they know of any new *houngan* in the Quarter. I will meet you at your hotel at dusk to join forces and scour the town for these abominations."

"I'm headed to the station," Ponté declared. "I'll see you at sunset."

I grabbed the last of the beignets while Amy took care of the check, then we walked through the Quarter back to our hotel. I felt actually relaxed as I stepped off the elevator, but all that went out the window when I saw the door to our suite standing just a hair ajar. With no cleaning ladies anywhere to be seen, my mind went to monsters and my hand went to Bertha before I remembered she was empty and so was my backup.

"Take these," I whispered to Amy as I handed her my coffee and the bag of beignets. I drew my Buck hunting knife from a sheath under the leg of my pants, reversed my grip on it, and slammed the door to our room open, barreling through with the same speed I used to use chasing quarterbacks.

Catherine sat on the couch in our small hotel room, reading an Anne Rice novel. She looked up as I crashed into the room. "Oh good, you're home. Let's talk."

Chapter Eight

I DON'T LIKE SURPRISES, WHICH IS A PRETTY STANDARD MINDSET FOR a man who carries around a fifty-caliber handgun. I don't like vampires, despite meeting a couple of them that were actually pretty decent people. And I sure as hell don't like being surprised by vampires when I'm tired and covered in zombie parts, and I'm supposed to be on vacation anyway and not have to deal with shit that goes bump in the night for just one week.

All that whining is to explain why I walked past Catherine to the bathroom of our hotel room and started taking off my clothes, completely ignoring her request for conversation. I kicked my boots off barely breaking stride, and turned on the water to somewhere between "scalding" and "rip the flesh right off the bone."

I don't know what kind of womanly "men, what can you do?" kind of looks go exchanged between her and Amy behind my back, but with a blur and a breeze suddenly there was a vampire sitting on the bathroom counter. Her hair was pulled back in a tight bun, and her black sweater had been replaced by jeans and a Marie Laveau's House of Voodoo t-shirt. Her bare feet hung a foot off the floor and she looked as much like a goth college girl than the ruling vampire of the Crescent City.

"Don't let me stop you," she said, looking me up and down like a farmer eyeing a prize hog.

"I wasn't going to," I replied, and dropped my pants to the floor. I stripped out of my shoulder holster and laid it gently on the back of the toilet, then peeled off my t-shirt and dropped it to the floor of the bathroom with a wet *thwap* sound.

"Hey honey," I called out the open door to Amy. "I was going to invite you to scrub my back, but we seem to have company. Since all my plans for enjoying the morning have gone to shit, can you have housekeeping send up some extra towels, jumbo trash bags, and something to burn my clothes in?"

"Just as soon as I get room service ordered," came Amy's voice from the bedroom area.

"Didn't you get enough beignets?" I asked.

"I'm ordering lunch. You're going to sleep after we deal with Catherine, and then we'll both wake up starving." She really is the smart one of the pair.

"Okay, Catherine, what do you want?" I asked, peeling off my socks and throwing my boxers into a corner of the room. I spent years in locker rooms with coed reporters and various women coming and going for various reasons real and imagined, so undressing in front of a vampire didn't bother me. That, and I was still a little pissed that she broke into our hotel room, so I figured she needed to put up with a little of my crap in return.

I stepped in the shower as she started talking. "The rogue is getting stronger."

"We know. I just left Ponté and he told us about the head thing."

"The 'head thing,' as you call it, is just part of it. Another of my establishments was attacked last night, and three of my soldiers were killed. That makes six true-dead just last night, counting the ones you killed, and we can certainly lay blame for those deaths at the feet of this rogue as well. If this keeps up, I'm going to have to launch a recruiting drive, and the Mayor won't like that at all."

"Yeah, I can imagine that tourists going home from vacation with new dietary restrictions would put a cramp on business in the French Quarter," I said, shampooing my hair and beard.

"Not only that, but if this rogue is turning humans, he's building an army at the same time he's thinning my ranks. We may be heading toward a war that I can't win."

"No offense, Catherine, but why do I care which vampire wins? Both sides look at me like a cheeseburger, so why do I give a shit who wins and who loses?"

"Status quo," she said simply. "I'm the devil you know. I've ruled New Orleans for well over fifty years. Through ups and downs, through storms and floods, through Katrina, and the hurt that did to the heart of my city… my city…this is *my* city, Bubba, and I'll be damned if I'll let some upstart take what I've built and tear it apart."

"Okay, that makes sense," I said. "We'll keep looking. There's some kind of connection between this bad voodoo priest and your vampire king wannabe, we've just got to find out what it is. And I think I know exactly how to do that."

"How is that?" She asked.

"Can't tell you," I said, pulling open the shower curtain and reaching for a towel. Catherine had the courtesy to vacate the bathroom so I could dry off, probably because I take up almost all the available space in a bathroom, and I've got almost as much body hair as a werewolf, so it takes a lot of towels to dry me off.

I stepped out of the bathroom a few minutes later smelling better than I had in hours and wearing a towel mostly around my waist. Catherine and Amy were sitting on the bed laughing and giggling like schoolgirls, but they fell silent when I walked in.

"Well, that's enough to make a man paranoid—the object of every fifteen-year-old boy's fantasy sitting in his hotel room, but they stop talking the second you walk in."

"Don't worry, Bubba, Catherine was just commenting on how different men were today from when she was turned back after the War."

"Civil?" I guessed.

"American Revolution," Catherine corrected. Holy shit, I was in my hotel room with an almost two hundred fifty-year-old vampire. That was some serious power. No wonder she was able to run New Orleans without any problems. Until now, that is.

"Let's revisit this plan of yours that you can't tell me about," Catherine said, leaning back against the headboard of my bed and causing all sorts of naughty ideas to run around in my otherwise completely empty skull.

"Plan? Oh yeah, the plan. I can't tell you about it," I said, walking over to the dresser. If there's one thing I've learned, it's that traveling with a woman is different from traveling alone or with all guys. For one thing, the dresser actually gets used, and not just as a place to put your car keys. Amy actually unpacked all our crap and put it in the dresser for the week we were going to be there. If I was traveling alone, I'd just wear the same jeans for a week and change underwear and t-shirts out of a duffel bag, or a trash bag if I couldn't find my luggage. That idea didn't go over so well with the girlfriend.

I pulled on my boxers and jeans, then turned to face the irritated vampire standing behind me. "I said I'm not telling you my plan, and I'm not. I don't trust your organization."

"Why not? And put a shirt on, I feel like I'm standing next to a grizzly bear."

"I didn't invite you in," I reminded her.

"That only matters for permanent residences, not hotels."

"I meant that I don't need to be all that polite to you, since you broke in."

"Oh. I suppose that's true. But why don't you trust me?" She gave me a little pout, and I felt a pressure behind my eyes, like someone poking around in my head.

I opened a drawer and pulled out a faded Langhorne Slim t-shirt, then reached back into the drawer and pulled out a silver stake. "Let's be real clear, Cathy. I understand that you're the baddest vampire in New Orleans, and we're working together under some kind of unofficial truce, but if you try to compel me, or anybody with me, to do anything again, I will shove this stake through your heart, then cut off your head and burn your head and body in two separate fires. Then I will scatter the ashes of those two fires on the grounds of different cemeteries and wash them into the earth with holy water. If that doesn't scream true-death to you, then I don't know what will. Now stay the hell out of my head."

She pouted at me. "Can't blame a girl for trying, can you?" But the pressure in my head relented.

"I don't blame you for trying, I just wanted to make the consequences real damn clear." I dropped the stake back into the drawer and closed it, then went to sit on the couch. "Did you want something else?"

"No. Since you won't tell me your little plan, I suppose you won't tell me when you're planning to perform it, so I can't have you over for a late dinner this evening, can I?"

I forget sometimes just how different from normal, breathing people the undead really are. Especially the ones that are starting to look at time in centuries rather than years. For a human, the most important thing in the world would be stopping a crazed vampire hell-bent on taking over your city. But to a vampire, planning a dinner party took precedence over keeping her city under control. I guess when you think life never ends, you kinda take the long view of things.

"No, I'm sorry Catherine, but we're going to be busy trying to keep your city from crumbling around you. Now if you'll excuse me, I need some sleep if I'm going to do that."

She gave me a little nod of the head. "Of course. I'll leave a pair of my security team here to make sure you're not disturbed."

"That's fine, but if they so much as press an ear to that door without my invitation, I'll put a hole in their head the size of a softball."

She smiled and glided out of the room, stopping to say something quietly to the goons standing outside. I guess they'd been on a concession run when I got there. I walked into the room, pressed my finger to my lips, and pointed at Amy's suitcase. I waved a finger around the room in circles, and she nodded.

Amy opened her suitcase and pulled out a small black plastic waterproof case. She dialed a combination on the case and opened it, taking out a small handheld device that looked like a carpenter's stud finder. She walked around the room waving it at the lamps, phones, windows. After a couple of minutes, she flicked a switch on the box and collapsed the antenna.

"We're clear," Amy said, sitting back down on the bed.

"Almost," I said. I walked into the sitting area of the room and flipped on the TV. I set the volume on MAX and went back into the bedroom. "Now we're clear," I said.

"So what's the plan?" she asked.

"Walk around Bourbon Street and try to attract a vampire." I tossed the plastic case back into her suitcase, then put the suitcase on that odd folding thing that hotels put in every room and only gets used when women travel. Guys just put their suitcases on the ground.

"That's the big secret plan?" Amy gaped at me from the bed.

"That's part two of the big secret plan," I said. I dropped my t-shirt on top of Amy's suitcase, then skinned out of my jeans.

"What's part one of the big secret plan?" she asked with a smile.

I scooped her up into my arms and threw her on the bed. "Make enough noise the security guards don't have any questions as to where we are and whether or not we're safe." I grinned and laid down next to her, pulling the covers up over both of us.

Chapter Nine

DARK FELL ON NEW ORLEANS, AND THE CITY REALLY CAME ALIVE. The bustling tourist city of daytime New Orleans shifted into something darker, more primal, dirtier, more *real.* In short, my kind of place. Amy and I stepped out of our hotel onto Bourbon Street and I stood there for a second, letting the primal urges of humanity wash over me.

"You love it here, don't you, Bubba?" Amy asked, a note of surprise in her voice.

"Darlin', I've only found a couple cities in my life where I really felt like I could stand to stay for a while. This is one of 'em. I guess in the back of my mind I always hoped I'd retire here, buy a little jazz club, make the best damn margaritas in town, and spend the rest of my days listening to incredible musicians and pouring drinks for tourists."

"I never knew that," she said, a little smile playing across her lips.

"Hell, Amy, don't feel bad. I've known him since before he could drive, and I never knew that." Skeeter's squeaky voice could ruin even the sweetest moment, and this one was no different. I turned, and my best friend had a good-looking police detective on his arm and smile on his face fit to beat the band. Looked like I wasn't the only one to get a nap this afternoon. Skeeter looked like a cross between a stereotypical tourist and The Joker from *The Killing Joke* in a Hawaiian shirt, bright pink shorts, and brown loafers with black socks pulled up almost to his knees. Detective Ponté was much more the picture of New Orleans dress casual in khakis, loafers, and a short-sleeved pastel dress shirt untucked to hide his service weapon, or so I assumed.

Amy wore a light jacket for the same reason, with her Sig at the small of her back in a paddle holster. I had my Langhorne Slim shirt from earlier, jeans and my Doc Martens, with a Hawaiian shirt of my own hiding Bertha in a shoulder rig. But I wore it better than Skeeter. Might have had something to do with the socks.

"What's the plan?" Ponté asked. "Catherine was plenty irritated when you wouldn't share it," he said with a grin.

"I already sent Eddie off to check the cemeteries, so we wander around together, then split off and try to look attractive to vampires," I said.

"That's it?" Ponté asked. "That's the plan you wouldn't share with Catherine?"

"Yep." I nodded.

"What's the big secret to that? It's kinda the logical thing to do," the well-dressed detective said.

"Yeah, but she pissed me off, so I was being petty."

"That could come back to haunt you later," he said.

"I doubt it," I replied. "I've got a long history of not being the thing you want to mess with in the dark."

"It's true, babe, I've seen it," Skeeter said. *Babe?* I looked at Amy, and she gave a tiny shake of her head. I made a mental note to ask about that later. In private. Where I could mock my friend mercilessly without my girlfriend coming to his rescue.

"Where's your preacher friend?" Ponté asked.

"Checking the cemeteries we didn't get to last night," I said.

"Is he gonna be okay on his own?" the detective asked with a raised eyebrow.

"He's packing, he's wired into our comms if he wants to be, and he said something about bringing along local backup, so I think he'll be fine."

"Fair enough," Ponté replied.

"So where do we start? I think I'll head off this way." Amy pointed over to a crowded meat market bar that masqueraded as a rock n' roll bar.

"Probably a good choice," I said. "I'm gonna walk down toward Preservation Hall and see what I can find that way. I doubt anything's going to pick me for a snack with all the easier prey around, but it's worth a shot." I started down Bourbon toward the legendary music venue.

"I'm a little too well-known in the supernatural community to be useful in an op like this, so I'll just walk my rounds and talk to my informants like normal. Skeeter can come with and poke around alleys and opportune snatch points while I talk to my sources," Ponté said.

"Sounds good. Everybody stay in touch at all times. The trouble word is 'Vermont'." I said. I checked my in-ear communicator. Everything was coming through, loud and clear.

"So if we think we've found the rogue, change the topic to how much we love Ben & Jerry's, got it." Amy gave me a mocking little salute and turned to go into the club.

I wandered Bourbon Street for a while, listening with half an ear at the inept pickup lines Amy kept shooting down, and with another half an ear at the awkward just-started-dating fumbling for conversation between Skeeter and the detective. I was happy for my buddy. It had been too long since he'd had anybody in his life romantically. I reckoned if things kept going the way they seemed to be, I might have to give the good detective a warning about the delicate feelings of my best friend and how protective I was of those feelings. I didn't mind them dating, but if he hurt Skeeter, all bets were off, and I was out of my jurisdiction.

I walked into The Famous Door to see if anybody I'd heard of was playing. It wasn't anyone famous, just a little three-piece tearing up jazz standards. The singer was a beautiful woman of indeterminate ethnicity with a voice that could knock your socks off, and I swore I felt a little magic when she sang. Then she turned to me at the end of a note and smiled, and for half a second, she dropped the glamour and I saw the elf standing there in front of me, pointy ears and everything. Then I blinked, and the elf was gone, replaced by the beautiful woman and her beautiful music.

"They say there's magic everywhere down here," I muttered under my breath, and I swear she turned and winked at me. I noticed a commotion out of the corner of my eye and turned to get a better look. A couple of vaguely familiar frat boy types were running down an alley across the street, chasing a goth kid who looked like he was scared out of his gourd. I chuckled a little, then caught sight of the stake in one frat boy's hand and started to move.

I pushed my way through the throngs jamming near-midnight Bourbon Street and finally broke through the crowd on the other side of the street. I heard faint yelling and the sound of glass breaking from deep within the narrow alley, and looked around at just how perfect an ambush site it was. I took a deep breath, let it out in a stream of profanity, and charged down the poorly-lit pathway, Bertha in hand.

I turned the corner to see three young guys surrounding one skinny goth kid. Recognition dawned on me as I remembered where I'd seen these idiots before. I stepped into the light cast by one very dramatically placed light over the back door to a business I probably didn't want to know too much about and cocked Bertha.

The sound of cocking a pistol is unmistakable to anyone who's heard it before, and the lead frat boy froze. He turned around to me, very slowly, and when his eyes met mine, I saw the same spark of recognition that I felt.

"Hello, Davis," I said, holding Bertha with her barrel to the sky. No need to escalate things much further. Davis had a wicked-looking black-bladed knife in his hand, and each of his buddies had broken beer bottles. The goth had a board that looked like he'd ripped it off of a busted pallet leaning against the brick wall of the building behind him. The kid was trapped, with buildings on all three sides, but I could tell from the look on his face that he wasn't planning on going down without a fight. His threadbare Marilyn Manson t-shirt and baggy black pants marked him as a wannabe, but he had way too much color in his cheeks to be a vampire, unless he'd fed in the last hour.

"Bubba," Davis nodded back to me. "We've got this covered, but thanks for the offer." He turned back to the goth, but his buddies didn't take their eyes off me. Good call.

"I'm not here to hunt him, kid. I'm here to protect him. From you."

"Say what? Since when does the big monster hunter protect the monsters?"

"Since the monster is just a stupid kid with shitty taste in music and not enough sunlight in his diet. This chump is no more a vampire than I am a vegan, and you can damn sure believe I still like a good steak."

"How can you tell? I mean, shit dude, he's even got fangs!" one of the other frat boys chimed in.

"Son, when I want your opinion, I'll beat it out of you," I said. I holstered Bertha and stepped into the circle of idiots. The goth kid stared up at me like he didn't know whether to wet himself or hump my leg, but I just held out my hand. "Fangs," I said, nodding at my open palm.

He reached into his mouth, and with a *click*, dislodged the bridge holding his fake fangs in place. It was a good prosthetic, but as soon as I knew he wasn't a real vampire, I knew they were fake fangs. He dropped them into my hand, and I turned to Davis. "You see? Fake as a stripper's boobs, which is where y'all oughta be, drowning your sorrows in cleavage and cheap body glitter. I'm sorry about your friend, but if you keep messing around in the alleys of New Orleans, you're gonna find something a lot less friendly than me."

"That's right, mortals," the goth kid hissed from beside me." The snake queen Nagaru will hunt you down and punish you for harassing her loyal servant. She will—" I didn't hear the rest of his babble because I flicked out a fist and knocked him out.

"Look, he's an asshole, but he's a human asshole. And since y'all obviously can't tell the difference, you probably oughta hang up the stakes and leave the hunting to those of us whose lives suck enough for us to actually live in this world. Otherwise I'm gonna end up having to save your ass from yourselves, again."

"And we saw how good you are with the whole saving people thing already, didn't we?" Davis spat.

"Yeah, I couldn't save your friend. And that sucks. He goes on the list of all the people I couldn't save, and that list runs through my head every night before I finally get to sleep. So let's keep your name from screwing up my shuteye, shall we?"

Before he said anything, my comm crackled in my ear. It was Amy's voice. "That doesn't look right. I'm heading in to get a better look."

"What is it, Amy?" Skeeter asked.

"I don't know," she said. "It might be nothing, it might be a mugging, I can't tell. But something feels off somehow."

"What's your 20?" Skeeter asked.

"I'm heading down an alley a couple buildings down from the Bon Maison, across from the Ambush Mag offices."

"I'm on my way," I said. "I'm down by Yesteryears, I can be there in a couple minutes."

"I've got this, Bubba, stay on your end of the Quarter. There's probably more action off Bourbon down by Pat O's anyway. Hey, what are you doing?" Her voice got louder. "Hey! Leave her alone!"

I turned away from the frat boys and headed back to Bourbon at a dead run. People scattered out of the way of the giant charging out of the alley. The sounds of struggle rang in my ear over Amy's comm as I pelted my way north on Bourbon. I turned left and bolted across the street into the alley she said she was going down, catching Joe out of the corner of my eye as I almost took out a hot dog cart.

"Amy, where are you?" I said into my comm. "Amy? Come in, dammit!" I burst through the crowd like it was an ACC offensive line and exploded into the alley, my head on a swivel looking for any signs of Amy. I heard a chorus of "excuse me's" behind me as Joe caught up and leaned against a wall, winded.

"Anything?" he panted.

"Not yet. Skeeter?" I said into my comm.

"Her comm is down, but she's moving east, and fast."

"You can track her?" I asked.

"I've got trackers on all of you. In all of you, if you want me to be real precise about it."

"I'll let you explain that in a minute. For now, keep tracking her while we check the alley for clues. Let us know when she stops moving and we'll be there," I said.

"Why don't you go ahead and send Ponté there ahead of us so somebody's got her in sight?" Joe suggested.

"Good idea. You get that, Detective?" Skeeter said.

"I'm on it. You said she was leaving the Quarter heading east?"

"Yeah, they just took a left on Rampart," Skeeter confirmed.

"Might be heading to St. Louis #1," Ponté said, naming a famous cemetery just outside the French Quarter.

"Can you get there first?" I asked.

"No? I'm too far away and I don't have super-speed. Or my car."

I looked at Joe, who was on his cell waving at me. "What's up?" I asked.

"Go that way, out to Dumaine Street," he said, pointing off to his right through a courtyard. "There's an alley. I've got somebody to meet you there. You'll know her when you see her. She'll get you to St. Louis #1 and keep you covered until Ponté gets there. I'll stay here and look for clues."

I stared at him for a second, until he grabbed my shirt and leaned in to me. "Go!" he almost yelled in my face, and I bolted through the courtyard and down the alley. It was a tight fit, but I came out on Dumaine just as a black Harley roared up onto the sidewalk in front of me.

The rider was a woman dressed completely in black motorcycle leathers, from her side-zipper boots to her jacket. She flipped up the visor on her helmet and said in that French-tinged English that speaks of a life on the bayou, "You Bubba?"

"Yeah," I said.

"Then get on, *cher*, Joey tells me you be in a hurry." I threw a leg over the back of the bike and grabbed on as she roared into traffic, weaving through cars and pedestrians like we were in a video game or a movie. I felt something bump into my leg and looked down. She had a Mossberg 500 in a custom-built holster on the side of her motorcycle. I decided right then that any chick that rode a Harley with a twelve-gauge shotgun strapped to it was good enough backup for me.

Chapter Ten

WE PULLED UP IN FRONT OF THE CEMETERY AND MY MYSTERY partner killed the engine. We got off the bike, and I walked up to the gates, which were hanging wide open.

"That ain't right," the woman said, walking up next to me with her Mossberg in hand.

"Yeah, I think we found the place," I said. "What's your name, by the way? I figure if I'm gonna let you help me out, I oughta at least know who you are."

"*Let* me help you? *Let* me help you? *Cher*, did yo boy Joey not tell you who I am? Hell, you lucky I'm lettin' you walk around in my cemeteries at all, much less packing that hand-cannon you toting under that shirt. I mean, damn, son, what in the world are you compensating for with that thing?"

I just stared at her. It was one of the few times in my life I've been legitimately speechless, and I was really glad Skeeter wasn't there to see it. He heard it though, since my comm link was open, and I could hear him snickering in the background. Finally, after a few seconds of gaping at her like a fish on the pier, I found my words again.

"No, Joe didn't tell me anything about you, so why don't you fill me in on why you call it *your* cemetery, and why you think you could possibly stop me from doing anything I damn well please wherever I damn well please to do it?"

She took off her helmet, and a mass of black curls spilled out and ran halfway down her back. She tucked her gloves into her helmet and put them both on the Harley's seat. She looked up at me with her huge, oval eyes of the deepest violet, and held out a mocha-colored hand. I took it, and we shook. Her grip was firm, and I had no doubt she could handle that shotgun and whatever else she had tucked away inside that black leather jacket.

"I'm Sister Evangeline, and this is my territory. I'm the Hunter for Louisiana, part of Texas, the panhandle of Florida, and the Mobile/Gulfport parts of Mississippi and Alabama. Basically, I've got the Gulf from Tallahassee to San Antonio, and all of Louisiana. I'm you, just smarter and a whole lot prettier."

"Well, I'll damn sure agree with you there, especially in those pants." Black leather pants make an ugly woman look good, and Evangeline was no kind of ugly woman. With milk chocolate skin, curves in all the right places, and a tight black turtleneck that revealed nothing but still left little to the imagination, she was a tall, athletic-looking woman with a strong jaw and cherubic heart-shaped face belying the steel in her eyes and the firepower in her hands.

"So you're the Hunter for this part of the world?" I mused. "I reckon that makes it as much your cemetery as anybody's. So, shall we?" I gestured at the gates, and Evangeline stepped through the open portal, her thumb going to the rail-mounted flashlight on the front of the shotgun and flipping it on. The bright xenon beam cut through the darkened cemetery, and we started down the main aisle toward the center of the graveyard.

"Skeeter?" I whispered into my comm. "You got anything?"

"Looks like she's stopped moving. She's about a hundred yards ahead and off to your left about twenty yards."

"How long has she been stopped?" Evangeline asked, and I relayed the question to Skeeter.

"Only a couple of minutes," he replied.

I passed the word along, and Evangeline nodded. "That's good news," she said. "If they were going to kill her, they would have done it in the alley. If it's a ritual, it'll just be starting, so we've got some time."

"But not a ton of it, so let's move," I said, starting forward. I pulled a small flashlight out of my pocket and drew Bertha, moving down the center aisle of the cemetery with Bertha in front of me, my flashlight hand under my gun hand in a crossed grip. Evangeline was right on my heels, moving through the leaves and twigs without so much as a whisper. We got to about the right place to turn left by Skeeter's tracking, and I held up a hand. Evangeline froze behind me and I stood motionless for a moment, listening hard into the darkness.

I clicked off my flashlight and pointed off to the left. I looked back at Evangeline and she nodded. She heard it too—the low, lyrical chanting off in the distance. I clicked my light back on, but kept it shuttered in my hand, just letting out enough light to keep me from stumbling all over the place.

We crossed several rows of headstones before we came to a huge crypt with the door standing open. There was a chorus of singing voices coming from within, so I took the chance and clicked on my comm. "Skeeter, are we at the right place?"

"Yeah. According to my tracker, you're within ten feet of her."

"Sounds good to me," I said. I turned back to Evangeline. "That scattergun will be all but useless in close quarters—"

She held up a hand. "Way ahead of you," she said, leaning the shotgun against a tombstone and drawing a pair of nickel-plated Colt 1911 .45 pistols from under her jacket.

"Good Lord, woman, who do you think you are, Deacon Chalk?" I asked, naming a badass monster killer in Atlanta I'd heard stories about. I'd never met the man despite living in the same state, but he sounded like my kind of guy. Hung out in strip clubs, blew up a lot of shit, had some family issues. You know, typical dude-that-hunts-monsters kind of stuff.

"I don't know who that is, but these belonged to my Daddy the Colonel, God rest his soul, and I've sent many a vampire and zombie to their final resting place with these pistols."

"Then let's do that again," I said. I stepped through the open door of the crypt to see Amy laid out on a sarcophagus surrounded by zombies all swaying in time to the chanting of half a dozen or so humans. The black-clad humans were arranged in a semi-circle around her with a gorgeous woman in a white robe standing directly over Amy's head and holding a wavy dagger that reflected candlelight all over the room. The zombies made a circle around the sarcophagus, surrounding my girlfriend and the humans. This seemed like a particularly bad idea to me, but since they weren't currently trying to eat anyone, I didn't mention it.

"So I heard there was a party tonight, and I wasn't invited," I said, stepping to one side to give Evangeline and her pistols plenty of room to work. "My feelings were hurt for a minute, but then I decided that I should probably just kill everybody in the room anyway, so no big deal, right?"

"Finish the ritual!" a pudgy dude in what looked like a black hoodie sewn onto a bathrobe shouted.

I pointed Bertha at his head and said, "Tubby, if you ever want to eat another beignet, you better haul your fat ass out of this cemetery right now. That goes for the rest of y'all, too. In about ten seconds, everybody in this crypt is either gonna be on my team, or dead forever, so if neither of those ideas appeals to y'all, you better run like hell."

I stepped to the side as four of the humans, amazingly not including Tubby, bolted for the open door. Tubby charged me, his head down like he was a bull after his very first matador. Too bad for him I'd seen that movie before. I side-stepped his charge, turned halfway to my left, and planted a foot in his sizable ass as he went by. He took the turbo boost like a '69 Charger just got a shot of nitrous, and dove into the stone wall of the crypt like he was rocket-propelled. He slid down the wall and collapsed in a heap amidst a couple of broken urns and some dried leaves. I heard a *thump* from behind me and turned to see Evangeline standing over the unconscious body of the other human chanter.

I looked at the blonde woman in the white robe standing over my girlfriend with a knife and said, "If you want to live, you should put that knife down."

"You can't shoot me fast enough to save her, idiot."

"I don't have to, dumbass. And don't call people names, it's not nice." I said, then said, "Amy, take her out." Amy, who had been playing possum the whole time, grabbed the sides of the sarcophagus and kicked straight up. Her right foot flashed back over her head and caught the priestess right between the eyes. The blonde woman took one wobbly step back, then sat down hard on the concrete and passed out against the wall. Amy rolled to her feet atop the sarcophagus and winked at me.

"Where's the vampire?" I asked.

"He didn't stick around, the little prick. He just dropped me off here, took some money off this idiot, and left."

"What were they trying to do?" Evangeline asked, and I watched Amy notice her for the first time. A definite chill entered the tomb as my girlfriend registered that I'd brought another woman to help rescue her, *and* that woman was hot, *and* now that woman was asking her questions like they knew each other.

I decided to step in and be the voice of reason in the situation, because that always works so well. "Amy, meet Evangeline, the Hunter for New Orleans and the Gulf Territory. She's here to help."

"Help with what?" Amy asked. "Looks like we have this pretty well covered."

"Except for that," Evangeline pointed at the priestess, who was awake and grabbing at her necklace. She pulled a crystal from around her neck, threw it at the far wall of the tomb, then ran out the open door. The crystal smashed, and all the zombies stopped swaying and turned their attention on us.

"What was that?" I asked, thinking I knew the answer and really hoping I was wrong.

"I'd guess it was her focus, the magical tool she used to keep these zombies under control." I hate it when I'm right.

"So now what?" Amy asked.

"Now a lot of this," Evangeline said, turning to the nearest zombie and opening fire. She put four zombies down in as many pulls of the trigger, and I dropped another three with Bertha before I heard the tell-tale *whizz* of a bullet buzzing by my ear. I looked around, alarmed, and saw Amy on the ground behind the sarcophagus and Evangeline crouched in a corner.

"Watch out for ricochet, you idiots!" Amy yelled at us. "Decayed flesh does nothing to stop those cannon rounds you're slinging around in here!"

She was right, so I holstered Bertha and drew my new KABAR Hank Reinhardt kukri, over a foot of black high-quality American steel and a razor-sharp blade. It took me all of thirty seconds to down the last few zombies, with Evangeline taking out one by crushing its skull with a funeral urn. I chose to believe that the dust spilling out of the urn was just dust, not a former member of the family.

"That was easy," I said, holding out my hand to Amy. She took it and stood, giving me a quick kiss and shooting a possessive look back at Evangeline. Then she froze in my arms, and her head sagged to my chest.

"Bubba, you gigantic idiot, when will you learn not to speak?"

"What do you mean?" I asked, looking around the room. All the zombies were dead, the priestess was gone, and all that was left were two voodoo wannabes sleeping off their first encounter with real badness, namely me.

Amy pointed out the door, and I said a few bad words. Then I said a few more. Then I invented a couple and said those. Then I said, "Well, good thing I brought extra magazines."

There were three zombies all trying to get through the door at the same time. If they were smart enough to come in one at a time, they would have gotten me from behind while I was dealing with the indoor zombies. Thank goodness dead things aren't very smart.

Chapter Eleven

"HOW MANY OF THEM ARE OUT THERE?" AMY ASKED. "AND *who* is she, again?"

"More than I can count," I replied, but before I could repeat my introductions, Evangeline stepped up and pressed a pistol into Amy's hand.

"I'm Sister Evangeline. I'm the Gulf Coast Hunter, and a Sister of Lupus, an order of militant nuns and priests that operate very discreetly in New Orleans."

"I've heard of the Fellowship of Lupus," Amy said, taking the pistol and checking the chamber. "I thought you were all lycanthropes?"

I shot Evangeline a look, and she laughed. "At one time we were, but membership in the Fellowship waned in recent years, so the elders opened up the ranks to a few non-shifters. The only thing that happens around me on the full moon is that no chocolate is safe." She gave Amy a half-smile.

"I know, right, especially chocolate ice cream. That shit is my kryptonite."

"Ladies, I hate to interrupt the meeting of the Yo-Yo Sisterhood, but could we return our attention to the zombie apocalypse taking place right outside our door?" I pointed back at the three zombies contorting in the doorway just as one shoved his way through, breaking free of the logjam that held back the flood of undead and spilling walking corpses into the crypt. We had about a twenty foot square room to work with, but the center was dominated by a four foot wide, eight foot long sarcophagus. I drew my kukri and decapitated the nearest zombie, taking up a position at the foot of the sarcophagus facing the door. Amy and Evangeline hopped up onto the stone coffin and started firing into the mass of zombies streaming through the door.

Every shot was a head shot, and every bullet found a home in a zombie's brainpan, but there was a shitload of zombies, and only a limited number of bullets. I chopped important pieces off zombies with every swing of my blade, but no matter how many I sent back to their rest, another two took their place.

I heard Amy's hammer click empty, so I drew Bertha and passed her back over my head. "Watch out for the recoil, she likes to test new shooters," I said, just before the fifty-cal roared to life. Not only did the zombie's head she was aiming at explode like a grape under a boot heel, the round traveled through the decayed flesh, inflicting damage on three more shamblers before its energy was finally expended.

"Damn, Bubba, now I see why you carry this monster," Amy said from behind me.

"Yeah, let's see how your wrists feel after a couple dozen rounds, then come see me," I said. I swung into the zombie throng like an old-school woodcutter—lift, chop, lift, chop. With every stroke, a zombie went down until there was a pile of true dead men and women piled up in front of me like a duck blind made of overdressed corpses. After several minutes of chopping, shooting, and general re-deadening of walking dead people, there was a brief break in the constant onslaught of zombies. For just a few seconds, nothing was trying to get into the tomb with us, and everything already in the tomb was at the appropriate state of dead (them) and alive (us).

"I'm gonna go see what's out there," Evangeline said and leapt from the coffin behind me clean over my head and rolled out the door, coming up in a crouch with her shotgun at the ready. I nodded in appreciation; if I'd tried that move, I would have ended up flat on my face with a shotgun pistol grip wedged up my ass.

She fired off three rounds, turning in a semicircle to clear the area in front of the door, then waved us forward. I held up a hand to help Amy down, but she took her cues from the new girl and vaulted me and the wall of corpses between me and the door. She didn't tuck and roll, just leapt halfway across the crypt like a blonde Lara Croft.

"Trying to prove something, sweetie?" I asked.

"I've got nothing at all to prove, babe. You coming?" She raised Bertha and stepped out into the cemetery.

I pushed, kicked, and stomped my way through the mess between me and the door, then stepped out and stopped, my mouth dropping open at what I saw. There were more damn zombies stumbling through that cemetery than nerds at a midnight *Call of Duty* release. Literally hundreds of undead shambled to and fro in every aisle and walkway of the cemetery. I hadn't seen that many brainless husks in one place since I ventured into the Clemson-Carolina football game one year on accident.

These weren't ordinary voodoo-controlled zombies, either. These were dumber than rocks, eat anything in their path, mindless walking stomachs, and if they ever got out into New Orleans, the city would know that everything it suffered in Katrina was just a warmup.

"What the actual fuck is going on here?" I muttered.

"When that bitch smashed her control gem, she didn't just set her dead free, the stupid bitch let loose a magical backlash that brought every corpse in this cemetery to its feet," Evangeline spat.

"With no one driving the bus," I said.

"Exactly," she replied. "This is every dead body in St. Louis #1 with enough connective tissue left to walk, and it's only a matter of time before some of them find the gate and wander into the tourist district."

I looked at my watch. "It's about four now, so we've got what, three hours until sunrise? That's too long to wait them out. I think we oughta make for the gate and set ourselves up on the other side, just shoot anything that gets too close."

"Stand on the sidewalk in downtown New Orleans and shoot zombies at four in the morning where God, the po-po and everybody can see? If that's your idea of keeping a low profile, it's no wonder they never let you come to the meetin's." Evangeline managed not to laugh in my face, but the struggle was apparent. I reached past her and crushed the skull of a zombie before it took a bite out of her neck, but she was still giggling.

"She's got a point," Amy said. "Even with my badge, I can't close a major downtown area without some blowback. And what does she mean, meetings?"

"There's an annual Hunter's conference every year. I was kinda uninvited a few years back after I had a disagreement with a bishop."

"Disagreement?" Skeeter's voice rang over all our comms like fingernails on a chalkboard. "Shit, Bubba, you threw the man off a fifth-floor balcony! You're lucky he didn't have you arrested!"

"I threw him into a swimming pool, and yes, before you ask, I knew the pool was there."

"In Boston. In February. Outdoors. That pool was froze over solid," Skeeter said.

"The ice wasn't that thick," I protested. "He broke right through without getting hurt or nothing."

"Except almost drowning," Skeeter pointed out.

"Except that," I admitted.

"And hypothermia," Skeeter added.

"And that," I had give him that one, too.

"And that broken ankle," Skeeter said.

"It was just a sprain, I swear to God!" I said, then took a deep breath. "Skeeter, how the hell are we gonna get out of here? We got wall to wall zombies and only so much ammo between us."

"I don't know, Bubba. I've got Joe almost at the cemetery, but I don't know what all he could do except pray over it and bring some more bullets."

"I don't think that's gonna cut it, buddy. And how do you know Joe's close?"

"He's got a tracker, too. We all do." Skeeter's voice sounded suspiciously nonchalant, and I've known him long enough to recognize when he's faking it.

"What do you mean, we all have trackers, Skeeter? I don't have a tracker on me." I said.

"Well, technically that's true…"

"Skeeter…"

"After the first fight with your brother, we all thought it would be a good idea to be able to keep track of one another a little better, so we all got these little subcutaneous tracking chips implanted in our wrists. They're tiny. But they power off body heat and transmit up to a mile, so as long as you're within a mile of a cell tower, or emergency broadcast tower, or basically any radio transmitter or satellite phone, I can find you to within a couple hundred feet." That explained a lot of inopportune phone calls I'd gotten over the last year right when things were getting interesting at certain gentlemen's clubs, but I still couldn't remember ever signing up to be microchipped like somebody's Cocker Spaniel.

"When exactly did I agree to this?" I asked. "And when did you put the chip in?" I looked at my arms and couldn't see any scars I couldn't account for and didn't feel any lumps under the skin.

"Well…" Skeeter put on his patented avoiding the question voice.

"Talk," I growled.

"Don't y'all have zombies to kill?" Skeeter asked.

"Amy and Evangeline have got that covered for now. They been dropping dead dudes the whole time we've been talking. That would be the conspicuous sound of gunfire behind me. Now spill it," I demanded.

"We planted it in the back of your neck under your hairline when you were in the hospital after Jason cut you up." He said it all fast, like the quicker he got it out the less pissed I'd be. It didn't work.

"You stuck a tracker in my *head*? While I was recovering from being skewered like a damn shish kabob with my own damn sword? Skeeter, we gonna have a long talk about this one day soon, but right now I need…aw, shit that's just what I needed."

"What happened?" Skeeter asked, his voice going all high and panicky. This time I didn't blame him. I was starting to think pretty strongly about cutting and running myself.

"Eddie just showed up."

"Eddie the voodoo priest from last night?"

"In his butt-nekkid glory with a dozen other nekkid folk walking behind him chanting and glowing."

"Did you say they were glowing, Bubba?"

"Yes, and before you ask, I only had three Hurricanes, they were half-strength and it was a couple hours ago, so yes I am sober, and yes, there are nekkid voodoo people walking through the cemetery glowing like somebody shoved a million candlepower flashlight up their hoo-has. Now if you will excuse me, I am going to go talk to a nekkid *houngan* about how to get two hundred zombies back in their graves where they belong without having to shoot each and every damn one of them in the face. Wish me luck."

"Good luck," Skeeter said, and I clicked off my comm to go deal with the weirdest damn thing I'd seen since coming to New Orleans, and that bar was getting higher by the minute.

Chapter Twelve

"EDDIE, WHAT IN THE SWEET HOLY HELL ARE YOU DOING OUT HERE? And why are you glowing?" I asked as I walked up to the naked voodoo priest and his flock. They walked single file in a line of nakedness down the aisle of the cemetery, all of them carrying bags slung over one shoulder or backpacks, and wearing sandals. I guess even nudists need to be careful of getting their feet cut up. Eddie had about half a dozen men and women with him, a couple of white dudes, a black dude, a grandmotherly black woman who reminded me of Ruby Dee, and a hot Asian girl who might have been twenty or might have been fifty, I couldn't tell. Each of them was framed with a pale white light that seemed to emanate from their skin, and the zombies never came within ten yards of them.

"We are here to help bring these poor souls to rest, Bubba," Eddie said, and I was very careful to only look him in the eyes. The last thing I needed was another reason to feel bad about myself.

"And how exactly are you planning on doing that?" I asked. "I thought making zombies was more your thing than putting zombies to rest."

"My zombies are not like these mindless thralls, Bubba," Eddie said, and if I didn't know him to be about half con man and half necromancer, I'd have believed that his feelings really were hurt.

"My zombies are men and women who follow my teachings in life and wish to continue to serve after death. No one is ever raised without permission before death, or the permission of a spouse, or next of kin. My zombies are well cared for, never left to roam like these poor souls. What was done here is an abomination, and whoever committed such an atrocity against the dead should be punished, and most severely." His voice went hard, and his eyes flashed with power. This was an Eddie I did not want to mess with. This Eddie manipulated the magic of life and death, and he packed a punch.

"Eddie, I think I'm out of my league," I admitted. "I can kill a bunch of zombies, but there's way too many of them for me to handle."

"Don't worry, Bubba," the priest said, and the kindly smile I was accustomed to returned. "You worry about finding the evil that brought these people back from the grave. My followers and I will see that they are returned to their resting places."

"There might be a couple in the crypt there that need some returning, too. And they might not be quite so mobile as these out here," I said with a shrug.

"Well, we will attempt to send those to a rest as well," Eddie said. He looked over my shoulder and his smile stiffened a little. "Sister Angel, it is good to see you once again."

"I told you, Eddie, my name's Evangeline now. New name, new job, new God. Even got a little bit of a new hair color, you like it? I put red highlights in." I looked, but couldn't see anything but jet black hair. Of course it was five in the morning in a dark-ass cemetery.

"You will always be my little Angel," Eddie said. "And there will always be a place for you with me."

"Not for a long time, Eddie," Evangeline said, and there was a melancholy in her voice like bayou blues. "There's not been a place for me with you for a long time. But if you can help lay these people to rest, I can help run interference with NOLA police department about y'all running around naked in the cemetery. Again."

"Much appreciated, Sister Angel," Eddie said, then turned to his followers. "Set the circle, children. Let us work toward bringing rest to these poor souls." The men and women snapped into motion, placing candles in a circle and scattering herbs and powders all around.

I stood there for a few seconds, then realized that I'd been dismissed. I turned back to Evangeline and Amy, who had stopped shooting when Eddie and his crew showed up, mostly because as soon as Eddie got near, the zombies found someplace else to be.

"You got something you want to share with the class, Sister Angel?" I asked the sassy leather-clad Hunter.

"Nope. Ancient history. Just here to shoot things that go bump in the night nowadays."

"I'll let that go for tonight, but we work together again, I'm gonna need to know everything about the Hunter at my back," I said, looking down at her.

She cocked an eyebrow at me. "Does that mean I get the whole story about your brother and daddy, Bubba? Or is this honesty a one-way street?" I didn't have a good answer for her, and she probably saw that on my face. She reached up and patted me on the shoulder, gave me the kind of gentle smile you only get from priests and nuns, and said, "We've all got baggage, big guy, it's what brings us into this job. Don't worry. When I say I've got your back, you're covered. Everything else is just noise."

"I can live with that. Now what do we do, watch? Help somehow? Hunt down stragglers?"

"How about meet Joe at the gate and make sure none of these guys get out before Eddie can lay them back to rest?" Amy asked.

"Good idea," I said, turning back toward the front of the cemetery and away from the naked voodoo people. Naked people I usually don't mind. Voodoo priests I usually can deal with. It's the combination of the two that got me all twitterpated.

We were almost to the gate when I heard the unmistakable clatter of one of life's truest tragedies—a Harley Davidson falling sideways to rest ungracefully on concrete. A Harley is more than just a motorcycle; it's a piece of the American collective consciousness, a piece of out zeitgeist as integral to the definition of America as John Wayne, Chevrolets, and rock n' roll. When a Harley is in motion, it's poetry on two wheels, Walt Whitman's ghost cutting through the air like a Great White prowling the ocean. Even sitting still, a Harley has a barely restrained look of speed and aggression about it, like it might burst into action, all bipedal Christine, and tear apart any little sissy sport bike or God forbid Vespa that happened to park within range of its chrome-plated rage.

But a Harley knocked to the ground, lying on its side like a beached whale, all denuded magnificence and ineffectual fury, that's a goddamned sacrilege—a defamation worse than flag burning, more visceral that ripping up a Bible, or wiping your ass with the Stephen Foster songbook. That's the sound that greeted my ears when we were almost at the gate. It was followed by the tinkle of broken side mirror glass, then the sharp handclap of a Sig Sauer .40 pistol firing off three quick rounds.

"That's Joe," I said, and broke into a run. Well, more of a limping lope, really. Apparently at some point in all the zombie crushing, I'd tweaked my old knee injury, so I wasn't moving at full speed. And really, my full speed was only every good for about twenty yards at a time anyway. I only ever needed to run from the line of scrimmage to about three yards past the quarterback. Usually by the time I knocked him back that far, the poor bastard quit struggling and I put him down.

Evangeline and Amy were better off than I was, so they sprinted the rest of the way to the gate. I heard more guns open up, along with some faint cursing, so I assumed Amy was okay. I didn't know Sister Evangeline all that well, but Joe wasn't much of one for profanity, and I figured it went with the whole "working for the clergy" thing. I limped along for a few more seconds, then I reached the gate and started some serious swearing of my very own.

Joe was the cause of the clatter because he was sprawled backwards across a pair of toppled Harleys. He was bleeding a little from the mouth, but he was moving and trying to get himself disentangled from the handlebars to get back in the fight. And the fight was pretty impressive, too. Amy and Evangeline were flanking a vampire, and they looked to have gotten a couple shots in already. Amy had a silver stake in one hand, and Evangeline had a retractable baton in one hand and a long dagger in the other. I took half a second to give her leather-clad form another once-over, wondering where the weapons had come from, but the vampire landed a punch on Amy that set me in motion. She rolled with the punch, but it still knocked her to her knees and sent her eyeballs to Glassyville. The vampire reached in to finish her off, but Evangeline launched herself at the monster's back, dagger flashing in the streetlight as she stabbed the vamp in the neck again and again.

I burst through the cemetery gate just as the vamp dislodged Evangeline and flung her into Joe, who had finally gotten back to his feet. They went down in a tangle, and the vampire turned back to Amy. I drew Bertha, stopped right outside the gate, and squeezed off one round.

I got a direct hit, and the vampire's leg below the knee disappeared. The monster flopped onto the concrete, screaming and holding its stump. Amy scooted back away from the writhing bloodsucker and pulled herself to her feet. She picked up her pistol off the ground and trained it on the vamp. I walked up to the screaming creature and booted him gently-ish in the side of the head.

"Shut up," I said. He didn't. I kicked him harder, and he stopped shrieking long enough to glare at me and pull himself into a sitting position.

"You shot my leg off!" the vampire yelled.

"You were going to kill my girlfriend," I pointed out.

"That was nothing personal, she works for DEMON," he protested.

"Just like it was nothing personal kidnapping her earlier tonight and handing her over to zombie priestesses to be killed or possessed," I said. I was keeping my voice calm, but the more we talked, the more of his leg grew back, and as fascinating as that was to watch, I needed to get any information out of him before he was ambulatory again.

"You idiots were getting too close. I needed to slow you down. Can't have you getting in the way before I finish with Cathy-poo." He grinned, and I knew he was stalling.

"And what are you planning for Catherine?" I asked.

"Nothing much, just the destruction of everything she cares about and then eventually, true-death. No big deal, really."

"Yeah, nothing much," I agreed. "And exactly how were you planning on doing that?"

"Is this the part where I lay here and give you my entire plan so you can figure out how to beat me? I don't think so, human!" He got his good leg under him and sprang up, claw-like fingers going straight for my throat. I hate it when they figure out my simple and clichéd plans.

Chapter Thirteen

I SIDESTEPPED HIS CHARGE AND KICKED HIM IN THE LEG HE WAS regrowing, chuckling a little at his scream of pain. Petty, I know, but there aren't many times I can actually go toe-to-toe with a vampire and hold my own, especially when I'm not carrying Grandpappy's sword, so I took my giggles where I could get them. Unfortunately for me, the pain spurred him to greater speed, and he whirled around and caught me upside the head with a backhand. I spun halfway around and dropped to one knee, the world suddenly gone all *2001: A Space Odyssey* on me, which is to say, it was full of stars.

I felt the rush of air over my back as Evangeline flung herself back into the fight, very literally. She planted a foot on my shoulders and launched her entire body at the vampire, and they went down in a heap of leather and blood. I shook my head to clear my vision, hoping I wasn't concussed. Evangeline was astride the vampire, stabbing again and again with that long dagger. The vampire blocked every blow, then bucked her off with a twisting flop that left Evangeline on her back, her knife a foot away from her grip, and the vampire on his feet.

He took two long strides toward Evangeline, reared back his foot, and kicked her in the ribs like it was kickoff at the Super Bowl. I heard ribs crack from ten feet away, and the scream she let out was bloodcurdling.

"How do you like that, human?" the vampire asked, rearing back to kick her again. I raised Bertha, but saw only empty hand in front of me—I must have dropped Bertha when I got my bell rung. I staggered to my feet and tried to charge the vamp, but he got another kick in before I got to him. Evangeline curled up in a little ball, trying to keep her ribs in roughly the right places while I bum-rushed the vampire and slammed him into the stone wall beside the gate.

He grunted on impact but brought both fists down on my back in a double axe-handle blow that drove me to my knees. I collapsed to the concrete and felt hands grab my head. *This is it*, I thought. *I'm gonna get my head ripped off by a vampire in New Orleans.*

Four quick shots rang out, and the vampire's body jerked with the impact. I turned and saw Amy and Joe standing, pistols leveled at the bloodsucker, just plugging away. I turned back to the vampire, still on my knees, and looked up. He was distracted by the bullets punching holes in his torso, so I did the most logical thing I could think of—I punched him in the balls.

I didn't really know if it would do anything, vampires being wired differently than they were when they were human, but apparently some things maintain because this vamp dropped like a stone. He fell to his knees right in front of me, and I shoved a silver stake into his chest. I intentionally didn't pierce his heart, just shoved the stake in enough to get his attention.

His eyes went wide and he froze. "What are you doing?" the vampire asked.

"I believe the term would be 'advanced interrogation techniques'," I replied. "I've got questions, you've got answers. Let's have those things meet in the middle, or else I'll have the point of this stake meet your heart. *Comprendé?*"

He nodded, so I started right in. "What's your beef with Catherine?"

"She turned me. I served her and her family faithfully for years, and my reward was to get turned into a bloodsucking monster! Well, if that bitch wants a monster, she's got one now."

"Who's helping you?" Amy asked, kneeling beside me.

"Nobody," the vamp spat. "I don't need any help taking out that insipid bitch."

"You know, I'm getting really tired of that word," Amy said. "Call me a feminist, but, oh wait, I am a feminist. So you use the word 'bitch' one more time, and I'll feed you your shriveled little vampire willie."

The vampire looked terrified, and I probably did, too. I decided to push on with the questioning before I said something that pissed her off and got that kind of attention turned on me. "Don't give me any crap, dude. I know vampires, and I know voodoo, and I know vampires can't do magic, so tell me who raised the zombies for you." I also knew that some vampires *could* do magic, but only the really old and powerful ones. This one was really young, less than a decade at my best guess.

"You took her out an hour ago, remember? She was in the crypt with your friend here."

"No way," I said, giving the stake a little wiggle. "That chick had about the magical power of my left pinkie finger and couldn't make dough rise, much less the dead. Now gimme the truth, or I'll just perforate you and keep digging on my own."

He said something, but it was so low, I couldn't hear him. I leaned in, and almost bumped heads with Amy, who leaned forward at the same time. I looked at her and chuckled, and that was all the time the vampire needed to turn shit upside down. When I turned to Amy, I relaxed the pressure on the stake just the slightest bit, and the vamp took advantage. He shoved me backward with one hand, and pulled Amy forward with the other, both blocking me from getting back in at him with the stake and getting her neck within biting range.

I fell down on my butt, and he chomped down on Amy's neck. I cringed, waiting for the spurt of blood, but all I heard was a *crunch* and a string of curses. I scrambled to my feet as the vampire did the same, shoving Amy away and wiping at his mouth in agony. Amy flew several feet and crashed into the stone wall around the cemetery with a sickening *thud*.

"You crazy bitch!" he screamed. "Who the hell wears a chain mail choker?"

"Somebody who hunts vampires, asshole," Amy said from the ground, shaking her head to clear the cobwebs. She drew her pistol and put four rounds into the bitching vampire's chest. "Those are silver-tipped rounds, you misogynist prick, so they oughta burn for a long time. I told you about calling people bitches."

The vampire charged Amy but ran into a stiff side kick from me and the rest of a magazine of silver-tipped 9mm ammo from Amy. He stopped cold just outside of my arm's reach, so I drew Bertha, pressed the Desert Eagle to the back of the undead asshole's neck and pulled the trigger three times. Fifty-caliber bullets tore through flesh, cartilage, and spine, and decapitated the vampire as effectively as any sword. Blood splashed all over Amy and me, with a fair amount just going every damn where, and the corpse dropped to the ground.

"That was subtle," Evangeline croaked from the ground.

"Subtle is not exactly what we prioritize with Bubba," Amy said. She tried to stand, but had to reach out to the wall for support.

"You okay, babe?" I asked, reading her side.

"I will be," she said. "I just took a hard shot when I hit the wall, and my vision's a little blurry."

"You've probably got a concussion, and Evie's definitely got some broken ribs," I said.

"I'll be lucky if I have any that aren't broken," Evangeline said from the ground. "It feels like I've got a chest full of daggers."

"That's basically what you have," Joe said. "I'll call the local parish for medical transport and cleanup."

"I'll search the dead guy and see if he has any useful information on him," I said. "Joe, you should go wherever the girls end up. They need someone to cover them while they're getting patched up."

"You're right," he agreed.

Amy started to protest, but I held up a hand. "Honey, just chill. You know you've got a target on your back, and there are probably a lot of things down here that would like a piece of Evangeline when she's not at her best."

The Hunter nodded and said, "Yeah, I'm gonna be wrecked for a while, and it'd be good if there was somebody to keep an eye out and make sure that nothing decides to turn the ER into a buffet."

"Sonofabitch," I said, standing up with the vampire's wallet in my hand. I was right, he was a young one, still hanging on to a lot of vestiges of his former life.

"What's wrong?" Amy asked, holding out her hand for the wallet. I passed it to her, open to the snapshot I'd found. "Oh shit," she muttered. She looked up at me, brow furrowed. "You gotta go."

I was already clicking my comm on and off to no avail, so I pulled out my phone and dialed "Skeeter." As expected, no answer. I picked up Joe's motorcycle from where it lay on its side and turning the bike around to point back to our hotel.

"What's going on?" Evangeline demanded.

"Ponté," I said. "He played us. He's the voodoo priest, he's the one trying to take over New Orleans. He's the one trying to get revenge on Catherine." I straddled the Harley and kicked the motor to life, feeling the hungry power beneath me. There was a well-dressed police detective about to answer some real uncomfortable questions.

"Revenge?" Joe asked. "For what?"

"For what he saw as the ultimate betrayal," I pointed at the pieces of vampire scattered on the ground before me. "For turning his baby brother into a vampire."

Chapter Fourteen

I CONTINUED TO PIECE THINGS TOGETHER AS I RODE FOR OUR HOTEL, Joe's motorcycle cutting through traffic and pedestrians with ease. Ponté said his family had worked for Catherine for generations. Apparently that went sideways somehow with Little Bro, whose name was Andrew according to his driver's license, and he got turned. Then he went rogue, and Ponté decided to use his insanity to keep Catherine's attentions diverted while he raised a shitload of zombies and took over New Orleans. Or turned it into an amusement park for the undead, I wasn't really sure what his overall plan was.

I pulled the bike up on the sidewalk in front of our hotel and ran for the doors. The valet took one look at me, wild-eyed, covered in blood and zombie guts with Bertha in my hand, and hid behind his key rack. The doorman held the door and pulled out his cell phone the second I was through, but I had Amy coordinating with local law enforcement from the back of her ambulance so I wasn't sweating getting arrested. The lobby security guy was obviously trained to be discreet, and he walked calmly toward me as I ran through the lobby toward the elevators. He fell into stride with me, trying to divert my attention and get me somewhere that I wouldn't drip blood on his carpets.

"Sir, if you could come with me, I'm sure there's—" His words cut off sharp when I shoved him into a square marble pillar and stuck Bertha into his nostril.

"I am a government agent in pursuit of a dangerous fugitive. I have shot a large number of very dangerous men tonight and my superiors will reward me by overlooking a little collateral damage. Unless you want to be that collateral damage, you want to get on the elevator with me, turn the knob to emergency, and get us to the fourteenth floor as fast as possible. Otherwise, I will be forced to turn this lobby into a goddamn abattoir. Do you understand me?"

He looked like he couldn't believe I knew the word "abattoir" but otherwise seemed sufficiently terrified. He nodded, and we covered the last twenty feet to the elevator in about eight seconds. I pushed the button, the doors *dinged* open, and we stepped in, along with a tiny elderly woman holding a toy poodle. She might have been five feet tall and a hundred pounds soaking wet, but she looked up at me without an ounce of fear in her eyes.

"You done been in a mess, boy," she said, disapproval heavy in her tone. Suddenly I was eight years old and back in Sunday School.

"Yes, ma'am, I have. And I'm afraid I ain't done yet."

"You gonna make a mess in this hotel?"

"I hope not, but there's a man upstairs that's liable to be hurting a friend of mine, and if he's still here, it's probably gonna get messy. And loud."

"Well, I'm on twenty-seven, and I need my nap, so you try to keep it down," she said, her lips pursed.

"Yes ma'am," I said. "I'm going to fourteen, so hopefully we won't disturb you."

"I hope not," she said. "It's been a long time since I had to put a bloodsucker down, but I still remember where the bastards keep their hearts and I've still got my stake in my purse."

I gaped at the little old lady as the doors *dinged* open for my floor. "You better go on now, son. You got ass to kick and I got a nap to take. Go with God, Hunter."

"And He with you, ma'am," I said as I stepped out into the hall on my floor. The security guard was looking at me with a grin he was barely holding back.

"Who was that?" I asked, staring at the elevator doors.

"That was Mrs. McGillicutty. She lives on the twenty-seventh floor, all expenses comped. Some sort of service she did to the city back in the day. She's a regular spitfire, that one."

"I reckon she is," I murmured. I'd never met a Hunter that old. Hell, she was the first one I'd ever heard of living old enough to think about retirement, much less really do it. I reckon Grandpappy was almost seventy when he died, but this old bird had at least a decade and a half on that. She must have been hell on wheels fifty years ago.

"Which room is yours?" the guard asked, snapping me back to reality.

"Head for 1430. It's my friend's room."

"I can't open—" He started to say something stupid about rules, but a good look at my face put a quick end to that. We walked single-file down the hall, me in front with Bertha drawn, the guard, whose nametag labelled him as "Pete," pulling up the rear with his master key card and a Mag-Lite. Skeeter's room was about four doors down from Amy's and mine, and across the hall. I saw from ten feet away that the door to his room was open and recognized the brown smear on the jamb instantly.

"He's gone," I said to Pete, holstering Bertha.

"How can you tell?"

"That blood is on the outside of the frame and high enough that it's right in my line of sight. Skeeter did that on purpose as he was being dragged or carried out of the room. Let's go see what other clues he left us." I pushed the door open and stepped inside.

The room looked pretty much together until you got to the sitting area, where the coffee table was covered in blood. A small computer chip lay in a pool of drying crimson, with a note in the center of the table. I picked it up. "Going Home" was scrawled on a sheet of hotel notepaper in a shaky hand. I picked up the chip, wiped it on the note, and slid it into my pocket.

"Shouldn't you leave that for the police?" Pete asked.

"Won't be any police, Pete. Won't be any mention of this anywhere. Sorry for the mess, but you should probably sacrifice a few towels to the blood on this table before the maids see it and flip out. Just put the linens on Mr. Jones' tab." All our rooms were on Skeeter's credit card, which was paid for out of some mysterious slush fund from the Vatican, so I knew there was plenty of cash to cover the bill.

"Where are you going? And do I have to go with you?" Pete asked as I headed for the door.

"No, you don't have to go with me. This is way better if I handle it alone. You stay here, clean up the mess, get the door fixed, and pretend nothing ever happened. I'm going to clean up and change so I can walk through the lobby without causing a general panic, then I'm going on a hunt to get my best friend back. He's being held by some bad people who want to use him as bait to lure me out, so I'm going to screw with their plans and give them exactly what they think they want."

Pete nodded and started for the bathroom for towels. Then he stopped and turned toward me. "Good luck. I don't know what you're messed up in, but if you're wearing that much blood and none of it's yours, I gotta assume you can handle yourself. But still…good luck."

"Thanks, Pete. Now remember, this never happened." I turned and went out the door, heading toward my room and pulling my key out with one hand and my phone with the other. My door was still locked, and the tape I'd put over the hinges was intact, so I felt pretty good about the place's integrity. I opened the door and scanned the room, but everything appeared untouched. Satisfied, I dialed Amy.

"Is he there?" she asked.

"No, are you close to Evangeline?"

"Yeah, she's right here. We're in the back of the ER. She's pretty looped, though."

"Get me Catherine's home address, for her main residence, and text it to me. I'm gonna get a little clean and go after Skeeter."

"You sure he's got him?"

"He cut the tracker out of Skeeter's arm, then left us a clue. He wants me to find him, he just doesn't want us to catch him before he gets where he's going. The destination is important to him. There's some kind of ceremonial significance to it."

"Now who's been watching too much *Criminal Minds?*" Amy teased.

"You detective types are rubbing off on me. How's your head?"

"I'm pretty sure it's fine. My vision is almost back to normal already, but Joe is making me go to the hospital."

"Good. It's not the worst thing in the world to get checked out, and it'll be good to have somebody there to keep an eye on Evie."

"You think she's hurt worse than she's letting on?" Amy asked.

"Nah, but if word gets out that the local hunter is laid up in the hospital, who knows what kind of critters might decide to pay her a visit. It'd be better if those critters were met by a heavily armed government agent than just a couple of nuns with rosaries."

"Fair enough. I'll text you the address."

"I'll call you when I've got our boy back."

Chapter Fifteen

TEN MINUTES LATER, I WAS ROARING NORTH ON I-10 ON MY borrowed motorcycle, my hair streaming out behind me like a flag. I was clean, in fresh jeans, a *Locke & Key* t-shirt with a black overshirt hiding Bertha from the rest of the world, wishing I hadn't left Great-Grandpappy's sword at home when we left for this "vacation." Amy had made a couple of calls and gotten me a police escort almost all the way to Catherine's place, a sprawling old plantation hidden away in the Big Branch Marsh National Wildlife Refuge. I left the blue lights behind me when I moved onto federal land and meandered my way down the narrow roads and almost deer trails until I pulled up to Catherine's house.

There was a Hummer parked out front, along with a Mercedes convertible and a Jag sedan. I assumed the Chevy with blackwall tires belonged to Ponté, so I was pretty sure I was in the right place. The four zombies blocking the door were also a dead giveaway, pun intended.

I pulled the Harley up beside the Hummer and put the kickstand down. I stepped over the bike and started toward the house, drawing Bertha as I walked.

"If those wandering corpses on the porch are important to you, they'd better be making a Bubba-sized path to the door right about now," I called as my foot hit the first of three steps up onto the wraparound porch. The house had seen better days, or better centuries, but it was still standing after a couple centuries worth of swamp rot and hurricanes, which was more than I could say for anybody else I knew. The glory of the four-columned porch had faded long ago, replaced by a patina of moss and funk covering just about everything. Kudzu and other vines twined along the floor, making footing treacherous. I just stomped my way up to the door anyway.

The zombies parted, revealing an open maw where the front door once stood. I stepped through the entrance into a grand foyer, complete with double spiral staircase leading up to the second floor. Candlelight flickered from my right, so I turned in that direction and stepped into the parlor.

If Skeeter weren't wearing his favorite *Big Bang Theory* hoodie, I might have thought I'd traveled back in time. The parlor was a study in antebellum elegance, with hurricane lamps glowing from side tables, antique sofas holding a host of living and undead guests, and Ponté standing at a roaring fireplace, holding court like a Mississippi plantation owner in 1850 or so.

"Welcome, Bubba! I am so glad you could attend the finale of our little performance," Ponté said, stepping forward as if to shake my hand.

I raised Bertha and leveled her at his nose. "I'm leaving. With Skeeter. Your problems with Catherine are your problems, but you come near one of my people again, there won't be enough left of you for the gators to care about."

"I don't think you're going anywhere until I decide you're leaving," Ponté replied, gesturing at the zombies behind me.

I turned, and there were four zombies blocking the doorway. I squeezed Bertha's trigger four times in the span of a single heartbeat, and there were four zombies decomposing on the floor.

"You want to tell me again why I'm not leaving?" I asked.

"Because by now there are a hundred more undead between you and your motorcycle, and you didn't bring that much ammunition." I looked through the open door and saw that he was right. The yard, empty when I pulled up to the house, was teeming with zombies now.

"Fine, Detective, why don't you tell me what you want, then we can all go home." I holstered Bertha but kept my arms loose, ready to draw at a moment's notice.

"I just want what's mine, the respect of this heartless bitch, and my brother back!" He gestured to Catherine, sitting stock-still in an armchair beside him. She was bound to the chair with what I assumed were silver chains, both because she wasn't moving at all and from the burns I could see on her wrists.

"I don't know about respect, but she's not the one that killed your brother—that was me. Just a couple hours ago, as a matter of fact. I put my pistol up against the back of his neck and performed the messiest damn decapitation I've ever seen." Skeeter wasn't talking, apparently bespelled into silence and paralysis by Ponté, but he could move his hands and was waving them frantically trying to get for me to shut my cakehole and stop poking the bear. I knew what he was trying to say, but I also knew my only hope of getting out of that room was to escalate things way beyond what Ponté could control.

I watched his face get red and saw the fight for control he was waging within himself. "She did that!" He pointed at Catherine again. "If she hadn't turned him, he never would have gone mad. My family served her for decades; three generations of Pontés have bent a knee to this bitch, and she repays us by turning my brother in a fit of hunger! What kind of master does that?"

"You know what you sound like, Detective?" I asked, trying to keep him grounded in reality as much as possible. If he went full-on voodoo priest on me, there was no way we were both leaving that room alive. "You sound like a whipped little dog that suddenly figured out it had teeth. Is that what you are, Ponté? You nothing but a whiny little dachshund that finally got tired of taking punishment and decided to nip at your master's heel?"

"You know nothing, you redneck trash!" The more agitated he got, the more the zombies scattered around the room moaned and rocked back and forth. Ponté took a deep breath, brought himself back under control, and said, "I just brought you here to be a witness to my ascension. You get to watch me destroy this bloodsucking bitch and release the city from her dominance once and for all."

"Then what?" I asked.

Ponté started, like I'd short-circuited something in his head. "What do you mean?"

"I mean what happens then? Do you quit being a cop to take over all her operations, because from what I've seen, being a criminal mastermind is a full-time job. And how are you gonna bring every other voodoo priest, witch, vampire, lycanthrope and whatever the hell else lives in New Orleans under your control? Do you have that kind of power, son? 'Cause there will be a Master, whether it's Catherine or somebody else. And right now, I'm leaning a lot towards the 'devil I know' camp than the 'devil I don't'."

"You mean to help her?"

"I mean to keep you from hurting my best friend. Then I mean to make sure this city is some kind of stable while your Hunter recovers from the injuries your brother inflicted on her. Then I mean to finish my vacation by getting drunk as a goddamn frat boy at a bachelor party and throwing beads off my hotel balcony at women of loose moral standing and spectacular breasts. And I plan on shooting the ever-loving shit out of anyone or anything that gets in my way. Are we completely clear on that?"

"Kill him!" Ponté barked and pointed in my direction. I sighed. I'd really hoped that just laying out the plan for the boy would have incentivized him to give up on his plan of mayhem and destruction, but in my experience, that never works. There were six zombies in the room, scattered around various couches and chairs, and one standing by a swinging door that led further back into the house. All of them started in my direction at the same time, so I sighed again and commenced to doing what I do.

All too often what I do is create maximum chaos in limited space, and this was no different. I drew Bertha and turned the nearest zombie, the one that had already been standing, into a headless corpse with one shot. The body kept walking for a couple feet, but when I reached out and pushed it over, it fell motionless to the buckled hardwood floor. I dropped three more with head shots before they really managed to get off the sofas, spraying brains all over the walls and furniture. I figured it would probably blend in after a few days of tremendous humidity and swamp moss.

That left two zombies, one of which was right on me before I could get Bertha around for a shot, so I put my gun arm across the thing's throat to keep it from chewing off anything I might want later. I reached around with my left hand, pulled my Buck 110 folder from my pocket, flicked the blade open, and buried it to the hilt in the monster's skull. The last zombie was either the longest dead or was just real stupid in life, because he was walking into a wall again and again. I left him alone.

I ejected the mostly-spent magazine and reloaded Bertha, then drew my new KABAR kukri in my left hand. I rolled my head, cracking my neck in a couple of places, and looked at Ponté. "I'm done with the appetizers. What's the main course?"

He pulled out a tiny doll dressed in jeans and a black shirt, with tattoos drawn all over its arms, and long hair and a beard. He then drew a pin out of a cushion on the mantle behind him and jabbed it into the doll's knee. I dropped to the floor, holding my knee and screaming in pain.

"This is the main course, you redneck trash." He jabbed the pin into the doll's left arm, and my kukri clattered to the floor. "I am the most powerful *houngan* in the bayou, you fool. My *loa* are more powerful than any! I will not be vanquished by some toothless hillbilly like a simple monster."

"First, asshole, I've got all my teeth, except for the one that got knocked out in a fight when I was in college. And two, you think your *loa* got power, jackass? I work for the Holy Roman Catholic Church, we *invented* resurrection." I picked up my kukri and stood. "And the *loa*? They serve *Bondye*, the Supreme Creator. A distant God, who leaves most of the world alone unless things get real jacked up. Sound familiar? Your *loa*, they're working for the same dude I'm working for, and they're all real pissed at you. That's why you can jab that doll all you want, I won't feel a thing. Because yea, though I walk through the valley of the shadow of death, I shall fear no evil. For God is with me. And I am the baddest son of a bitch in the valley."

I'd been slowly walking toward Ponté since I got up off the floor, and now I was right in front of him. I sheathed my kukri and took his doll, not a terrible likeness really, and threw it into the fire. Then I holstered Bertha and backhanded the trim detective right across the mouth. He spun almost all the way around and went down to one knee.

I saw his hand move toward his right ankle and said, "If you touch that backup piece on your ankle, I'm gonna have no choice but to kill you before you clear leather. And if you doubt I can do it, just look around. I'm big, and sometimes silly, and I ain't never been known as the smartest man in any room, but I draw clean and I shoot straight and I don't have to hit you in the kill zone with Bertha, she just blows off any part of you she hits. So why don't you stand up and press your back up against that mantelpiece while I take these chains off your boss?"

Ponté did as he was told, and I took the chains off Catherine. "Ma'am, your boy there has been a little unruly, playing with things above his pay grade. I'm gonna take my friend here, and we're gonna drive back to the city in that big old Hummer. You deal with the good Detective however you see fit, but I would appreciate it if somebody would deliver the motorcycle to my hotel tomorrow. I borrowed it."

Catherine stood with that unnatural grace that vampires have, no wasted motion in anything. "You don't want vengeance on Louis for the pain he has caused you and your friend?"

"He ain't really done much to me but make my vacation a little more exciting. And as for hurting Skeeter…" I looked over at my little buddy. He had a busted lip and a good-sized bandage on his arm, but it was the hurt in his eyes that made me see red. He'd liked Ponté, and the good-looking asshole had used his vulnerability against him. One of the things I loved most about

Skeeter was how trusting he was, how ready he always was to see the best in people. Ponté had hurt that part of him, and that was unforgivable.

"As for hurting Skeeter, he kinda deserved to have that tracker carved out of his arm for putting one in me without telling me," I said.

"It was for your own good!" Skeeter said, whatever spell that had held him silent and motionless obviously broken.

"Yeah, and this is for yours," I said, then reared back and flattened Ponté's perfect nose with a big right hand. His head bounced off the wall behind him and he fell to his hands and knees, blood pouring from his shattered sniffer. I leaned down next to him and whispered in his ear. "You hurt my friend, you son of a bitch, and I don't mean with a knife. If I ever hear of you stepping out of line or you ever leave New Orleans for the rest of your miserable life, I will cut you into little pieces and bury you in a dozen holes all over my backwoods mountain property where won't nobody ever look for your miserable, worthless ass. Are we clear?" He nodded, flinging drops of bloody snot across the floor.

I stood up. "He's all yours, but he stays in New Orleans until he dies. I ever hear of him outside the Crescent City, and his ass belongs to me. We clear?"

Catherine smiled a brittle smile. She was obviously not a woman accustomed to taking orders, and she didn't like it, but she also didn't want to take me on in her current condition. "Crystal clear, Mr. Brabham. Thank you for your assistance in this matter. Now, if you'll excuse me, I have some discipline to mete out."

"Um, I don't mean to be a pest," Skeeter said, actually raising his hand to get attention.

"Yes, Mr. Jones?" Catherine asked.

"There's still a shitload of zombies in your front yard, and they're gonna make it real hard to drive."

"Oh yes," Catherine said. "You. Disperse them," she commanded Ponté. He made a couple gestures, then pulled a knot of weeds out of his pocket and threw it into the fire. A sickly-sweet smell filled the room as the knot blazed to life, and in seconds all the zombies were shambling off, presumably back to their resting place.

Skeeter and I walked out to the Hummer, put it in gear, and headed back towards the city. After a few miles of riding in silence, Skeeter cleared his throat.

"Uh…thanks for coming to get me," he said.

"I don't leave my people behind. You're my best friend, Skeet. I couldn't just let him zombify you, or whatever he was gonna do."

"Thanks. I didn't know, you know, what with me acting all…"

"All what? Acting all horny? Acting like you liked him? Shit, Skeeter, how many titty bars and cathouses have you pulled me out of? If we didn't save each other from our own bad decisions, we'd have both been dead years ago."

"Yeah, I reckon that's true. Like that time you insulted the bartender at that strip club in Tampa?"

"You might have to be more specific, brother. I been to a *lot* of strip clubs in Tampa."

"The one you knocked down the whole DJ booth fighting with the bouncer and the bartender. Remember that one?"

"Oh yeah, and you hacked the fire alarm so I could get out the back without getting shot!" I chuckled. "Those were good times." I pointed the nose of the Hummer into the rising sun, and we told stories all the way to Cafe du Monde, where we stopped for beignets before we went to see the rest of the gang in the hospital. I've always found that if you go visit people in the hospital, especially if they're in the hospital because they tried to help you out, it's better to bring pastries.

Night at the Museum

Chapter One

ONE OF THE GREATEST THINGS ABOUT LIVING ON THE SIDE OF A mountain in Georgia miles away from civilization, aside from pretty much everything, is the freedom to build a shooting range on the bank of the creek behind my house. There's not a whole lot better than an afternoon with my girlfriend sewing hundreds of rounds of ammunition into the targets with a twelve-pack of beer sitting in the creek to stay cold.

So that's exactly where I was on a warm April afternoon, up to my ankles in cold mountain runoff, the sun beating down on my bare shoulders, wearing nothing but a pair of cutoff overalls and a shoulder holster, raining fiery death upon a dozen spinner targets I had spaced along the opposite bank, some fifty yards away. I was blaming all my misses on using Agent Amy's 9mm pea-shooter instead of my more familiar Desert Eagle, Bertha. I was indeed putting a lot more slugs into the dirt in front of the targets than I was into the targets themselves, but the eight empty beer cans littering the sandbar behind me might have contributed to that situation as much as overcompensating for the lighter weapon.

"Sumbitch!" I spat as another plug of dirt exploded three feet in front of the untouched target.

"I hope you still own a necktie, Bubba, because another couple of misses and you're going to have to take me somewhere *nice* for dinner. Like, maybe Atlanta nice." Agent Amy Hall mocked me from her shooting spot ten feet to my left. She was the other reason for my distraction, standing there in a bikini top and a pair of cutoff shorts that would have given Daisy Duke concern for her modesty. I'm pretty sure there was more pocket hanging below the waistband of those shorts than there was denim, and I'd made it a point to look pretty hard all afternoon. Her blonde hair was tied back in a high ponytail that bounced as she laughed, which was a lot this afternoon. These were the moments that I really loved, the times we could forget all the shit we'd seen and lived through, forget about my psycho brother and the other monsters in the world, and just be normal people, drinking beer and shooting shit on the side of a creek in the springtime.

"I've got a tie somewhere, but it might be taking the place of the fan belt on Pop's old tractor. I'm sure it's fine, though. I'm only down about fifty bucks." I grinned at her.

"Math isn't your strong suit, is it big guy? I'm ahead by seven, and at twenty-five bucks a shot, I think that smells like about one seventy-five. And since you've only got four rounds left..."

"Five," I said, raising the pistol and squeezing off five quick shots. Each report from the pistol was followed by a quick *spang* sound as the slug found the center of a four-inch hanging steel disk.

I holstered the pistol and turned to Amy. "I had five rounds left. So I think that leaves me down fifty bucks. And that means we can eat local. I'm thinking sushi."

Amy laughed, and all sorts of interesting things shook in her top and shorts. "Sushi, huh? Has Mr. Kim recovered from your last trip through his all-you-can-eat sushi bar?"

"Mr. Kim and I have come to an understanding. If I just want a snack, I pay regular price, and he decides what's 'all I can eat.' If I'm hungry, I pay double and he'll keep rolling fish in seaweed until I get tired of eating or his hands give out."

"That sounds fair. I can do sushi, and it'll be good to see Lee Kim again. Let's get this crap cleaned up and head home." I liked hearing her call my place "home." Amy had her own apartment in Washington, D.C., where she worked for DEMON, the federal Department of Extra-dimensional, Mystical and Occult Nuisances, and yes it always sounds like somebody wanted to call it "DEMON" real bad. She spent most weekends with me, either at my cabin just outside of Dalton, Georgia, or on a case with me.

I picked up the spent shell casings scattered all over the bank and the sand bar, tossed the brass into a backpack along with the shoulder holster and empty pistol and magazines, and pulled out a tattered "Austin 3:16" t-shirt. Just as I got my shirt on and was looking around for my flip-flops, I heard the buzz of an engine.

"You hear that?" I asked, moving toward the tree line. The throaty rumble of the motor sounded like an ATV of some type, probably a four-wheeler given what the local hunters liked.

"Yeah, what's up?" Amy picked up on my posture right away and shimmied into a t-shirt and a pair of Tevas. The engine was getting closer, and moving fast.

"You got any ammo left, or are you for real out?" I asked.

"I've got one mag. What's up?" she asked again, more serious now.

"Load up and get to the trees. Cover me. I found a patch of weed in the woods last week and the owners might have reason to be unhappy with me."

"You didn't turn it in?" she asked.

"Nah, it wasn't hurting anybody," I said. "But I did cut it all down and leave it to rot with a note saying to stay the hell off my property."

"Subtle."

"Yeah, subtle ain't my strong suit," I agreed. "But it's no secret who lives here, so if they're looking for me, they're probably gonna want to have a chat about that crop."

"How much weed did you cut down?" Amy asked, pulling her pistol and slamming home a fresh magazine.

"Twenty or so plants, I reckon. I don't know how much money that is, it's been a long time since I smoked, but I figure it was enough to be upset over." I picked up a four-foot branch lying at the base of a pine tree and gave it a couple experimental swings. The roar of the ATV came closer, until Father Joe, my handler for the Catholic Church and my best friend Skeeter's uncle, burst through the brush at the top of the trail and roared down to the creek where we stood.

Joe pulled up to where I stood staring at him and turned off the four-wheeler. It was one of those real fancy ones, with seating for four, like a big-ass golf cart with a roll cage and a beer shelf on the back. I reckon somebody somewhere might find something else to put on it other than beer, but it was the first thing I thought.

"Hey, Bubba," Joe said, stepping out of the four-wheeler. I just stood there, gawking at him. "Where's Amy?" he asked.

"I'm right here, Joe. How are you?" she asked, stepping out of the woods and slipping her pistol into her backpack.

"I'm good. Been trying to reach Bubba for two days, though. He doesn't answer his phone anymore." Joe gave me what was probably a withering stare to his parishioners, but I was still poleaxed by my preacher friend rolling up in a twenty-thousand dollar hunting ATV when as far as I knew, he'd never been hunting a day in his life.

"Where the hell did you get that thing?" I finally found my voice and pointed at the ATV.

"This? Oh, I borrowed it from Lincoln. You know him, he's always got to have the latest thing for his hunting trips. I told him I thought I knew where you were, but I couldn't get there on my bike, so he let me borrow this. It's kinda fun. I might get one."

I laughed a little bit at the picture. Joe looked just about right in a pulpit with the robes and sash and all that, and honestly, he looked pretty much at home on his Harley, too, with his kinda-long hair flying over the collar of his leather jacket. But no matter how hard I tried, I couldn't picture him with an orange vest over a set of camouflage coveralls and a Carharrt hat and Wolverine boots stomping through the woods and climbing a deer stand at five in the morning trying to find a comfortable way to sit with a chemical hand warmer tucked under his taint so his nuts don't freeze off.

"You taking up deer hunting, Joe?" I asked.

"No, it's just a lot of fun to ride around in," he replied, blushing a little.

"You might want to ask Lincoln what these things cost before you go trading in your Harley, pal. But what's so important that you've got to come all the way out here and track us down?"

"Well, we've got a job," Joe said.

"Yeah, but it's Sunday. Your Sunday job is looking after the metaphysical well-being of a couple hundred people in the Church of the Holy Redeemer down in Dalton. My Sunday job is drinking beer and wishing it was football season, and Amy's Sunday job is—"

"If you say a word about cooking or dishes, you will never see me naked again," my spectacularly hot girlfriend interrupted.

"Amy's Sunday job is getting a pedicure or whatever girls do when we're drunk." I corrected my course in mid-sentence.

"All that may be true, but I've been trying to reach you since Friday afternoon." Joe leaned on the fender of the four-wheeler, then reached around to the cooler Uncle Lincoln had bungeed to the luggage rack. Joe pulled out three beers and passed them around.

"I stop answering that phone Friday at four. It keeps me from getting pissed off when you get a last-minute call and ruin my weekend. This way I don't get pissed off until late on Sunday. See how well this works?" I popped the top and sat down on a rock. Amy followed suit, and Joe sat sideways on the seat of the four-wheeler.

"It works great, except we need to be in Orlando tomorrow at the latest. So now instead of flying, we have to drive, and we'll probably have to drive all night to get there," Joe said.

"Wait a minute," I said. "There's a few things I don't get here. One, Orlando ain't but about eight hours from here, and that's driving like Skeeter's mama, God rest her soul. Two, there's a whole bunch of 'we' in that sentence, and last I checked…" I looked over at Amy.

"Yeah, babe, I've got a meeting with a couple of Senators tomorrow, so I'm on a chopper back to DC at six in the morning," she said.

"So, are you coming along as my backup? Because if that's the deal, we gotta talk about the traveling music." Joe was one of about three people not called Bubba that I'd let drive my truck, and I hadn't met the third one yet, but if I had to listen to Taylor Swift's *1989* on repeat the whole damn way to Orlando, I might as well just drive my F-250 right into the Atlantic Ocean.

"You can control the radio, Bubba, but I am coming with you. This case has some personal connections for me, so I want to be there to help." Joe had a set to his jaw that told me not to push, so I figured I'd adhere to the bro code and let him tell me about his feelings when (1) there weren't any womenfolk around, and (2) when he damn well felt like it.

"Okay, then. I reckon we oughta get home and get packed. If we're driving through the night, I'm gonna need some Red Bull, ammunition, and pants," I said, standing up.

"Don't be in no hurry, hillbilly. We need to have us a conversation." A new voice came from behind me, and I turned to see three men step out of the woods. Two of them carried shotguns and were dressed for the woods in flannel, jeans, and work boots that had seen some wear. The one who spoke held a pistol in one hand and looked a little like a misplaced yuppie, with an expensive haircut and a polo shirt. His boots were new, his jeans were clean, but he carried the gun like he knew what it was used for, and his eyes were cold, like a snake. The two thugs with him were third-generation trailer trash twin brothers Bart and Marty Turner. I knew them in grade school 'til they flunked enough years to finally drop out. Word was they got most of their money running dog fights, selling a little dope, and working protection for some gangster out of Atlanta, making sure his shipments didn't get jacked.

Looks like I found the owners of that little patch of weed I wrecked.

Chapter Two

"WELL, HOWDY, STRANGER, WHAT CAN WE DO YOU FOR?" I asked, putting on my biggest "stupid redneck" grin. It was hard to see under all the beard, but it usually got city folks to underestimate me a little. All Yankees think if you sound like Foghorn Leghorn, you must have an IQ to match, and all city folk think if there ain't a sidewalk in front of your house that you probably ain't figured out indoor plumbing yet. This was one of the times I thought I might use people's prejudices against them.

"Hey, Bart. Hey, Marty." I nodded to the brothers. We'd been friendly back when we played Little League baseball and rode the school bus together. We even got spankings together in Mrs. Dickson's third-grade class for tying bottle rockets to the class turtle and trying to make it fly. I think with a couple more fireworks we could have got there, but that poor turtle was so damn stressed after our experiment that he didn't come out of his shell for a month.

"Hey, Bubba. How you doin'?" Marty asked. Bart just grunted. He was always the less vocal of the brothers. In fact, I'm not sure I'd ever heard Bart actually speak.

"I'm okay. Just doing a little target practice, you know. How's your mama? I heard she's been down."

"Aw man, the doc says it's her heart. Congestive heart failure, he called it. I think it's when fluid builds up around the heart and makes it hard to pump. Makes you tired as shit all the time."

"Shit, son, that's terrible. Is there anything they can do for her?" I asked.

"The doc told her she had to quit drinking, quit eating fried food, and quit smoking, even weed. He told her if she did all that, she'd live another twenty years."

"That's rough," I replied.

"Yeah," Marty said. "When the doc told her that, she looked that old sumbitch right in the eye and said, 'If I can't drink, eat, or smoke, what's the damn point of being alive?'" We shared a good laugh, then his face went still. "I reckon you know why we're here, Bubba."

"Your boy there has some objection to me chopping down them marijuana plants I found growing on my property last week, I reckon," I said, looking up the hill at the skinny man with the pistol.

"Do you have any idea how much money you cost me, you ignorant redneck? I oughta just take it out of your ass, but I'm a nice guy, so I'm going to give you one shot to come up with my money. You pay me what I'm losing out on that patch, and maybe I decide not to kill your stupid ass."

"Well, I'm not a fan of getting shot," I said. "It's happened once or twice, and it's never as much fun as it looks like on TV. How much money do you think I chopped down in those, what, twenty plants?"

"Yeah, twenty plants. I can get a pound out of a plant, and I sell an ounce for a hundred bucks, so that's what, sixteen hundred dollars a plant?" I love how drug dealers become math professors when it comes time to talk money. "Twenty plants at sixteen hundred a piece comes to something like twenty-three thousand. Add in the irritation of not having supply for my customers, and potential lost business, and we'll call it twenty-five grand and I let you walk out of here."

I laughed at him, then pointed at my cutoff overalls. "Where the hell do you think I've got twenty-five cents in this outfit, much less twenty-five grand? Now I've got some cash back at my place, and we can go get that, or you can start shooting, but you know Joe over there is a preacher, right? You kill him and there's no way you don't go to hell when you die."

He stepped forward and pressed his pistol into my gut. He almost had to break his neck looking up to glare into my eyes, but he managed. "You think I give a shit about heaven and hell, redneck?"

"You keep saying that like it's a bad thing, son. I'm proud to be a redneck, and I reckon these boys are, too." I pointed at the Turners, who glared at their city-slicker friend.

"I don't give a shit what you like, asshole!" He fell into that old Yankee habit of talking with his hands, and as soon as he waved that pistol off to my left, it was on like Donkey Kong. I wrapped my left hand around his, gun and all, and brought my right fist down on top of his head like I was pounding a fence post into the ground. His eyes rolled back in his head, and he slumped to the ground.

I plucked the gun from his lifeless fingers and looked at Marty Turner. He held his shotgun low to the ground and didn't look too thrilled with the idea of shooting me, or getting shot, so I figured he was the one to talk to. Also, Amy had his brother on the ground with her service weapon in his ear, so Bart was out of the fight. I love a woman who can kick ass.

"Marty, this can go down a couple of ways, and they're all your choice, buddy," I said.

"I reckon don't none of them choices include me getting the five large that little shitbird promised us, do they?" Marty asked.

"Well, son, that's between you and him. Way I see it, you did your part. It ain't really your fault you ran into an armed federal agent and the meanest sumbitch in twenty square miles."

"You got a point, Bubba, but you gonna send this jackass to jail, and then he ain't never gonna be able to pay me! I shoot you, at least I get something out of the deal. I kill you and I get to drink for free in every werewolf bar in Georgia."

"And Tennessee," Bart said from the ground. Some people choose the strangest times to get chatty.

I thought for a second. I didn't know how Marty and Bart came to know that werewolves were real, but most hill folk are a little more in tune with the supernatural than your average Joe. I figured on a counter-offer. "I bet that boy's got himself a couple grand in his wallet, and that watch he's wearing looks expensive. How about I let you roll him, then y'all go on home, and we'll take care of this dumbass."

"That sounds fair," Marty said. "That okay with you, Bart?' Bart grunted, keeping the total number of words I'd ever heard him speak to two. I lowered the pistol, and Marty knelt by the unconscious weed farmer. He took his watch, a couple of rings that I thought looked fake, but I'm no jeweler, and pulled a wad of bills out of that boy's front pocket big enough around to choke a horse. "Can I have the credit cards, too?"

"Nah, just take the cash," I said. "We don't want y'all to get in no identity theft trouble."

"Okay," Marty said. He stood up and held out his hand. I shook it. "Thanks, Bubba. We didn't much want to help him rob you, especially since you was always decent to us growing up and then turned out to be so damn big. But he offered more money than we make in a month, so we kinda had to do it."

"It's alright, Marty. I know how it is." Bart was on his feet by now, and I shook hands with him, too, then I tied the city slicker's hands and feet together with his boot laces and dumped him onto the back of Joe's ATV.

"Let's get back to the house. Amy's gonna have some paperwork to do with this asshole and I reckon I need to pack a bag to go to Florida." I gave Amy the thug's pistol to put in her bag and we rolled off to the house. Joe parked his four-wheeler next to my truck, and Amy called the Sheriff to come pick up our little Junior El Chapo.

I grabbed a quick shower, threw some clothes in a bag, and was back out on the porch to see the Sheriff's car rolling down my driveway in a cloud of dust. "Everything cool?" I asked Amy.

She was sitting on my porch in a rocking chair, her feet propped up on the porch rail, pink toenails shining in the afternoon sun. "Yeah, it's all good. Sheriff's gonna stick him in a holding cell for twenty-four hours while I get somebody down here to charge him with possession, intent to distribute, concealed weapon, conveying threats, and whatever else I can get him on. I don't get the big charge, which would have been nice, but somebody mulched all the evidence."

"Sorry," I said.

"It's fine. He threatened a federal agent, even if he didn't know it at the time. So he'll get the book thrown at him on everything else, and my testimony should be plenty to put him under the jail for years." Amy stood on tiptoes and gave me a kiss. "Now get in the truck and find out what's got Joe so riled up about Florida. I've called the office and they're sending a chopper for me in a couple of hours. I'll stay at my place in DC tonight and check in with you tomorrow."

"Alright, we'll get rolling. I bet Joe's pacing my living room like a lion in a cage."

"I'm surprised he's not sitting in the passenger seat honking the horn." Amy grinned up at me, then hugged me again. "Be safe, you big idiot."

"Yeah, I love you, too," I said, then hollered back into the house. "Joe! Let's roll!"

He burst through the back door, a duffel bag in hand. That boy was ready to *go*. I bent down, kissed Amy again, and hopped into the truck to go to Florida and find out what was so important to Joe in the Sunshine State.

Chapter Three

THE SUN WAS COMING UP AS WE ROLLED OFF THE INTERSTATE AND onto International Drive. According to Joe, this new Museum of Antiquities was in one of the old parts of the convention center, so I turned into what looked like the right parking lot, found a spot near the back door, and turned off the truck. Joe reached for his door handle, but I pressed the "lock" button before he could escape again.

"Open the door, Bubba, I need to use the bathroom."

"You peed less than an hour ago at that Waffle House, so you can hold it for a minute. I been in this truck for most of eight hours, and you ain't said a word yet about the case, or why it's so all-fired important that you be here with me. Matter of fact, aside from singing along to *Blank Space*, you been silent as a monk since we left the mountain. Now spill it, or we're gonna sit in this parking lot all day."

"It's complicated, and I'd rather you hear the details of the case from the museum personnel," Joe said, then turned back to try the door again. Wasn't happening.

"That's fine. I don't really give a shit what we're after. It's bad, we'll hunt it down, I'll kill the shit out of it, we'll go home. That ain't what's important here. What's up your butt, Preacher?" He flinched a little at the word "preacher," and I was even more confused.

"It's about that, actually..."

"For God's own damn sake, Joe, if you don't tell me what the hell is going on, I'm gonna whoop your ass 'til my arm hurts!"

"Fine, fine, calm down." He sighed and ran his fingers through his curly black hair. He wore his hair too long for most mountain-type preachers, but The Church cut him a whole lot of slack because he was the only one who could kinda keep me in line. They cut me a whole lot of slack because I killed everything they sent me to kill, and sometimes brought back bonus dead bad guys, too.

"There's someone working here in the museum that I used to know. That I used to...be friends with. Before I was a priest." Joe very studiously did not look at me while he said all this. Somehow, the mirror outside my passenger window was suddenly very interesting.

"Okay, so there's a chick here you used to bang, back when you banged chicks and didn't save it all for Jesus. Who probably doesn't want all your sweet lovin', by the way. But that's another conversation. What's the big deal?"

"Well...we haven't seen each other in a very long time, not since we broke up, and I'm afraid that she might have..."

"Are you scared that she moved on and got married, or are you more scared that she didn't?" I asked.

"I don't know," he said. Now he looked at me, and the regret and pain in his eyes was so raw, so open, that I almost couldn't take it. I'm not much for sentimental. A good fart joke is as close to sentimentality as I usually get, so seeing Joe bare his soul like that was really shocking.

"Well, shit, Joe," I said. "You loved her!"

"I thought I did. Then I felt the call. So I left school and transferred."

"Without telling her," I added.

"Without telling her," he confirmed.

"And you didn't return her calls." I tried not to condemn with my tone.

"Or her texts, or her emails," he agreed. "I cut her out of my life without warning, and I've felt horrible about it ever since. But I was twenty years old, I had no idea what I was doing, and now..."

"The world has played a nasty trick on you and you have to deal with the shit you pulled when you were a stupid kid," I finished his sentence for him. Probably not in the words he was planning on using, but I got my point across.

"Yeah, pretty much." He sagged into the seat of my truck and looked up. "What do I do?"

"Sack up and deal with it," I said.

"Excuse me?" He turned to face me. Pretty sure that's the first time since he put on that collar that anyone told him to "sack up."

"Put on your big boy pants and get in there. You screwed up, you feel like shit about it, so go in there, be a professional, and the first chance you get to talk to this girl in private, apologize."

"Apologize?"

"Apologize."

"Apologize?"

"A. Pol. O. Gize. It ain't hard, Joe. I've seen you fight elvish warriors, werewolves, vampires, snake-dudes, and all sorts of nasty critters. Just yesterday you stared a pissed-off drug dealer in the face and didn't flinch. I'm pretty sure this woman, no matter how much you crushed her heart, is less interested in killing you than anyone else on that list. So reach deep down into your socks, find your balls, and strap 'em on. Let's go." I unlocked the doors and got out of the truck. Joe didn't budge, and I didn't press him.

I opened the back door of the crew cab and shoved my duffel into the floor. Then I flipped up the seat and opened the top drawer of the gun case I had built into the truck. I grabbed Bertha, my Desert Eagle, and slipped on her shoulder holster. I checked to make sure she was loaded and confirmed regular ammo in the gun. Then I slipped three magazines into the other side of the shoulder rig. One was silver, and the other two alternated between cold iron and white phosphorus rounds. Anything that could stand up to cold iron usually really didn't like getting set on fire from the inside out, and vice versa.

I grabbed a paddle holster and clipped it to the inside of my waistband at the small of my back. My Judge revolver went there, with three holy water and silver .410 shotgun shells and two cold iron .45 long rounds. I liked the versatility of the Judge, and there was something reassuring about having a shotgun just hanging out at the small of my back for tough situations. I tossed my caestus into a backpack with a few flash-bangs, a couple smoke grenades, half a dozen yew stakes and three Dasani water bottles full of holy water. I strapped a pair of silver-edged kukri to the outside of the pack and slung it over both shoulders. Feeling loaded for bear, I looked up in the front of the cab. Joe was gone. I buttoned up the gun case and closed the door.

He was standing by the front bumper, still looking a little green.

"You gonna make it?" I asked, using what I thought was my "tender voice." In other words, the only voice I had that didn't send small children running for the hills whenever I spoke.

"Do I have a choice?" he asked, a sickly little smile on his face.

"Sure," I said. "You can wait in the truck. I ain't gonna leave it running, but I'll crack a window for you, like you're my dachshund or something."

"The day you own a dachshund, I'll go out and get a mastiff," Skeeter's voice came into my ear over our Bluetooth connection. Joe's head snapped up as he heard his nephew.

"Hey, Skeeter," Joe said.

"Uncle Joe," Skeeter replied. "Now, are y'all gonna go in there and find out what needs killin', or are y'all just gonna stand outside and hold hands some more?"

"We're going," I said, and started walking toward the door. I didn't look back at Joe. He was either going to get his shit together about this girl, or he wasn't. And if he wasn't, I didn't want him watching my back anyhow. But I was relieved to hear the clump of his engineer boots on the asphalt behind me as I got close to the Employee Entrance.

The security guard at the back door either thought he'd nabbed The Big One or that he was going to die when I walked up, bristling with artillery. "Hey," I said, stopping at his station.

"C-can I help you?" he asked, and I'm guessing this was a good day for him to be wearing the brown pants.

Joe stepped up, back to his smooth self. "We're here to see Rebecca Knowles. We're here to consult on the religious significance of some artifacts she may have recently acquired. My name is Dr. Joseph MacIntyre. I believe she is expecting me."

"For some time, Dr. MacIntyre," came a silky female voice from the now-open door into the body of the museum. She was a good-looking woman, medium build, with a dark brown or maybe auburn pixie cut. She wore jeans and sensible hiking boots, with a dress shirt tucked into her pants. A pair of wire-rimmed glasses set atop her button nose, and she had a splash of freckles across her cheeks that made her look younger than she probably was.

She stepped forward and held out her hand. Joe shook it with a mute nod, and I stuck out my big paw. "Robert Brabham, Miss…Knowles?"

"Doctor," she corrected. "Doctor Rebecca Knowles, but you can call me Becca. Everybody around here collects PhDs like some people collect baseball cards, so if you just call out 'Doc,' you're likely to get half a dozen answers. Including your friend, Dr. MacIntyre." She gestured to Joe, who still hadn't spoken since she stepped through the door. I felt like the polite thing to do was to hold up his end of the conversation, too, but I was gonna have to make a wisecrack sometime in the next two minutes or I might explode.

"Nah, he knows if I'm looking for him, I'd holler 'Padre' or something like that." That didn't count, even though Becca faked a little laugh. We stood there shuffling back and forth for a couple minutes until I said, "So, I understand you've had some strange stuff going on? You want to show us where the weird shit has been going down?"

She snapped to like I'd pinched her, which I swear I didn't. Hell, as small as she was, if I pinched her, it was liable to leave a bruise. "Yes, of course. Let's get you some visitor badges and take a look at the site of the disappearances."

We had pictures taken and the guard printed out little laminated ID cards. Apparently they had a deal on laminated cards, or somebody thought this was going to be more than a one-night gig. Becca led us through the back door into the body of the museum, pointing out some of the back-room kinda stuff as we passed, like storage rooms with uncategorized donations. I filed that away for future reference, since all kinds of stuff ended up donated to museums, and we might find the answer to all our problems in some box of Mrs. McGillicutty's knickknacks.

The museum was all but abandoned, with a few workers here and there touching up exhibits. I'd never been to a museum right before it opened, but I'd been to a bunch of other construction projects, and this one felt weird somehow. There was none of the buzz of activity that accompanied the final stages of a building project, and nothing in the people around me said "We're in a hurry, we open soon." Everybody just seemed semiconscious, or like they were sleepwalking.

"Becca, I don't mean to sound rude or nothing, but don't y'all open in a couple days?" I asked.

She did have the courtesy to blush, which I appreciate in someone who has conned me into driving all night for a fake grand opening. "We…don't really open Friday. I mean, not this Friday. We open next Friday. That's… just what I told your people so they would pass our request directly to your team. Directly to…'

"Me," Joe said. "Directly to me."

"Yes," Becca admitted. "I knew, well I hoped anyway, that if you saw my name as the client that you would push me to the top of the list."

"So you manipulated the system using your past relationship with my handler to get me down here sooner than normal," I said.

"Yes, and I'm sorry, but there really is something going on, and I really do need your help." She was almost in tears after admitting her lie.

"I don't mind," I said. "Hell, I respect somebody who's willing to lie a little bit to get what she wants. So what's the deal? What's going on around here?" I looked around, but the place looked just like every other museum I'd ever been to—a whole lot of boring in one address. One of these days, somebody's gonna build a museum to boobies and beer, and I'm gonna be all over that shit. Until then, I pass.

Chapter Four

"THE PROBLEMS STARTED WHEN WE CHANGED THE OPENING exhibit from a history of early American coin-operated games to an immersive exhibit on fictional and fantastical monsters throughout history. Our board of directors felt that we needed something with broader commercial appeal for our grand opening, so we made the change over the protests of some of our curators, several of whom had invested quite a bit of time bringing in coin-operated games from all over the country," Becca said, looking way, way up at me.

"You mean like Pac-Man, and pinball and shit? How hard could those be to find?" I asked.

"We're actually talking about games much older than those, from toy banks from the turn of the century, to replica Batmobiles and hobby horses that stood outside grocery stores to extract that last quarter from your mom's purse after a shopping trip." She corrected me with a grin, and I started to see what Joe liked in her. She was a sharp one and would have made a good match for my preacher buddy, except for that whole not getting married and celibacy thing.

"What kind of problems have you had?" I asked. By then we were standing in front of a big sheet of plastic with strips of yellow caution tape crossed over the surface in a big "X." A couple of the nearby workmen were giving us the side eye, so I found the split in the plastic and held it open. We stepped through, and Becca walked over to the wall and turned on the overhead fluorescents.

I could see how the place would be creepy as shit with the dim exhibit lights as the only illumination, but like so many things that are creepy in the dark, pouring a ton of light on it made it all seem harmless. Skeeter's dance moves are one exception to that rule. The darker it is when he's flailing about like an epileptic giraffe, the better for everyone.

"You getting all this, Skeeter?" I asked, turning around slow so he could get a good look. I wasn't wearing my sunglasses, which was how he usually got a camera shot, but a couple weeks ago my little super nerd came busting into my house holding a pretty badass skull belt buckle and grinning like the cat with a bellyful of feathers. Turns out the skull is a Wi-Fi camera, so now wherever my belt went, Skeeter went. This made for more than one uncomfortable moment at a urinal and a real long lecture about my behavior during a lap dance over a weekend where Agent Amy had to stay in DC for work and I was left to my own devices. I am not a man with a strong moral compass, so when the opportunity to drink beer and look at boobies arose, I was there. I forgot that wherever my pants went, Skeeter went. And my pants went to Jolene's Landing Strip out by the airport for about six hours and forty-seven beers. At least Skeeter drove me back to get my truck after he finished bitching me out.

So anyway, I turned in a circle so my belt buckle could see the whole room and started talking to the air, exactly the kind of professional assistance I'm sure Dr. Becca was looking for.

"I'm sorry," I said by way of explanation. "I've got a Bluetooth comm set up with my tech guy back home, and he put a camera in my belt buckle so he could see what I see. Or what I would see if my eyes were down where my—"

"Bubba," Joe cut in, probably just in time going by the blush on Dr. Becca's face. "Does anything look odd to Skeeter?"

"Well?" I asked.

"Nothing in the visible spectrum. Gimme a second to switch to infrared… nothing there. UV looks good, too. There's nothing the camera can pick up, fellas," came the report into my ear.

"Skeeter says the camera doesn't see anything out of the ordinary, and apparently my belt buckle can do infrared and ultraviolet. Cool, huh?" I kinda thrust the belt buckle out at Joe and Becca, then realized how that probably looked through the translucent plastic and pulled my crotch back. "Sorry," I said.

"Don't worry about it," Becca replied. "So you didn't find anything?" she asked.

"Well, no, but that was just a quick scan across a couple of spectra. Now we get down into the investigatin' part of things. Let's start with provenance on the artifacts."

She gaped at me. "Excuse me?"

"Provenance. It means where did all this shit come from," I said.

"I…know what provenance is, I just…"

"You just didn't expect *me* to know what provenance is." I finished her sentence for her. "Don't worry about it, Doc. I know I sound like what you get if Buffy banged the cast of *Duck Dynasty*, but I do know what I'm doing. There's some nasty shit out there, and I'm the best there is at hunting it down and killing it."

"How do you know?" she asked.

I grinned at her. I didn't hold back, I gave her the full-blown "I have been through the shit and come out the other side" crazy grin. "I know 'cause I'm still alive. And all the sonsabitches that tried to kill me ain't. I've killed more monsters than any other Hunter working for the Vatican, except for that old boy that got the Black Forest in his territory, and can't nobody compare to the shit that comes out of that place. But as far as America goes, you have standing before you the baddest mother in the valley. So I don't fear no evil. Now, about that provenance?"

She looked at me, a little wide-eyed, then turned her gaze to Joe. He just shrugged and said, "He's right. There's really nobody better."

"Okay, then," Becca said. "Where do you want to start?"

"Let's start at the oldest and work our way forward. If there's anything really powerful here, it's unlikely to be all that recent in origin. Meanwhile, you can tell me what's been going on."

"When we first made the change, it was small things. Paint rollers and pans left out where people would step on them in the dark, ladders leaned precariously against doors so they fell on people when they walked through, the kind of things that are annoying, and painful, but nothing really harmful. We had a few people get bruised, and few shoes and skirts get ruined from paint, but we all just assumed that the contractors had left things lying around. But when we came in on a Monday and cases were smashed, we knew the contractors had nothing to do with it."

"It happened over the weekend?" I asked.

"Yes," she replied, leading me over to a remote corner of the exhibit. "This is the starting point of the exhibit. You enter from there—" She pointed toward a pair of sliding doors. "And begin here, with ancient Japanese dragon masks." She pointed to the wall. "The masks are to hang just off the wall and be backlit, so there's very little seen but the eyes, until you step here, and hit a pressure pad in the floor."

She stepped into place in front of where the mask should hang, and a set of lights came on aimed at the wall, revealing a colorful dragon mural painted about twenty feet down the wall. A pair of bars hanging from wires started to jiggle, indicating where the masks would move. A recording came in over the speakers in the ceiling, and I started to get a lesson in Chinese and Japanese Dragons. I didn't know there was a difference. Something about toes was all I got from the recording 'cause I wasn't paying a whole lot of attention.

"So these masks are the oldest things in the exhibit?" I asked. "I might need to see them."

"We can do that, but they're in our secure storage until the exhibit is almost ready to open. They are very old and valuable, so we don't want to just leave them hanging around while we're under construction."

"That makes sense," I said. "What's that thing?" I pointed to a case a little further into the exhibit.

"That's the next stop," Becca said, sliding past me to go stand in front of the case. Just like with the dragons, when she stepped on the right spot on the floor, lights clicked on. These all focused on a two-foot square case on about a four-foot high pedestal. In the center of the beams of light was a gleaming white skull, and what I saw on the skull made me gasp.

"Skeeter, do you see that shit?" I murmured.

"I do, Bubba. I do indeed, but I can't imagine how I'm seeing it."

"Yeah, it don't make no sense to me, either. I thought they turned to dust when you chop their heads off." At least, every bloodsucker I'd ever killed turned to dust, or at least bloody slush, when I killed it. Actually, come to think of it, I'd never killed one old enough to turn to dust. The ones I killed always made a mess that needed way more of a Shop-Vac than a Dust Buster.

"Oh, it's not real," Becca said with a little laugh. "I mean, obviously it can't be real because…wait, what?"

I nodded at her, and Joe stepped forward to look closer at the human skull sitting in the case with extended fangs protruding down over its lower jaw. "Yeah, this is fake, Bubba. The fangs are in the wrong place, and they're obviously snake fangs just added onto the real teeth. It's a good fake, but it's fake. Look here, Beck." He motioned her over and pointed to the skull. "On a real vampire, the fangs are the first canines, closest to the incisors, but you're got them on the second canines, which puts them too far apart to actually bite someone. Also, the fangs don't look like this when they're down. They just look like long pointy teeth, only a little more so. They don't look like snake fangs, or even a cat's teeth. They don't make those neat little puncture wounds like in the old movies. It's more that they rip a hole in the victim's carotid and just catch the spray and drink it." He stood up quickly, as if he realized all of a sudden that he was close to a girl and was afraid of getting cooties.

I was obviously going to have to lock these two in a broom closet with a bottle of scotch before this case was over. I cleared my throat. "I'm pretty sure the fake vampire head isn't causing any of your troubles, so what's next?"

"Next we move to the djinns and rakshasa. Rakshasa are—"

"I know what rakshasa are," I interrupted. "They're invariably Clemson or LSU fans, so they're among my least favorite monsters. They're also universally mischievous assholes, so if it's mostly pranks, you might very well have a tiger-man running around here in disguise."

"Well, I thought that might be the case as well, so I installed a lot of extra mirrors around the exhibit, but so far I haven't seen anyone paying extra attention to themselves." I grunted a little at the idea. She *was* smart. Rakshasa are shapeshifters whose natural form is male human bodies with the heads of tigers. Being part cat, they are incredibly vain, complete assholes, and prone to shit in your shoes if you do something they don't like. I made that last part up. They won't shit in your shoes; they'll just rip you to shreds or cast a spell that turns you into a mouse or something equally unfortunate.

If you don't think being a mouse is unfortunate, remember that these are essentially six-foot tall cats, so it's a pretty unfortunate place to be a mouse. Since they are so vain, a rakshasa can't ever pass a mirror without stopping to admire itself, fix its hair, and generally be a pretty pretty princess for a minute. Becca installing mirrors all over the place without anyone noticing the creature probably means there wasn't a rakshasa nearby. Especially if she used good mirrors. Good mirrors still use silver backing, and silver is rough on magic, so a rakshasa looking into a silver-backed mirror would reflect its true form for anyone to see.

"And yes," she answered my unspoken question. "I used silver mirrors." Yup, smart chicks will be the death of me.

Chapter Five

"OKAY, SO WHAT'S NEXT?" I ASKED.

"After the rakshasa, we move on to the Western European section of the exhibit." Becca led us through a hallway that was a lot narrower than anything a dude my size really wanted to walk through, and we came out into a replica of what looked like the biggest Brothers Grimm mashup you've ever seen. There was a cabin big enough to walk into made out of candy, and the trail led right up to the door, so we went in. Inside there was a whole Hansel & Gretel setup, complete with an animatronic witch, huge oven, and a couple of kid mannequins in a cage.

We stepped through a door in the witch's cabin and came right out into Little Red Riding Hood's Grandma's bedroom, complete with a werewolf in the bed and a woodsman wielding an axe at the monster. We stepped through another door, and I saw the base of a giant beanstalk. I looked up, and tucked away within the rafters of the building was Jack, a dummy rigged to slide down the beanstalk with a golden goose under his arm.

"Y'all went all out on the robots in here, didn't you?" I asked.

"We designed this exhibit for the maximum interaction with our patrons, yes," Becca replied. "This is where the trouble started getting more serious. We came in one morning and several robots were malfunctioning, and the woodsman was reoriented so his axe swung right at head level every time the door opened."

"So you've got a monster that's good with robots? That don't make any sense," I said. "Look, usually either you have a monster, in which case you have a bunch of dead bodies and blood and people pieces strewn everywhere, or you have a human, and you've got a bunch of people scared shitless but mostly not hurt. People *want* something. Monsters just kill shit. And they're real good at killing shit, and not so good at picking around with electronics. I think you've got a human problem, not a monster problem."

"That's what we thought, too. Then we started finding bodies," Becca said.

"Bodies?" Joe asked, finally shaking off the funk he'd been wallowing in since we arrived.

"It started with small animals, mice and rats. I thought maybe some of the mice from the animal lab downstairs got loose, but these weren't white mice. They were just random field mice, then a few rats, then a dog."

"Where were these animals found? Was there a pattern to their arraignment? Any sort of ritualization of the killing, or did it seem to be random?" Joe fired off questions rapid-fire, like a machine gun. It was good to see him engaged, but a little unnerving how quickly he snapped back to himself once the specter of evil magic was raised.

I left the two lovebirds talking about rat blood and finger-painting in entrails and started poking around the exhibit myself. I whipped out my Leatherman and popped a back panel off the woodsman's torso. The wiring was clean, with no apparent cuts or splices, so whoever messed with the big guy really did a killer job. This part of the drama was looking more and more like a very corporeal culprit, as opposed to something attached to one of the artifacts, but I kept poking around just to be sure.

I wandered through Contemporary America, pushing buttons that made Robert Pattinson's eyes light up and his skin sparkle, and turning a knob that made a computer-generated Taylor Lautner get really hairy and even shorter than normal, but I didn't see anything that didn't look way more like it was man-made than anything touched by a monster. "Skeeter," I said, tapping my Bluetooth.

"Yeah, Bubba?" He sounded like he was doing something, and I couldn't tell if I interrupted his nap time or his porn time. Either way, I didn't much care.

"I'm bored. Is there anything in any of this shit that looks haunted?"

"Nope, nothing."

"Possessed?"

"Uh-uh."

"Magical in any way?"

"Not even a little bit."

"Then what the hell is going on here?" I asked the air.

"If you ask me, that mouthy little bitch is getting what's coming to her, and it's about time," came a voice from the other side of a display case. I stood up on tiptoes to see over the case full of props from *The Walking Dead* and peered into the beady eyes of a very sour-faced old dude. He looked like he'd spent the last two years chewing lemon rinds raw, and the fifteen before that getting his ass kicked in high school. He was every stereotype of the kind you expect to find working in a museum. He was skinny, short, maybe 5' 8", with a short-sleeve blue dress shirt, a darker blue tie, horn-rimmed glasses, and I shit you not, an honest-to-God pocket protector.

"And who might you be?" I asked Mr. Personality.

"I'm Dr. Douglas Cornwell III, senior exhibits programmer and expert in early twentieth-century amusement paraphernalia." He stepped around the case and held out his hand. We shook and he said, "I apologize for being snippy earlier. It's been a very trying period throughout the entire facility."

"And I assume the mouthy little bitch you were talking about is Dr. Knowles?" I asked. I didn't like this dude, and not just because he was slagging Joe's ex, who seemed okay for a big-brain type. Something about him just irritated the piss out of me, probably the way he managed to stare up at me and still look down his nose at me.

"Dr. Knowles-it-all?" He almost spat when he said the name. "Yeah, that's her. She's the little upstart that got my exhibit bounced until later this year, and out of the main halls, too! Now I'll only have two little rooms to display the entire depth and breadth of Americana toy-making. That's almost impossible, but I'll figure it out."

"I reckon it's good you've got more time to plan, then," I said.

"Oh, is that what you 'reckon'? Well, that just goes to show what you know, which is nothing. She didn't bump me from the calendar to give me more time; she did it to get herself more money. My exhibit won't come online now until well after the budget for the next three years' worth of capital expenses is approved, not to mention this year's raise cycle!"

It all made sense suddenly. "So you're really just pissed at her because now you won't get a raise, or a new computer, or whatever," I said.

"That bitch's machinations—"

"Evil plans, maneuvering," Skeeter whispered in my ear.

"—have cost me an opportunity to acquire several priceless pieces for the museum's collection already, and without a significant increase in my departmental budget, my conference travel plans may have to be curtailed, or even cancelled. And several buying trips I had planned for New Mexico and the Southwest may be put on hold as well, all because of Dr. *Knowles* and her monster exhibit. Well, I, for one, am glad to hear it's being shut down."

"Shut down?" I asked. "Nobody's said anything to us about a shutdown. We just got here to look into things. There's no need to shut stuff down before we get a chance to poke around and find out if there's a supernatural element in the stuff that's been going on around here."

"Well, of course there isn't," the snotty little curator scoffed.

"And you know this how?" I asked. "Are you behind all the troubles Dr. Knowles has been having?"

His pasty face went half a shade whiter at my question, but he recovered enough to splutter, "Of course not! I simply meant that as there are no monsters, these supernatural theories will quickly be disproven, then we can go on about the business of running a museum, not a theme park!" He waved a finger in the air, for emphasis I guess, then stormed off past me. Well, truth is, he tried to, but when he stormed by me, he kinda ran into my shoulder and bounced off. I reckon he was accustomed to people yielding the right of way to him a lot more than I did, because he tried it again, and bounced off again. This time he turned sideways and scooted between me and an exhibit case and vanished into the bowels of the museum.

"I see you met my biggest fan." Becca's voice came from my right, over by the entrance to the exhibit.

"Yeah, he's a dick," I said. Joe glared at me a little, but Becca just giggled. "What's his beef with you? You steal his parking place, or make them convert the cigar lounge to a women's restroom?"

Becca laughed again, then her face went serious. "I honestly don't know the root of his problem with me. Maybe he just hates educated women. But he's worked against everything I've tried to accomplish since the day I got here. He tried to get funding blocked for the monster exhibit, then tried to stir up community sentiment against the exhibit saying I was promoting witchcraft and Satanism."

"Are you?" I asked.

"Bubba!" Joe shot me a look, but I ignored him.

"It's a valid question," I said. "So are you promoting witchcraft and Satanism?"

"No," Becca replied with a lopsided smile. "The exhibit does culminate with a display of occult and Satanic paraphernalia, but we very carefully neither endorse nor condemn any belief system in the exhibit. We talk about the origin of the Devil myth, from Biblical stories, to the Jersey Devil, to the stories of old blues men selling their soul at the Crossroads, to the Satanic Panic of the 80s and 90s, and the backlash against things like Dungeons & Dragons and Judas Priest."

"I can understand hating Judas Priest. I was always more a Motorhead guy myself, but when they started messing with D&D, they went too far. Where's this devil worship exhibit?" I asked with a grin.

"Right through here." Becca stepped past me and led us through the rest of the Contemporary American Horror section, including a Wall of Fame featuring life-size photos of horror luminaries like Stephen King, Dean Koontz, Joe Hill, Tom Savini, Robert Kirkman, and Lady Gaga.

I tapped the pic of Gaga on the chin as I walked by. "Now that's something I don't want to face in a dark alley."

"I love Lady Gaga," Joe protested.

"I know," I said. "But you have the iPod of a fourteen-year-old girl. Or a forty-year-old hairdresser. I can't decide which."

We walked down a short hallway lined with arcane symbols and snippets of spells. "Skeeter, any of this gibberish on the walls mean anything?" I asked over the comm.

"No, it's Latin translation of Chinese takeout menus and the text for two spells—one supposedly summons a giant pug/poodle mix, and the other removes dandruff. Both spells are missing some key parts to make them work, not that I think the dandruff one would work anyway. I'm pretty sure the Latin word for dandruff isn't 'flakos'."

I caught Becca's shoulders shaking ahead of me and said, "You did that on purpose, didn't you?"

"Of course," she said. "There's always that one jerkoff who back checks everything about an exhibit just so he can point out all the pieces you screwed up. So this time we wanted to really give him something to focus on. Since much of this whole thing is a trip through the darkest parts of our subconscious and unconscious, we wanted a few Easter eggs in there to make us smile. Especially leading into this, the darkest hole in our little house of horrors."

With that, she pulled open the door and we stepped into Hell.

Chapter Six

Of course we didn't really go to Hell. First of all, we weren't dead. Second, I was pretty sure that Joe had about as much chance of going to Hell as I had of going to a Skrillex concert. And lastly, I'm pretty sure Hell isn't still under construction. Unless maybe you're a carpenter. That might be Hell for you—a job site that never ends. And it wasn't really even a room made up to look like Hell, just a gateway to the big Down There. When you walked into the room, you could go right or left. Go right, and you walk through some of the most disturbing occult-themed crime scenes in history, from Nazi Germany to the Son of Sam. Go left, and you're treated to a walk through the "Satanic Panic" of the 20th century—when everything was supposed to lead kids and adults straight into the arms of the devil. There was a group of nerds dressed all in black playing Dungeons & Dragons. There was a display of a group of misfit nerds throwing the goat at a Black Sabbath concert. There was a couple of nerdy kids playing horror-themed video games.

As we walked through the exhibit, I cleared my throat. "Uh, Becca?"

"Yes, Bubba?"

"I've got this whole Satanic Panic thing figured out."

"Oh?" she asked.

"Yeah," I said. "Look around at all these displays. What's the same in all of them?"

"There are young people in all the displays. That was one of the main tenets of Satanic Panic, that evil forces were trying to infect the minds of our youth."

"Yeah, that's just the thing," I said. "The youth are the problem! It's not evil forces trying to get *into* the minds of teenage boys, it's that fact that teenage boys *are* evil forces that should never be unleashed on the world! I solved it!" I stood there looking smug for a second before I realized that she wasn't picking up what I was laying down.

"You get it?" I asked. "Because it's all about teenage boys? 'Cause teenage boys *are* the devil?" She just gave me a blank look. "Never mind, let's just find something for me to shoot."

"Like yourself?" Joe asked, abandoning the Guy Code completely and leaving me twisting at the end of a terrible joke. Damn ministers make shitty wingmen.

We followed the hall through to the back of the exhibit, where Becca's *coup de grace* stood. She had a full-sized demon summoning altar built at the back of the museum, and there was a robotic demon climbing up from behind it. At least I hoped it was robotic. I might have slid my hand around my back to rest on the butt of my pistol just in case.

The altar was about six feet long and about four feet wide, the perfect size to lay a body on and cut it into little pieces. The altar was streaked with fake blood, some old, some new, all in varying shades of brown and red. There was a skinny dude with a black robe on standing at the head of the altar, hands held high above his head with a shiny ceremonial kris catching the minimal light in the room. His robe had slid down his arms to the elbows, revealing frighteningly accurate tattoos of mystical glyphs and runes. I recognized a couple of letters of Enochian, but most of it looked like Led Zeppelin or old Dio album art. Lying on the altar was a writhing blonde woman, apparently representing a virgin, but built like a stripper. The robots writhed and twitched, then the knife plunged down into the female robot's chest and a gout of blood spurted out across the wall.

Behind the priest, an eight-foot demon clawed its way out of a hole in the wall painted to look like a gap between dimensions. The demon had a skull face, bat wings, and backward-hinged knees like an insect. Its skin was bright red with streaks of black and purple, and its face narrowed into a snout filled with hundreds of small, needle-like teeth. It had four arms that we could see, and a bunch of its body was still bursting through the wall, but all four arms were a good five feet long and tipped with razor-sharp, lobster-like claws. It looked like a cross between an H.R. Giger painting and a nightmare *SpongeBob* supporting character.

"That's nasty," I said.

"Thank you," Becca replied. "I designed it myself to incorporate many of the stereotypical elements of the demon summoning mythology. I think I got it pretty close without putting too much information out for the public. It's not my place to break down their delusions of safety, just to entertain. Let them think these creatures only exist in TV and movies. They don't need to know the monster under their bed is real."

"When did you first realize these creatures exist?" Joe asked, his voice soft. I looked up, and his gaze was locked on Becca, concern written all over his brow. He'd heard something in her voice, something I missed entirely. That's why he was the salvation guy, and I was the "Punch Things Until They Explode" guy.

She looked at Joe for a long time, then looked at me. I nodded, in what I hoped was an encouraging manner. It's hard to know how my gestures will be taken by normal-sized people sometimes, so I hope I was being encouraging and not terrifying. Becca took a deep breath, then went to sit on the foot of the altar, the sacrificial robot's feet twisting behind her making a bizarre backdrop to our conversation. Then again, conversations with bizarre backdrops are kinda my life. At least there were no naked Sasquatch or voodoo priests in the museum.

"It was grad school, a couple of years after we...after you..."

"Vanished? Ran out like a coward in the middle of the night?" I offered.

Becca let out a little laugh and Joe shot me a dirty look, but the tension was broken, and that was all I was interested in. She went on with her story. "I was going to say 'heard the call,' but you can use whatever words you like. We weren't together any more, and I wasn't dating anyone. I threw myself into my work and concentrated on completing my master's degree in two years, then my doctorate in another two. It meant cramming a lot of classes into a short time, and that meant a lot of late nights studying and researching at the library, which was all the way across campus from my dorm, if you remember." She glanced up at Joe, who nodded.

"I was coming back from one of those late-night study sessions when a man stepped out of the shadows in front of me. He *materialized* more than anything, I guess, and he scared the crap out of me. I let out a little scream, and he grinned at my fear. When he smiled, I saw that his canines were longer than normal, and his eyes didn't look quite right. I thought he was a theatre kid or something out playing hide and seek, or dressed up for something, so after my initial fright, I just pushed him aside and kept on walking."

I couldn't help it, I laughed. Becca and Joe both turned to me, and I said, "Sorry, I was just thinking about that poor vampire, all ready for his meal to faint or flee, and she just blows him off. Probably the first time *that* had ever happened!"

Becca gave me a little smile, and said, "Probably so. Anyway, I kept walking, and suddenly he was in front of me again. Now I was concerned, because I was walking pretty fast, and I hadn't heard him running to pass me. But it was still possible for him to catch and pass me, I guess, so I pulled out my pepper spray and let him have it."

"You pepper sprayed a vampire?" I asked.

"Yep," Becca replied. "I gave him a solid shot right in the face, and he cut loose a scream like nothing I'd ever heard on Earth. He dropped to his knees, and I bolted past him, leaving my library books lying in the grass. Not a good idea, as I learned later. But at the moment, I just wanted to get away from the crazy stalker-rapist guy and get to my room where I was safe."

"Except…" I said.

"Except it doesn't work that way," Becca said. "Apparently dormitories change residents so often that many of them, like me, never really consider it home. Without a sense of home, and all the little feelings that go into that, the threshold of a place isn't protected from intrusion by those with ill intent."

"Like vampires," Joe said.

"Like vampires," Becca confirmed. "He picked up my books, followed my scent to the dorm, talked his way into the front door, and knocked on my door."

"Which you didn't open," Joe said.

"Which I didn't open," Becca agreed. "Which I stood on the other side of and dialed campus police, and then dialed the girls on either side of me and told them to stay in their rooms, then dialed the front desk and called for help, then…"

"Then?"' I asked.

"Then I started screaming because he ripped the door off its hinges, deadbolt be damned, and walked into my room. I threw a chair at his head, but he caught it and smashed it to kindling. I threw my laptop at him, but he just knocked it out of the air. And the whole time, he was smiling at me, this cocky, cold smile that said he could do anything he wanted to me and there was nothing I could do about it. He got closer and closer, then…" Becca paused and closed her eyes for a second. It was obvious that reliving this had a cost for her, but we needed to know her background with the things that go bump in the night.

"Then?" Joe prompted, his voice soft and low.

"Then I heard a motorcycle roar up outside my window, which explodes inward, and suddenly I'm not trapped between my window and a batshit crazy Lestat wannabe. I'm trapped between a—"

"Batshit crazy Lestat wannabe and a nun dressed like a fetish party and packing a twelve-gauge."

Becca's eyes went wide, but I motioned for her to go on. "Exactly. The motorcyclist was some crazy woman who called herself Sister Evangeline. She'd followed the vampire all over campus since he was turned, just waiting for the right place and time to take him out. And when he came after me, she realized the time was right now."

"I didn't know you went to Tulane," I said.

"I never said I…" She just stopped and looked at me.

"I know Sister Evangeline. She's the Hunter for that part of the country. So she took out your fine fanged friend?" I asked.

"With prejudice and a hell of a lot of noise. But with no interference or interest from campus security, my RA, or anyone on my hall. I never quite understood how she managed that."

"We work for the Vatican," Joe said. "There are a lot of people out there who just do it when the Church asks for a favor. That and Evangeline is well-connected with the local authorities."

"So after that night, I didn't just become a believer, I became obsessed. After I got over being terrified, that is. I tracked Evangeline down and got her to tell me all about the monsters and magicians in New Orleans, and I changed my doctorate to Paranormal Studies."

"So how did you end up here?" Joe asked.

"Well, there's not a whole lot of money in paranormal investigation," she said.

"Then you're doing it wrong," I said. "You see, you got to either find yourself a religious group with deep pockets, or a super-secret government agency with an off-the-books budget. Or both. Preferably both. Then you work freelance for both of them, and you pretty much get to double-bill anything you kill, and they reimburse for ammunition, too!" I grinned as I dropped this little bit of knowledge on her. But my grin disappeared like Skeeter at a musical theatre festival when she spoke her next words.

"Oh, Bubba, I didn't want to hurt the creatures. I wanted to understand them." I didn't groan. I'm at least 75% sure I didn't groan. I might have groaned a little bit. But I, at least, tried not to groan, and that counts for something.

"What the hell is there to understand, Becca? They eat people. We don't want to be eaten. So we kill them. End of discussion," I said. "This exhibit doesn't have anything to do with you trying to make contact with some damn Florida Gator-Man or some other swamp-dragged local legend critter I ain't never heard of, does it?"

"No, nothing like that! Nothing at all, I swear. The exhibit does serve two purposes—to let the local paranormal population see that the museum understands that they exist and wants to build a bridge between our communities," she said, sounding like, well, like something you'd read in a museum guidebook.

"Build a bridge? With something that looks at you like a hot fudge sundae? Damn, girl, you sounded smart 'til you started talking like you're in love with a damn werewolf or something."

"Well, at the time, my human relationships hadn't been exactly brilliant, so who could blame me if I..." Her words trailed off and her cheeks flamed. Joe very studiously didn't look at her.

"Please tell me you didn't, um...'interview' any vampires," I said.

"No! Nothing like that. Vampires still scare the crap out of me," she protested.

"Good," Joe said. "I've never met one that didn't deserve to be decapitated on the spot."

I kept my mouth shut, remembering a family of vampires I mistook for a chalupa, no, a chimichanga...no, a chupacabra one time. Turns out they were just on their way to Disneyland and stopped for a snack at the wrong farmer's field, drained a couple of goats and cows, and got everybody all up in a tizzy. I gave them some gas money to get back on the road, and they were fine. But Joe was mostly right. Most of the vampires I'd ever seen needed to be staked and chopped into bits at the first sight of them.

"But there are a lot of decent voodoo priests and witches in and around New Orleans, and a couple of very nice were-jaguars living on the outskirts of town. There is even one necromancer who taught me a lot about death magic and zombies. The magical kind, not the epidemic kind. But I didn't become some kind of crazed fangirl. I approached all my interactions with the nonhuman populace from a very anthropological point of view, just as I would have a tribe of primitive people, or dangerous animals. I studied these beings for years, and finally when this museum opened up, I found someone willing to listen to my ideas about paranormal creatures, and how humans and the beings we've historically thought of as monsters—"

"Because they have this nasty habit of trying to eat us," I mumbled.

Becca ignored me. She was getting the hang of being around me. If she wanted to get her point across, the only way to do it was to ignore me. She went on. "—are really complex social creatures, and often as intelligent as humans. She allowed me to put together this exhibit ostensibly to bring in new visitors and donors, but also to open ourselves up for deeper interaction with the local supernatural communities."

"So you want the vampires to come in here and feel understood or something?" I asked.

"That was part of the initial goal, but we may have underestimated the animosity these creatures feel for our species," she said.

"You think?" I asked. I turned and started to walk away. "Joe, you stay here and get more of the backstory out of your ex here. I gotta go take walk and get away from the stink of stupid. Thinking you can safely co-exist with vampires. Somebody's been reading too many teen novels. They don't sparkle, they don't fall in love with humans, they don't play baseball, and they don't live and let live."

I stomped off to calm down and collect myself before I said something real rude to Joe's ex-girlfriend and got us thrown out of the museum once and for all.

Chapter Seven

I LEFT THE BLACK FOREST SECTION OF THE EXHIBIT AND WANDERED into the Contemporary America section. I knew that's where I was because everything looked familiar, tech-wise, and there was a big sign on the wall that said "Contemporary America" as I passed into the hall. I tapped the Bluetooth in my ear and spoke to thin air. "What do you make of this, Skeeter?"

"It all looks and sounds like human assholery to me, Bubba. I haven't seen anything that makes me think it's more than somebody who really wants this exhibit to turn out like crap."

"Like maybe some of those other museum nerds who wanted to show off tin toys from ancient Egypt, or whatever the hell?" I asked.

"That's where I'd start, but it might be better to catch them in the act," came the nasally voice in my ear.

"Then pull their mask off like an old Scooby-Doo episode?" I asked.

"Yeah, you can be the meddling kid, except huge!" Skeeter agreed. I laughed and went back to join Joe and Becca.

Or I tried to, at least. I thought I headed back in the direction I came from, but I ended up turned around and started wandering through what looked like a bamboo forest. I crossed a wooden footbridge, and halfway across, I looked up and there was dude in full armor standing in front of me.

He was a little dude, especially compared my six-and-a-half-foot height and three hundred pounds and change. But the sword he held looked wicked sharp, and the second he looked up at me, he flashed that thing around his head in a series of complicated slashes and whirls that left me dizzy just looking at him. He stepped onto the bridge and started walking across.

"Hey buddy," I said. He stopped and looked at me. He wore one of those masks that attached to the front of his helmet, with a Chinese dragon for a face. He didn't speak, just stared at me through those deep black holes in the mask.

"This bridge ain't built for two, pal. You wanna scoot back a little bit to let me through?" I made a shooing motion with my hands, but he didn't move. Instead, he put his sword out in front of himself and making like it was a broom, "swept" me backwards.

"So that's how it's gonna be, huh?" I asked. I drew my kukri and grinned. "Good. It's been a few days since I got to hit something, and with all that armor you're wrapped in, I don't see a whole lot of reason to pull my punches."

Apparently neither did he, because without a word, he sprang at me, sword flashing in the dim light of the museum. He got some air, too, clearing a solid fifteen feet of ground in one leap. If I'd been expecting a normal man, he would have caught me completely off-guard and wrecked my face. But I know that in my life, the odds of me fighting a human are less than the odds of me winning the lottery. And I don't even buy lottery tickets.

So I got a good judge of his leap and took one huge step forward, putting my shoulder right about the spot where he wanted to be landing. Samurai Slim hit me like a ton of bricks, but I was ready for him. I planted my feet and twisted to the left as he came down, and he flopped into the artificial stream under the bridge, armor and all. I dumped him on his back quicker than Jenny Newell after my junior prom. He wriggled around in the shallow water like a turtle for a few seconds while I stood looking down on him and laughing, but then he turned to smoke and vanished.

"Now that ain't fair…" I said, then pain exploded in the lower part of my abdomen, and I almost blew chunks over the bridge rail into the little fake river. As it was, I went high enough up on my tiptoes to almost take a header over the handrail before I grabbed onto the railing with one hand and my balls with the other. My kukri clattered to the wooden bridge, completely forgotten as my testicles swelled up to four times their normally impressive size, and I saw all the colors of the rainbow flash in front of my eyelids as I screwed my lids shut to keep my nuts from flying out through my eye sockets.

I collapsed to the bridge, pressing my face into the wood trying to find an inch of my body that wasn't completely occupied with my genitals. That's hard enough under normal circumstances, but in the minutes after a man is kicked so hard in his nuts that he seriously contemplates castration, because it would hurt less, there was exactly zero chance of me thinking of anything other than my exploded nutsack.

I lay there on my side gasping for breath and very conscientiously not puking, and eventually my vision cleared. When I could see through the tears, which was much like driving through a North Georgia July thunderstorm as far as visibility was concerned, I saw a pair of red boots standing shoulder-width apart about eighteen inches from my nose. I rolled over a little farther, and those red boots were attached to the same red devil armor that my opponent for bridge supremacy was wearing before he found himself half-buried in mud and silt.

Looking farther up, I saw the grinning devil face had vanished right before my eyes. His shoulders were shaking with laughter as he leaned on his sword and watched me writhe in pain. My shoulders were shaking, too, but it was more from abject agony than amusement. That changed a little as the tips of my flailing right fingers brushed the hilt of one of my discarded kukri. I wrapped my fist around the hilt of the big curved knife and brought it down overhand onto the bridge of the laughing jackass's foot, burying the tip through the arch of his right foot and about two inches deep into the wooden bridge.

He let out a howl that I'm pretty sure rattled the roofing tiles all over the museum and bent almost double clutching at his foot. I met his face coming down with a fist as I stood up, and the combined momentum of his skull and my cantaloupe-sized right hand converged on the nose of his grinning devil mask with a thunderous *crack*. The mask shattered all over the bridge, my knuckles split all the way to the bone from the impact, and his head snapped back hard enough to reverse his entire forward motion into a backflop onto the wooden bridge. His head hit the boards with an almost hollow-sounding *thunk*, and he lay completely still.

I thought for a second that I'd killed him, until I looked into his helmet and found nobody home.

"What the literal shit," I muttered. "Skeeter!" I hollered at the air.

"What happened, Bubba? I lost comm for the last few minutes," Skeeter's voice came right into my ear, which most days was like wearing a functional dentist's drill for an earring.

"Yeah, apparently Japanese ghost armor makes our technology shit the bed. And in case you were wondering, Japanese ghost armor hits like a goddamn Mack truck. I swear to God he kicked my balls up into the bottom of my lungs," I wheezed. I picked up my kukri and re-sheathed them, then picked up the now empty helmet and sword. "I wonder if this shit was expensive," I mused.

"Just at a quick glimpse, I'd say it was probably crazy expensive. That style of sword didn't come into being until the fourteenth century, but they were prized for their sharpness and durability. And a complete set of armor like that would be worth millions. Until it ran afoul of you, of course."

"He started it," I protested. "I was just walking across the bridge."

"And you didn't yield to the samurai, did you?" Skeeter asked.

"Yield? What, like go back and let him just walk across when I was almost halfway done? Hell no, I didn't do that."

"Then the ghost of the samurai was honor-bound to battle you in single combat."

"Was he honor-bound to try and castrate me, too?" I asked, still rubbing my sore junk.

"I think that might be the least of our problems here, Bubba," Skeeter replied.

"Says the guy who, thanks to me, hasn't been hit in the balls since middle school," I grumbled. "But what's the other problem?"

"The fact that you just fought a suit of haunted armor in a museum that we thought wasn't haunted."

"Shit," I said. "I reckon we're in the right place after all."

"And that's how it went down." I finished relaying the story to Becca and her boss, the Museum's Executive Director, Ms. Harrell. Ms. Harrell was a pinched-face woman who looked like she had fun once, but got over it quick. She wore a dark pantsuit with no jewelry, no adornment of any type, with long brown hair and pretty much no makeup. She had quick green eyes that missed nothing, and a tendency to point out exactly how stupid something sounded to her in no uncertain terms. She'd already made it clear to me and Joe that Becca overstepped in calling us in, that there was nothing supernatural at all in her museum, and if there was, she still wouldn't believe it.

"So you expect me to believe that a six-hundred-year-old suit of armor came to life and dueled you, kicked you in the testicles, and then fell prey to your superior wit and strength?" Harrell asked.

"You wanna see my balls?" I asked, reaching for my zipper. "I'm pretty sure the swelling hasn't gone down yet." She opened her mouth to speak, and I held up a hand. "I'm sorry. That was uncalled for. But yes, your six-hundred-year old suit of armor came to life, kicked me in the balls, and I broke its face with my fist. Then it fell down and didn't get back up."

"But that's not the real problem," Joe added.

"Tell that to my nuts," I said, but I kept my voice so low that it sounded like I was clearing my throat. At least that was the intent, anyway. Becca was sitting next to me and might have gotten a little more uncensored version of things than I'd planned.

"And what do you see as the problem, Dr. MacIntyre? Surely the destruction of a three-million-dollar artifact is an insurmountable problem?" Ms. Harrell sat back in her chair, arms crossed against her chest."

"Ma'am, if you'd seen half the shit we've dealt with, you'd understand that a little wanton property destruction in the name of saving the world from big nasties is a small price to pay." I decided to chime in, mostly because I was getting irritated with this lady. I saved her museum from a pissed off ghost in a suit of armor, at great personal suffering, and she not only wasn't thanking us, she was kinda chewing us out for it. That shit wasn't going to stand, especially since I was gonna need stitches to get my hand to quit bleeding and at least a case of beer to get my nuts to stop throbbing.

"And if you had to deal with the people I have to deal with, you would understand that no matter what stupid story you've cooked up to excuse your ramble through my museum, the fact remains that I have a multi-million-dollar suit of antique Japanese armor that's now only good for some fanboy to wear to ComiCon and pretend that he might someday touch a girl. Now if you *gentlemen* will excuse me, I have an exhibit to redesign, a subscriber base to mollify, and an associate curator to terminate, not necessarily in that order." She motioned for us to leave, but extended a bony finger to Becca.

"Doctor Knowles, a moment please." I gave Becca what I hoped was a reassuring pat on the shoulder, but with the day I was having, I probably broke her collarbone. Me and Joe headed out of the office and started walking to the truck, taking about as much time as we could justify.

"You think Cruella in there is gonna shitcan Becca?" I asked.

"I don't know," Joe replied. "She was pretty pissed. I guess that suit of armor was really expensive."

"Yeah, I heard. Three million dollars. Shit, Joe, I didn't think it was worth that kind of money, or I would have tried not to break it too much. Hell, as it is the only thing that's really beat to shit is the mask. They could super-glue that back together, and it'd be just about good as new. But she wouldn't let me get a word in edgewise, so I couldn't even tell her that. Oh, shit, sorry, dude." That last bit wasn't to Joe. It was to this real skinny fellow that stepped in front of me, not looking where he was going. That didn't end real well for him, as he kinda bounced off my belly and flopped to the floor right on his ass.

I managed to keep from laughing, and I did reach down to try and help him up, but he wasn't having none of that. He twisted around on the floor like a dog covered up in fire ants and finally clambered up to his feet.

"Don't touch me, you filthy barbarian!" He got as much up in my face as a skinny bastard that's at least a foot shorter than me could manage and poked me in the chest with one really long, skeletal finger.

I don't like being poked. I don't really like being touched that much, unless it's people I like. It comes from always being the biggest kid in school. The one that people always stared at, always thought was stupid, and *always* picked the fights with, knowing that I'd get in way more trouble than a normal-sized kid because I'd hurt somebody and "should know better."

I don't know better anymore, and I was in a bad damn mood. My hand hurt like a sonofabitch, and I'd just had some ivory tower intellectual asshole treat me like a moron, and here was another overeducated douchecanoe who couldn't change his own tire with two jacks and a AAA card, and he was poking me. Because the little bastard hadn't stopped. He was poking me in the chest again and again, going on about how I should watch where I was going, and how he had very important work to do, and how could he get anything done with giant lummoxes like me around.

I reached out with my left hand, the one that wasn't currently dripping blood on the carpet, and wrapped it almost completely around his face. I covered his mouth and nose with my hand, leaving just enough space between my fingers for him to breathe, but not enough for him to be comfortable, or speak, or bite me.

I leaned down and stared right in his bugged out little green eyes. "Don't poke people," I said. "It's not nice. And just because what you've got going on feels important, it doesn't mean that other people don't have important shit happening, too. You got me?" He nodded, his head bobbing like the Virgin Mary Pop used to have stuck to the dashboard of his pickup truck when he worked for the Church. He wasn't blasphemous—that was Pop's idea of paying tribute.

I let the wriggly little bastard go, and he ran away into the bowels of the museum. "Can we leave?" I asked Joe.

"We'd better, before you kill somebody. Let's get that hand stitched up and get some food in us."

"I know a great little steak place just about a half mile from here," I said, and my mouth started to water like I was a Russian lab dog or something.

Chapter Eight

"I HATE GETTING FIRED," I SAID AROUND A MOUTHFUL OF MASHED potatoes. Between the Darvocet the doc-in-a-box gave me after he put twenty-seven stitches in my right hand, the four Stellas I started my meal with, and the first filet mignon settling in my belly while I waited on my half-impressed, half-terrified waiter to bring me another one, I was feeling pretty righteous. I usually start with a medium steak, just to make sure that it'll be hot. Too many places think medium rare means cold as shit, and I ain't in for a cold piece of meat. I deal with enough of those at work.

We were at Charley's, one of the top ten steakhouses in the country, and to my mind the only damn redeemable quality in Orlando. Charley's is an old-school steakhouse, the kind where you walk in and there's a giant damn flaming pit with steaks scattered around it. The kind of place where they bring you a cut of meat to the table to show you what your steak looks like before it's cooked. The filet is about the size of my fist, which is to say almost the size of a normal human's head, and it is as tender a cut of meat as I've had in my life. Joe got the same thing, only he got asparagus with his. I reckon he thought he might need a toothpick or something. He'd polished off half a bottle of a pretty solid Coppola blended red, but I stuck to beer.

"It makes me feel like I done something wrong," I continued. Joe just nodded. "And I didn't do anything wrong. I mean, sure I busted up a couple million dollars' worth of armor, but that only goes to prove that there's something out of the ordinary going on in that place." I waved my fork over the table, maybe a little enthusiastically, so Joe grabbed my arm and brought it back into our airspace.

"I know, Bubba," he agreed. "I hate that we were tossed out right when we were getting close to some answers."

"Well, I don't know about all that," I said. "I didn't even know what questions we were supposed to be asking, but I do know that if there's an empty suit of antique armor whooping your ass, then something hinky is going on."

"I was able to get a little more specific information," Joe said. He pulled out his phone, swiped a couple times, tapped the screen, swiped again, and handed it to me. I looked at it for a second, then picked it up, fully expecting somebody to jump out of the bushes and tell me to do the Hokey Pokey. The screen was full of pictures of squiggles. I turned it sideways, and the squiggles rotated, but stayed squiggles. I turned the phone around a few times, but no matter what I did, it was still just a bunch of writing in a language I couldn't read.

"What's this, Padre?" I asked, handing the phone back to him. Just then, the waiter came in with my second steak and some more mashed potatoes, and I dug in while Joe talked.

"These appear to be recent writings, but in a very ancient language," Joe said.

I swallowed a piece of the best steak I'd had since the last time I'd been here, and said, "Yeah, but doesn't that make sense? It's a new exhibit, but Becca would have researched old shit to make it all look right, wouldn't she?"

"Yes, but she wouldn't have found this in any of her research. At least, not unless she has some contacts with real magical connections. This is written in a variant of ancient Aramaic that's only been seen a few times throughout history, and the last time was on the tablets that Moses brought down from Mount Horeb."

"Sinai," I corrected, then gawked at Joe for getting that one wrong.

"Horeb," he repeated. "Don't ask. I can't explain unless you become a Jesuit priest and go through a couple of doctoral programs in ancient religious history. But the real Ten Commandments came down Mount Horeb, not Sinai."

"Shit," I said. "Next thing you'll tell me that Jesus wasn't a white dude with blue eyes and blondish-brown hair."

Joe narrowed his eyes at me for a second, but I figured he wasn't going to punch me right in the middle of a couple-hundred-dollar dinner, especially since his dessert just arrived, a slice of cheesecake tall enough to get its own gimmick in little people's wrasslin' back in the day. Joe took a deep breath, then let it out slow while I watched him count to ten in his head. English, French, German, Spanish, Russian—they all rolled across his eyes before he could look at me without wanting to punch me. I just sat there, laughing as close to silently as I could manage.

"Regardless of the origin of the tablets, this language is far older than anything Becca should have access to, so I think there's no coincidence that someone is inscribing ancient Aramaic rituals into the exhibit here, to what end we don't know."

"But we're pretty sure it ain't good," I said.

"Oh, it definitely isn't good," Joe said. "The pieces I could decipher were parts of a summoning ritual for a fairly nasty demon."

"Is there any other kind?" I asked. I knocked back the last of my beer and motioned our waiter over. He brought the check, then got some clean plasticware for Joe's dessert doggie box. "Gimme a bite of that before you wrap it up and forget about it." I loaded up my fork with cheesecake, strawberries and syrup and had it almost to my mouth when my cell rang.

"Shit," I said, taking a quick bite to remind myself of what I wasn't going to get to eat while I was killing whatever that phone call was about. I pulled out my phone, but it was a number I didn't know. I pushed the green button and brought it to my ear.

"Hello?" I said.

"Bubba? Oh thank God! He's here, Bubba. I was staying to finish up some signage in the zombie exhibit, just in case they changed their mind about the exhibit, but I heard something out there, and when I went to look, it...it was horrible! It chased me into the exhibit, and now I can hear it. It's coming." She dropped her voice to a whisper so the thing wouldn't hear her, but then there were sounds of a scuffle, and her phone clattered to the floor. I heard screams through the phone's speaker, and I stood up.

"Let's go. Becca's in trouble." Joe never asked questions, just threw three Franklins down on the table to cover dinner and started for the valet stand. I grabbed my keys from the startled kid in the red vest, and we drove over the curb and peeled rubber out onto I-Drive. I whipped a U-turn the first chance I got and pointed the nose of the truck back toward the museum. Tourists and Canadians were laying on their horns all around me, but I was the biggest, meanest dude on the road, driving the biggest, meanest truck, so I didn't care about the opinions of a CPA in a Prius. He could lead, follow, or end up like the Guest of Honor at a monster truck show.

"What's going on?" Joe asked, fighting with his seatbelt. I never wore mine, but Joe had faith in different places than me. He put a lot of faith in God and the Bible, but next to none in my driving.

"I don't know," I replied, taking the corner into the museum parking lot on two wheels. "She called, said she needed help, then I heard screams. Skeeter?" I said, pushing a Bluetooth button in the dash.

"Yeah, Bubba? What you need? I got the call on Becca."

"I need the museum alarm to go away," I said.

"I don't know, Bubba. That sounds illegal…" Skeeter couldn't hold it together and broke up laughing. "Sorry, I couldn't even say that shit with a straight face. Gimme a second."

"You got thirty," I said. I parked the truck and hopped out. Joe did the same, and we both popped the back doors and flipped up the seats to get at the weapons underneath. I went light, grabbing Bertha in a shoulder holster, Great-Grandpappy Beauregard's sword, and the silver-spiked ceastus Agent Amy gave me for Christmas. I slipped the leather-and-steel gauntlets on and flexed my fists I felt the stitches in my handstart to give, and knew I'd had a glove full of blood after the second punch. It felt kind like having five-pound bags of sugar tied to my wrists, only these bags of sugar were studded with one- to two-inch spikes along the back of the hand and the knuckles. Sturdy wrist wraps and bracing in the gloves let me hit harder than ever before, and with those things on, I felt like I could bash right through the wall if Skeeter didn't get the alarm down.

Which, of course, he did. "Alarm's taken care of," Skeeter's voice rang in my head. I looked across at Joe, who had a bandolier of shotgun shells slung across his chest and a .45 in a shoulder rig under his left arm. He held a Mossberg 12-gauge with a pistol grip and a flashlight strapped to the barrel. I grabbed a light of my own and a couple of chemical glow sticks, jammed them into a pocket, and closed the truck door. I heard Joe do the same, and we turned to the back door of the museum. The little guard room was empty now, and I took a good look at the door, something I hadn't bothered to do the first time through it. Typical hollow metal door, perfectly capable of keeping out all but the most insistent of criminals. And me.

I reared back with a foot and planted one size sixteen right beside the lock. Metal bent and snapped, and the door bent outward enough for me to pull it the rest of the way open. The hallway beyond the door was empty and dark. I reached over and flipped the light switch. Nothing.

"Skeeter, we got no lights," I said into the comm.

"Yeah, looks like something has knocked out power to that whole side of town, including the convention center across the street."

"That shouldn't even be possible," I said. "All them big-ass hotels have to have generators, and I know damn well nobody would spend that kind of money on a convention center without backup power."

"Most days I'd agree with you, but something has everything north of The Magic Kingdom darker than an elephant's butthole, Bubba, and every first responder in the city is busting ass trying to keep Yankees and snowbirds from killing themselves at stoplights."

"So there ain't no backup, is what you're saying."

"There ain't even gonna be an ambulance if you screw this up. So try not to screw it up. And I can't do a whole lot for you because without power, I'm as blind as you are. No building plans, no security cameras, nothing."

"We're on our own," I said to Joe. "Alright then, Skeet. We'll try not to get dead, you see if you can remote into something and get some lights back on in here."

"Will do," Skeeter said, then clicked off. I pulled a flashlight out of a pocket and clicked it on.

"No lights coming?" Joe asked.

"No lights, no backup, no medivac," I confirmed.

"Well, then let's not need those things," Joe said, pointing his shotgun down the darkened hall in front of us. He started down the hall, and I followed. I let him take point because it was pretty easy for me to shoot over and around him, and there wasn't enough room between me and the walls for him to shoot past me without putting a lot of buckshot in a lot of uncomfortable places.

We made our way down the deserted hallway and into the main body of the museum without encountering another living soul. We walked side by side through the halls until we finally came to Becca's pride and joy. A sign over the door proclaimed "Here be monsters," so I figured it was where we needed to be. I pushed into the exhibit, and an even deeper darkness reached out and swallowed us up.

Chapter Nine

IF I THOUGHT IT WAS DARK IN THE REST OF THE MUSEUM, THE MONSTER exhibit was a damn black hole. Situated in the main gallery of the museum, there wasn't a wall anywhere in the exhibit that touched the outdoors, and the few skylights scattered throughout the rooms were blacked out with thick black fabric and plywood.

"Give her a call," I said.

"Huh?" Joe just stared at me.

"Joe, call the girl. It ain't normal that we can't hear anything out of her. It's not like this place is *that* damn big. If she's still in the building, she should have heard us crashing around like a pair of drunken rhinoceroses. So call her, and let's figure out from the sound of her phone ringing just where she is and what's messing with her."

"Good idea," Joe said.

"I know," I replied. "I said it."

Joe rolled his eyes and dialed the phone. Almost immediately, I heard Justin Timberlake's "Sexyback" blaring from a nearby phone. I looked over at Joe, who shrugged.

"We were young," he said simply. "And ringtones were kind of a new thing."

I forgot all about Joe's continued poor musical choices almost as quickly as I realized the ringing was close. "Follow me, and try not to shoot me too much," I said to Joe.

"I'll think about it," he said.

We pushed farther into the darkness, our flashlights narrow beams pushing back a couple of feet of darkness at a time, and that just barely. This wasn't normal dark—this blackness was palpable, fighting back against our LED flashlights like a formless, angry thing defending its territory. I looked behind us, but the blackness enveloped us so completely that I couldn't even see the red EXIT signs that I knew were hanging over every door.

"Call her again," I said after we'd walked some twenty feet into the exhibit. We should have been right about where her phone was, but I couldn't see my feet, much less Becca or anything that might have ahold of her. A couple seconds later, the dulcet tones of Justin Timberlake blared through the silent room, and I saw a flash of light out of the corner of my eye. I turned and ran to it, before the ring cut off and it was swallowed by the darkness again. I stood over the phone, shining my flashlight all over the floor, the walls, and the ceiling.

"Nothing," I reported.

"I don't know that I would say that." Joe's voice was more of a croak, and I spun around, tracking Bertha and my flashlight to the sound.

"Please put that away." The thing that held Joe looked mostly normal, except for being even taller than me and skinnier than Skeeter. And Asian, which made the whole super-tall thing seem even weirder.

I holstered Bertha, then said, "Okay, the gun's away, now let my friend go."

"I don't think so," the guy said, then bent his head toward Joe's neck. I watched as a pair of fangs extended from the tall dude's mouth and stretched to several inches in length. Tall Guy bent down, I guess to pierce the carotid, but got a rude awakening as soon as his teeth touched Joe's skin.

The vampire's teeth actually started to sizzle, and he jerked his head back with a shriek that sounded like a million teenage girls at a One Direction concert. He flung Joe away from him, and I intercepted my flying friend before he crashed into a big glass display case off to my left. Of course, that meant that *I* crashed into the glass display and showered myself with tiny bits of safety glass and a couple of, no doubt, priceless parchments.

Joe was lying on the floor, struggling to get to his feet, and making strange wheezing sounds. I crawled over to him. "You all right, Joe? You didn't break nothing when you crashed into me, did you?"

"N-n-no, I'm good," he said, and it was then that I realized he was *laughing*.

"Are you laughing?" I asked.

"Oh my God, yes," Joe said. "That was the best idea in the world, Bubba. I'll try to remember to paint my neck with holy water every time I think I might be going into a vampire fight. Did you see the look on his face? Oh Lord, that was hilarious." Joe rolled to one knee, still laughing, then he went quiet as he looked around. "Where is it?"

"I don't know. It bit you, screamed, then ran off. Part of me wants to believe that it ran all the way back to Ancient Japan to soak its teeth in the blood of its ancestors, but the rest of me is waiting for him to—" I never did find out what I was waiting for because all of a sudden there was an iron cable wrapped around my throat lifting me off my feet. I kicked and thrashed, but this thing was *strong*. I finally got Bertha loose and put four rounds in a semicircle behind me, the Desert Eagle unleashing thunder and fire throughout the pitch black room. The thing holding me let out an *oof*, and I dropped to the floor. I landed on my feet and kept dropping, bending my knees and tucking into a forward roll to get some separation from the giant bloodsucking bastard behind me.

I came up to one knee and spun around just as Joe cut loose with his Mossberg. The unexpected roar on the twelve-gauge startled me, and I collapsed right onto my ass, which ended up saving a big part of my scalp. Between Joe's low-flying buckshot and the slashing arms of the vampire, something was trying to take my head off. I maneuvered around so I was at least out of Joe's line of fire and took half a second to get a better look at the monster.

This might have been the ugliest damn vampire I'd ever seen in my whole life. Like I said, it was easily seven feet tall if it was an inch. And maybe two hundred pounds of gaunt, yellowed skin stretched taut across high cheekbones and a forehead high and slanted back like a bicycle ramp. Its face was narrow, like the old *Nosferatu* movies, and dominated by four needlelike teeth. Its arms were preternaturally long and tapered to fingers twice the length of human digits. This thing had started out human, but years and a steady diet of human blood had erased any hint of that heritage from its black eyes.

It turned to me and blurred into movement almost faster than I could follow. But not quite. I drew Bertha and stuck the barrel in the general vicinity of where I expected him to stop and pulled the trigger twice. The first shot went wild, but the second caught it in the shoulder like a sledgehammer mated with a stick of dynamite. The hole going in was the size of two fingers, but the hole coming out was about the size of a good cherry pie. The vampire flew backward about three feet, landed flat on its back, bounced once, then popped back up to its feet like its ass was spring-loaded.

"Well, shit," I said. "Can't it be easy just once?"

The vampire grinned at me, those front fangs going everywhere like a parody of bad orthodontics, and said something in a language I didn't understand.

"What was that? I'm sorry, I only speak English, Redneck, and Whoop-Ass." I brought Bertha back to bear on the monster, tracking him one-handed and squeezing off a quick five rounds. The recoil on a Desert Eagle makes it almost impossible to hit anything when you're shooting one-handed, but I really needed to slip my left into the ceastus hanging from my belt. I aimed at the beastie's knees, hoping the recoil would kick the barrel up and I'd land a lucky shot on its center mass.

I've done a lot of things in my life, but getting a lucky shot on an ancient Asian vampire in the pitch black with a hand cannon like Bertha is not anything I've ever managed. I kept to my streak and missed every shot, but the muzzle flash gave me enough light to see the onrushing creature. I slammed Bertha back into her holster and got my hand back up between the monster's face and my neck just in time.

He was close enough I could almost count his fillings, if he'd had any. His breath smelled like something crawled up out of the grave, rolled around in a sewer, then went swimming in sulfur. To say it made my eyes water was a helluva understatement. I pushed against its throat with my right arm while I bashed it in the side of the head again and again with my silver-clad left fist. Every blow rocked the creature, and after four or five shots, I felt another impact slam into the thing and looked past it to see Joe slam his shotgun into the vampire's spine. The beastie let go of me and turned its attention to Joe, which gave me the distance I needed.

I took one step back, yanked Great-Grandpappy's sword from the sheath over my shoulder, and ran that three-foot steel blade right through the middle of the vampire's heart. It dropped to its knees, then fell forward, sliding off my blade as it collapsed to the ground.

"Is that going to kill it?" Joe asked. "I know sometimes—"

"Yeah," I said. "Sometimes you gotta cut the head off before it—what the shit?" I grabbed Joe and yanked him out of the way as the weirdest damn thing I ever saw came flying at him.

You know, I've fought nekkid Bigfoots, gotten drunk with rakshasas, set fairies on fire with hairspray, gone bar-hopping with a half-snakeman, and beat the shit out of a dude who changed his form to look like Elvis Presley, so when I say it was the weirdest damn thing I ever saw, that bar's set pretty high. But when a vampire reached up with its hands, pulled its head off its shoulders and threw it at Joe, that took the cake and the whole damn bakery besides.

The vampire head flew past Joe, then spun around in mid-air and came back at us. It had those damn crooked-ass fangs chopping like some kind of demented Pac-Man, so I nudged Joe out of the way and set myself up right in the path of the critter. It got close. I sidestepped about two feet and swung the family sword like a Louisville Slugger. The blade caught the vampire's face right about its nose, and thousand-year-old vampire brains splattered all over me, Joe, and every artifact in the exhibit.

"If that woman was pissed about me wrecking her suit of armor, I can't wait to hear what she's gonna have to say about me getting brains all over her freshly-painted walls. Hey Joe?"

"Yeah, Bubba?" Joe asked from the floor about ten feet away. I might have shoved him a little harder than I thought.

"Is the rest of that vampire still over there?

"No, but there's a puddle of really smelly yellow stuff on the floor in roughly the shape of the vampire, and these rags in the puddle look kinda like the clothes it was wearing, so I'm pretty sure you killed it."

"I woulda thought that before it threw its head at me, but you're probably right. Quit laying around, we gotta find your girlfriend," I said, reaching down to help him extricate himself from the display cases that he fell into.

"There are so many things wrong with that sentence I don't even know where to start," Joe said, brushing himself off and reacquiring his shotgun. "What next?" he asked.

"If I remember right, it's the rakshasa and djinn part of the exhibit, which I hope we don't have to fight our way through."

"Why's that?" Joe asked. "I thought you had fought rakshasa before."

"I have, but they're a lot like fighting cats, and you know how cats cheat."

Chapter Ten

THE RAKSHASA ROOM WAS CLEAR, AND I WASN'T STUPID ENOUGH TO even brush a sleeve against any of the jars, bottles, or flasks in the djinn display. Djinn are powerful, old, smart, devious, conniving, and any other unpleasant adjective you could think of. I didn't want to fight one on my best day, with Amy right beside me, and every weapon I could think of in arms' reach. I sure as hell didn't want to fight one in the half-dark of the museum while I still needed to find Becca and keep Joe safe.

We came to the door that led into the Black Forest exhibit, but it looked different somehow. There were odd symbols drawn into the frame, but I didn't recognize any of them. I put my hand on the knob, and something felt *off*, like there was something on the other side of the door, and it didn't like me very much.

"I think you oughta hang back a little, Padre," I said to Joe, my voice pitched low so as maybe not to piss off whatever was on the other side any more than it already was. I turned the knob and slipped through the smallest opening I could manage. I left the door open behind me for Joe to follow but felt something pull the door out of my hand and slam it shut the second I was completely through it. I heard pounding on the door for a second or two, but then nothing. I turned around, shining my light at the door, but it was gone. The only thing behind me was a brick wall, weeping moisture and covered in thick green moss.

"I reckon I ain't in Kansas no more, huh, Toto?" I said to the air as I looked around. I was in what looked to be a sewer, at least judging from the smell and the water around my boots. It was mostly dry, at least, with water not even cresting my ankles. The walls were old brick, with decades of moss and fungus and other shit growing on them. There was a dim light coming from the tunnel in front of me, and my flashlight seemed to do better against the darkness down here, for some reason.

I pressed the comm button in my ear. "Hey, Skeeter?" I said. No response. I pushed the button again. Still nothing. So wherever I was, I wasn't anywhere that Skeeter could find me, and I couldn't see a way to get back to Joe. I reckoned I was really flying solo on this one. I thought about it for a few seconds, then slipped on my other ceastus, carefully drew Bertha, used both hands to get her situated in my now-gloved hand, and started down the tunnel toward the light.

I've never been what anyone would consider stealthy, but I managed to turn the corner and find myself staring at the back of one of the biggest damn werewolves I'd ever seen. He had to be seven and a half feet tall, and easily four hundred pounds. And from what I could see, it was all muscle. It was in its half-shifted state, stuck between man and wolf, and all grumpy badass. I stood in the doorway for a few seconds, trying to find a way past the beastie, but there was only one door leading in and one door leading out. I took a deep breath, steadied Bertha, and squeezed a round at the back of the big furball's head.

Except the head wasn't there when the bullet got there. Fuzzy heard something, or smelled something, or just had a premonition or something, because he ducked under my shot and swung around at me, his long claws reaching out to disembowel me as he spun around. I sucked in my gut, and his claws flickered past my midsection, one nail just leaving a razor-thin line across my belly.

"Hey!" I shouted as I stepped back and brought Bertha to bear on the monster's face. It locked eyes with me over the barrel of a fifty-caliber pistol, and I swear I saw the wolf grin at me. It threw a punch, but the power of the fist was somewhat lessened by getting punched in the chest with a big-ass bullet. I knew the lead round, even blessed as it was, would only provide a few seconds' pause to the monster, but that was all I needed. By the time the werewolf was back on its feet, the flesh already knitting back together over the gaping hole in its chest, I had dropped the magazine from Bertha's handle, pulled a spare magazine from my shoulder rig, and slammed it home.

"Last chance, furball," I muttered, but the wolf couldn't hear me over its own snarling. It charged, and I squeezed the trigger three times in quick succession. The first bullet, normal lead left over from the last magazine, provided just enough impact to slow the creature down. I side-stepped his charge and put two more in the back of his head as he barreled past. The first round from the new magazine had no effect, but the second one, a fifty-caliber sterling silver bullet landed right above the junction of his skull and spine. Werewolves aren't renowned for their brains, but I can honestly say that this guy had a head full of 'em. I know because some of the backspray got on my boots. The wolf dropped like several hundred pounds of ground chuck onto the floor of the sewer with a wet *thwack*.

I heard a rustle of wings behind me and spun around to see a shadow flicker around a corner. I shrugged and pushed forward into the room, figuring that I may as well follow it, then stopped cold at what was around me. I turned back to look at where I'd come from—yep, still looked like sewer. But the room I was standing in looked enough like the landscape of Eastern Europe that the next thing I did was look up.

There were stars. Not only was I not in Kansas anymore, I wasn't *indoors* anymore. I had no idea where that doorway had taken me, but now I was outside, in a deep forest, with a dead werewolf at my feet. I thought about it for a minute and realized that standing there wondering about shit wasn't going to get me any closer to going home, so I set off through the woods in the direction I'd seen the shadow flicker. I tromped through the darkened forest for what felt like hours before I broke through into a clearing. It wasn't even really a clearing, just a wide spot at the end of a road leading up to a castle rising up out of the mists high on a hill above me.

"What the ever-loving hell?" I asked the hordes of nobody around me, then dove back into the woods as a horse-drawn carriage roared past me out of nowhere. I turned to see where it had come from, and the forest I'd just walked through was gone, replaced with a long dirt road, a gloomy, rainy thing stretching far off into the night. The road wound down the side of the hill I had just looked up, so it only surprised me a little when I turned around again and saw that I was standing in front of a pair of huge wooden doors.

"This place needs a guest spot by Lon Chaney," I muttered. I reached out for the demonic-looking knocker on the door, then decided against it. Whatever was running this simulation obviously wanted me indoors, and I didn't feel like waiting for RiffRaff to limp his skillet-wearing ass down to the front door to let me in. So I tried the knob, which was locked, of course. Fortunately for me, I brought a couple of different style lock picks with me. I reared back with my right lock pick and slammed my foot into the door, just to the right of the lock. The doors shuddered in the frame, and I heard a few small cracks, but the doors held fast. I nodded to myself, drew Bertha, checked the chamber, saw a red-tipped bullet ready to go, and stepped back a safe distance. Like twenty yards.

I leveled Bertha at the door and squeezed off one shot. The white phosphorous round slammed into the wood with a resounding *crack*, then the doors burst into flames as the phosphorous reacted with the air. I let the doors burn merrily for a minute or two, then walked back up the steps, kicked the lock again, and this time was rewarded with both doors flying inward, showering sparks around the deserted entryway. I shined my flashlight all around, but no one had come to investigate the ruckus. I shrugged and went inside, following the script that was being written for me.

The entryway opened into a small study on the right, but a quick once-over showed it was empty of people—just a desk, a couple of comfy-looking chairs, a huge rug in the center of the room, and a huge fireplace with a few logs crackling merrily in it. There were more books lining the walls than in my high school library, and the place was lit with hurricane lamps and candles. Looked like wherever I was, there wasn't a whole lot in the way of utilities. So, of course, that's the moment my bladder decided to remind me that I drank seven beers with dinner and that indoor plumbing was gonna be real important real soon. Or at least a ficus tree or something.

"Welcome to my home," came a heavily accented voice behind me. So heavy, in fact, that I kinda didn't understand what he'd said until I turned around to look at him.

"Huh?" I asked. "What'd you…" I trailed off. I couldn't help it. I had nothing. I've quipped with werewolves, engaged in witty repartee with fairies and troll, shot the shit with a love-struck rakshasa, and parried triple entendres with a butt-nekkid Sasquatch, but I just stood there like a beach bluegill when I turned around and Count Friggin' Dracula was standing in front of me. And I mean old-school Drac, not looks like a euro-trash omnisexual pansy from *Buffy* Drac. I mean wearing the cape and the tux and the slicked-back hair and I thought he'd be taller and—

"Is that a *girdle*?" The words just came out, like Skeeter in seventh grade, with nothing holding them back.

Dracula looked offended. "It is a waist cincher, I'll have you know."

"How the hell does a vampire get fat?" I asked. "All the ones I've ever met were super-skinny and hot as hell. But dude, no offense, you look kinda like everybody's weird uncle. You're not real tall, you got that funky receding hairline thing going on, and now I find out you're wearing a *girdle*? Damn, my illusions are shattered all to shit."

"What are you babbling about, peasant? I am taller than…" He looked up to meet my eyes, since he was almost half a foot shorter than me. "Well, regardless, my hair…" He trailed off again, running his fingers over the encroaching flesh where his forehead was growing rapidly into an eight-head.

"None of that matters, human. I am Vlad Tepes, Count Dracula, and a specimen of your size will make a lovely slave for my wives!" He locked eyes with me, and the room got a little swimmy at the edges. I felt a sudden desire to go visit his wives, to roll around nekkid with three beautiful Eastern European vampires for a decade or two, then a disapproving blonde face swam into my vision, and I realized exactly how pissed off Agent Amy would be if I screwed myself to death in some weird-ass knockoff Dracula's Florida AdventureTime Castle. I shook my head, and the desire to frolic with fanged chicks vanished (for a little while, if I'm being honest).

"Nah, I got a girlfriend," I said, and Dracula's eyes went wide.

"How are you resisting my compulsion? What magic is this?"

"The magic of a man who knows his woman will cut his nuts off if he so much as looks at another woman. I think they call it love. Now look, Drac, pal. I don't know who conjured your ass here, or what the hell is going on, but I got a museum lady to save, and somehow I gotta figure out how to get your castle out of Orlando and back to Transylvania. And back to fiction, for that matter. So if you could just point me to the exit, I'll get out of your hair…heh, sorry about that one…and you can go back to doing whatever it is you do here. Alone. In this big, creepy-ass castle." I turned and headed back toward the door to the study, and that's when Drac made a tragic error. He grabbed my arm.

Now for a little fella, he was strong. He latched onto my arm, and I wasn't moving until he let go. Problem for him was, he grabbed onto my left arm, and that meant my right arm was free to reach up over my shoulder and draw Great-Grandpappy's sword. I drew and spun around, bringing that sword down on Drac's forearm as I did. The blade cut through muscle and bone just like it was butter. I stepped back, and I took Drac's lower arm and hand with me. He kept a couple inches past the elbow and a spurting wound.

"What?!? You dare assault the Lord of the Undead?" He stared at his stump for a second, and I watched the wound close, and skin grow back over the cut. I think I even saw new flesh start to grow as the arm regenerated, but Drac was coming at me, so I had to shelve my fascination with his arm to pay attention to his mouth. Said mouth was wide open, with fangs prominently on display, so I did the most logical thing I could think of—I raised my sword and let him run onto it. With his wide-open mouth. The razor-sharp blade combined with his momentum to shove the sword through the back of his skull. Gray stuff splattered onto the rug, and his eyes went really wide.

"You're still alive?" I asked. His eyes blinked, and he flailed at the blade in his head with his remaining hand.

"I don't think that's a good idea," I said, and swatted his hand aside. He moaned a little, then started to walk backward, sliding his head off the sword.

"Oh, that is just *nasty*," I said. "You have got to be kidding me." Drac kept walking backward, but I just walked with him, keeping his melon speared on the blade of my sword. After about ten steps, he walked backward into a bookshelf, burying the blade into a book with a deep *thunk*. Drac grinned around three feet of steel and reached out with his hands to shove me back. I reckoned he figured if he got me off the hilt of the sword, he could pull it out of his head and kill me. Which is a great idea, unless the dude you're shoving has a height advantage, a leverage advantage, a hundred pounds or more weight advantage, and is holding the sword buried in your head. His shove was more like a light stroking of my chest, which I found awkward but not particularly terrifying.

"You want this out of your head?" I asked. "Don't try to nod, just blink twice for yes." He blinked twice, and I yanked the sword out of his head with a wet, squelching sound. A line of gray matter ran down Drac's forehead, and he wavered on his feet for a second, then he locked onto me and charged, fangs and claws outstretched.

"Damn, son, that didn't go so well last time, so what makes you think this is gonna go better?" He answered by turning to mist and reforming behind me, all his wounds healed and his arm regrown.

"I believe my magic is what makes me think such things, peasant. Now prepare to die!" He raised both hands and came at me again, but this time I was ready, or at least a lot more ready. I raised my sword to meet his charge, and he turned to mist again. But this time when Drac turned to mist and flew past me, I spun around and raised Bertha. I put a white phosphorous round right through the middle of the cloud. He solidified about the same time the bullet hit where he should be, and the energy transfer when that white phosphorous bullet hit Drac right in the sternum was like nothing I'd ever seen. The fire started immediately, and it started *inside* Drac's chest. He had just about enough time to throw me a confused look, then his chest exploded in flames.

It was pretty impressive, I gotta say. His head flew up about six feet, bounced off the ceiling and landed on the desk. His arms blew off in opposite directions, his chest just blew slap damn to pieces, and his ass and legs stood there for a second like they were expecting the rest of Drac to pull back together. He didn't. Pull back together, that is. His legs just toppled over, and I spent a couple seconds stomping out fires on the expensive rug. Once I got all the little fires out, I looked around, saw the study door now led into a gray mist, and headed that way. I stepped into the mist, wondering if wherever I came out could possibly be as screwed up as Dracula's Castle. I should never wonder these things.

Chapter Eleven

I STAGGERED THROUGH THE DOORWAY AND COLLAPSED ON THE FLOOR in front of Joe. I lay there for a minute gasping for breath and wishing I'd remembered to stash a flask in my jeans while Joe stared down at me.

"Bubba, are you okay?" he asked, holding out one of those aluminum water bottles that hippies carry so they don't ruin the environment or something. I didn't care about his ecological motivations; I just unscrewed the cap and sucked the sides flat on that bottle. I handed it back to Joe, who turned and refilled it from a water fountain on the wall.

I drained the next bottle of water, then waved off a third. "I'm good. You figure anything out about that door while I was gone?"

Joe laughed. "I'm good, Bubba, but even with Skeeter's help, I'm just the pastor, not the miracle worker."

"What do you mean?" I asked.

"Be reasonable, Bubba, nobody could have uncovered anything in the few minutes you've been gone."

"Few minutes?" I thought it through. I'd fought a werewolf, got lost in the woods, found Dracula's castle, whooped Dracula's ass, and come home. No way could I manage that in less than a couple hours. "Joe, I have to have been gone at least two hours, probably four."

"Bubba, I swear on the Bible that you stepped through that doorway less than five minutes ago."

"He's right Bubba," Skeeter's voice rang through my ear, and I almost dropped to my knees I was so happy to see his sorry ass. Or hear. Or not, really, because hearing his ass usually meant something unpleasant was happening. For a little dude, Skeeter can fart with the best of them.

"So y'all are saying I went through that door less than five minutes ago?"

"Yep," they said in unison.

"And I'm saying I fought a werewolf and killed Dracula, and that it took me way longer than a few minutes to manage that. I friggin' hate magic." I sat there for a second, checking myself for injuries and generally catching my breath. "Hey Joe?"

"Yeah, Bubba?" He gave me the look that said no Jimi Hendrix song lyrics were welcome in this situation, but for once I was not going to follow up my address with "where you going with that gun in your hand?" Instead, I jerked a thumb at the door I'd just come through. "Can you do something about those scribbles on the doorframe? I think they're magic something-or-others that make the door into a portal through space and time."

Joe raised one eyebrow at me and said, "Portal through space and time, huh?" But he reclaimed his water bottle and used his handkerchief to start scrubbing the symbols off the door.

"Leave me alone," I protested. "I know about time-travelly stuff! I've watched *Doctor Who*! I know that it's all timey-wimey wibbly-wobbly, or whatever the hell that little dude said. I fell asleep halfway through. But I watched some of it, anyhow."

"I don't think this is the time to discuss whether or not half an episode of *Doctor Who* is adequate education on the behavior of the space-time continuum, but regardless, removing these sigils from the doorframe seems to have returned this to a mundane portal once more," Joe said, opening the door to reveal the Black Forest exhibit I'd expected to find the first time I barged through.

I stood up off the floor, knocked back another big slug of water from Joe's bottle, checked Bertha's ammo situation, and stepped through the door. I was almost disappointed when the exhibit stayed all fake around me instead of teleporting me to Germany or someplace cool. But it did stay a normal museum, well, as normal as it can be when the exhibit is dedicated to monsters.

We passed through the Black Forest exhibit, then came to another locked door, this one leading into what Becca had called her *coup de grace,* the demon summoning room, complete with creepy-ass altar. I wasn't really looking forward to spending any time in this joint, but let's face it—bad guys aren't that original, and monsters are even less so. If Becca was still in the museum, she was behind this door.

"You got a plan?" I asked Joe.

He shook his head. "Isn't this the part where you laugh at plans and do whatever you want anyway?"

"Yeah, but I thought maybe we'd try something different this time."

"Like what?" Joe asked.

"Maybe you kick the door down and get the crap knocked out of you, then I come in and kill everything that's not nailed down?"

"That plan sucks, Bubba."

"Now you know why I don't do plans," I said, then I got a running start and blew through the locked door like it was the Duke O-line at my junior year homecoming football game. The home of the Blue Devils is known for a lot of things, but football is pretty far down the list. The door splintered just like their tackle's ribcage, and I burst into a scene straight out of a nightmare. It took everything I had not to turn around and head right back out the shattered door, but I figured there wasn't anybody better equipped for a hundred miles to deal with the shitshow in front of me, so I took a deep breath and got ready to do some serious killing.

My first target was the skinny bastard that I'd bumped into earlier, Professor Pokey. The skinny little assclown was standing at the head of Becca's oh-so-carefully constructed to be accurate altar, holding what looked like a pretty damn accurate knife high in the air.

"Put it down, asshole," I said, drawing Bertha and pointing the giant pistol at his skinny bird chest.

"Go to hell, redneck!" he shouted, and his voice made Skeeter sound like a baritone, it was so high and thready.

"I'm in a museum, ain't that bad enough for somebody like me?" I asked, and pulled back the hammer. I didn't need to—the action of the pistol is fine if I just pull the trigger—but there's a certain sound a pistol makes when you cock it that sometimes can convince a bad guy to give up if he's only moderately insane.

This was not that time. The look that the mad scientist turned to me was crazier than a shithouse rat. His eyes were rolling around in his head like marbles, and sweat poured off him like a madam in Sunday School. He went up on tiptoes to get even more power behind his stroke and brought the knife down at Becca's chest as I brought the pistol up to point at his. I didn't hesitate, didn't even think about it. I pulled the trigger and blew the son of a bitch six feet backwards.

Bertha sounded like a cannon in the tiny space, and the smell of gunfire laid heavy over the stink of incense, candles, and a couple of bowls of entrails placed at the points of a crudely drawn pentagram. I motioned for Joe to stand back until I could get a good look at what we had going on in there, a little voice in the back of my head screaming at me that I had just shot a human, for God's sake, not a monster, and what the hell were we going to do about it? I didn't have an answer for the little voice in my head, and I sure didn't have an answer for Skeeter, who was screaming questions in my ear at about the speed of a NASCAR driver on a beer run. I reached up and took the Bluetooth out of my ear, then dropped it to the floor and stepped on it.

"There," I said. "Now Skeeter's out of this. Joe, you stay back there so you're clear, too." I kept walking the room, blowing out candles and turning over bowls of blood and other things that I couldn't, and didn't want to, identify.

"Clear of what?" Joe asked from the threshold. He had enough training and experience to stay out of a room when I told him to, because too often the magical backlash of the crap we dealt with could be deadly.

"Clear of whatever's gonna happen to me for killing that nut bar," I said. "I think I can get off without doing any time because he was one hundred percent gonna kill Becca, but there's gonna be a lot of questions. You probably want to get the Church's lawyer down here pretty fast."

"Could we untie me first?" Becca asked from the altar.

"Oh shit, Becca, I'm sorry," I said, stepping over the lines of the pentagram and holstering Bertha. I flipped out my Kershaw pocketknife and cut the ropes holding her feet, then freed her wrists. She reached up to a cut on her shoulder and wiped away a thin line of blood left from when Professor Apeshit dropped his knife, then sat up.

That's when it all went completely and utterly to shit.

In sitting up on the altar, Becca used her right hand to steady herself on the stone. The same right hand that had a little blood on it from the cut on her shoulder. The cut made by the sacrificial blade in the middle of whatever summoning ceremony Doctor Crazyass had started. So she put the blood of the sacrifice, released by the charmed blade in the midst of the proper ceremony, onto the altar, the gateway to Where the Bad Things Are. The second her hand touched the altar, the blood completed the spell, and the altar began to glow with clichéd but still scary as hell red light. I picked Becca up, threw her over my shoulder, and jumped back over the lines of the pentagram on my way out.

I put her down just in front of the door and looked up at Joe. "Keep her clear. I don't know what that asshole was summoning, but it's on the way through right now."

The altar split down the middle with a resounding *crack* and a pair of skeletal arms reached up from the glowing interior far past where human arms should have stopped. What pulled itself out of the glowing crimson portal was obscenely female, with pendulous breasts sagging almost to its knees and long hair hanging past its shoulders, but it was just as obviously not human as it was an obvious mockery of femininity. Its skin was cracked and blackened, like it had just pulled itself from a fire, and gray slime oozed through the cracks. It fixed a pair of yellow eyes on me, and when it grinned, I almost threw up. Only the memory of exactly how much that steak cost kept it down as I looked at a forked tongue licking over a double row of pointed teeth.

"You rang, humansssss?" it said, those teeth splitting its face into a terrible grin. Its voice was like fingernails down a chalkboard and the screams of pigs being slaughtered, all set to a Rob Zombie soundtrack. It sounded like every terrible thing that had ever happened, rolled up into one nasty voice.

"Nah, nobody called for a bucket full of ugly. You can go home," I said, hoping like hell my voice wasn't shaking as bad as my knees were. I was pretty sure I hadn't pissed myself, but it wasn't for lack of absolute terror. This thing was a whole different league than anything I'd ever faced, and I knew in my gut that I couldn't beat it. My only hope was that in hopping in and out of that magical circle, I hadn't broken any of the lines, and whatever spell Doctor Dumbass cast to summon this thing could hold it until either sunrise or Joe could perform an exorcism or banishment or something.

"I ammmmmmm home, now, human. I am hommmmmmmme, and I ammmm hunnnngggrrryyyyy."

"Well, too bad I left the Corn Nuts at home. You'll just have to settle for a couple of ounces of lead wrapped in holy water," I said as I drew Bertha, ejected the normal rounds that were in her, and slammed home a magazine full of blessed bullets. I squeezed off three quick rounds and caught the demon in the center of its chest with each one.

Let's be clear. The Desert Eagle is one of the most powerful pistols ever created. It is not intended to do anything except wreak havoc on whatever you point it at. It is not a target practice pistol. It is not a trick shot pistol. It is four and a half pounds of death and destruction in a beautifully constructed package, and that's before you put the bullets in it. Getting shot by a Desert Eagle is nothing a human being gets up from. Even with a bulletproof vest, a chest shot from a fifty caliber bullet is like getting hit in the chest with a sledgehammer by a very strong, very angry, very large man. So I laid three good sledgehammer strokes into this monster's chest. The kind of damage that would have blown most vampires into four or five pieces, left a werewolf lying in the dirt wondering where his legs went, and given a troll serious second thoughts about remaining in the same zip code as me.

This demon laughed at me. It plucked the bullets from its hide, dropped them onto the floor, and laughed at me. That's when things got bad.

Then I noticed something I hadn't seen before. When I shot Professor Demonsbuddy, he flew backward for several feet before hitting the ground. But then he slammed into a wall and bounced forward to lie, and in very short order die, on his stomach. With his left hand stretched out across the boundary of the summoning circle, thus breaking the magical barrier that kept the demon locked away from the world.

I hate magic. I said that, right?

Chapter Twelve

I DID WHAT ANY REASONABLE PERSON WOULD DO WHEN FACED WITH A seven-foot tall demon in a small space. I drew my sword and ran right at it. And she (it? Hell, I don't know, I'm pretty sure it was a "she") did what any self-respecting seven-foot tall demon would do when faced with a six-and-a-half-foot tall idiot with a sword. She reared back with one big fist and knocked the piss out of me. She backhanded me across my face without even a grunt's worth of effort and spun me around almost out of my boots.

"You think you can sssssstop meeeee, humannnn?" She drew back a hand tipped with needle-like claws and slashed it at my guts.

"I don't know, but I'm gonna try," I said, with maybe a grunt of my own from blocking her disemboweling stroke with my blade. I held onto the sword, but it wasn't without effort. I ducked under her other hand as it swept out to take my eyes, and stabbed upward with my sword, hoping to land a lucky shot and nail her in her softer underbelly. Except her underbelly wasn't even the least little bit soft. My sword skittered across her flesh, and I followed the line of the thrust, bringing me way closer to her torso than I ever wanted to be. I dropped the sword as the demon reached out and pulled me close.

She crushed me to her chest, slamming my face into one gray-skinned breast. Every bad experience I'd ever had with a boob came back to me, from seeing my mom changing when I was eight, to finding out in the back row of the Mountain View Drive-In Movie Theatre that Julie Anne Margraves had three nipples. I know the third nipple thing isn't a real big deal, but I was sixteen and had no warning. I just found it while exploring under Julie Anne's shirt in the middle of *Crouching Tiger, Hidden Dragon* and was a little freaked out over the whole experience. The demon's cracked gray skin raked my cheek and her arm pressed into my back, threatening to break a rib. I could almost feel the thing's other arm raising to the sky for a killing stroke, and I scrabbled frantically at the back of my jeans for my Judge revolver. I yanked the pistol free of the paddle holster in my pants and jammed it into the demon's thigh, the only part of the monster I could reach. I squeezed the trigger again and again until all five rounds were spent, and I'd fired three .410 shotgun shells full of silver shot and a pair of .45 long rounds doused in holy water into the hell-bitch's leg.

She let go of me and shoved me back a few feet. I tossed the empty pistol off to one side and rolled my shoulders as I stared at the demon. She stood there grinning at me, a tiny line of black ichor running down her leg the only hint that I'd even scratched her.

"Ouch," she said, in that voice that let me know in no uncertain terms that she wasn't the least bit injured by my popgun, but was just insulted enough to make my death hurt for a very long time. Oh well, I knew when I signed up for it that this gig had a shit retirement plan. I jammed my hands into the caestus hanging from my belt and raised my spiked fists. The demon grinned again and raised her hands.

"Joe, get Becca out of here. I don't know how long I can hold this thing off," I said. Then the demon grinned, and for the first time since she crawled out of the shattered altar, I noticed the tail that arced several feet over her head and ended in a scorpion's stinger.

"Scratch that," I said. "Get Becca out of here fast 'cause I ain't gonna be able to hold this thing off more than a few seconds." The tail flicked out, and I knocked it away. The demon lashed out with one hand, and I blocked with an iron-clad fist. She drew back both clawed hands, and I took in a deep breath as she lunged, both claws and tail all coming straight at me, full speed. I stepped inside her stroke, spun around, and grabbed her tail with both hands. I took a battering from her forearms, but she missed with all the claws, so I called that a win and yanked on her tail with every ounce of strength I had. I whirled around inches from the demon's body, holding her tail in both hands, and shoved it into her midsection until the stinger popped out the other side.

"Take that, hellbitch," I said as the demon's eyes went wide. She stood frozen for a half a second, then she just laughed. The stinger slid out of her torso without any apparent effort or pain, the tail clipping me on the jaw as it went past. I hit one knee and was trying to regain my footing when a giant demon fist caught me right on the point of my chin. That uppercut stood me up perfectly straight onto my tippy toes, then my eyes crossed, and I fell straight back like an overweight redwood. I crashed to the floor and stared up at the ceiling, wondering when I had fallen, and why I couldn't get up. I was lying there, working out the physics of my situation, when the demon loomed into my vision. She stabbed straight down at my chest, and my last thoughts on Earth were "Amy is gonna be *pissed*."

At least those would have been my last thoughts if those claws had hit me. Because they were definitely intended to rip out my heart, and that's not on the list of things that I can get over. Fortunately for me, the claws never touched my chest. After several seconds of not being dead, or being dead hurting a lot more than it had any right to, I opened my eyes.

"Sonofabitch," I whispered. There was indeed a demon's claw hovering a couple of inches from my torso. And a few inches past that, at the demon's wrist, was a hand in a long-sleeved black dress shirt. The hand glowed with a white light that was almost painful to look at, but I forced myself to follow the hand up the arm to the shoulder, and then over to…Joe's face?

"Joe?" I just said his name, but there were about fifteen questions in that one word.

He looked down at me, and his eyes glowed with a pure white light. "You should probably move, Bubba," he said, but it wasn't entirely his voice. I mean, it was Joe's voice, but it was more than that, too. There was a power behind his voice, and a weight to it, and I couldn't exactly put my finger on it, but there was definitely something else in there with my friend. I pulled myself out from under the grasped hand of the priest and the demon, and scooted on my butt back over to the wall. I tried to stand, but the room was still spinning way too much from the demon's punch, and I was still trying not to puke up my dinner, so I just sat there.

I sat there and watched my very normal-sized priest friend, all six foot and two-hundred or two-hundred-twenty pounds of him, wrestle the demon's hand up to hold it between them. The demon just stared for the first few seconds, but then she began to pull and thrash against Joe's grip. I saw smoke start to seep out from between Joe's fingers, and the demon started to fight harder to get away. She swung out with her other hand and bashed Joe in the shoulder, but he didn't flinch.

Now I'm a big dude, and I've taken some epic punches in my day, but standing still while a demon whales on me is not in my skill set. But at least today, it was in Joe's. The more smoke billowed out from his fingers, the more blows the demon rained down on his head and shoulder. And Joe never flinched. It was like he didn't even notice the punches, until one caught him right on the point of his jaw. That shot turned his head to the side, at least. He still didn't let go of the demon, just cracked his head from side to side, then flicked out his left hand and caught the demon's other wrist.

She let out a shriek that left no doubt as to her origins, because anything that can make that noise is definitely straight from Hell. Her scream was the stuff of nightmares, mixing banshee shrieks with ear-splitting yips and yells, high ululating cries that rang through the little room in deafening waves.

"Stop."

With one word, Joe silenced the demon. He didn't raise his voice, didn't threaten or cajole. He just said "stop," and the monster quit screaming. The silence was almost worse than the shrieking because under the hiss of the air conditioning you could hear the slight sizzle of the demon's burning flesh.

"Sit." Joe spoke again, and released the demon. I scurried backward and sat on the edge of the altar.

"Whaaaaatttt arrrrree you, morrrrrttttallll?"

"I am more than I seem, demon, but I speak with the authority you've always recognized," Joe replied. "You have a choice, beast. Choose swiftly, and choose wisely."

"A choice?" it rasped.

"Since the beginning, Fallen One, there has always been choice. Do you choose to return to Hell, or do you choose to die here?" Super-Joe never raised his voice, never moved to threaten, never even touched the demon. He just stood there, his eyes glowing with an unbearable white light.

"I'll go home, angel. But not until I've sssssated my hunger, and nevvvvverrrrr without a fight!"

And with that, it was on. The demon literally ripped its own arms off to get away from Joe, planting a foot in the center of his chest and jerking its body backward, leaving Joe holding a pair of five-foot-long arms tipped with brutal claws. He raised an eyebrow and tossed the left-hand arm aside, then gripped the remaining arm like a Louisville Slugger and used it to parry the tail strikes the demon was throwing. That chitinous appendage flashed up, down, and sideways, but every time it lashed out, Joe knocked it aside with the demon's own severed arm.

But the literal bitch from hell was just stalling, just killing time until she could grow a new pair of arms to add to the mix. Soon Joe dropped the severed arm and was moving faster than my eye could follow, swatting aside tail jabs and claw slashes like he was a divine Chuck Norris, which may or may not be redundant, depending on your views on Chuck Norris.

The demon backed up to the far wall, then leapt over Joe's head to land between me and where Becca stood, frozen with terror since the demon crawled out of her exhibit. I'm pretty sure that was never in her design pitch to the board of directors. The monster flicked out a claw and wrapped it around my neck, pulling me to my feet like I was no more than a rag doll. It held me off the ground, choking me with one claw while it held the other poised to rip my guts out. It stretched the stinger out to press ever-so-gently into Becca's chest, right where it could skewer her heart in half a second, then stopped.

"You mentioned choisssssse, angel," the demon hissed with a toothy grin. "Now the choice is yours. Your friend…or your one true love? Who lives, and who dies? The choice is yoursssss, morrrrrrtal."

Joe looked from Becca to me and back again. I wracked my brain for something useful, but came up empty. The demon's grasp tightened around my throat, and I watched as it wiggled the tip of its stinger over Becca's heart. I was out of guns, my sword was lying ten feet away against the altar, and my Jedi powers weren't pulling to me no matter how much I held out my hand and wished really hard.

Joe looked at me, stricken. He didn't know what to do. Hell, even I could see the easy answer, and my idea of being on the right side of morality was tipping the girl extra after the second lap dance. I tried to speak, but couldn't even get a croak out.

The demon turned to me. "Trying to say ssssomethingggg, human? Impppplorrrrring yourrrrr friend to ssssavvvvve the girrrrrl and let you die in herrrrr place? Howwwww foolishly noble." At those words, something clicked in my head, and just like a really bad light bulb going on, I knew how completely and utterly screwed we were.

Chapter Thirteen

I KNEW IT JUST LIKE I KNEW MY NAME—THE DEMON WAS GOING TO kill us both no matter who Joe picked. All he was going to do was use Joe's decision to torture him even more. I saw Joe's eyes tighten and knew he heard the same thing.

"Foolishly noble?" Joe asked. The demon jerked a little at the iron in his voice and turned its head almost completely around without moving its body at all. I continued to not throw up, but this time the only thing holding my gorge down was the demon's own hand, clasped tight around my throat.

"There is nothing foolish about sacrifice, monster, but if you understood that, you would not serve who you serve, and you would not belong where you belong. So now it is time for you to return there. Begone!" With his last word, Joe raised his arm and pointed his open hand at the demon. A beam of purest white light burst forth from his palm and struck the demon square in the chest. It let go of my throat and flew backward several feet. I dropped to one knee, then sprang forward and shoved Becca out the door to the exhibit. I couldn't exactly slam it shut behind her after the destruction I wreaked on it getting into the room, but there was enough metal and wood there to give her some cover at least.

I looked back at Joe, who stood over the smoking hulk of the demon. "Get up, you filthy piece of spawn-trash." He prodded it with his foot, and the demon writhed in pain. Smoke rose from its chest, and its arms and legs didn't seem to be working together.

"Get up." Joe kicked harder. The demon scrambled to its feet, ducking its head like a whipped dog. Joe's hands still glowed with power, and his eyes still were pupilless white. "Now," he said, and there was power beneath his words like I'd never heard. "Either you crawl back into the hole you came out of, or I destroy you. As I said, it all comes down to choice." Joe smiled, but it was a cold smile, full of stoic authority and judgment.

"I'll go," the demon said, then whirled back to me, its claws flashing in the dim candlelight and flickering overhead exhibit lights. It shot out an arm long enough to do Inspector Gadget proud, with razor-sharp fingers aimed at my throat. "But not without this one!"

I expected treachery. It was a demon, after all. So when the claws came flying at my admittedly hard to miss gut, I just had to sidestep the thrust and pull the last thing I had on me that could be considered a weapon, and even that only by the TSA. I pulled my Kershaw pocketknife, flicked the blade open, and stabbed the demon through the wrist. I stuck it to the wall like a kid's butterfly collection, then caught an elbow to the jaw and spun around to sit on the floor and look at the pretty stars.

Joe walked over to the pinned demon and put a hand on its chest, pressing it flat into the wall. "Leave this place, monster, or I will be forced to destroy you utterly."

"Asssssss if you coulddldd, huuuummmmmannnnnn," the demon hissed.

"Human?" Joe asked. "Think again, hellspawn." His hand was pressed flat against the monster's chest, and I watched as the muscles in his neck and shoulder bunched, then Joe, or whoever he was, *pushed*. Smoke rose from the demon's flesh, and as Joe pushed, his hand sank into the thing's chest. There was no ripping, no cutting, just *pushing*, and his hand slowly disappeared into the demon's chest as though he were pushing his hand through mud. The stench was spectacular, sulfur laced with shit and blood and sweat and all the nasty nightmare smells of melting demon-flesh. The beast let out a shriek that had me screaming along with it, even with both hands clasped over my ears. After what felt like a year, probably fifteen seconds, Joe relaxed his arm and pulled his hand out of the monster's chest.

My friend, the Catholic priest, the kindest man I know, the man least likely to ever raise a fist in anger, the man who used humane mouse traps then released the vermin out into the wild, wiped demon blood off his finger onto his jeans, leaned down right in the demon's face, and in a voice that would give Christopher Walken nightmares, said, "Do not doubt what I can do, demon."

The creature's eyes went wide, and it nodded feebly. "I'll go, but we'rrrrrrre not finisssssssshed," the monster hissed.

"Likely never will be, fiend. But for today, we are done." Joe waved a hand, and the altar glowed red again. Thick, black, oily smoke poured out, wrapped the demon from head to toe, and when the smoke sucked back into the cracks in the altar, the stone rectangle was restored to one solid piece, and the demon was nowhere to be seen.

He turned to me and reached out his hand, this man who wasn't a man, my friend who was suddenly something *more.* I didn't hesitate until I'd already grabbed it and he pulled me to my feet, then I looked down to see if I was on fire. I wasn't. I also wasn't dizzy, or nauseated, or hurting from any of the places I'd been punched during the day.

I looked at my friend, who stood there looking at me with glowing eyes. "Something you want to tell me, Joe?"

The angel smiled, and it used Joe's face to do it. "No, Bubba, I don't think so."

"You always in there?"

"No. I come when His need is greatest."

"Joe's need?"

"No."

"Oh. Him." *That* Him. Joe's ultimate boss. And I don't mean the Pope.

"Yes, Him."

"So He needed you to possess a priest and fight a demon?" I asked.

"He needed me to keep you alive, and keep Joe working. And we can't have the Fallen just wandering around the world's happiest place, can we?"

"I don't get it," I admitted.

"Mysterious ways isn't just a catchphrase, Bubba, it's the truth. You can't see everything He sees and certainly not what is to come. The world needs men to stand up and throw back the darkness. Men like you, and like Joe. This man," he pointed to the corpse of Professor Pokey, lying facedown on the floor with a Bertha-sized hole in his chest, "this man made a very bad decision. His jealousy of Dr. Knowles' success led him to consort with the forces of darkness. And as so often happens in these cases, he was given the letter of their agreement—Becca's exhibit was cancelled and his exhibit was scheduled as its replacement."

"But he didn't read the fine print where a demon was coming through from Hell to…what was she coming here for, anyway? Vacation? I mean, everybody loves a good roller coaster, but…"

"You noticed it was a female demon, then?"

"Yeah, kinda hard to miss with all those floppy boobies flying all over the place." That's when I remembered that in its demon form, it had at least four breasts, maybe six. In the rush to not die, I somehow missed the extra mammaries. I shuddered a little. That was a set of mammary memories that I was going to carry with me for a while.

"And what do you think a female demon would want with a supply of human men coming through the museum?"

"I don't know, was she going to...oh man, that is *nasty*." My stomach did a few unpleasant flip-flops, and I lost hold on the steak I'd worked so hard to hold onto through the whole damn demon fight. I mean, I can handle getting my ass beat by a nasty demoness without throwing up, but the idea of that *thing* banging her way through the visitor's log of the museum was more than my digestion could handle. I grabbed a jar off a shelf and filled it with recycled steak and mashed potatoes.

Several long moments later, I put the jar back on the shelf and turned back to Joe, or whoever was riding around in his skin suit. "I could have gone my whole life without that thought ever crossing my mind, thanks."

"Sorry," he said. "Sometimes I overshare."

That did it. That oh-so-human, oh-so-*Joe* confession from the angel walking around in my friend's body, was all I could take. I sat down on the floor, laughing my ass off, until Becca and Joe joined in and we sat and stood around the ruined exhibit, laughing hysterically until tears rolled down our faces.

Epilogue

"So you're re-hired? And the exhibit is a go?" We were in Becca's office the next morning. The museum looked very different in the light of day, much less like the set of a horror movie and much more like the cross between a theme park and an academic center that it really was. Joe and I sat on one side of a big conference table, with Becca on the other side and Skeeter on a big monitor on the wall. He hadn't quite forgiven me for stepping on our comm unit, but he chalked it up to me being distraught at taking a human life and was cutting me some slack.

He was right, too. I'd killed a lot of monsters, and some of them might have worn human skin from time to time, but the nutjob curator was the first straight-up human I'd ever killed, and it didn't feel right. It didn't matter that he was about half a second from skewering Becca like a kabob at a Fourth of July cookout, or that he literally raised hell in the middle of Florida. He was a human, and my job was to protect humans, not kill them. This was the first time I'd crossed that line, and even if I hadn't spent most of the night talking to the cops, I didn't see me having much in the way of restful sleep.

The cops took me in, of course, and had quite a few questions about what I was compensating for with a gun like Bertha. Joe's statement helped, and so did Becca's, but the call from the Director of Homeland Security at three in the morning claiming jurisdiction of the case, the museum, all evidence, and me was what really did the trick. Amy worked her magic from Washington and buried the local police precinct in so much paper it looked like a snowstorm as I walked out, with every fax machine and printer in the building running at full capacity. So I wasn't going to prison, but I wasn't going to get away from the image of the professor flying backward off the altar, his eyes wide with shock as a hole the size of a dinner plate appeared in his chest. He was dead before he crashed into the wall and flopped to the floor like a beached sunfish, but his eyes stared at me every time I closed my own.

"And even Marisol made it home last night!" I shook my head and dialed back into the conversation in the room. Becca was saying something that was obviously good, and I dug around in my memories until I remembered there was a missing cleaning lady named Marisol, who apparently was now home. I didn't want to think too much about where she had been because that would lead to thinking about what she might have brought back with her, which would mean a home visit, which would likely mean another fight, and I didn't think I had another fight in me right that minute. I filed it away in the "shit to look out for" mental file and turned my attention back to Becca.

She was looking at Joe like she had a lot of shit to say, and he had a similar look, so I put my hands on the table to stand up. Joe held up a hand, and I sat.

"Please stay, Bubba," Joe said. "You should probably hear this, too."

I leaned forward onto my elbows. "I always did love story time."

Joe shook himself, popped his knuckles, and looked Becca in the eye. "I loved you," he said, and she opened her mouth to reply. "No, let me finish. I know it's been a long time, but after this week, I'm pretty sure you'll believe what I'm saying." Becca closed her mouth and leaned back in the chair, arms folded across her chest. If I read her face right, she really wanted to believe him, but there was a lot of years' worth of baggage she was carryin' around.

Joe started again. "I loved you, I really did. I could see us settling down somewhere with me being a high school teacher and you running a little craft shop, or art studio, or whatever you wanted to do. I didn't care, I just wanted us to be together forever. Then one night in my senior year, everything got turned upside down.

"I was walking home from the library, and I passed the art building. A young woman came out of one of the side exits and walked in front of me for a while. She was maybe twenty yards ahead of me, but when I turned around the corner of Tillman Hall, she was gone. I looked around, but she was gone without a trace. I didn't think anything of it, figured she had gone into Tillman to use the bathroom or something, and kept walking. Well, when I got past the big steps in the front of the building, I heard something coming from the bushes by the building. I was a curious young guy, so I turned into that little courtyard to see what was making the noise. It sounded like a raccoon or something rustling in a garbage bag, but when I got back there away from everything, what I saw changed my life.

"The girl was there, but she was lying on the ground, her art supplies strewn all across the ground. She had a long white scarf, and that was laying beside her, unspooled from her neck and the tail flapping in the March breeze. It was dark back in that alcove, and it took a minute to register that she wasn't moving and that her throat had been torn out. I looked more closely, and there was blood everywhere, like if Jackson Pollack was the set decorator for *Carrie.* Standing over the girl was something I'd never seen before. It was about three feet tall, with arms longer than its body, and it was covered in thick black hair. At first I thought she'd been attacked by some kind of escaped gorilla or chimp, but then it looked up at me."

"And showed you a mouth full of pointed teeth and a hand holding a hat dripping with the dead girl's blood," I said.

"Exactly," Joe said.

"Wait, what?" Becca looked from Joe to me and back again. "What was it? And how did you know about it? Did you fight it later or something?"

"It was a redcap," I said. "A nasty little fae bastard with a taste for human flesh, particularly young female flesh. They hang out in shadows and pick off solitary walkers. They're cowards but have teeth like needles and are really strong for their size. Joe got lucky the thing didn't rip his throat out, too."

"It was more than luck," Joe corrected me. I raised an eyebrow at him, and he went on. "The redcap growled low in his throat, and that's a sound I've never forgotten. I heard that growl and knew that I was going to die beside that administration building that night. But just as the goblin leapt at me, a pistol shot rang out, and it dropped like a stone at my feet."

"A Hunter with cold iron bullets. Wait a minute, you were in college? Was this Pop?" My father had never mentioned killing any dark fae in Upstate South Carolina, but he didn't exactly keep a blog.

"No," Joe said. "It was quite a few years later that I found out how closely our fates would be entwined, Bubba. The man who killed this redcap wasn't a Hunter; he was a Guardian."

"Oh, that makes sense," I said.

"To you, maybe," Becca said. "But to the Muggles in the room, it doesn't make a damn bit of sense! What's a Hunter? What's a Guardian? And how or why does somebody become one?"

"I think you want the singular of Muggle, sweetie," said Skeeter from the monitor. "We're all Hogwarts-certified, so to speak. But to answer the question at hand, a Hunter is like Bubba—somebody who goes from town to town within a certain region of the country hunting down things that go bump in the night."

"And shooting them," I added. "Or stabbing, decapitating, exploding, dismembering, disemboweling, or defenestrating them. I like defenestrating. That's one of my favorites."

"You're just proud you know a word with five syllables," Skeeter said.

I counted *de-fe-ne-stra-tion* out on my fingers, then nodded at the screen. "You ain't wrong," I said.

"A Guardian—" Skeeter did what he did about half the time, which was pretend like I hadn't said anything. That felt like forgiveness, so I decided we were okay again. "—is someone assigned to a particular place for a certain time to protect one or more people. If the Church feels that someone has potential, they may be assigned a Guardian to make sure they live to adulthood."

"Yeah, I had one at Georgia. No matter how hard I tried, he wouldn't do my Physics homework," I said.

"Sometimes they are assigned not on potential but on the sheer amount of destruction that one young person can wreak if left untended. But in Joe's case, it probably had something to do with his potential to become a liaison between a Hunter and the Church," Skeeter said. I wasn't sure if that was a shot or not, but I assumed it was and flipped his image the bird.

"Actually, the Guardian was hers," Joe said. "He was there to protect the girl, but he got tangled up in a consultation as part of his cover story, and she died."

"Who was she?" I asked.

"I never found out," Joe said. "The Guardian killed the redcap, then gathered up the girl's body and ran off into the night."

"How did you find him again?" I asked.

"I went to his church the next day. There weren't very many Filipino Catholic priests in Rock Hill, South Carolina, in the nineties, so I recognized him instantly. I showed up on his doorstep, and after I beat on his front and back doors for an hour, he let me in."

"Yeah, I had that happen with a cheerleader once in college. She just stood there kicking and pounding on my dorm door for hours. Eventually I got up and let her out." I looked around the table, but nobody was laughing. "I let her *out*, get it?" Nothing. "Because she...oh never mind. Y'all just don't appreciate comedy." I leaned back in my chair and motioned for Joe to go on with his story.

"There's not much more. The Guardian was drunk, convinced that he had failed in his sacred duty. I was terrified, convinced that I had seen Satan himself on my college campus. So he let me in and told me about faeries while I tried to catch up to him in the drunk department. Then he told me about Hunters, and Guardians, and Liaisons, and that we were the modern-day Knights Templar, protecting the world from the evil on the other side of the veil. Then he made me swear a solemn vow not to tell anyone about any of what he'd told me, and passed out. I sat at his kitchen table trying to process everything I'd heard and seen in the last twelve hours and drank myself into oblivion. When we woke up the next morning, I had a Guardian to teach me the ways of the Templars and a hangover that made me swear off gin forever."

"Wait a minute," I said, holding up a hand. "You're a Templar Knight?"

Joe shrugged a little, made a few noises like he didn't really want to answer, but after a minute or so said, "Yes, I am a member of the Knights Templar. But it's not something we talk about."

"Like Fight Club," I said.

"Only a lot older," Joe added.

"And way more badass," I said.

Skeeter laughed. We all turned to the TV and he said, "What? I just think it's funny that your real title is Sir Uncle Father Joe."

We all laughed at that, and a lot of the tension in the room dissipated. Joe looked at Becca and said, "So that's why I vanished. I didn't hear the call like most ministers. The call sought me out and tried to eat my liver. I never found out who the girl was or why she warranted a Guardian, but without her there to guard, he was reassigned, and as his student, I went with him. And I've been with the Order ever since. I've thought about you often, but never had..."

"The balls," I muttered.

"A *reason*," Joe corrected, "to find you. I thought you'd be better off without me opening old wounds, not to mention safer if my line of work was nowhere near your life."

"Until the things that go bump in the night found me," Becca said.

"Yeah, shit happens," I said.

"What now?" Becca asked.

"Now we go back to normal," Joe said.

"Are you kidding me? I don't even know if I'll recognize normal if I see it after this."

"Good news," I said. "You live in friggin' Orlando. You ain't real likely to run into a whole lot of normal around here." Joe and Becca both shot me a dirty look, so I held up my hands and made little locking motions with my lips.

"Anyhow, I meant with us," Becca said.

"Well, there might be certain vows you need to know about…" Skeeter said.

"Actually…" Joe said. "The Templars have always been exempt from the vows most priests take regarding chastity. It was long thought that we needed to breed true in order to continue the line of Guardians and Hunters."

"So you can…date?" Becca asked.

"It's actually encouraged," Joe said. "There are a lot more monsters than there are Hunters and Guardians, so the more we…date, the better."

"That sounds a lot like my cue to get the hell out of here and let y'all get reacquainted for a couple days," I said, standing up from the table. "Skeet, our work here is done. Can you book Joe a rental car for a week and then a plane ticket back to Atlanta? I'm gonna go get my truck headed north and hope to get home by Friday so maybe I can spend the weekend with my girlfriend, leaving Skeeter as the only dateless one in the crowd, as usual."

"Actually, Bubba…" Skeeter said with a shy grin. "You remember that new choir director for the Methodist Church? Well, we're going to see *Deadpool* Sunday evening if you and Amy want to double-date?"

"Sure," I said. "I hear it's pretty good, even with Ryan Reynolds in it. Y'all behave yourselves, and I'll see you back at home, Joe." I turned away from where Joe and Becca were doing a whole lot of talking without any saying words and walked out of the museum to where my F-250 waited for me. I flipped down the sun visor, spent a minute looking at my favorite picture of Agent Amy, in full tactical gear holding an MP-5 with a barrel-mounted flashlight, and pointed that big blue pickup toward home.

Midsummer

July 25th, 6PM - 30:00:00

"I EVER TELL YOU I HATE NECKTIES?" I SAID, PULLING AT THE OFFENDING garment around my neck. I'm a big dude, with about a 22-inch neck, so ties are not part of my normal attire. Hell, shirts with collars are usually only something I put up with when somebody I care about dies or gets married. And given recent history, there's a lot more dying in my kin and friends than there is marrying.

The last time I remember wearing a necktie was at Aunt Marian's funeral. There was a lot of dead bodies lying around after my last big fight with Jason, but most of them weren't in any condition to bury. Besides, my brother was dead to me long before I finally killed his sorry shape-changing, murdering ass, so I didn't bother throwing him a funeral. I burned his body, pissed on the ashes, and went to the bar with Amy and Skeeter. That's how I celebrated my brother's life.

But anyway, all that to say that neckties are damned uncomfortable when you're normal sized, much less when you're built like a defensive lineman, which I am, and have a beard like the fourth member of ZZ Top, which I'm not. My neck's just too damn big to wear one of the things without it drawing up so much it looks more like a bowtie than anything else, and I tend to get the end of my beard caught in the knot. But none of that was any concern to my partner.

"Shut up, Bubba," was the response from my loving girlfriend and partner, Agent Amy Hall. She works for DEMON, the Department of Extra-dimensional, Mystical and Occult Nuisances, which always felt to me like somebody really wanted the letters to spell "demon," to paraphrase the movie.

"I know you're uncomfortable, but I can't do anything about that right now. If we're going to convince these people that you're legit, you have to look legit."

"And looking legit means wearing this ugly cheap suit and a damn necktie?" I asked.

"We're pretending to be FBI agents, Bubba. Cheap suits and neckties are pretty much the uniform. Now shut up and let me get us past the front desk."

We walked through the front doors of the Nashville Police Department headquarters, and Amy strode to the front desk like she owned the place. I reckon entitlement and arrogance are just another part of the FBI agent costume.

"Agents Hall and Brabham here to see whoever is in charge of the Sanders case," Amy said, flashing her credentials. They were pretty good-looking fake FBI badges. I was impressed. I was more impressed when Amy opened a bag in the back of her black Suburban and pulled out one for me, complete with my driver's license picture. I looked like a cross between a Hell's Angel and Bigfoot in my license photo, but terrible pictures just made it look more realistic.

I snuck a peek in the bag before she closed the door and saw at least a dozen other badges and credential wallets. She probably had badges for us for every alphabet agency in DC, plus every major police department in the South. Yeah, DEMON covered their bases, even for their "adjunct agents" like me.

"That would be Sergeant Yates," the bored-looking desk cop said. He barely looked up from his *Sports Illustrated* to reply. He kept his balding head tilted toward us while Amy stood there, silently steaming.

After a long minute, he looked up. "Can I tell him what this is regarding?" His head went back to the magazine before he even finished speaking.

Amy's eyes got big as she put on her affronted face. "No, you can not, you officious little peckerwood. You can get his ass out here and show me the damn professional courtesy befitting a fellow officer standing in front of your desk asking nicely instead of me just making a phone call and the FBI taking over this whole damned investigation in the first place!"

The cop's head snapped up, and he blushed, crimson creeping up his neck and face, all the way to the tips of his ears. "I don't—"

"I don't give a damn what you do or don't," Amy cut him off. "There are children missing, and the first forty-eight hours are critical. Enough time's been wasted before we even got here, and if we don't get that kid back in the next..." she looked at her watch, "thirty hours, the odds of finding her alive drop to less than twenty-five percent. Do you want to be responsible for a little girl's death, or do you want to help me?" Amy tweaked her voice at the end of the diatribe, going from ranting drill sergeant to concerned, wheedling little girl.

I don't know which tactic worked best, her masquerading as a douchebag FBI agent, or her masquerading as a helpless woman. Neither one was anything close to her personality, and they were both pretty hilarious if you actually knew her. But the poor guy behind the desk didn't know her, so he didn't know whether to scratch his watch or wind his ass. Finally, he decided to just do what she asked—it would be less painful for everyone. I coulda told him that. He got up and walked back into the station, shaking his head and muttering about "feds" and "mouthy women." I looked over at Amy, who was pretending not to have heard anything.

"That wasn't very nice," I said.

"It was better than your plan," she replied.

"How do you know what my plan was?"

"Because you only ever have one plan, Bubba. You hit things until they do what you want."

"You're not wrong," I admitted. I guess after dating somebody for a couple years, they start to figure out a few things about you. Then I started to wonder when I'd figure out anything about Amy.

My brief bout of self-examination was interrupted by the return of the desk cop, who I now saw wore a nametag pronouncing him "Brown," and a large African-American man in a suit, who I assumed was Sergeant Yates. I looked him over and knew him immediately. He was like me, an ex-jock, probably football, but smaller. I'd guess running back or tight end, maybe a safety if he played defense. Linebacker at a stretch, but he wasn't quite bulky enough for that. He looked about forty, without too much of a gut. His suit was better than mine, but that wasn't saying much.

"I'm Sergeant Yates," he said, holding out his hand to Amy, then to me. We all shook, and Amy handed him a business card.

"Special Agent Amanda Hall," she said. "This is my partner, Agent Brabham. We're here to help."

He smiled, but it was the smile of a man who just stepped in shit and had somebody telling him to his face that it was chocolate syrup. "I'm sure that's how you see it, but I reckon I'm the one who's supposed to call you folks if I need your very special brand of 'help.' Or have the rules of jurisdiction changed?"

"They change all the time, Sergeant. But this one hasn't. Kidnapping is an FBI affair, and that's why we're here. I don't care who gets the credit, but I do care about getting Tamara Sanders back to her family alive and intact."

I watched the big man bristle and held up a hand before he started to respond. "Look, man," I started. "I know the deal. I've been a local guy and had the feebs come in and take over my investigation. And I've been the fed coming in taking over an investigation from incompetent local cops."

Amy gave me a "what the hell are you doing, that's not helping" look. I ignored her, which I decided a long time ago was the best way to avoid some fights.

I went on. "But right now, I want to be the guy that helps you do your job, and we just want to stay out of the way and give you access to our resources, our crime lab, and our tech experts. Not to mention another couple of feet on the street and eyeballs on the crime scene. So what do you say? Can we just work together, or is Agent Hall gonna have to get all official up in here?"

I could almost hear the thoughts running through the big detective's mind as he mulled over his options. His shoulders sagged a little bit, and he looked at Amy. "If I fight this, you just take over the whole show and kick me to the curb, don't you?"

"Probably."

"And now I have your word that you'll keep me apprised of anything you find?"

"I'll go one better. You lead any press conferences about the abductions, talk to all the press, and all we do is get named as 'assistance from federal agencies.'"

He laughed, a short bark that sounded not at all amused. "I get to talk to the press, huh? Thanks a lot. If there was one part of this shit-show that I'd want to hand over to the feds, that's the one."

I grinned right back at him. "Little assholes, aren't they? It's the same all over."

"It's worse when you're on the force in a town you grew up in. The asshole covering the crime beat nowadays is the same scrawny little shithead that hated me in high school."

I didn't bother mentioning that the reason most "scrawny shitheads" hate us jocks is because we treat them like crap. When my best friend Skeeter and I first met, he was about to be run up the flagpole out front of our middle school by his underpants at the hands of a few of my fellow football players. But I put that aside for now in the spirit of getting along with the locals.

"Fine, y'all come on back and take a look at what we've got. It's not much, but if you've got some super-tech out there that can help us find this girl, I'm all in favor." He grabbed us a couple of visitor badges from the desk guard and waved for us to follow him into the back.

He led us to a small conference room with a large table covered in takeout coffee cups, photos, file folders, and a few napkins scattered with pizza crusts on them. He gave Amy a chagrined look and started picking up the scraps of what looked like the whole investigative team's dinner.

"Don't clean up on my account, Sergeant. I've been in these rooms too many times to be bothered by the smell of stale pizza and staler coffee. Are these photos from the crime scene?"

"Yes, ma'am," said a young woman in a polo shirt and khakis. "I'm Jessica Clark, CSU."

Amy and I shook hands with the tech, and Amy said, "What did you find?"

"A whole lot of nothing, if I'm being honest. We've got video of her with her friends all along Broadway, then entering Riverfront Park. The park is closed at dusk, but that's never stopped teenagers. We have a few cameras in the park, but they're mostly clustered around entrances and attractions, like the dock or the amphitheater."

"Is there a chance that she slipped and fell into the river?" I asked. "I hate to ask, but..."

"We know," Yates said. "There's a chance, and we have divers working the river now, but we're coming up on dusk, and they'll have to come up soon."

"Plus, we don't think she fell in the water," the tech interjected.

"Why not?" I asked. Yates shot her a dark look, but the slender redhead ignored him and bulldozed right ahead.

"We have video from the entrance to Fort Nashborough. We're not sure what it shows, exactly, but it's definitely something."

"We don't know that, Jess. It might just be a camera malfunction. None of the other kids saw anything."

"Those little shitheads were so buried in their phones they wouldn't see shit if they stepped in it," Clark shot back. She looked at me and Amy with a start. "Sorry about that."

"Don't worry about offending me; I played college ball. If there's a cuss word I haven't heard before, then it was invented since I left college in 2002,"

I said with a grin. I hoped it put her at ease. Sometimes my grins have the opposite effect, like people are scared I'm gonna eat them or something.

"Where did you play?" Yates asked.

"UGA."

"Defense?"

"Yeah, I wasn't pretty enough to play offense." I smiled when I said it so he'd know I was joking. I wasn't, really.

"I think I remember you," the sergeant said. "They called you Bubba, didn't they?"

"Still do," I said. I was really hoping I didn't put him out of a game, or a season. I left a few bodies in my wake on the rare occasion I got onto the field.

"I remember you!" He broke out into a huge grin. I played for the Commodores 2001-2004. Y'all beat us like a drum my first couple years. I only got in for the fourth quarter, but I caught a pass over the middle in one game and you made me regret ever putting on pads. Man, you could put a lick on a brother." He shook his head and rubbed his chest like his ribs still hurt. I understood that completely. My knee still twinges every time it's gonna rain.

"Yeah, I remember playing Vandy. Y'all weren't real good those years."

"We sucked, man. I was third-string on the Commodores and wouldn't even make the cut on a top-tier SEC team."

"Heh, which means you coulda been a starter for the ACC." We both laughed. If there's anything that'll bring old ball players together, it's making fun of a rival conference. "Sorry about the beating. I was just so damned excited about getting to play finally that I felt like I had to make every hit a highlight reel."

"I understand that. So, how did you end up working for the government? I thought you were gonna go pro for sure, even with Pollard playing in front of you."

"I blew out my knee, then went home and got into the family business. But speaking of..."

"Yeah, I know. Clock's ticking. We can take a trip down memory lane later. Follow me. We'll take a look at the video in our Nerd Room."

"Nerd Room?" Amy asked, one eyebrow climbing.

Yates held up both hands. "Not me, I swear. Our techs named it themselves. Put a sign over the door and everything. They've got this place wired up like it's Microsoft headquarters or something. Come on, I'll show you." He turned and walked out of the conference room, and we followed him, off to see the nerd wizards.

July 25th, 7PM - 29:00:00

He wasn't really wrong to call it the Nerd Room. It was a lot like Skeeter's office downstairs, to be honest, just with more geeks in it and no fridge full of Red Bull and Mountain Dew. The overhead lights were either disconnected, or just out, so the whole room was lit by small task lights and huge monitors. The walls were ringed with half a dozen workstations, each with a pair of huge monitors on the desk, and one even bigger one mounted on the wall. The big monitor was about the size of my TV, and at least one of them was running a four-way split-screen program that let the tech scan a bunch of video sources at one time.

Yates led us to one workstation, then waved CSU Clark forward. "Okay, Jess. You're in charge."

"Been waiting a year for you to realize that, Sergeant," the young tech said with a grin. She pulled an elastic tie from her waist, yanked her red hair back into a ponytail, and sat down at the desk. A couple minutes later, the big monitor split into four displays, each with a grainy black and white image on it.

"These are the video feeds from the security cameras around the park. You can see Tamara Sanders enter the park here," she pointed to the display in the lower left, "at ten-thirty. Then she heads over near the Fort Nashborough historical site." She pointed to the screen at the top left.

I held up a finger. "Hang on a second. I'd like to have my tech take a look at this as well. Is there any way we can get this to him?"

"The files are pretty huge, but we do have a secure login that other agencies can utilize. Just have him call in to the—" We were interrupted by a phone ringing at her elbow and every cell phone in the room going off simultaneously.

"That'll be Skeeter," I said, shaking my head a little. Sometimes Skeeter feels the need to out-nerd everybody in the room. It's usually not even a close race, but this Clark kid looked like she might be able to give my little buddy a run for his money.

She answered the phone. "Clark," she said, keeping any hint of being impressed out of her voice. "You must be Skeeter. Yes, we have a secure line that I can give you...okay, yeah, that's pretty good. Okay, then you'll need to... oh, okay. That's also pretty good. So if you just...oh." This time she couldn't keep the "oh shit" out of her voice or off her face.

Clark turned to us, her eyes a little wide. "Um...he says he..."

"Is already in your system and you can just sit back and let him drive?" I added. She nodded. "He's just showing off. Ignore him, and he'll stop being a little douche soon."

"I heard that!" Skeeter's shrill voice rang through the speakers on the desk in front of Clark. "Ms. Clark, Sergeant Yates, I'm Agent Jones. Pleasure to meet you both. Ms. Clark, if you'll narrate the action, I'll run the video. This way everything copies to our servers here as it runs, and we have a copy in case anything happens."

Or in case there's something on that footage that DEMON doesn't want civilians to know exists outside of Halloween stores and Hollywood, I thought. But for once I kept my mouth shut. Clark reached over to press a button on her keyboard, but the video started to roll before she touched it. Skeeter was showing off again.

"As I was saying, we have her on camera entering the Fort Nashborough site, but we don't have her on any camera leaving. We can track the entrance and exit of the three girls she was with, but we don't know what they were doing, or why they wandered aimlessly around the Fort for an hour, then left without touching anything."

"You don't know?" Skeeter's voice sounded incredulous over the speakers. "You're totally going to have to turn in your nerd card. They're playing FairyQuest Live!"

"The video game?" Yates asked. I turned to him, question written all over my face in big letters.

"What?" he asked, shoulders raised. "I've got two daughters. It's all they can talk about. How many fairies they snared today, how big they are. And where's the best place to go to hit toadstools for more fairy dust."

I must have looked at him like he had two heads, but Skeeter's voice called me back to the screen, where a colorful display now dominated, swirls of glitter and sparkles all over the screen with the words "FairyQuest Live!" floating in the middle of the display. "It's a mobile game," Skeeter's disembodied voice explained. "You play it on your phone and wander around cities trying to find different types of fairies. Then you find different magical fruits to give them new spells and powers, and eventually you put them in a Fairy Ring and claim it for your tribe. There are four different tribes, for each of the legendary Fairy Courts—the Summer, Winter, Fall, and Spring."

"There are only two courts of the Fae," I corrected. "Summer and Winter. There are no courts for Spring and Fall—they either belong to Summer, as Spring does, or Winter, which Fall pays homage to." I looked around, and Clark and Yates were staring at me, along with every other Nashville cop in the room. "I minored in anthropology at Georgia; world mythology was my concentration." Complete bullshit, of course. I majored in football and minored in beer, but they wouldn't know that. Besides, it's fun to show off a little bit and let the smartasses know they underestimated you.

"In the game, there are four courts," Skeeter continued. "So you wander around towns looking for Fairy Rings, which are landmarks where the game has placed resupply stations."

"Landmarks like historic places?" Amy asked.

"Historic places, unique outdoor artwork, public gathering spots with interesting features, that sort of thing," Skeeter said.

"So Fort Nashborough probably has one of these Fairy Rings in it," Clark said. "It's definitely a national historical site. And the amphitheater in the park has that light sculpture out front, and the fountain that kids like to play in, too."

"Yeah, both of those are the kinds of places where the developers put Fairy Rings," Skeeter agreed.

"Okay, so she was playing a game on her phone," Yates said. "What does that get us? We're no closer to finding her than we were five minutes ago."

"No, but we have another piece. We know she wandered off from her friends because of the game, not because she was lured away by a predator," Amy interjected. "But you're right, we need to see the rest of the video."

Skeeter started the video rolling, with Clark narrating. "She leaves the view of the entrance cam at the Fort here," she pointed to one screen, "and we pick her up coming into view here. And this is where things get weird."

"If she thinks this is weird, she should go to a museum with Joe," I whispered to Amy. To her credit, she held her laughter. Or maybe it's less to her credit and more a statement on my joke. Whatever.

We watched the screen as the girl walked around the small grassy areas between the reconstructed Revolution-era stockade. She stopped dead center in the courtyard, looking around and frantically tapping her screen."

"What's she doing?" I asked.

"She's found a Fairy Castle, and she's waging a Wizard Duel to overthrow the Fairy Queen or King that rules it. You match up your best fairies against the fairies that are left there to defend the castle and get experience points for beating them," Skeeter said.

"I don't think I understood a word you just said, at least not in the order you said them," I said. I would usually think Skeeter was just making shit up to give me shit, but he wouldn't do that in the middle of a case where a girl's life was in danger."

"She's fighting a monster in the game," he said.

"Oh. Why didn't you just say that?" I grumbled. The only answer was a patented Skeeter Jones "Bubba's a tech-ignorant savage" sigh. He had a bunch of different sighs, and I knew them all by heart.

I turned my attention back to the screen just in time to see the display flare to nothing but white for ten or fifteen seconds, then restore to static for another thirty seconds or so, then back to normal. Except for normal without Tamara Sanders anywhere on the screen. Her phone was lying in the grass, abandoned.

"Well, we know she didn't go anywhere voluntarily. No teenage girl would leave her cell phone lying in the grass," Amy said, her voice somber.

"What the hell happened?" I asked. "Skeeter, can you fix the image?"

"There's nothing to fix, Bubba," Skeeter replied. "The lens was blown out by whatever made that light. The image was so overexposed the chip in the camera stopped taking in signal. That's what made the snow when it came back online. It had to completely reset and iris out to operate in the low light. There's literally no image data for me to enhance."

"That's the same things our guys here said," Clark added, a glum look on her face. "I was hoping you could do something they couldn't. They even took the cameras apart and worked from the chip level, and they got nothing."

"Sorry," Skeeter said. "I wish I could add something, but whatever blew out the camera didn't leave a trace."

"Not that could be seen on camera," I said. "Now it's time to do things the old-fashioned way."

"We've been over the scene with a fine-toothed comb," Yates said.

"Yeah, but another set of eyeballs never hurt, did it?" I asked.

"No, you're right. Let's go out to the Fort and take a look around. Clark, you coming with us?" Yates asked.

The young crime scene tech perked up like she's just been invited to a party, not a crime scene. "Hell yes! I mean, yes, sir. I don't want to let this one go. There's a girl's life at stake."

"We agree completely, Ms. Clark," Amy said. "Let's get out there."

July 25th, 8PM - 28:00:00

IT WAS GETTIN' ON TOWARD DARK BY THE TIME WE GOT TO FORT Nashborough, and security was just closing the front gate as we walked up. Yates badged us through, and we walked into the courtyard between the reconstructed wooden buildings that held prisoners in the dawn of the United States. I could almost feel the ghosts of Revolutionary soldiers and British sympathizers that were held there.

"They came in over here," Yates said, walking us over to a wall that looked completely secure. I must have shown my confusion on my face because he gave a little chuckle and pushed on a section of the wooden palisade wall. It swung up smoothly, opening a portal about six feet high by six feet wide that led straight out onto the street behind the old fort.

Yates laughed at the incredulous look on my face. "It's for the lawn care company. They have to get lawnmowers in and out of the compound and wanted to be able to leave their trucks out there and just roll the mowers off the trailers and ride in. So the city built them this little doggie door. Apparently the girls knew about it and used it to break in last night."

"Everybody knows about that door, dude." We turned back to the opening. The speaker was a kid of about thirteen or fourteen, a skinny white kid with a baseball cap and baggy pants. A t-shirt blazoned with some anime character and bright orange sneakers completed the outfit. He stood just outside the wall with his phone in hand.

"You playing FairyQuest?" Amy asked, nodding at the phone.

"Duh. Everybody's playing FairyQuest. Even old people like you are playing it. And this is one of the best places in town to hunt. There's like four

Fairy Rings within two blocks, and there's always a bunch of fairies around. I heard somebody even found a Puck last night!"

"What's a puck?" I asked. I was proud enough of myself that I knew he wasn't talking about Predators hockey. I didn't need to pretend I knew crap about this game.

"Puck's like this total badass fairy. He's super rare, and only comes out at night. You've got to find him, and then make Offerings to get him to stick around, and then you almost always have to spin a SuperSpell to catch him, even after you've given him an Offering."

"So if you heard a rumor there was a Puck in this fort, you'd be willing to break in at night to catch him?" I asked.

"Dude, yeah, totally. I'd be all over it. Hell, I'd climb the stupid gate if I couldn't get the secret entrance to work."

"Some secret," Amy said. "If everybody knows about it, it's not much of a secret."

"Yeah," the kid agreed, "but nobody really cares 'cause nobody messes anything up and there's nothing to steal. Usually it's just older kids coming in to drink beer or have sex."

"Because that's what you want happening in a place that's probably as charged with supernatural energy as an abandoned war prison," Skeeter said over our comm. My usual Bluetooth set had been replaced by a high-powered in-ear unit that automatically paired with my phone but could also jump frequencies to find better signal if I had poor reception. I understood about one in three words Skeeter said, but as long as I had a working comm, and it was a lot smaller than the old thing, I didn't care how it all worked. Hell, he could have told me that it was a babel fish and I wouldn't give a single damn. I nodded at his assessment of the situation but kept my attention on the kid.

"Were you out hunting last night?" I asked.

"Yeah, but not here. I live over in Hillsboro, so my parents took me and my cousin to Belmont University to hunt. There's a lot of people playing there, and they usually put Sparklers on the Fairy Rings to draw more fairies, so we just wandered around campus catching new ones all night."

"Alright, that's fine. But look, kid. A girl was abducted from here last night while playing this game, so please be careful. Always stay with other people, and stay near an adult," Amy said.

The kid's face lost every hint of the preteen smirk that hadn't wavered during our whole conversation. "Did you find her? Is she going to be okay?"

"Not yet," Amy said. "But we're doing everything we can to figure out what happened to her and to bring her home safely. Now we've got to go keep looking for her, but please be careful. Is there anyone out here with you tonight?"

"Yeah, my cousin is just around the corner. I'll go find him now. Please find the girl." The boy looked genuinely upset as he turned and ran up the street.

Yates reached up and swung the portal closed. "Well, now we know how they got in, and we know that most people with any interest in the game knew about this entrance."

"And that there would be a lot of kids here," Amy said.

"But none of that explains the flash of light and the disappearance. All of that is just normal predator stuff. Not that it's not terrible, but it doesn't really address the elephant in the room," I said.

"But there's nothing here," Clark pointed out.

"Maybe there's nothing that we can find," I said. "But apparently there are fairies all around us."

"Are you suggesting that we play that stupid game to try and find the girl?" Yates had a look on his face like I smelled bad or was spectacularly stupid. Since I showered before putting on that godforsaken necktie and pretending to be an FBI agent, I knew I didn't smell bad.

"It's actually a pretty good idea, Sergeant," Clark chimed in. "The game uses augmented reality to overlay in-game treasures, monsters, and battles onto real landmarks, using the phone's camera. It's entirely possible that there's some kind of clue in the game world that doesn't exist in the real world. Maybe there's a sign or a clue in there, and we'll find Tamara hiding in some forest on the edge of town after she got lost looking for a super rare fairy."

"We can hope," Amy said.

"Well, let's download the stupid game and go chasing fairies," Yates said. "It's not the dumbest thing I've ever done to close a case, but it's close."

"Then we oughta hang out more, Sergeant," I said. "This shit barely cracks the Bubba Top 40 list of stupidest things I've done to solve a case."

July 25th, 8:30 PM - 28:30:00

I downloaded the app, with a little help from Skeeter. We all decided that since Yates and Clark knew the city, they would go get one of Tamara's friends and follow the route they took from the Sanders home to the Fort. This would make sure they didn't miss any clues or evidence along the way that only popped up in the game, and it would get them away from me and Amy for a while in case we found whatever beastie snatched the girl and had to deal with it. A lot of what we do is better if it's never seen by the local law enforcement. They don't usually believe in what we fight, and that leads to a lot of confusion, and sometimes hospital bills when I start killing monsters that aren't supposed to exist. It's just easier if I only work with people who already know about the dark side.

We started outside the fort, walking the perimeter. It was now full dark, but there were plenty of streetlights so we didn't feel like we were in any danger walking around staring at our phones. I don't ever feel like I'm in any danger just walking around, but I'm better than six-and-a-half feet tall and a little bit north of three-hundred-fifty pounds. Between the beard, the ponytail, the tattoos, and the Desert Eagle pistol tucked under my arm, there's not much in the world that wants to mess with me. Amy's a lot smaller, a lot blonder, a lot prettier, and doesn't look like she can kick near as much ass as she does. So she stays more alert than I do. I mean, let's face it, when you've survived hand-to-hand combat with a damn sasquatch, getting mugged in an alley doesn't worry you too much anymore.

Until it happens to your girlfriend. Then it's a bad scene. Especially for the mugger. And this mugger looked like he'd seen better days. He stepped out of a shadowed doorway in the one twenty-foot stretch between working streetlights, a knife in his shaky hand and a stutter in his voice.

"G-g-gimme your wallet, or I'll cut you, bitch!" He tried to sound tough, but Amy Hall has stared down vampires, werewolves, sasquatch, and me with a tequila hangover. That woman ain't scared of any skinny-ass tweaker with a ripped Members Only jacket, busted Chuck Taylor high tops, and Levi's so threadbare they liked like they might disintegrate in a strong rain. I couldn't tell if he had a scraggly blond mustache, or if he just didn't wash his face very often, or what. And if I really needed to change the oil in our Suburban before we left, I reckoned I could just hold his head over the engine block and squeeze. All told, he was not an impressive specimen of criminal.

"How about you run away, and I don't kick your ass?" Amy counteroffered. I thought it was a pretty fair offer, but Greasy apparently didn't 'cause he came at her swinging his knife. If it had been a bigger knife, I mighta been worried. If he'd been a bigger dude, I mighta been worried. If he hadn't looked like his last meal came out of a dumpster three weeks ago, I mighta been worried.

None of those things were true, so I wasn't worried. And it turns out I was right. Amy shifted her weight onto her back foot and threw a quick roundhouse kick, hitting Greasy on his wrist and sending the knife flying. She let her momentum carry her into a spin, kicking Greasy on the jaw with her other foot. His head spun around like the Big Wheel on *The Price is Right*, only without Bob Barker or Drew Carey handing out cars. He dropped to his knees in the alley, and Amy kicked him one more time, this time right under his jaw like she was Ray Guy all pissed off about waiting so long to get into Canton. I heard a *crack* as Greasy's jaw broke, then another one as he flew back and landed on his head on the concrete sidewalk.

I walked over to him and knelt down, putting a couple fingers on his throat. I felt a pulse, strong despite the probable concussion and maybe skull fracture he was gonna be dealing with. I peeled up one eyelid and saw that there was very much nobody home at the moment. He was out *cold*.

"Skeeter, you better call and ambulance to our location. Amy got mugged," I said.

"Holy shit, is she okay?" Skeeter sounded real worried over the comm.

"Skeeter," I didn't bother trying to hide the "dumbass" written in my tone, "have you met Amy?"

"Oh yeah," he replied. "Is the dumb bastard breathing?"

"Yeah, he'll live. As long as he doesn't wake up and try to do it again," I said, grinning at Amy.

"If he comes at me with a knife again, I'll just shoot him," she said. "I've had my workout for the night, and we've got a kid to find. Time to stop screwing around with junkies."

"Yeah, we've got fairies to catch," I said.

"I wish I had that on tape," Skeeter chuckled. "I'll get an ambulance rolling for your friend. Do you want it to be official or anonymous?"

"Make it anonymous," I said. "I don't want to screw around with the paperwork."

"Done and done," Skeeter said. "Now go bring that kid home. If it's a mundane kidnapping, you've got less than thirty hours left." He didn't bother to add that if it was something supernatural, we were probably already out of time the moment she vanished.

We finished our loop around the fort, and by the time we got back to the front gate, I had gained three levels and figured out how to spin spells, catch fairies, morph them into bigger fairies, and battle. I'd also spent a hundred and fifty bucks on upgrades, extra spells, better spells, super fairy catcher things, and all kinds of other in-game crap that I really hoped DEMON was going to reimburse me for.

We walked through the gate, eyes glued to our phones, and shut the gate behind us. Looking through the screen, the stockade was transformed into a magical land full of trees and sunshine, with a stream running right through it, and tons of fairies running around, almost begging to be caught. I stood by the gate, turning in almost a full circle looking through my phone, and finally caught a glimpse of a dark figure darting between two small cottages off to my left.

"I think I saw the Puck," I said to Amy, pointing in the general direction of the sprite. She nodded, and I headed off in that direction. She walked the opposite way, tapping her screen in rhythm and cursing when one of her fairies busted loose.

I walked around to the side of an old stockade building, which was new and built of glittering marble in the game, not an old wooden replica of a wartime prison. The light from the street lights dimmed, and soon it seemed as though the only light around came from my phone. Then he was there—right in front of me stood the rarest of the Fae—a black-clad, rapier-wielding fairy with blue- and green-spattered black wings jutting out from his back. He was tall for a fairy, nearly five feet, but had the slender build, narrow chin, and pointed ears that all the fairies in the game had.

"Gotcha!" I said, readying a spell. I tapped the screen ten times in rapid succession, making the spell coalesce into a star and shine like a miniature sun. I swiped my finger sideways across the screen, spinning the spell towards the Puck dancing on my screen, and grinned as it hit him square in the chest.

"Gotcha, indeed!" The voice came from right behind me, a high, reedy voice, shrill in my ear but still oddly alluring.

I spun around and there stood the Puck, grinning at me in real life, not through the augmented reality of my phone.

"Aw, shit," I said.

"Indeed," the Puck replied. Then he snapped his fingers, and everything disappeared in a flash of intense white light.

I came to lying on the grass in sunlight. The temperature was perfect, the grass was soft, and my head was absolutely damn killing me. I sat up, then lay back down thinking better of it for a minute or two. Then I sat up again, this time taking it more slowly. I managed to get to my feet and looked around. The Puck was sitting on a thick stump a few feet away, watching me with a sideways grin on his face.

"Well, I must admit, this is unexpected," said the slender fairy. He sat with his legs folded beneath him and his elbows on his knees, bent over at odd angles, all pointy elbows and knees. His features seemed to be drawn with razors, sharp edges everywhere and points on his chin and ears. Those ears. They weren't the gently swooping elfin points of a Peter Jackson film. No, these were great, savage-looking pointed things, more like bat ears than anything beautiful. His hair was an unruly shock of black and blue and purple and blood red all sticking out every which way, but it was his eyes that commanded my attention.

He stared at me with eyes of wall-to-wall black. No pupil, no iris, no sclera (shut up, I went to college!), just unrelenting black staring back at me from that angular face with the over-chiseled jaw and cheekbones just a little too sharp to be attractive.

"You're telling me," I said, sitting up on the grass. "I thought I was trying to catch a Puck, but..."

"It seems the Puck caught you," he replied.

"Yeah."

"And now you want to know what I plan to do with you."

"Yeah."

"Do you think I'm going to eat you?" He opened his grinning mouth to show off a double row of pointed teeth.

"Nah, too much fat and gristle," I said. "Besides, if you wanted to eat me, you wouldn't let me wake up. You'd just bring me here and start carving off chunks."

"I have to admit, you're not wrong. Who are you, human?"

"They call me Bubba. I hunt monsters."

"And what do you do with them when you find them, Bubba?"

I got the distinct impression that life could get very uncomfortable for me if I answered wrong, but I also didn't know if he could tell when I was lying or not. *Screw it,* I decided. I told the truth.

"Sometimes I shoot them. Sometimes I throw them off tall places. Sometimes I stab them. Sometimes I set them on fire. Sometimes I shoot them, stab them, set them on fire, and THEN throw them off tall places. And every once in a while, I talk to them, figure out why they're doing things they shouldn't be doing, and send them on their merry way. That last bit doesn't happen very often. Usually I end up killing something."

"An honest human?" Puck mused. "Will wonders never cease?"

"And who are you, fairy?" I tossed his question back at him.

"I am just who you called me," he tossed back. He stood up on his stump, and it looked more like a spider unfolding itself than anyone standing up. "I am Robin Goodfellow, at your service. But you, dear Bubba, may call me Puck."

"Puck," I repeated.

"Puck."

"Like Shakespeare, Puck?"

"One and the same."

"Like Titania and Oberon, Puck?"

A shadow flickered across his face. "I would prefer you not mention those names again. Names have power, Bubba. Names draw attention. If you say the Summer Queen's name too often, she may notice you. And you don't want to be noticed by the Summer Queen."

"And the Summer Queen is—" I caught myself. "The person I named?"

"Very good!" He clapped his hands, his overlong fingers flapping like he was double-jointed. "You catch on fast, Bubba"

"I'm not just a pretty face," I replied. "So what are you doing bringing me over here? And more importantly, did you bring anyone over here last night?"

"Oh. We don't exactly measure time the same way you do on the other side, so I'm not sure." He looked sad, like he really wanted a little nighttime. "But I did acquire a new gift for my queen recently. A human girl, about this tall." He held his hand out about the right height above ground for it to be Tamara Sanders.

"Do you remember her name? Was it Tamara?" I got up and realized that he wasn't a very big fairy. I looked him in the eye, even with him standing on a stump.

"Humans have names?" he asked, a confused look on his face. "Who knew? I don't know what she called herself. I simply delivered her to my queen. But it wasn't enough to buy back my lady love. And now I've caught you, and you're no good to me. I suppose I'll have to send you back." He started waving his arms in midair, and sparkles flew from his fingertips.

"Wait!" I shouted. "You can't send me back. I have to find the girl and take her with me. Her parents are worried about her. And you can't just steal children."

"Why not? You humans make so many of them. It's not like you'll miss one or two. Now go away, and let me find another girl-child, one that will please Her Majesty."

He started waving his arms around again, and a portal spun open in the air behind me. I felt it start to suck me in, but I knew I had to stay. This might be my only chance to find Tamara and bring her home, not to mention any other kids this freak had taken. The pull of the portal grew stronger, and I couldn't move forward against its draw. I strained against the force, switching very quickly to Plan B.

Plan B looks a lot like the rest of my Plans A-Z, only I use a different tool. This time I drew my second favorite tool from her holster under my left arm. I leaned forward against the magical portal's draw and put three rounds from Bertha in the center of Puck's chest.

The portal winked out of existence, and I staggered forward, all force behind me suddenly gone. When I looked up, Puck was off the stump, the force of three fifty-caliber rounds sending him sprawling in the grass a good four feet away. I watched with my mouth hanging open as he sat up, reached into his chest to remove the bullets, and tossed them aside with a sneer.

"That was my favorite shirt," the angry fairy said, getting to his feet with three brand-new holes in his favorite shirt and murder in his eyes.

Oh, shit.

Chapter Four

OH, SHIT.

That's all I had time to think before I was covered up in pissed-off fairy. He was all sharp elbows and pointy fists, and the little bastard was strong out of all proportion to his size. He hopped to his feet, then jumped onto the stump a few feet away, using that as a launching point to clear the ten feet between us without any apparent effort. He leapt from the stump to my shoulders, raining blows down on my head with his little fists that felt more like somebody pelting me with rocks than flesh.

I reached up behind my head and got a good double handful of his abused shirt, yanking him over my head and slamming him to the ground. I raised a foot to stomp a muddle in his ass, but he blinked out of existence right before my oversized hiking boot slammed into the turf. That left me off-balance, which is my excuse for falling down like a felled redwood when he appeared behind me and kicked me right in the ass.

I planted my face in the green, green grass of Fairyland and quickly learned that getting slammed to the ground hurts just as much in a magical friggin' wonderland as it does everywhere else. Bertha went flying, which was fine, since obviously fairies were immune to my preferred method of inducing lead poisoning. I pushed myself up to my hands and knees, then went straight back down on my belly, curling up into a fetal position as a pointy little fairy foot launched my nuts up into my ribcage. I swear I felt my left testicle bounce around between my spine and ribs like a goddamn pinball while I writhed in breathless pain.

My vision cleared just enough to see Puck standing beside my face, bent at the waist so far that his head almost touched the ground.

"You had enough, human?" he asked, a smug grin plastered across his pointy face.

"Screw you, fairy," I growled. Okay, it was more like I squeaked, but if I hadn't been an unnatural soprano, I would have growled. I wrapped my big right paw around the little bastard's neck and started to squeeze.

"Let's see you vanish out of that, asshole."

"Okay," he croaked. He couldn't get much air, but he sure as hell could vanish right out of my fingertips. I kinda felt the air move on the other side of my head, then definitely felt my brain slosh around in my skull when he kicked me right in the temple. My vision went all sparkly, then the grey tunnel started to close in on me. I rolled over a couple times, came up on my knees, and shook my head, fighting off the symptoms of the concussion I was pretty sure I had.

Puck popped into view right in front of me, and this time I nailed him on the chin with an uppercut. He sprawled straight back, his bell rung for a change, and I made my wobbly way to my feet. He clambered to an upright position and looked at me with a little respect for the first time.

"You're not like most humans. You can fight."

"I've stood toe-to-toe with a troll, been gutted by a damn werewolf, and gone three rounds with a buck-naked sasquatch. You ain't got shit, fairy. I would say you hit like a girl, but you don't. Girls know how to lay a hit on somebody. You hit like a damn *quarterback*." I didn't want to be insulting. I coulda said he hit like a placekicker.

He looked confused. "I don't know what that is, but it doesn't seem like a nice thing to say." He waved his hand in the air, and a sword appeared.

Well, shit. Good job, Bubba, you pissed off the armed magical creature.

"Bring it, little dude." I held out both hands and made a "come at me" gesture. He did. He ran at me, his sword coming in low to sweep up and disembowel me. But I learned a long time ago that if you've got to fight somebody who has a sword, and all you've got is fists, there's only one safe place to be—in real close.

As he started his swing, I didn't take up the defensive posture he expected. Nah, I stepped *inside* his sword stroke, using my big body to get in the way of his arms and foul his killing stroke. Then I put my hands on either side of his head and slammed my forehead down into his face, shattering his nose and blinding him for a moment.

The sword fell to the grass and winked out of existence. Puck staggered back, blood pouring from his nose and tears streaming from his eyes. I followed him, raining punches that he couldn't see to block. Jab, jab, jab, hook, jab, hook, uppercut—I hit the little bastard ten or twelve times, big, solid punches that made a good connection with a fist the size of a small Honeybaked ham, and he still didn't go down. Finally, I reared back for a haymaker that was either going to mash his face pancake flat or leave me so open to a retaliation that he'd just conjure up a sword and gut me like a catfish.

To my surprise, neither one happened. The little dude's eyes cleared enough for him to see the fist coming for him, and he blinked out of existence. I did exactly what I knew I'd do if I missed and overbalanced flat onto my belly in the grass. I lay there for a couple of seconds, waiting for the feeling of a blade running through my body. Again.

When it didn't come, I got to all fours and pulled myself to my feet. I looked around and saw Puck sitting on the stump again, his head down between his pointy knees and a fancy handkerchief pressed to his nose. He saw me looking at him and waved the hanky at me.

"I surrender, human. Just stop hitting me."

"You know you're supposed to wave a white flag for surrender, right?"

"It was white before I bled all over it, is that good enough?"

"Depends. You gonna try to send me back?"

"Are you going to shoot me again if I do?"

"Probably not. Didn't seem to do much good the first time. But I will beat the shit out of you again."

"Then do you mind terribly if we avoid that particular course of action?"

"Nah, I think I can do without another concussion or having you wear my nuts on your toes for jingle bells."

"Truce, then?"

"Yeah, I'm okay with that." I lowered myself back to the ground and sat. My balls hurt like a sonofabitch, and my ears still rang from the punched I took to the head, but my vision was clear, so I probably wasn't really concussed. I still had to find Tamara Sanders, though. I suppose the only good news was that I didn't have to sweat the whole forty-eight-hour thing anymore. That was only the rule of thumb with human abductors. Fairies and other supernatural critters ran by their own set of rules.

"Are you starting to feel better?" Puck asked after a minute or so.

"Yeah, I am, actually. What's that about?"

"We're in the Summer Lands, human. Injuries heal very quickly here. You'll be right as rain in no time; then you can leave."

"Not without Tamara," I said, my voice flat.

"Oh yes, the new girl. I forget you name yourselves. I'm just so used to calling you 'boy' or 'girl.' Well, she's well out of reach. I sent her to the queen. I'm sure she's a kitchen drudge by now, or maybe a scullion."

"What do you mean, you sent her to the queen?"

"I sent her to the queen to serve her in the castle. She did just what you did—she tried to catch a Puck, and the Puck caught her." He grinned like he was the cleverest asshole in the forest. Which he probably was, but I still didn't like him pointing it out.

"So the whole game is a trap?" I asked.

"You are very bright, for a human," he said in a tone that made it clear that "for a human" meant about the same thing as "for a houseplant." "The game leads human children on a merry chase looking for rarest of fairies—the Puck. Whenever they think they've caught a Puck, I've caught them instead! And I bring them here and give them to my queen."

His face fell, and some of his obnoxious pride fell off. "But it's not enough. It's never enough."

"What's not enough?" I asked, even when the little voice in my head screamed *DON'T ASK.* But if I listened to that little voice, I never would have done half the cool things I've done in my life. I also would have avoided a couple of nasty rashes and at least three courses of penicillin, but that's beside the point.

"Nothing I do is enough," the now-mopey Puck replied. "I bring her human children, and it's not enough. I design an addictive game to suck the creativity and desire out of thousands of human children *and* bring more human children, and it's not enough. Nothing I do will ever get her to free my Silvara."

"What's a Silvara?" Again, the little voice in my head doing cartwheels and telling me not to ask. Again, me ignoring the little voice. If I were my little voice, I'd be really irritated with me most of the time.

"Silvara is the fairest of fairy maidens. She is the sunlight on my face in springtime, the honey in my tea, the wind in my willows. She is the most lovely, delicate, enchanting creature I've ever seen. And Titania keeps her locked away in a dungeon just to torment me."

"So she's your girlfriend."

"She is the love of my infinitely long life, you mortal imbecile. Titania has sworn that if I make a significant enough offering, she will release Silvara to me. And the Fae cannot lie, so she is bound to do as she promised."

"Let me guess," I said. "She hasn't bothered to tell you exactly what constitutes a significant enough offering."

He looked up at me, a heartbroken little fairy with a now-crooked pointy nose. "Exactly."

"I had a boss like that once. It sucks."

"What did you do?"

"I probably wouldn't follow my example on this one."

"Why not? What did you do to solve your problem with your heartless ruler?"

"I broke a beer bottle over his head, shoved another one up his ass, and left him doing a handstand in the shitter of the strip club I was bouncing at. Like I said, I don't think you want to try that with a magical fairy queen."

"No, I don't think I should attempt to break anything over Titania's anything. If she didn't strike me dead on the spot, Oberon would squash me like a bug."

"So you're screwed. But I still have to get this girl home. Now, how do I find her?"

"You don't. I sent her to the queen. She's at the capitol and has likely already been drafted into service as a kitchen drudge or scullion."

"I don't know what those are, but it doesn't sound like very much fun. So I'm gonna have to go get her." I struggled to my feet. "Which way to this queen?" I looked around, but we were in a clearing in the middle of a forest, without any apparent trails or roads leading out.

"You can't possibly hope to sneak into the capitol, much less the castle, and smuggle out one human girl. Besides, how will you even know which one to take?"

I stopped looking around the clearing and turned back to Puck, very slowly. When I spoke, my voice was very slow and controlled. Because if I didn't keep my shit together, I was pretty sure I was going to turn him into a smear of fairy juice on the nearest tree.

"What do you mean, which one? How many human girls have you brought over here with this damned video game?"

"Not many. I think the one you came looking for was the sixth. Maybe seventh. I lose track after a while, and you humans really do all look alike."

"The only reason I haven't gone back to the plan of beating you into a bloody smear of fairy-juice is that I think I need you to get back home, you know that, right?" I didn't wait for an answer. "You mean to tell me that you've brought half a dozen human children over into Fairyland, sold them to the queen, and you don't have any idea what happened to any of them?"

"No, not at all. That's nothing like what actually happened."

"Then what happened?" I was genuinely confused now. I have a pretty good grasp of basic English, and he didn't use any fancy words, so I was pretty sure I knew what was going on.

"I could never *sell* human children to the queen. They were intended as gifts. I *gave* them to her."

I just sat down on the ground, in front of the smart-ass fairy kidnapper, put my head in my hands, and bemoaned my choices in life.

Chapter Five

I ONLY TOOK A MOMENT TO THINK ABOUT EVERY BAD DECISION I ever made; then I sucked it up and got back to the task at hand. Besides, there's nothing *illegal* about sleeping with your high school girlfriend's mom, especially if you were already eighteen at the time. It probably wasn't my most morally sound choice, but I was pretty sure I was on solid legal footing. And her sister was totally over eighteen. The mom's sister, not my girlfriend's sister. Well, she was, too. So I was covered on all fronts.

I stood up, took a deep breath, and squared my shoulders. "Nothing has changed, Puck. I just have to rescue a lot more human children now. So I need you to point me the way to the castle so I can get on with this rescue operation. And any intel you can give me about the place would be helpful, too."

"Intel? I'm sorry, my friend, but I can no more grant you intelligence than I can make you more attractive. Hmmm, now that I think about it, making you more intelligent could be a far simpler matter."

"Kiss my ass. If I want to take shit from a skinny fairy, I'll go home and talk to Skeeter."

"What is a Skeeter?"

"Never mind. Where's the castle?"

"Tisa'ron, the capitol city, is three days' ride south of here. Just walk east unto you find a wide road through the woods. Follow that south until you get to the city. I'm not sure how you expect to talk your way through the gates since humans are usually only brought into Fairy as slaves or breeding stock, and you aren't exactly what Fae women look for in a mate. No offense."

"Have you ever noticed that those two words usually either precede of immediately follow the most offensive thing the speaker can possibly come up with?"

Puck smiled at me, all innocence, sunshine, and rainbows. "Why no, I've never realized that, human. You are truly an intellectual giant among your people."

"Whatever," I said. I turned and started walking in the direction he indicated.

"Wait!" he called from behind me. I turned around to him, arms folded across my chest.

"What?"

"Are you convinced that this is the only possible course of action?" he asked.

"I don't see anybody else jumping in line to bring that little girl home, so yeah, I reckon it's the only thing I can do."

"Then perhaps we can be of use to each other." I didn't trust the glint in his black eyes, or the tiny grin playing around his lips, but I also felt pretty short on options, so I walked over to another stump nearby and sat down.

"Talk," I said. "What did you have in mind?"

"I might have mentioned that Her Majesty Titania, may she rule forever in her unwavering beauty and grace, has my beloved imprisoned in her castle. The same castle that you are determined to storm."

"I wouldn't say storm so much as walk into and ask nicely, but go ahead."

"If you are determined to continue down this foolish path, then perhaps I may lend some assistance. In exchange, of course, for your help with a little problem of my own."

"You want me to reduce your maid when I grab the human girls and bring her back here so y'all can run away together, or whatever fairies do when they elope. That pretty much it?"

He hemmed and hawed for a few seconds, then said, "Yes, as much as I loathe anything that straightforward, that is an accurate assessment of the situation."

"You coulda stopped at 'yes,'" I pointed out.

"No, I really couldn't." He shook his head. "But yes, if you agree to rescue my Blossom, I will give you information that will make it much easier to get in and out of the castle. And if you return here with her, I will return you and all the other human children I have captured with my game to the same location you crossed over from."

"That sounds fair. Now what can you tell me about the castle?" I leaned forward as the little love-struck fairy started talking.

An hour or so later, my head full to bursting with information on the castle, its defenses, the gate guards, the best escape routes, which girls at which taverns have particularly loose morals and a fascination with "creatures from other realms," and all sort of other stuff that may or may not be useful in a rescue op, like how many guards patrol the city and which ones can be bribed. I also had a small coin purse (not the kind your great-aunt carried when you were a little kid—think more like a leather dice bag) with a few gems and gold and silver coins to help grease a few palms and maybe put a little food in my belly.

I stood up, ready to get going, and Puck stopped me. "Your weapons are useless here. Take this, it's dangerous to go alone." He unbuckled his sword belt and held it out for me.

That phrase sounded familiar somehow, but I couldn't quite put my finger on it. Filing that away for later, I took the belt and strapped it on. Somehow the same belt that went around a hundred-twenty-pound fairy also managed to fit around my waist, which probably weighs a hundred-twenty-pounds by itself. *I hate magic*, I thought, then held out my hand to Puck.

"Good luck, human. You'll need it."

"If you're so sure you think I'm gonna die, why did you give me your sword?"

"I can call the blade back to me if need be. If you haven't returned in a week or more, I'll activate the belt's magic, and it will return to me instantly."

I still hate magic. But that's pretty cool. "Neat trick," I said. We shook hands, and I headed into the woods, hoping I'd be home ever, much less before dark. The second I passed the tree line, I got a creeping sensation between my shoulders, a feeling of being watched, but whenever I looked around, I saw nothing.

"Well, Bubba, you didn't think you were gonna be able to just traipse around through Fairyland without anybody noticing, did you?" I said out loud, then chuckled a little at me thinking out loud just to break the silence. I gave one last look around, then went back to walking.

And walking.

And walking.

And walking.

I swear I would have thought that I was walking in circles if I didn't grow up in the woods and mountains of North Georgia and had some rudimentary woodcraft drilled into me before I learned to drive. I used my pocketknife to leave small marks on the trunks of trees as I passed, and since I never passed those marks again, I was at least twenty percent convinced I wasn't walking around in circles. I walked for a couple hours through pretty dense forest, mostly oak, maple, and other hardwoods, but the occasional patch of pine and even a little spruce scattered here and there.

The walk was even pretty pleasant, all things considered. The trees above wove together to make a thick canopy of leaves and branches, and the light that filtered down dappled the ground in beautiful patterns. It wasn't too hot, or too cold, and no matter how long I walked, it didn't get any hotter or colder. I remembered what Puck said about it never turning to winter in this part of Fairyland and thought that I could do worse than living somewhere perpetually seventy-five degrees. I'm Southern, and I'm a big dude, which means that six months out of the year, I travel with an extra shirt and a couple sweat rags behind the seat of my truck. It's hell getting people to let you in the front door of super-secret government facilities with acronyms like DEMON if you look and smell like a college locker room.

After what felt like three or four hours, not that I could tell anything about my travel outside the slight change in the trees around me, I stepped out of the woods and onto a well-maintained road. It was a straight swath of hard-packed dirt running as far as the eye could see in either direction.

I sat down on a small hillock of grass and took inventory. In my world, it was moving toward sunrise, if time moved the same there as it did here. But here it was just moving into evening, with the trees casting long shadows across the road and making the forest look and feel a lot less inviting than it had just a few hours before.

I checked my pockets and did a quick inventory. I hadn't exactly planned on crossing between dimensions when I got dressed this morning, so I wasn't what anyone in their right mind would call prepared. I had Bertha, of course, but we saw how useful the standard rounds were against Puck. The impact of a fifty-caliber round was nothing to sneeze at, but that's all it was going to give me—impact. I checked the magazine and found five rounds left. I popped that mag and set it aside for a moment, ejecting the round from the chamber and slipping it in atop the other five.

I pulled the two spare magazines from my shoulder holster and checked the loads, gratified to find that I remembered everything right for once. One magazine held ten silver rounds, but the other one was the winner in my book. It had five white phosphorous rounds—not tracers but literal balls of fire. Those Dragon rounds alternated with what I hoped would be my ace in the hole in Fairyland—five cold iron rounds. I ejected the Dragon loads and the cold iron bullets, as well as the regular lead bullets from the other magazine, and reloaded my weapon. I put the five cold iron rounds into one magazine and topped it with a regular load. Then I set up the other magazine with three regular rounds, four alternating regular/Dragon loads, then three white phosphorous bullets to finish off anything that needed more fire.

I didn't know if you could catch fairies on fire or not, but I've never known any monster that appreciated being hit with a flaming ball of lead, so I figured worst case they'd get me in close enough to finish the job with either my knife or my fists. My knife was just a regular Kershaw Blackout spring-assisted folder, clipped to the inside of my front pants pocket, but it was sharp, and it was steel. I wasn't sure if steel counted as cold iron, but I also figured if anything got close enough for me to cut it with my pocketknife, I had bigger things to worry about. My little Pelican LED flashlight clicked on, so apparently Duracell batteries are good for inter-dimensional travel. That's always good to know.

But as far as gear, that's all I had. My cell phone wouldn't even turn on, much less make a call, and my comm was useless as well. Apparently other planes of existence are out of range of even black-ops government issue communications devices. Nothing in my wallet was going to be useful, unless I suddenly needed to slice someone to death with a Vatican-issue black Amex, and the small plastic vial of holy water I carried for emergencies wasn't looking too useful, either.

I did have a Clif bar in one of the cargo pockets of my pants, and a Werther's Original caramel candy in another pocket. I was pretty hungry, but not terribly so, and trying to eat a chocolate and peanut butter Clif Builder Bar without anything to wash it down is a less than optimal meal, so I unwrapped the Werther's and sucked on a caramel as I started down the road, heading south toward the capitol of Fairyland and my date with Titania.

Sometimes my life even sounds weird to me, and I'm the one living it.

Chapter Six

THE SOUND OF CREAKING WOOD AND JINGLING METAL ROUSED me from sleep. I jerked awake, trying my best to leap to my feet and deal with the threat, but my back was so damn stiff from sleeping on the ground propped up against an ancient tree that my leaping was more like a geriatric crawl and clamber. My old knee injury from college let me know in no uncertain terms that it did not approve of sleeping outdoors anymore, and my neck wouldn't quite let me turn my head all the way to my left. So I staggered to my feet like a roadie on the tail end of a two-week bender, which is to say any roadie on any given day, and held myself upright with my left hand on a tree trunk and my right hand clutching Bertha.

"Well, that's not exactly the good morning I get from most fellow travelers, there sonny." The voice came from my left, and a good eight feet off the ground. Thanks to my jacked-up neck, I had to turn my whole body to see the speaker and was relieved out of all proportion to see a rotund fairy man sitting atop a two-horse cart.

Oh good, not a giant was my first coherent thought. It says a lot about how I feel in the morning that I could wake up beside a road in the woods and hear someone talking from ten feet in the air and immediately expect to have to fight a giant before coffee, instead of assuming that the voice belonged to someone sitting on top of a wagon. I holstered Bertha and looked up at the driver.

He was an older fairy, looking to be about seventy in human years. For all I know, he might have been two thousand years old—I don't know how long fairies live. But this one was obviously living well. His beard and mustache flowed down to his chest, and the bright red vest he wore over a plain white shirt didn't meet in the middle, and didn't look like it ever had any aspirations of doing so. He looked like any merchant, harmless and pleasant, but his clothes were clean, and his wagon looked to be in good repair, and the sword on his belt looked like it had seen some use, judging just by the hilt. The two horses pulling the wagon were brushed and healthy-looking, and the cart behind him was piled his with casks and kegs.

Praise be to Shakespeare, I had just been discovered by the Fairy Beer Guy. This whole case was starting to look up.

I holstered Bertha and held up both hands. "Sorry about that. You surprised me, and I'm not the most pleasant guy when I first wake up."

The portly fairy laughed, and his everything shook like the proverbial bowl full of jelly. "Me neither, lad. Me neither. But what are ye doing sleeping by the road? Are ye daft? Or just too poor to afford an inn?"

I looked at him again, then decided on an unusual course of action for me—honesty. "I'll tell you straight, friend. I was brought here by a mischievous fairy, set upon a quest that's probably completely hopeless, and turned out onto the road without a map, any food, a bedroll, or any money except what I brought with me from my world. I'm trying to get to the capitol, and Puck told me this was the road, so I slept where I could. And that's the God's honest truth."

"Which one?"

"Which what?"

"Which god, lad, are ye daft? Some of those ruttin' bastards don't have any more truth in 'em than me pecker, and that damn thing'll as soon lie to you as look at you, and it's only got the one eye!" He laughed, slapped his knee, and almost fell off the wagon in his glee.

"Sorry," I said. "Not much of a pantheon where I'm from these days."

"Well, be careful who ye be swearing to, boyo. Ye never know who might be ridin' up on ye."

"Are you telling me you're a god?" I raised an eyebrow. I'll admit to a little cultural bias, but in the movie in my head, I never pictured a god with a beer gut. I guess there's always Bacchus, but this fairy sounded Irish, so that was probably out. And was this guy's accent getting heavier with every sentence?

The little round man laughed again, wiped his eyes, and looked down at me. "No, son, I'm no kind of god. I'm just a beer merchant, toting me cargo to the city to sell to the taverns and inns. Now I might be of mind to offer ye a ride to the capitol in exchange for some service that might need to be rendered at a moment's notice."

"What's that?" Usually when someone offered me a gig right after meeting me, it either has something to do with moving a piano, changing a lightbulb without a ladder, or beating the shit out of something. I didn't see a piano on his cart and there was no electricity, so that narrowed the field a little.

"There's been reports of bandits along the road to Tisa'ron. They shouldn't be a problem for a big, strapping young lad like yourself, but they could destroy my whole livelihood with one attack."

I thought about it for about a second and a half, then held my hand up to the man. "You take me to the capitol; I'll make sure bandits don't steal all the beer."

He grinned and motioned for me to climb up into the cart, so I took the seat next to him, taking a minute to arrange Bertha and Puck's sword so they were in easy reach.

"What's your name, traveler?"

"Bubba," I replied.

"Pleasure to meet you, Bubba. I be Oakroot, master brewer and master sampler, too!" He laughed again, a hearty rumble that shook the whole cart. He shook the reins, clucked his tongue at the horses, and we were off.

The road was mostly shaded, so the ride in the open cart was cool, if a bumpy trek sitting on a couple of two-by-fours. We rode for a few hours, then stopped at a small village with a couple of picnic table sitting in a clearing in the middle of a dozen or so houses. The cart was surrounded by fairy children as soon as we stopped, all of them clamoring for some trinket or candy. Oakroot laughed and reached into a pocket, pulling out a handful of colorful treats.

"Catch, ye wee ragamuffins!" He tossed the candies into the air, and half a dozen children sprouted wings and launched themselves into the air, snagging candy on the wing. The rest of the children grabbed and scrambled for the few sweets that fell to the ground, then unfurled wings of their own and flew off after their friends to enjoy the delicious distraction.

"Nice," I said, climbing down and popping my back. I rubbed my ass, which hadn't seen that kind of abuse since Grandpappy caught me sneaking a cigarette behind his barn. He laid into me with his belt, whooping my ass 'til his shoulder hurt, then he switched arms and tore my butt up some more. I didn't sit down to eat for most of a week, but I also never smoked cigarettes again. We won't talk about some of the smoking I did in college, but I passed all the mandatory drug tests to play football, so that's all that mattered to me anyway.

"Not used to riding that long, lad?"

"Not in a wagon with a board for a seat," I replied. "Where I'm from, we have seats padded fit to beat the most luxurious chair you've ever seen."

"You must truly be a pampered lot, then. I hope you can actually use that blade if we have need of it."

"Worst comes to worst, I'm pretty good at just punching things until they fall over," I said. "You need me to do anything?"

"Well, I thought this might be a good place for some lunch, so why don't ye get that small keg from the tail of the cart and set it up over on yon table? I've got some food and plates and such in my pack." He walked over to one of the picnic tables and set his small knapsack on it. I went to the tail of the wagon and grabbed the little keg, throwing it onto one shoulder and carrying it easily.

"Nice, lad. Ye've got some use to you after all," Oakroot said as I set the keg on the table. He laid the keg on its side, pulled a couple of wooden wedges from his pack, and jammed the wedges under the keg to keep it from rolling. He reached into his pack again and pulled out a wooden spigot, then pulled a cork from the end of the cask and tapped it with the spigot. The whole process took about ten seconds, and that included him rummaging around in his pack. I was obviously dealing with a professional. Once again into the pack he went, this time emerging with a pair of tankards, plates, and forks.

"What else do you have in there?" I asked with a chuckle.

He looked up at me. "Well, lad, our food is in here, as well as most of me tools, me bedroll and cloak, a few trinkets I've picked along the road for me lady love and a couple of items that I've acquired in me travels that I thought I might be able to sell for a pretty penny once we get to Tisa'ron."

"In that little pack?" I gave him a look. The pack wasn't any bigger than a child's bookbag, with a drawstring top and a couple of shoulder straps. All the stuff he described would have taken a steamer trunk, especially if he was bringing enough food to keep us both alive, and since he set out two plates, I assumed he was planning to share.

"Oh, lad, I forget ye aren't from around here," he laughed. He did that a lot, but I didn't mind. It was a rich, hearty laugh, full of amusement and good cheer, not a malicious laugh at the ignorant hillbilly. Or I guess ignorant human in this case. "This be me sack of many things. It's got a wee piece of magic attached to it. When I reach into the sack, me arm comes out in a room back at me house. Me wife keeps everything I like to have when I travel laid out on a table, so it's just a matter of feeling around until I find what I'm looking for. Or, if she's home, she hears the bell and comes to put whatever I need right into me hand."

"Bell? You've got some kind of magical alarm in your house so she knows whenever you open a portal to your house?"

"Well, after a fashion," he agreed. "When I had the wizard who sold me the sack set the portal in our spare room, I rigged a bell just off to the side of it. So now, if it's daytime when I'm using the sack, I reach out and smack the bell first thing. Then Thistledown comes running to help out. Sometimes she even kisses the back of me hand. That's nice when I've been on the road too long." He wore a lovesick little smile when he talked about his wife.

"Oh. Yeah, just hanging a bell is probably much easier than some kind of magical alarm," I said.

"Indeed, lad. Indeed. Spell maintenance is quite expensive, don't you know. But now, enough jabbering, let's eat before those little sprites get back here and harass me for candy again!"

Lunch was delicious: a nice little plate of sliced ham, or something that looked and tasted like ham, bread, and some vegetables of various colors. It was all rich and full of flavor, and filling, but not heavy like so much food back home. And Oakroot's beer was good enough to send the Pope on a bender. It had a nice crisp flavor, with just a hint of oak in the aftertaste. The beer had a pleasant side effect, too. It made my ass stop hurting but didn't get me drunk or make me tired. When I was done with the meal, I felt rejuvenated and re-energized, like I could ride for days. Which I really hoped I wouldn't have to do.

We packed up our leftovers, Oakroot untapped the keg and put the cork back in, and I loaded it back onto the cart. I had just turned back to the table when I saw a tall fairy walking to the table, a scowl on his face and an air of authority surrounding him like the cloud of a broccoli fart. He marched over to the table and stood over Oakroot, who just calmly kept packing away plates, cups, and utensils like he didn't have a care in the world. Or like he didn't give a single shit about the newcomer.

I leaned on the side of the cart to watch. There didn't seem to be any imminent danger, unless getting bitched at suddenly became physically damaging, in which case I'm gonna be in traction the next time Amy gets pissed at me. That woman is way too smart for me, and she uses her vocabulary like a weapon when I get under her skin.

The grumpy fairy stood there, arms crossed and toe tapping, as Oakroot finished tidying up. When the last plate was scraped over near where a dog napped by the base of a tree and my companion slung his pack over one shoulder, he finally snapped.

"Were you planning to speak to me, Master Oakroot?" His voice even sounded officious and pissy, all high and nasal. I didn't like him from the moment he stomped up all pissed-off looking, but when he started talking with a voice like Gilbert Gottfried, I decided I might have to punch him after all.

"I wasn't, actually, Master Redfern. I was hoping that ye would be so occupied with your brewing that ye wouldn't notice that I was in town at all. And now, look! I be almost on me way."

"You cheated, Oakroot. You are a cheat and a liar and I demand satisfaction." The puffed-up man drew himself up to his full height, which was probably all of five-eight. Tall for a fairy from what I'd seen, and certainly tall compared to the almost spherical Oakroot, who barely crossed five feet, but he still didn't cut a very imposing figure. And Oakroot was certainly in the "gives no shits" category.

"Then ye should return to your home and satisfy yourself, Redfern. I have no interest in you that way, so I certainly won't be taking care of it."

I tried. I really tried to keep my composure and not laugh. I knew any sound I made was just going to escalate things, and I also knew that I needed to get my ass to the capitol so I could actually start the hard part of this task, the breaking into the capital and rescuing the human children part. But I couldn't do it. One jerk-off joke, and Oakroot had me braying laughter like an oversized donkey.

Redfern glared at me, his pointy ears trembling with rage and his manicured black eyebrows running for his hairline. "What. The. Hells. Is. That?" he asked, disgust dripping from every word.

That was a poor choice on his part. Or maybe I was about to make a really poor one on mine. I don't like condescending assclowns, and I really don't like being sneered at. I walked over to the assclown and stuck out my hand.

"I'm Bubba," I said.

Assclown just stared at my hand like it was something really nasty. And it wasn't. It had a little ham grease on it, but I'd wiped most of it off on my jeans, so I was relatively clean. For someone who'd slept in the woods and hadn't bathed since yesterday morning. But he didn't need to know that.

"What is a Bubba?" Redfern asked me, his lips curling so far up into a snarl that I thought he was trying to show off his dental work.

"A Bubba is a human. What is a Redfern?" I kept my hand there, just hanging out. I could hold that pose for a while before I started to stiffen up, and I thought I might enjoy making things as awkward as possible for this douche.

"I am Kyreon Redfern, and I am the Master Brewer of the District of Haf'narion."

"Good to meet ya," I said, reaching out and taking his hand and forcing a shake on him. He looked like he didn't know whether to throw a punch, run away, or piss himself.

"Now, what can we do for ye, Redfern?" Oakroot asked. "We've got business in the capitol and really shouldn't dally."

"I will have you know that I have lodged a formal complaint about you with the Brewer's Guild and am traveling this day to Tisa'ron to present my evidence." He gestured to a pony tethered to a post a few feet away.

"Evidence? What evidence, you daft bastard?" Oakroot asked. His face, calm just seconds before, started to turn red at Redfern's accusation.

"I have evidence that you cheated in this year's Spring Brewing Festival, and I'll be presenting that to our queen herself. If you'd like to accompany me, I'm sure she will give you an appropriate opportunity to defend yourself." He crossed his arms and looked down his long, pointy nose at Oakroot.

Wait a minute, this tool was going to present his case to the queen? In person? I'm not a terribly religious man, despite taking a paycheck from the Catholic Church, but in that moment, I thanked everything I'd ever believed in. This scrawny bastard might be a doucherocket, but he was a doucherocket that could get me into the castle.

Chapter Seven

BY THE TIME WE WERE A MILE OUT OF THE VILLAGE, I REGRETTED my decision. By the time we were two miles out, I regretted taking this case. By the time we'd traveled two hours, I regretted ever being born. The two brewmasters bickered constantly, and about everything. And I do mean *everything*. Redfern had to stop to piss, so Oakroot griped about how slow our progress was now that we had this asshat slowing us down. Oakroot's wagon was loaded down, so Redfern bitched about the cart slowing us down. Then Oakroot started bitching about Redfern bitching, so I just climbed down out of the cart and walked ahead.

The loaded cart was moving along at about a brisk walk, so I jogged a hundred yards or so to get ahead of the two grumpy fairies, or at least to get them out of earshot. I rounded a bend in the road and just barely caught a glint of metal in the trees off to one side of the road.

Ambush.

Shit.

I turned to the side and faced the nearest tree, whipping out Little Bubba and taking a long piss while I listened intently for any noise coming from ahead of me. The bandits were quiet; I had to give them credit for that much. If one dude hadn't screwed up his camouflage, I never would have known they were there. But I did, and that gave me all the advantage I needed.

There's only one thing to do when you know you're walking right into a trap—spring it. But springing the trap on your terms flips the script on the bad guys who think they have the element of surprise. The element of surprise is now in your favor, and that's real important when you know from the get-go that you're outnumbered. Being three times the size of your opponents also helps ease the burden of being outnumbered. I tucked Little Bubba away and zipped up, then turned back to the trail. The cart was still out of sight, a couple hundred yards behind me on the road, but I knew they'd be coming into earshot soon. And that was human earshot, not even taking into account if fairies had better hearing because their ears are bigger. I knew I had to act fast, so I walked out into the middle of the road, weaving a little like I was drunk.

Then I started to sing. Now, for the record, I don't sing. Ever. There's a reason for this. My voice has been described as the sounds of two cats screwing in a dishwasher. Now I've never heard two cats screw in a dishwasher, but I can only assume it's not a pleasant sound. That's the unfortunate thing about my singing—everything. But I belted into the theme song for all intoxicated rednecks everywhere—Lynyrd Skynyrd's Southern National Anthem—"Sweet Home Alabama." I sang it loud, and I sang it as proud as if I actually was from Alabama, which thank God, I am not.

I made it all the way to mangling the line about Neil Young before a slim fairy dude leapt from the trees beside the road and intercepted me. He was slim, like every fairy, besides Oakroot, that I'd encountered, and short even for one of the fair folk, barely five feet tall. He might have weighed a hundred pounds soaking wet, and his rapier looked a lot more like an overgrown toothpick than anything I should worry about, but I knew better than to ignore the potential a sword has for inflicting damage.

If it sounds like I've got a little bit of a hang-up about getting stabbed since the whole deal with my brother Jason, then it's only because I do. If you have any problems with that, I'd like to refer you to the story where I had a foot of steel sticking out of my back, and then almost died at the hands of a succubus nurse while I was "recovering" in the hospital. It's the billing department of the hospital that's supposed to suck out your soul, not the nursing staff. So yeah, I've got some issues with swords. At least with other people having them. I have no problem swinging one myself, as evidenced by me drawing mine when the second mini-Dread Pirate Roberts leapt into the middle of the road, black bandanna mask and all.

"Hand over your purse, traveler, and I won't be forced to kill you," he said, twirling his blade in a moderately convincing fashion. I probably would have been worried if I was unarmed, if he'd surprised me, and if I wasn't three and a half times the little bastard's size. As it was, I figured I'd had worse fights than scrapping with a fairy holding a pigsticker in the middle of a dirt road.

"I don't think so," I said. "Why don't you give me that little toothpick and I won't wedge my foot so far up your ass you taste shoe leather every time you eat a meal?"

"What?"

"I said I ain't giving you my money. So piss off before I give you an ass whoopin'."

"Human, do you understand how this works? I jump out of the trees, wave my sword around, you give me your purse, and run away screaming. That's the natural order of things between bandit and traveler. Don't start thinking and screw up the way things are supposed to run, now. Just hand over the loot and no one gets hurt."

"Let's try this," I said. I took three quick steps up to him, putting myself right in front of him and inside his sword's swing. Then I balled up one fist and laid it across his face with extreme force. In other words, I punched the little wannabe bandit right in the nose.

"Ow!" He staggered back and sat down on his ass right in the middle of the road. "That hurt!" he hollered, looking up at me. I took another step forward and planted my foot across his blade, pinning it to the road.

"It wasn't meant to tickle, shithead. Now give me your purse and get the hell out of here." This had to be the worst ambush in the history of bandits. This guy would get written out of any decent dashing rogue story, no question.

"No problem, giant. Just stand there for another few seconds until...ah, there we are." The fairy's demeanor changed completely. The foppish bravado was gone, replaced by a cunning grin. The same time he turned off the stupid kid act, I heard shouts from back down the road. It sounded like something was up with Oakroot...son of a *bitch.*

"You were the decoy," I said, looking down at the thief.

"I'm the smallest. I get the jobs that require the least actual fighting. I climb things, slit the occasional throat, and act helpless. Then the briers go in and kick ass. We all have our jobs." He grinned up at me again, and I kneed him in the mouth. His hands flew back to his face, and I raised the foot pinning his sword to the ground. I reared back with that foot and put my size sixteen in his chest. I heard at least three ribs crack, and this time when he fell back onto the dirt road, he wasn't faking the whole writhing in pain bit.

I picked up his rapier, took the hilt in one hand and blade in another, and carefully bent the sword in half, making sure not to cut my fingers to shreds. "If you try to follow me, I'll break every bone that's big enough for me to fracture. Do you understand me?"

He nodded, and I turned to the noise. I put on the gas and sprinted the length of two football fields until the fracas came into view. I was pretty blown up by this point, between my little scuffle with the other fairy and running back to this fight. But I sucked it up and drew my sword as I rounded the last bend.

There were six fairies total, with two of them holding Redfern and Oakroot at sword point while two of them rummaged through the cart, looking for something that wasn't beer or wine. Another fairy was going through a pack I recognized as Redfern's, and given the fact that it was still sitting on the ground, no one had gone through Oakroot's bag yet. A magical bag like that was far too valuable for anybody to leave laying around, even in Fairyland.

The last bandit sat on a horse surveying the action, and of course, he was the one to notice me first. Great, not only was I bone-tired, but now I had to fight a fairy, and his horse, too. And the horse was looking like the bigger problem, what with all the hooves and teeth and everything. Then the fairy turned to me and started waving his hands in midair. A glowing ball of purple light materialized over his head, and he pushed his hands out at me like he was shoving me right in the chest.

The ball of purple energy flew toward me like a cannonball, and I revised my opinion about the horse being the bigger threat. I dove to the side of the road, rolling to one side and crashing into the trunk of a huge maple. I tried to stand, but my knee buckled, and I went right back down on my belly.

That probably saved my life. Another blast of energy, red this time, flew over my head and crashed into the tree. The maple tree, bigger around than my body, blew apart, showering me with splinters.

Now the other bandits were looking at me, and one of the sword-wielding ones started running my way. I fast-crawled forward, ducking behind another big tree as yet another blast of magic came my way. This one melted the tree like it was a candle in a forest fire.

"Okay, screw this shit," I muttered, diving forward into a clumsy roll. I didn't win any invites to *American Ninja Warrior,* but I also didn't get blown to pieces by the bolt of lightning that struck the ground where I'd stood seconds before. I came up on one knee with Bertha in one hand and leveled the big pistol at the fairy. He started waving his hands again, and I lined up my sights carefully. I squeezed off one round, and it blew that spell-slinging sonofabitch out of the saddle and a couple feet to the other side of his horse.

The road fell silent as all eyes turned to me. The Desert Eagle is, as Ray Wylie Hubbard said, one bad-ass pistol. And it makes a big damn boom. And a big damn impact. Puck got the shit knocked out of him, and he was immune to the effects of a lead round. This guy wasn't hurt by the bullet, either, on account of the first round being a lead "warning shot" of sorts. But he was lying on his back six feet away from the horse, and he was holding his chest like he had a couple broken ribs. Which he probably did, given the fact that I just hit him in the center mass with a sledgehammer, then he fell off his horse.

I had everybody's undivided attention now for damn sure. I stood up, dusted myself off, and looked at the bandits and merchants. I held Bertha high where everybody could see her and started talking. "Now that I've got your attention, let me explain what just happened. This here's Bertha." I turned the gun from side to side, letting them see what they were dealing with.

"Bertha don't like bandits. But Bertha also don't like killing folks if she can help it. So I'm gonna make y'all an offer. You put everything back where you found it in those wagons, apologize to my friend Oakroot there, and promise to stop robbing folks. Then you ride on down the road, and we continue on our merry way toward the capitol. Sound good?"

"If we don't agree?" The speaker was an older fairy, with a long, twisted scar running from his forehead down over one eye. I pegged him for the leader, on account of the scar. That and on account of the other robbers looking to him to do anything.

"Then I reckon we go back to fighting. I've only got five more bullets in Bertha, but every one of them is cold iron. Do you want to take the chance that I spend the first one on you?"

Chapter Eight

WE HAD US A REGULAR STANDOFF. THE FAIRY BANDITS DIDN'T want to leave without Oakroot's money, gear, and cart of beer. I had some strenuous objections to that, not the least of which was that not having that cart would make it a lot harder to get to the capitol and rescue Tamara Sanders. Then there was the thought of losing an entire cartload of beer, which hurt my very soul.

The wizard bandit got to his feet, slowly, and started waving his hands again. I pointed Bertha at him and shook my head. "No, no. We're still talking. You so much as think about throwing a spell my way, I will put an end to your precious little fairytale life."

He froze, but his cohorts didn't. The other four fairies rushed me, covering the last ten yards between us in a blink. I still didn't want to kill anybody, so I slammed Bertha's butt into the nearest dude's forehead. His eyes crossed, and he dropped like a stone. I holstered Bertha and put my hand on the sword Puck loaned me. I saw how close the fairies were and thought better of it.

There were three still standing in a ring around me, plus Scar hanging back waiting to deliver the *coup de grace*. I grabbed the nearest fairy and slammed him into one of the others, sending them both to the ground in a tangled heap. The third fairy looked around, wide-eyed, suddenly on the wrong side of outnumbered against a man three times his size.

He started to draw his sword, but I grabbed his forearm and squeezed. He dropped to one knee as I heard things crack inside his wrist. I pulled him forward, lifting my knee into his jaw at the same time. His eyes rolled back into his head, and he went down like a sack of potatoes.

The other two had disentangled themselves from one another by that point, and they came at me, swords drawn. I drew my own and parried both attacks. I kept moving and pushing toward them on a diagonal, forcing them closer together and foiling their footwork. After a couple of feints and lunges, they got so tangled up that the farthest one fell down on his butt parrying one of my strikes, and the other one tripped over him.

One fairy was down on his butt, and the other was on his hands and knees. I looked from side to side, heard the roar of an imaginary crowd, and dropped a People's Elbow on the back of the second dude's head. He went from hands and knees to kissing dirt in half a second, and I hopped back up, dragging the last fairy with me. I picked him up, held his body over my head, and hurled him at Scar. The bandit leader ducked, and his minion crashed to the dirt.

"Not even going to try to help him out?" I asked. "Damn, that's cold."

"I have other things to deal with. One other thing, to be specific." Scar drew his sword. Make that swords. Instead of one rapier like most of the fairies I'd encountered up to that point, he pulled a pair of short swords from his belt, wicked-looking little things with a curved blade that looked custom-made for opening guts like zippers.

Scar advanced on me, twirling his blades like a damn food processor. I looked at the blade in my hand, a slender longsword for a fairy, but barely more than a dagger for me. With a silent apology to Puck for mistreating his blade, I reared back and chunked the sword at Scar. He knocked it out of the air, but that moment's pause was all I needed. I drew Bertha with my right hand and a spare magazine with my left, ejecting the cold iron rounds and slamming the magazine full of silver rounds home. I racked the slide and leveled the pistol at Scar, who was almost close enough to make me nervous about his blades now.

"Stop," I said. "Or this is gonna hurt."

He didn't. I knew the silver wouldn't kill him, but when I shot him in the knee, he went down just like a human. Or troll. Or sasquatch. Or vampire, zombie, rakshasa, ogre, leprechaun, or any damn thing else when you bash its kneecap to a hundred pieces with a fifty-caliber silver bullet. Both curved swords dropped to the dirt, followed by a scar-faced screaming fairy who rolled around with both hands on his left knee. I'm pretty sure some of the things he screamed at me were not only physically impossible, but in violation of about thirteen laws of nature and seven laws of physics.

"I told you to stop," I said, not at all sympathetic. After all, I didn't kill 'em. The fairy that I dropped the elbow on got to his feet, looking a little wobbly. He took one step in my direction, then stopped when he saw all his buddies lying on the ground. He put his sword on the ground, then sat on the side of the road with his hand held high in the air.

"Good boy," I said. "But you forgot to empty your pockets and your purse, and to take off any jewelry and put it in a pile right there." I pointed to a spot a few feet from my foot. "Then take off your belt and sit on your hands."

He did as he was told, then I wrapped his belt around his chest and arms at the elbow and repeated the process with the other bandits. By the time I got to Scar, I had a nice little pile of swords and jewelry lying in the road, and a pile of dejected highwaymen sitting on the edge of the woods in fairyland.

I sent Oakroot ahead with the cart to get the fairy I left behind with broken ribs, and when everyone was sitting in a line looking glum, I stepped up in front of them.

"You guys are assholes, and you need to find another job," I said, pacing back and forth in front of them. "Now I don't have room in the cart to carry you along, so I'm going to have to leave you here while we travel to the capitol. As soon as we get there, we'll be reporting this encounter to the first guard we see that we think might give a damn and send them back here to collect you. I think it's important to make sure nobody wants to be a good Samaritan about you guys, so we'll just do this—" I found a scrap of wood lying around, quickly carved "BANDITS" on it, and tore off a strip of one dude's shirt and used it to hang the sign around his neck.

"Now hopefully no one will be inclined to help you idiots out. I'll also be taking all your money and gear, and your boots." I motioned at Redfern, who started de-shoeing the would-be robbers. "Now if you manage to get loose before the bears or guards get here, I'd suggest you find a better line of work. Because obviously the whole King of Thieves thing isn't working out for you."

I started sorting through all their shit, but finally just motioned for Redfern to toss it all in Oakroot's Sack of Stashing Stuff, and headed toward Oakroot and the cart. I'd put my foot on the first step when Scar spoke.

"You know we'll be free in minutes and come after you. You'd better not sleep, human. We live forever, and we don't forget an insult."

I put my foot down and walked back to where Scar and the rest of his scowling bunch sat on the dirt. He glared up at me, hate in his eyes. I bent down and grabbed the belt holding his arms tight to his chest with one hand. Then I stood up, lifting him high enough to look into my eyes. His feet dangled a good foot off the ground, but we were eye to eye.

"Look here, you little pissant. I've got enough ammunition to shoot you in the knee every day for a month and not even get tired," I lied. I had three magazines with ten rounds each, and I'd used some ammo already. I had enough bullets to shoot him in the knee every day for three weeks with a couple left over, but I counted on him not figuring that out, and me not being in Fairyland for a month. "And if you really start to be a pain in my ass, I've got cold iron bullets that will put a hole in your chest big enough for me to put my fist through. So you put any ideas of revenge out of your head, or you won't see another sunrise. Remember, shithead, being immortal means that you won't ever die, but it doesn't mean that nothing can ever kill you."

I dropped him to his feet, then gave him a little shove to send him sprawling onto his crew. He spluttered at me, but I turned my attention to the wizard. Bertha was already in my hand by the time I fully locked my gaze on his, and I lined up the barrel with the center of his face. His eyes got big, and his lips stopped moving.

"Am I going to have to shoot you in your damn head? You've already been shot once; you know how bad it hurts. Now imagine if I pull this trigger right now." I saw him thinking about how much damage the force of the bullet would hit him with, then he pressed his lips tightly closed.

"Good boy," I said. "Now I don't have to kill you. Look, I expect you idiots to try to escape. But I also expect you to run like hell in the opposite direction from where we're going, and I expect never to see any of you again. And if I do, I won't be shooting to wound, or screwing around with y'all. If I ever see any of you again, I'll kill your sorry ass and apologize to your mamas afterward. You got me?"

Wizard-boy nodded. I look at Scar, who nodded. Once Scar nodded, the rest of them looked like a collection of bobblehead dolls on a dashboard. I nodded once, stopped myself, and went over and climbed up into the cart.

Redfern mounted his pony and drew up alongside the front of the wagon. I leaned over and grabbed the pony's bridle, pulling Redfern right up beside me. "Let me be clear, you officious little prick," I said to him, my voice low. "We are going to have a pleasant, or at the very damn least, silent, ride to Tisa'ron. If you cannot be nice to Oakroot, or at least keep your damn mouth shut, I swear by all I hold holy, I will smack you in the mouth so hard your children will lisp. Do you understand me?"

He opened his mouth, eyes blazing, but I raised my hand. "Think hard before you speak to me in anger, Redfern. It's been a long morning."

He looked me in the eyes for a long moment, then finally decided better of whatever he was going to say, and just said, "I understand."

"Good. Oakroot, let's roll. I told Redfern if he can't keep a civil tongue in his head, that I would slap the taste out of his mouth. But that kinda depends on you not provoking him, no matter what level asshat he is. Does that work for you?"

Oakroot looked at the red-faced Redfern and smiled. "I think I can manage that." He shook the reins, and we were off for the castle. Again.

Chapter Nine

THE SUN WAS LOW THE NEXT DAY WHEN WE FINALLY MADE IT TO the gates of Tisa'ron. The green and yellow spires were visible in the distance, slowly shifting to orange and purple as the light changed and the sunset painted the sky in brilliant colors. As we drew closer, I saw that a high wall ringed the entire city, with guards atop the stop battlements. At least half a dozen archers and crossbowmen clustered over the main gates, with a few others walking patrol atop the rest of the visible section of wall.

A cluster of eight guards stood on either side of the gate, leaning against the walls casually, but with their swords loose in the sheaths and a pike or halberd leaning beside each man. A pair of older guards without polearms stood just in front of the portcullis, speaking to everyone who passed into the city and inspecting every cart and horse.

"Do you have money to pay the bribes?" Oakroot asked me when we were within a few carts of the front of the line. The look on my face must have been classic because the fat little fairy almost fell out of the cart laughing.

"Don't worry, lad, I be pullin' your leg. While there are indeed cities and towns with guards on the take, this lot be as honest as the summer is long. And we be in the land of the Summer Queen, so that be long indeed."

I relaxed a little, but still kept my purse close at hand. It was full of coin from the bandits, since we'd split up their haul when we made camp the night before. Redfern tried to play the moral outrage card and shame us for dividing up stolen goods, but when he saw exactly how much the highwaymen had on their persons, he was happy enough to take a one-third share.

We moved to the front of the line. Redfern, as a lone man on a single horse, peeled off to the right for a more cursory inspection and passage through a smaller gate. I clucked the horses to a stop and prepared myself for the questions and searching.

"Business in Tisa'ron?" The guard looked up at our cart with sleepy eyes. Other than having a human driving, our cart was just like every other one in line. And it wasn't that uncommon to have a human at the reins. We'd met a caravan on the road, and several of the wagons were driven by humans. None of them were wearing a tattered dress shirt and Levi's, but they were still human.

"Deliveries, Sergeant," Oakroot replied. "I have wine for The King's Table and beer for The Thirsty Dryad, The Weeping Niskie, and Bert's Place."

The guard nodded and walked around the wagon, peering under it and looking under the small tarp thrown across Oakroot's bedroll and cooking utensils.

"Bert's Place?" I whispered. "What a boring name. What's the owner, a fairy accountant?"

"A dragon," Oakroot said softly. "His real name is something like Bertorinix-something-something-something, a string of completely incomprehensible syllables that no human or fairy could every remember. So when dealing with lesser species, he answers to Bert."

"Lesser species?"

"His words, not mine."

"Is that polite?" I asked.

"He's a dragon. He gives not a single shit if he's polite or not, lad. Nor does he need to."

The guard meandered back to the front of the wagon and handed Oakroot a pair of shiny badges on leather thongs. "Wear these at all times when you're inside the gates, except in your rooms at whatever inn you choose for lodging. If the badges get hot, then we need to speak with you and you should find the nearest guard. Return them when you leave. If you try to take them more than a mile from the city walls, the magic will combust, burning anything touching it to a crisp. So don't forget."

Oakroot put his badge around his neck and dropped it down inside his shirt. I did the same, albeit with some concern. I don't like putting things that might catch fire or even just heat up that close to my nipples. It brings back bad memories of a night with three strippers, a veterinarian, the road crew for The Spin Doctors, and three dozen flaming shots called Bailey's Comet. It took almost a year for my chest hair to grow back after that one. I know most people don't have flashbacks to nights of partying, but most people have never run up a thousand-dollar bar tab drinking Mind Erasers in Birmingham, Alabama.

We had almost made it through the gate when a skinny guard ran over from the sally port that I saw Redfern enter. The little dude planted himself right in front of us, his pike leveled at me and a scowl on his face.

I reined in the horses and looked down at the man. He was big for a fairy, which made him about five-eight and maybe a hundred-fifty pounds. So less than half my size. And while he was holding a pike, it was still only about seven feet long, so it was barely long enough to reach me on the seat of the cart. He stepped forward, and the tip of the pike came a little closer to my belly than I liked, so I reached out with one hand and pushed it aside. I was even almost gentle about it.

"Don't touch that!" the guard screeched. His face was red and his pike was vibrating his hands were shaking so hard.

"Are you okay?" I asked. "You seem a little worried about something."

"We have reports that someone matching your description was in an altercation along the Queen's Highway. Was it you?"

"Probably," I said, trying and almost completely succeeding in not laughing at the excitable little dude. "Was this altercation me whooping the shit out of half a dozen or so highwaymen that tried to rob and murder me and my friends?" A little exaggeration, honestly. I don't think they wanted to kill anybody until I screwed up their plans to get rich quick. Or at least to make me poor quick.

"Our reports describe you attacking a band of merchants and making off with all their jewelry and gold, breaking one poor craftsman's arm, and leaving them tied up alongside the road."

"Part of that is true," I admitted. "I did break one of the robber's arms, and I did leave them tied up on the side of the road. The bit about them being merchants? I don't think so, unless merchants have developed a habit of attacking other merchants' wagons and trying to steal their wares."

"Well, we have to get this sorted out," the fairy said. "You'll have to come with me to the castle, right away."

I almost protested. I almost said I was innocent and how dare he assume that his random sources, who I didn't even have the guts to stand in front of me to make their baseless accusations, were right and I was wrong. Then I remembered that I *wanted* to go to the castle, and I got much more agreeable.

"You're right," I said.

"I am?"

"Of course you are. The only way we're going to get this whole mess figured out is by going to the castle right now, without any further dilly-dallying." That was a first for me. Never, in my thirty-some years on this planet, had I used the phrase "dilly-dallying." And I thought I never would. But if I'd ever met anyone, human or otherwise, that looked like they would be opposed to dilly-dallying, it would be this dude.

I climbed down off the wagon's seat, grabbed my pack out of the footwell, and reached up to shake Oakroot's hand. "Don't worry about Redfern," I said. "I peed on all his evidence last night. He won't even be allowed inside the castle, and you won't have to deal with the blemish on your reputation."

"Why thank ye, lad," he said, gripping my hand in his. "Ye've been a most pleasant companion, and a stalwart protector. I have complete faith ye shall overcome whatever obstacles await ye at the castle."

I barely knew what he said. I think it boiled down to "kick ass out there." "Yeah," I said. "You too." I nodded to Redfern but honestly had no interest in saying goodbye, or anything else, to him.

"Lay on, Macdougal," I said to the guard.

"It's Macduff, sir," he corrected.

"Not if you're talking about the liquor store nirvana in South Carolina," I replied. I waved off his confused look and motioned for him to lead on. I followed the guardsman through the streets of Tisa'ron for a solid half hour before we came to the gates of the castle. These ten-foot double doors were also guarded by a passel of men with crossbows, longbows, polearms, and battle axes, and they all looked very much like they knew how to use those weapons.

"Please stay close to me, and please don't speak," my escort said. "I gather from your running commentary as we passed through the city that you find yourself amusing. It will all go better for you if you assume that everyone here is completely lacking in a sense of humor." I wasn't exactly sure what he meant by saying that I find myself amusing, but I kept my mouth shut until we entered the throne room.

Then I couldn't help it. My jaw hung open like an automatic flycatcher, and my head spun around like a bearded Linda Blair as I tried to take everything in. The throne room was everything I'd ever imagined about a magical fairy castle, and more. It was like somebody hired Walt Disney and J.K. Rowling as their decorators. The room was huge, easily the length of a couple basketball courts end to end, and tall. The walls climbed up and up to a huge vaulted ceiling, and every single surface was decorated somehow.

Every wall was hung with tapestries or painted with murals, and this wasn't the kind of boring shit you see in old movies or castles back home, this was some straight up Hogwarts shit right here. The tapestries depicted battle scenes, and the scenes played out on the tapestries. The images were trapped within their own tapestries, but there were fairies, dragons, humans, centaurs, dryads, dwarves, elves, and all sorts of monsters and beings that I didn't recognize. They flew, fought, and wreaked havoc within their borders for minutes at a time, then reset themselves to the beginning of the scene. I stood there watching one scene of knights jousting on dragons several times before my escort got impatient.

"Come on," he said.

I ignored him.

"You need to move," he said, his voice a little lower and tighter.

I stuck with what I was good at—ignoring him.

"Move, *now*, human."

Nope. Didn't happen.

"Fine," he huffed. I felt a sharp pain in my right butt cheek and whirled around. The guard was holding his pike and grinning a nasty grin at me.

"Can we go now?" he asked.

"Yes," I said. *Asshole* stayed unuttered. Now that I was facing him, he had a spear pointed at my johnson. I'm brave, but I'm not that brave.

We walked half the length of a football field, then my escort motioned for me to stop a good fifteen feet from the throne. Four guards flanked the dais, and a pair of thrones sat upon it. One throne stood empty, but on the other one was the single most beautiful creature I'd ever seen. Titania, the Summer Queen, sat on her throne with a regal dignity that shone through without her saying a word. She was a tall fairy, and even seated, her presence was undeniable.

Her hair shimmered down over her shoulders in waves of blonde, light brown, and streaks of strawberry blonde. Her perfect complexion was enhanced more than marred by a light sprinkling of freckles across her delicate nose, giving her the impression of someone perpetually in the bloom of youth. Her long arms had a delicate strength to them, and her posture held the quiet grace of someone accustomed to being the center of attention.

The guard beside me dropped to one knee when he got to about ten feet from her, and I did my best to do the same. The effect was ruined when my knees rang out like rifle shots and the guardsman beside me dropped his pike to draw his sword. The polearm fell to the marble floor with an echoing clatter, and the guards on the dais sprang into motion. Two of them leapt in front of the queen, a short sword in each hand, while the other pair charged down the steps at me, double-headed axes poised to strike.

The smaller guard beside me reached for his sword, but since I was the only one not surprised by the sounds emanating from my kneecaps, I had the presence of mind to grab him by his sword arm and his belt buckle, lift him off his feet, and hurl him into the path of the charging axemen. The three fairies went down with a clatter of silver chain mail and bronze weapons, and I was relieved to see that none of them fell on the blades or anything. They were just doing their jobs, no need for them to get hurt over it.

One of the other guards left the queen's side and rushed at me, his swords held low and ready. I picked up the fallen pike and jabbed him in the belly with the butt of it. He ran into the wooden pole at full speed and dropped to the floor like a sack of very battered potatoes, all the air gone. He made it back to one knee without a long enough pause for me to explain what happened, so I rapped him on top of the head with the pike. His eyes crossed and he dropped back down to the floor, flopping onto his belly and probably breaking his nose when he landed.

"Now stop it," I bellowed. Time froze around me as the sheer volume of sound I produced registered with the delicate, fair folk. I'm a big dude, and that means I can move a lot of air when I put my mind to it. And my mind was definitely to it just then because I knew if the guards untangled themselves from one another, I was probably going to have to seriously hurt somebody to keep them from burying a big axe in me.

"I am not here to hurt anybody," I continued speaking in my best drill instructor voice. I've never been in the service, but I watched *Full Metal Jacket* a bunch when I was a kid, so I know how yell. "I will put the big stick down." I did.

"I am just here to clear up a misunderstanding about me and some bandits I beat the hell out of on the road." *And break a bunch of humans out of your dungeon,* I didn't add.

"Misunderstanding? I think I understood you perfectly when you laid hands on the queen's cousin, robbed me, and left me tied up in the woods, you round-eared human piece of dung."

I knew that voice. It meant all kinds of bad things for me. I peered past the lone guard protecting the queen and saw the owner of the voice standing on the dais beside her. The queen's cousin was my old buddy from the highway, the fairy that I lovingly called Scar.

Shit.

Chapter Ten

SHIT.

I looked at him again. Yep, still the same little bastard I beat up, robbed blind, and left tied up in the dirt beside the road.

Shit.

I beat the hell out of the queen's cousin. I shot the queen's cousin. I knew it wouldn't kill him, or do any permanent damage, but I'd still shot him.

Shit.

Amy'd been telling me for years that my shoot first, ask questions never attitude was going to have consequences. Now it looked like those consequences were sitting on a throne in front of me in the form of a gorgeous fairy queen.

Oh well, in for a friggin' penny, as they say...

"Hey, Scar, how's the leg?" I asked, pasting a big grin on my face.

Scar's face went instantly red and his hand drifted toward the leg I shot. He got control of himself, but I saw it. And I knew by the look in his eyes that he saw me seeing it, and that pissed him off even more.

"Your Majesty, this human piece of excrement just admitted to assaulting me on the highway! I demand that he be executed immediately!" Scar screeched.

"You make demands of the queen, Scar? That's pretty brazen, even for a cousin. That's the kind of bold, rash behavior I'd expect from a man who would lead an attack on a merchant's wagon in broad daylight. But I'll give you credit, I didn't see this coming. I didn't expect you to be royalty. I just thought you were a common little pissant robber. Now I see that you're a royal little pissant robber."

He flushed even further and took a step toward me, his swords clearing their sheaths with a hiss that echoed through the silent throne room. I drew Bertha and pointed the barrel straight at his chest, cocking the hammer back with a loud *click.*

"Take another step, dickhead. I don't give a shit if you're the queen's cousin, her boyfriend, or her damn manicurist, you come an inch closer to me with those skewers and I'm going to put you on your ass." He froze, then smiled and stepped back, sheathing his blades as he did.

"You see, Your Majesty? He's obviously violent and deranged. He threatened my person right in front of you. What kind of idiot does that? What species of moron comes into the queen's throne room and makes threats against her family?

"What kind of royal cousin attacks a wine and beer merchant on the road to Tisa'ron? What kind of royal cousin leads ruffians and thugs to prey on innocent citizens? What kind of royal cousin isn't man enough to face a mere human in single combat, but hides behind half a dozen allies and minions, then comes running to the queen when he gets his ass beat?"

"STOP." Titania stood up and glared at both of us. "Chauvan," she turned to Scar, so I reckon that was his name, "you have long been a smear on the honor of this family. You have all the morals of a jackal, without the redeeming qualities. But you are my blood, and an insult to you is an insult to the throne, and that cannot be brooked."

"But," she went on, "robbing travelers on the Queen's Highway is an insult to queen and kingdom, and that is tantamount to treason. The penalty for striking a member of the royal family is fifty lashes, while the penalty for treason is death."

I stared at Scar. Fifty lashes for beating up a bandit? That was gonna suck. But not as much as him getting his ass *killed* for playing Robin Hood in the woods. Without the whole giving away the money thing, of course. Scar looked like something he ate disagreed with him. Probably that heaping spoonful of reality that Titania had just poured down his throat.

"But," the queen said after Scar and I had a moment to process the depth of the shit that we were in. "But, we have a festival tomorrow to celebrate the one-hundred-fiftieth anniversary of my coronation, and I need entertainment. The past several anniversaries have been painfully dull affairs, with hardly any bloodshed. I think the two of you should remedy that."

Shit. It was really starting to be my favorite word, at least as far as fairies were concerned. I bet whatever the queen had in mind was gonna hurt at least as much as fifty lashes.

Titania sat back down on her throne, assured that she had our full attention. Her guards were back on their feet now, if a little wobbly. The one I poked with the pike had blood streaming down his face from his jacked-up nose, but he stood his post without blinking an eye.

"I offer you a choice. You can accept the punishments handed to you by the laws of the land, or you can compete against each other in a public duel, tomorrow at dawn." She looked at Scar and smiled. "You have long touted your skill as a warrior to whomever would listen, cousin, so I am certain that you have no qualms about battling a mere human before your peers, your family, your business associates, and the entirety of Tisa'ron."

She turned her gaze to me, and I felt my knees buckle a little. I've heard of women that can freeze men with a look, but this chick straight melted me. I managed to tune back in when she started to speak.

"And you, human. You seem larger than most, and if you bested my cousin the first time you fought, you must have some proficiency in combat. So I assume you find this an acceptable option?"

"That depends," I said.

One perfectly sculpted blonde eyebrow climbed so high on her forehead that I thought it was scaling Everest. "It depends? On what?"

"On how the fight is supposed to go," I said. "Are we fighting to first blood, unconsciousness, death, or some other random thing? If we're fighting to the death, I should probably take my chances with fifty lashes. I've got a pretty good chance of living through that, better than my chances of surviving a fight to the death with a lying, cheating, stealing shitbird of a fairy like your cousin, anyway."

The queen looked at me for a long moment, then laughed. "You are correct, human—"

"Bubba," I corrected.

"Excuse me?"

"You keep calling me 'human' like it's a synonym for 'asshole,' so I figured I should just tell you my name. It's Bubba."

"Bubba, then. You are correct, *Bubba*, that my cousin is a well-trained warrior and ruthless in battle. So your weapons will be magically blunted, and you will fight until one of you is unconscious or otherwise unable to continue."

"Sounds good to me," I said.

"I suppose it is what the humans call a 'win-win situation,'" Scar said. "I avoid summary execution at the hands of my favorite cousin, which could make future family gatherings awkward, and I get the added pleasure of beating some manners into this giant clod of a human. I shall return on the morrow and deliver your thrashing, human." He gave his cousin a florid bow, his nose almost touching the stone floor, and swept out of the room like he owned the place.

I looked around and bowed to the queen. I wasn't as grandiose as Scar, mostly because I don't bend that far, and partly because if I tried, I'd almost certainly fall on my own face, and I'd already seen how that worked out.

"I reckon I'll go find me a bar and a bed for a little while. I'll see y'all in the morning." I turned to go and found a couple of big fairies with big axes looking at me with murder in their eyes.

"Hey guys," I said, "sorry about that whole beating you up thing. No hard feelings?" I stuck out a hand. They both just stared at it. Either the handshake was a foreign concept in Fairyland, or there might have been some hard feelings.

"And just where do you think you're going?" the queen asked from behind me.

I turned back to her. "I thought I should probably get prepared for tomorrow. By drinking a lot. And maybe sleeping. But definitely drinking."

"The only thing you'll be drinking is water, human. And I'll provide you with very secure sleeping quarters. *Very* secure." She nodded to the guards, and they each grabbed an arm.

I shook them off easily, then said, "Look boys, I don't go for the holding my arms and marching me places thing. If you want me to go somewhere, one of you walk in front, one of you walk in back, and we'll go there, easy-peasy. But you put your hands on me again, I'm gonna take those axes away from you and shove them where the sun don't shine. We clear?"

The guards looked at me, then looked at Titania, then back at me. "Your Majesty, would you tell your boys here that it's okay not to manhandle me? Otherwise I'm going to have to break them, and you don't want to replace guards over something this trivial, do you?"

"It's fine," the queen sighed. "Just escort him to the dungeon. Bubba, please don't hurt the guards or try to escape. I find you somewhat amusing, and I would hate to turn you into a frog before you pummel my cousin tomorrow morning."

I nodded at the queen, bowed again, and turned back to my escorts. "Let's go, boys. I can't wait to see what's for dinner. I'm starving."

"The service in this restaurant blows," I grumbled a few hours later. I was in a cell in the dungeon of the castle of Tisa'ron. The cell was pretty clean, as far as dungeons went. Admittedly, it was my first time inside an actual dungeon. I'd seen the inside of drunk tanks, holding cells, even a week in a county jail in Myrtle Beach, SC, after a weekend involving twelve strippers, the UGA defensive line, seventeen cases of beer, eight pounds of weed, and a goat.

Don't ask.

But I'd never been inside an honest-to-God dungeon before. I don't think there are any dungeons left in the U.S. Well, I was damn sure in a dungeon now. Like I said, it was relatively clean, for a jail cell underneath a castle. It was dry, the bunk had a mattress on it, and there were two buckets. One was full of almost clean water, and the other was empty. It didn't take me long to figure out what the empty one was for.

The only real problem I had was the lack of electricity, Wi-Fi, or anything human-sized. Even human-sized stuff is usually too small for me, but since the average height of a grown male fairy seemed to be about five-six, I was a foot taller than the people the bed was made for. I was actually a foot taller than the people the *ceiling* was made for. I didn't quite have to stoop to walk down the central hallway, but the cell itself was at least four inches shorter than I was.

So I sat. Then I laid on the bed for a while with my legs hanging off. After a while of my feet going to sleep, I pulled the mattress off the bed and laid it onto the floor. At least then my feet weren't really dangling. I had just rolled over to try and catch some z's when a voice came out of the darkness.

"Hey mister, are you human?"

"Yeah," I replied.

"But are you a human from here, or from somewhere else?"

"I came from somewhere else," I said. "I came here looking for someone."

"Who are you looking for?"

"A human girl named Tamara. She fell into a trap that Puck set."

"I'm Tamara! Oh, thank God! I thought everyone had given up on me. It's been so long I just assumed everyone had forgotten about me. I'm so glad to hear your voice."

"What do you mean, it's been so long? It's only been about three or four days. I got here two days ago, and I got sucked into Puck's trap the night after you went missing."

"Dude, I don't know what you've been smoking, but I've been in this cage for like almost a month."

"Huh. I read some shit like this in a book once. Time moves differently here than in our world, so it's been a month for you, but only a couple days back home. So you can stay here as long as you want to, and everybody will still be happy to see you when you get home."

"Yeah, I'm sure they'll be thrilled. All my dad will do is bitch about how much money it's gonna cost him to replace my cell phone."

"You don't even have to worry about that. The cops found your phone. You can get it back when I get you home."

"You got a plan for that, genius? In case you missed it, you're locked up in the friggin' dungeon."

"You know, I thought I'd see a little more gratitude, seeing as how I jumped into another dimension to find your snotty little ass."

"Yeah, sure, dude. I'll be grateful as soon as you do something worth a shit, like getting us out of here."

"Us?"

"Yeah, dude. I'm not gonna, like, leave without my girls, right?"

Shit. There are more of them. "This would be a really good time for you to tell me that you're talking about one or two fairy girls you made friends with since you've been in here."

I heard a little snort from the cell. "Yeah, they're about as much fairies as you are, dumbass. There's like half a dozen of us that got kidnapped by that little rat bastard Puck. From all over the country, man. That dude gets around."

"Well, that complicates things, but it doesn't change anything. If I came here to get one human girl out of the dungeon, getting six out shouldn't be any more impossible."

"So what's the plan, Stan? What do we do?"

I laughed a little. "*We* don't do shit. *You* sit in this cell, keep your head down, your mouth shut, and think about how video games rot your brain and get you kidnapped to Fairyland where an evil queen tosses your dumb ass into a dungeon. *I* am going to sleep for a little while, then I'm gonna get up, stretch, do a little warm up like pushups or something, then I'm gonna go out there and beat the holy shit out of the queen's cousin. After that, I'm going to talk the queen into letting all y'all go home."

"How are you going to do that?" A new voice came from the other side of my cell.

"I reckon you're one of the other human girls?" I asked.

"Yes, I'm Emily Mocaten, from Indianapolis. I don't suppose you know if anyone is still looking for me, do you?"

"I'm sure they are, sweetie. Don't you worry about that, I'm gonna get you out of here. I'm gonna get all y'all out of here."

Now if only I had a single clue how I was going to do that.

Chapter Eleven

MORNING CAME TOO EARLY, AND STILL NOT SOON ENOUGH. I stood up to the sound of keys outside my cell and promptly bumped my head on the low ceiling.

"Ow, goddammit."

"Come along, let's go," said the fairy guard outside. He had a bandage over his nose, so I assumed he was one of the ones I met the day before.

"Hang on, I gotta pee," I said, then turned to the empty bucket and did just that. The morning's pressing business attended to, I stepped out of the cell and wiped my hands on the guard's bright green tabard.

"What the hell do you think you're doing?" He jumped back and started to brush at the fabric, then looked at his bare hands and thought better of it.

"This hotel sucks. The bathroom didn't have any towels in it. And the mattress was lumpy. You're really overdue for a renovation." I turned left and walked toward the stairs. As I went, I took some time to peer into each cell I passed. Seven or eight of the ten I walked past each held a single occupant, always a human girl.

"What did they do?" I asked the guard.

"No talking," he barked, poking me in the back.

I stopped dead in my tracks, and he crashed into my back. I whirled around and slammed him into the bars of one cell. I wrapped one hand around his throat and the other around the wrist of his sword arm. I leaned down into his face and spoke, very low and very slow.

"Look here, you irritating little prick. Up there with all your guard buddies, you might be King Shit of Turd Mountain, but down here, you're just the scared little dude who's got a giant breathing in his face. Now answer the damned question before I rip your head off and shit down your neck."

"They are not citizens. They were in the city without papers or badges, so they'll be sold next week."

"Sold?" I didn't know it was possible to get more threatening, but judging by the look on the guard's face, I managed.

"There is an auction in the square once a month. These girls are scheduled to be put on the block next week. I assume they'll be bought as pleasure slaves, but the ugly ones might be bought as lady's maids."

I reckon it's a good thing I'm busting these girls out of here today, then. I put the guard down and motioned for him to walk ahead of me to the stairs.

"I'm not supposed to—"

"I didn't squish your head like a grape. But that doesn't mean I trust you behind me with a sword. Now go." He stared at me for a moment, then he apparently decided that survival is the better part of valor and went down the row of cells and preceded me up the stairs into the wide entryway of the castle.

We walked through the huge foyer and out the front doors; then we were joined by a quartet of other guards. One handed me my sword belt and the blade I got from Puck, not that I expected to use it. Another handed me Bertha in her shoulder holster, along with my Judge revolver in a paddle holster. I checked the pistols, made sure they were both loaded for bear, or in this case, fairy, stuck the Judge in the back of my waistband and strapped on Bertha.

I got my pocketknife back from a third guard, and the last one just looked a little disappointed that I didn't have more shit, so he could have something to do. The four new guards took up position all around me, with the one from the dungeon leading the way.

We walked through the city to the central plaza, where I saw a twenty-foot circle laid out on the cobblestones. Scar stood just outside the circle, flanked by all his bandit fairy buddies. One of them had his arm in a sling, and another one looked like he was having a fair bit of trouble moving. I pegged him for the spellcaster I shot out of the saddle.

"What are the rules of this scrap?" I asked my escort.

"If you keep your mouth shut and your ears open, you might find out."

At least when I make jokes about Skeeter being a pissy fairy, I'm making a damn joke. This pissy fairy didn't have a single scrap of a sense of humor. Maybe I knocked it out of him in the dungeon. I shrugged and took a spot opposite Scar and his cronies outside the circle.

Like a wave, the entire crowd dropped to a knee as Titania entered the square. I went ahead and did it, too, even though the last time I tried it, my knees popped and I ended up scrapping with the whole damn royal guard. She waved for us to stand, and I made it back to my feet without causing an interspecies incident. The queen made a gesture, and the cobblestones shifted and flowed like water into a throne right behind her. A fairy from her entourage placed a cushion on the seat, and she sat down.

I reached up and closed my mouth with my hand. I've been around some magic now and then, but this was *power* like I'd never seen before. I suddenly felt very much out of my league. *Oh well, I'm in it now. Gotta see it 'til the end.*

An old fairy stepped forward, a white-haired man with a Gandalf beard and a walking stick topped with a large yellow crystal. He pounded the walking stick on the stones and began to speak.

"As these two prisoners have committed offenses against the dignity and reputation of the crown, Her Majesty, Titania the Graceful and Kind has decreed that they shall do battle for the entertainment of her citizenry. The combatants shall duel in single combat, with no outside assistance, until one or both of the criminals lies dead."

Shit. It all flashed suddenly clear. She didn't give a single damn that I hurt her cousin, and she gave less of a damn that he was robbing people. But his actions were embarrassing, and I was the first person to be able to whoop his ass. So she was using me to clean up her mess. If I lost, no big deal, I was a human and not one of her subjects that she had to protect. And if I killed Scar, even better, because she was rid of a problem and she didn't have to hurt her relative. This was the very definition of screwed.

"The combatants shall enter the circle, and a magical barrier will surround them. Anyone attempting to cross the barrier while both prisoners live will be destroyed. If either prisoner tries to leave the circle while the other lives, he will be destroyed. If both combatants are still alive after one half hour, both will be destroyed. Prisoners, enter the circle."

I didn't move. Now I not only had to beat Scar's ass, I had to kill him. And I only had thirty minutes to do it. Of course, if he got me in a tight spot with those two swords, I might not last thirty seconds. I let out a deep sigh and stepped into the ring. As soon as Scar and I were both in, a curtain of slightly shimmering light sprang up all around the perimeter of the circle. I was trapped with a pissed-off fairy wielding dual short swords and a whole lot of attitude.

"I don't want to do this, Scar. Talk to your cousin, maybe you can convince her that nobody needs to die today," I said to the fairy.

"Oh, don't worry, human. Someone needs to die, just not me. You embarrassed me in front of my men, and my family. I don't take that lightly. You have a debt to pay, and I intend to collect right now!" He sprang at me, swords whirling. I decided that I didn't want to be wherever he was with those swords, so when he leapt for me, I rolled underneath him, coming to my feet on the other side of the circle.

"Don't make me do this, Scar," I warned him again. He didn't listen, again, just charged me with those +3 spinning blades of redneck chopping. I drew my own sword, and he grinned. He knew there was no world in which I beat him in a sword fight.

I knew it, too, so I threw the sword at his face. He knocked it aside, and when he looked back up at me, I had Bertha pointed straight at him.

"Your human weapon can't hurt me, fool! I'm a prince of the Fae, and I will have your heart!" He charged again.

I shook my head and pulled the trigger. Scar flew back, knocked on his ass by the impact of the biggest damn bullet you can run in a semiautomatic handgun. He stood up, the anger on his face replaced by confusion, then pain. He gave me a questioning look, then fell to his knees. His swords clattered to the ground, and a hush fell over the crowd. A huge red stain spread across his chest, and he knelt there for another couple seconds, then keeled over sideways, stone dead.

The barrier around the circle dropped, and the crowd fell silent. The bandit wizard raised his hands, and I pointed the pistol at him.

"You twitch, and I'll put one in your damn head." He stopped moving.

I turned to the throne and stepped out of the circle. Titania's guards stepped forward to make a wall between us, but I just knelt in front of her, holstering Bertha as I went down.

"Your Majesty, I have solved the problem of bandits on the road to Tisa'ron. I am sorry to report that your cousin did not survive our discussion on the matter."

"You have proven victorious in single combat, Bubba the human. You may go freely within my city as you desire."

"Your Majesty, I would ask a boon for my service." I figured since I was here, I might as well try to get the girls out of the dungeon the easy way.

The corner of the fairy queen's mouth twitched up a little, like she was amused that I would even think of asking her for a favor after killing her cousin right in front of her. But I knew that she wanted me to kill her cousin, so in the movie in my head, she knew that I knew, and she wanted me to keep from telling everyone what I knew, and she certainly didn't want me to tell people that I knew that she knew what I knew, so I knew she'd pay a little price to keep me quiet.

"What is your boon, human?"

"I would ask for the release of the humans in your dungeon. They are not of this world, and I would take them home to their families." I didn't know exactly how this was going to get Puck's girlfriend out, which meant I also didn't know exactly how I was going to accomplish the whole "take them home" part of the plan, but I figured getting the girls out of the dungeon would be a good step.

Titania laughed, and it wasn't an "oh you silly human, of course I'll release everyone in my dungeon into your hands" kind of laugh. It was way more of a "you stupid hairy sack of crap, I wouldn't open my dungeon for you if you promised me a golden carriage drawn by unicorns that shit glitter and piss rainbows."

She looked down at me, even though I was about the same height on one knee as she was sitting on a throne. "Those human children are worth a lot of money to me. Money that I can use for the betterment of my cities, my roads, my kingdom. I would be a terrible ruler if I allowed you to take money out of my coffers and food out of the mouths of my subjects. No, Bubba, I will not release the human children. I will, however, grant you a boon." She motioned to one of her guards, who walked over to me and handed me the pack I had with me when I entered the castle. The pack I'd taken off her cousin's men when I beat their asses. Her boon was giving me back my own stolen shit. This woman was more conniving than a Las Vegas stripper. And hotter.

I took my pack and slung it over my shoulder, then took a step forward. "Your Majesty—"

She raised a hand to silence me. And it worked. Well, the hand made me pause. The six guards with crossbows that stepped out of the crowd at her gesture made me stop.

"Choose your next words carefully, human. They may very well be your last."

I dipped my head. "I thank Your Majesty for your gracious gift and for giving me freedom to explore your fair city."

She put her hand down and smiled a wry little half-smile. "I am glad to see that we understand each other." Titania rose from her throne, which melted back into the stones of the plaza at a gesture. Then she turned and walked away, just like nothing ever happened. Four guardsmen walked over to Scar, picked up the body, and took it to a cart waiting nearby. I guess they knew it was going to have a passenger today, no matter who.

The crowd dispersed, vendors going back to their shops and stalls, shoppers going back to their shopping, guardsmen going back to their guarding, children going back to their urchining. Within a couple minutes, the only people left in the square were me and Scar's crew.

They were a confused bunch, milling around mumbling at each other, glaring at me, and generally looking like they had no idea what to do next. Every so often, one of them would look at me with a scowl, then go back to talking with his buddies. I'd seen this shit before, in every redneck bar in the world. They were trying to talk themselves into enough of a frenzy to come at me.

Well, screw every bit of that. I stomped over to the lot of them, looked at the biggest one of them, then popped him right in the jaw with a big right hook. He went down like his strings had been cut, and I turned to the wizard.

"You in charge?" I asked. I knew that just by asking him that, I put him in charge. And he was probably the smartest surviving member, so he's who I wanted to deal with.

"Yes, I am," he replied. He opened his mouth to continue, but I backhanded him across the mouth. He spun around and dropped to his ass.

"I assume I have everyone's attention?" I asked. "Now here's the deal. I whooped y'all's asses on the road, and your boy Scar decided he wanted to throw his semi-royal weight around and cause trouble for me. What he didn't figure on was his cousin being a lot damn smarter than him, so she used me to get rid of an embarrassing problem. Now Scar's dead."

I pointed to the wizard. "This dude says he's in charge, and that's fine. I don't give a damn who's in charge of your little bunch of dumbasses. All I care about is this—y'all leave me the hell alone. If I ever see any damn one y'all again, I will beat you so bad your own mama won't recognize you. And if you try to ambush me, or throw magic at me, or shoot me with a damn arrow? Then I will put a cold iron bullet between your eyes and drop you deader than I did Scar. Are we clear?"

I looked around the circle, and every eye met mine, and every head nodded like a bobblehead on the dashboard. "Good. Now I'm gonna go about my business, and I suggest you go about yours. And go about it some damn where else."

I turned and stomped off, heading to the one place I knew I could find some peace, comfort, and people that didn't want to kill me on sight. I took my happy ass to the nearest bar.

Chapter Twelve

I STEPPED INTO THE TAVERN, AND IT WAS LIKE ALL MY TROUBLES melted away. In times of great stress, and a significant amount of ass-kicking, there are few things in life that will relax a man like copious quantities of alcohol. And boobies. But now that I'm in a committed relationship with a woman who shoots straighter than me, can kick my ass, and has the authority to send me to Gitmo, my time at strip clubs is severely curtailed.

That, and I don't even know if they have titty bars in Fairyland. I mean, if they don't, what's the point? It begs an existential question—if you don't have strip clubs, how do single fairy moms make a living? And where do ballet dancers go to get jobs when they grow up? And what will all the fairy women with daddy issues do? But that's beside the point because I didn't step into a fairy strip club, I stepped into a fairy *bar*.

This was a place for serious day-drinking. This is where the professionals went, the men who woke up in the morning, rolled out of the gutter, wiped the chunks of last night's party off their chests, and headed straight back into the ring for more punishment. This was the kind of establishment that served so many drinks before lunch in the name of "hair of the dog" that you wondered if there was a single scrap of hair left on a dog in a ten-block radius. In short, it was my kind of place.

It was dark, so dark that when I first walked in, the only things I could make out were the coals glowing in the fireplace and the light emanating from the whiskey bottles behind the bar. I went straight for the booze like a moth to a flame, stubbing my toe on a chair that I didn't see and bumping into a table that I didn't see. I heard an angry shout from beside me and saw a shadowy form lurch to its feet at my right elbow. I reached out with my fist and thumped the outraged fairy on the head, and he collapsed back into his chair.

My eyes had adjusted by the time I reached the bar, and I nodded at the stocky bald fairy who stood there, bar rag in hand, polishing a metal tankard. I wasn't sure which was dirtier, the tankard or the rag, but I didn't really care. I've found in my life that alcohol makes a really good disinfectant.

"Whiskey," I said, pulling a ring from the purse at my hip. I placed the ring on the bar, and the bartender walked over.

"What's this?" He picked it up and examined it closely. He placed the band between his teeth and bit down, nodded, and put it back on the bar.

"Payment," I said. "How much will that buy me?"

"Two bottles, four meals, and my best room for two nights. Plus, all the beer you can drink, if you're of a mind not to drink whiskey."

"Done. Give me one bottle now, and keep the beer coming." I took the shot glass and the bottle and made my way over to a table in a corner away from the fire. I try not to sit too close to the fireplace in bars. It's not that I start fights. I really don't. But there's a certain segment of every bar population that likes to fight, and those people very often want to start fights with *me*, so I have to end a lot of fights. And if I happen to do that ending too close to open flames, it ends with people getting hurt. Or buildings burning to the ground. Or sometimes even really bad things, like spilling my drink.

I sat with my back against a wall in a corner opposite the fire and downed a couple of shots in quick succession. The fairy liquor was strong, and I felt the ache in my muscles from trying to sleep on a fairy-size cot ease almost immediately. A cute little fairy girl in a flouncy top brought me a beer and leaned forward a little more than was necessary to deliver it. I took note of the fact that the top wasn't the only flouncy thing she had going on but turned my attention to my drinking. Remember, committed relationship to a woman who is an expert marksman.

I sat there drinking and watching the room for about an hour until the barmaid came back with another beer and a tray laden down with meat, cheese, and bread. None of it was terribly exciting food, but it was very tasty, and just basically a solid, well-prepared meal. Nothing to write home about, but nothing to complain about, either.

I made some small talk with the barmaid, who became a little more honestly friendly when she realized that I would tip her even without the cleavage and I wasn't going to put my hands on her. I even wandered back up to the bar as the afternoon dragged on, and I had no better idea than when I walked in how I was supposed to get into the castle. The bar was a long wraparound affair with most of its length facing the door but a couple of shorter segments at right angles to the entrance, so if I took up a spot in one corner of the bar, I was not only far enough away from the fireplace and the postage-stamp-sized stage where a bard was tuning his lute, I was also somewhere I could put my back to a wall.

Which became much more important the further into the bottle of fairy whiskey I got. For a bunch of little bastards, they brewed some strong damn liquor. I only had about half the bottle, but I was as close to tore up as I'd been since the first Lynyrd Skynyrd reunion tour.

The bar started to fill up after lunch, and I sat in my corner chair with my back pressed against the wall and some moderate level of equilibrium achieved, and started to quiz the barkeep.

"Have you ever been inside the castle?" I asked, trying to keep my voice casual.

"Yup," he said, wiping down the bar. I reckon being a bartender means you've always got something to do with your hands because everyone I've ever known spent as much time polishing the top of the bar as they did pouring drinks.

"How did you get in?"

"Through the front gate, how else?"

"Yeah, that's the problem. Those dumbass guards won't let me in."

"Why not?"

"I might have killed the Queen's cousin this morning. And now, even though I killed the little bastard at her unspoken but very politically savvy request, she can't allow herself to be seen giving me any favor. She can't just randomly have me killed because I won the duel fair and square, but the thieving little shitball was royal blood, so she has to at least act like the whole thing wasn't her idea. Regardless of the fact that it was all her idea."

"I'm not sure I follow, friend."

"You can call me Bubba," I said with a magnanimous wave of my hand. My magnanimity might have been a little poorly timed since my hand was holding a tankard of beer, a fair amount of which sloshed right in the bartender's face.

"Sorry," I said.

He stood there, not moving for a long moment. Then he shook his head and wiped his face with the bar rag. "Don't worry about it. But I'm not giving you any more booze."

"That's fair," I agreed. "What about when I get sober?"

"You get sober, and we can talk about more booze then."

"What about when the bard starts to play? He looks like the type that requires a lot of alcohol to appreciate."

"When he starts, I'll start drinking with you," the barkeep said.

"Fair enough. Now about the castle..."

"What were you saying about trying to break into the castle?" There was suddenly a new voice beside me. I had been pretty focused on the barkeep, and just about drunk enough to only be able to focus on one thing at a time, so I didn't notice that the guy sitting on the other side of the bar so as not to put his back to the door was a castle guard.

I have never been the most discreet or restrained person. Add a little whiskey, and I become somewhat less restrained. Add a lot of magical Fairyland whiskey, and the whole idea of restraint goes right out the window.

"I was asking the bartender, in a private damn conversation, mind you, if he knew a back way into the castle, or if he knew which ones of you dumb bastards could be bribed into letting me into the castle. There's somebody in the dungeon I need to bust loose."

He looked at me like a dog that caught a car and now didn't have a damn idea what to do with it. "You're admitting to one of the Guard that you are planning to break into the castle and free a prisoner from Her Majesty's dungeon, and that you intend to bribe a guard to do it?"

"I know you asked that like it was a question, but was there a question there?" I asked.

The guard went from confused to pissed off in a couple seconds. I have that effect on people sometimes. "You're under arrest. Come with me."

"No."

"What?"

"No. I ain't going with you, and ain't none of you sawed-off bastards able to make me."

"You should look again, human," the guard said, and he stood up. And up. And up.

"What the hell are you, part troll?" I asked, staring at the seven-foot guard standing in front of me. Through my beer goggles, I realized that he didn't have the fine features of every other fairy, but looked like he'd been carved out of rough granite. He had a thick brow and a jaw that stuck out with a pair of short fangs curling over his lip. He was huge, not just tall, but big, too, and had fists the size of coconuts.

"Half ogre, asshole. And you're under arrest. Now come with me and I won't have to hurt you."

"Okay, okay," I said, holding up both hands. "I mean, hell, I wanted to get into the castle anyway, right? This is probably the most efficient way."

I stood up off my barstool and promptly lurched left, staggered over to a table, flopped belly-first onto the table, and belched loudly. The two fairies sitting at the table sprang up and bolted for the exit, and in the confusion, I stood up, grabbed one of the chairs, and broke it to kindling over the guard's head.

He took a step back, shook his head to clear the cobwebs, and punched me in the gut. I dropped like a boulder to the floor, hitting my hands and knees and trying not to puke. Ogre-boy yanked me up by the back of my collar, and I sprang forward, burying my shoulder in his gut and crashing him into the bar.

He thumped both fists into my spine, and I almost went down again, but when he reared back to do it again, I jerked back and stood up quick, nailing him on the point of his chin with the chair leg I still clutched in one hand. I swung that chair leg like I was Babe Ruth calling my shot, and his eyes rolled back into his head and he collapsed.

I looked around the now-empty bar and grinned at the stunned fairy standing there holding his rag staring at me. I tossed him another ring from my purse and grinned. "Sorry about the table, buddy. But no worries about helping me get into the castle. I got it figured out."

Chapter Thirteen

A COUPLE OF MINUTES LATER, I STEPPED OUT OF THE BAR, TUGGING at the tabard on my new guard uniform. Or the parts of the uniform I'd stolen, anyway. I didn't take all of the dude's clothes, just his mail shirt, the tabard, his gloves, helmet, and sword belt. I felt a little bad leaving the belt and sheath Puck gave me behind, but I jammed his sword into the guard's belt and hoped nobody would call me on the different hilt.

Instead of walking along the edge of the crowd like I'd done since I got into Tisa'ron, this time I almost strutted down the middle of walkway, expecting everyone to get out of my way. And they did—they scattered like rats in front of this giant in a guard uniform. Nobody even noticed that my hauberk was a little too long in the sleeves because nobody stayed in my way long enough to notice.

I walked through the gates of the castle without anyone even looking at me twice, just nodding as I walked past. I made it all the way to the keep before anyone challenged me. I was in the entryway just about to turn and head down the stairs to the dungeon when a voice hailed me.

"Torg! What are you doing back? I thought you'd be knee-deep in a game of dice or cards by now!" The cheery fairy quick-walked over to me, clapped me on the back, then froze as he looked at my face.

"Who are—" I punched him in the face, holding onto his belt as his eyes rolled back in his head. He sagged into my arms, and I looked around the foyer, wondering if I was just going to end up in the dungeon the old-fashioned way. We were alone, so I threw him over one shoulder and hauled him down the stairs with me. I set the unconscious guard on a landing halfway down to the dungeon, patted him on the head, and used his sword belt to tie his feet together. Hopefully it would slow him down just enough for me to get free, and he wouldn't fall down the stairs and break his neck.

I walked down the steps like I owned the place and never paused as I walked between the two guards at the bottom of the steps. I walked over to where the keys hung on the wall and picked them up, turning to the cell that held Tamara. I kept my face down as much as I could, hoping that I could avoid a fight with the four guards in the dungeon.

"What are you doing, Torg?" a guard sitting at a table playing cards with his buddy asked.

"Queen wants to see this one," I said, trying to pitch my voice into the low rumble that Torg had.

"For what? She's to be sold at dawn."

"I don't ask questions. I just do as I'm told," I said.

"I can't let you in there, Torg," his buddy said, and for the first time, I noticed the gold braid on his uniform. *Well, at least I know who's in charge, and it ain't my old buddy Torg.*

The sergeant, or whatever Gold Braid was, came over to me and reached for the keys. He froze when he saw my face. "You're not Torg," he said.

Shit. Oh well, it was mostly a good plan. I grabbed Gold Braid by the front of his tabard and yanked him around into the bars, slamming his face into the steel. He didn't go down, so I did it a couple more times until his nose *crunched* into a flat mass, and with one more slam against the bars, he passed out.

I dropped Gold Braid, tossed the keys to Tamara, and said, "Get yourself and the other girls free. I'll take care of the guards, and then we'll get the hell out of here."

I turned to the other guards, trying to figure out exactly how I was going to take out three armed guards in a small dungeon without killing anybody. This was not going to be pretty.

The other guard at the table was halfway out of his chair when I charged him. My forehead caught him under the chin, and he went over backwards, chair and all. I sprawled on top of him, driving him into the floor and crushing the air out of him with a *whoof!* I pushed myself up to my hands and knees and smashed my elbow into his face a couple of times until his eyes rolled back in his head.

With booted feet rushing my way, I scrambled upright and grabbed the guard's helmet off the table. I flung it at the first guard, who ducked. In a moment right out of a slapstick comedy movie, the helmet nailed the second guard right in the face. It clanged off his helmet, and he went down flat on his back just like he'd been clotheslined.

The odds were suddenly even, but I was still way more hampered by the close quarters than the guard. Of course, he was a fairy and could actually stand all the way upright, so he had that going for him. He also carried a sword like he knew how to use it, which was way more than anyone could say for me. I grabbed a thick broadsword from a downed guard and fended off his strokes as best I could. I parried a couple with the blade, then stepped back to get out of his reach. Of course, I stepped right on the chest of the guard I tackled, and I went over backwards like a redwood, if redwoods have a shitload of tattoos and swear a lot.

I landed flat on my back and lost my sword and my wind at the same time. My head thumped into the stone floor, and my eyes crossed. I hadn't taken a lick like that since I played for the Bulldogs. Or training with Amy, but she didn't pull any punches. I lay there for a second trying to clear my vision and get those damn birds whirling around my head to shut up, then rolled over just in time to not get my head cleaved in two. The guard's sword drew sparks from the stones he swung so hard, and I smelled the unfortunately familiar and never-pleasant scent of singed beard hair.

I lashed out with one leg, catching him in the knee and making it bend backward. I had to hand it to him, he didn't go down and cracked that sword down across my thigh, making me very glad I decided to take the thigh guards off of Torg after I beat his ass. I still felt that strike way down deep in my leg, and I knew I was going to limp for a couple days. I rolled back the other way and spun to my feet in a really, really clumsy version of fat white breakdance. I really only made it to one knee, then launched myself at the guard when I got to that one knee, bulling past his guard and planting my shoulder right in his solar plexus. I straightened my legs and picked him up, running to the far wall and ramming him into it like he was a tackling dummy. Or an ACC quarterback, which are really the same thing to a defensive player in the SEC.

I ran into the wall with a full head of steam and a guard in a tin can as my cushion. I heard a bunch of cracking sounds from his ribcage, a hollow *bong* as his helmet slammed into the stones, and a loud *pop* from my shoulder as it dislocated. I collapsed to my knees, really hoping that I'd just smeared the last of the fight out of this dude like jelly on peanut butter.

I looked around to see if anybody was actively trying to kill me, and it all looked good. The four guards were out, but the one who took a helmet to the face was starting to stir.

"Tamara," I called out.

"Yes?" came the tremulous reply.

"I need you to get a couple of the girls and drag the guards into a cell. Take their weapons and tie them up, then lock the cell. Make sure you gag them, too."

"Can you help us? What if they wake up?"

"If they wake up, hit them with something heavy. I can't help you right now. I have to put my shoulder back in the socket."

"Oh, let me help you," one of the other girls said. "I took first aid in school, and they taught us how to do this."

"Did you take it in this decade?" I asked.

"I'm seventeen, I took it six months ago."

"That's a lot better than the last time I took first aid. Come on over here."

She came over, an athletic looking girl with a long brown ponytail and a deep tan. "I'm Elle," she said. "This is going to hurt."

"Everything always hurts, kid. It's kinda my job."

"You should look for a better job," she said. "Now give me your sword belt and lie down on your stomach on the table."

I did as she instructed, and she wrapped the belt around my wrist and buckled it. Then she slid on her back underneath the table and grabbed the belt. "Okay, I'm going to start pulling on 'three.' Ready?"

"Yeah."

"One...two..." She pulled on my wrist right after the "two," and it felt like somebody stabbed me in the shoulder. But after a few seconds, I felt a *thunk*, and my shoulder slipped back into the socket.

"That was mean," I said, standing up and rubbing my shoulder.

"Yeah, well, I'm a teenager, I'm supposed to be terrible." She grinned and got to her feet. She handed me back my sword belt and said, "You really should wear a sling until you can see a doctor, though."

"This is my sword arm," I replied. "And my gun hand. I think those are two things you all want me to have access to if we run into any more guards before we get out of here."

"You mean guards like that one?" the girl asked, pointing toward the stairs. The guard I knocked out and left on the stairs was standing at the door, his mouth hanging open. I drew Bertha, wincing at the weight of the gun. I really hated to think how bad it was gonna hurt if I actually had to shoot anything. I wouldn't put good odds on me keeping hold of my gun for a second shot.

"Don't move," I called out. The guard's eyes snapped to mine, and then to the barrel of the gun. "You saw what this did to Scar earlier, right?"

"Scar?"

"The queen's cousin, the royal asshole I killed in the circle this morning."

"Oh yes, Chauvan. I saw."

"Good. So you know what it will do to you, right?"

"I do."

"Then take off your sword, put your hands in the air, and go join those nice fellows in the cell. Tamara, tie him up."

The second she got within arm's reach of him, it all went to shit. He grabbed the girl and, using her as a shield, ran for the stairs.

"Sonofabitch!" I shouted. "Get your pointy-eared ass back here!"

The guard wasn't listening. Just trying to make it to the stairs before I killed his ass. But he didn't count on the fighting spirit of one Tennessee teenager who had been taken away from her whole world, jammed in a cell, and told she was going to be sold into slavery. Not to mention made to pee in public and spend days on end without a working cell phone. Little Tamara was *pissed.*

She bit down on the guard's hand, locking her teeth into his palm right in the webbing between his thumb and forefinger. He turned his attention to her, and the second he looked down at her, she jabbed her fingers at his eyes. He jerked his head back, but he had to separate a little from the girl to get out of range. She raked his cheeks with her nails, leaving four bloody furrows down one cheek. He dropped her completely, so she turned around and rammed her knee right in his balls.

That would have been way more effective if he wasn't wearing armor. As it was, she kneed him right in the chain mail overskirt, which still wasn't comfortable, but didn't have quite the effect she was looking for. What it did have, however, was a hell of a motivating effect on her fellow prisoners.

The other five girls swarmed the guard like frat boys on a free keg, and he went down under an avalanche of flailing fists, elbows, and knees. One girl mounted the side of his head and started laying in knee strikes like Ronda

Rousey's pissed off baby sister, while a tall black girl stood over him with his ankle in both hands and one foot planted in his crotch. She just stood there, grinding one foot into his jewels and twisting his foot almost off with both hands.

They beat that poor guard until I reckoned he didn't have a spot on him that wasn't bruised, scratched, bloodied, or downright broken. He finally passed out, and I hollered for them to stop.

"That's enough fun for one night," I said in my best "coach voice." "Now throw him in the cell with the others and let's get the hell out of here."

Then I remembered Puck and his girlfriend. I looked around at all the cells. They all stood empty except for the one full of unconscious or pissed off guards. "Was there anybody else here with y'all?" I asked Tamara.

"No, nobody."

"Is there another dungeon?"

"Not that I know of, but the others have been here longer." I turned to the other girls, but they all shook their heads "no."

"Well, shit," I said. "Oh well, let's get y'all out of here, and I'll figure out the rest when it comes to it." I sent one of the smaller girls up the stairs to scout ahead, and when she came back with the all-clear, we walked up the stairs and out the front gate of the keep. We were almost to the front gates when one guard cocked his head to the side, then leaned over to the man next to him, obviously asking him a question.

"Run!" I yelled, and we hauled ass out the gate before the guards got their shit together enough to drop the portcullis. I laid one out with a tackle, and almost went down myself as my shoulder exploded in pain. Tamara helped he back to my feet, and we burst through the gates into the night.

Free! For the moment, at least. We still had to get out of the city gates, and we had every guard in Tisa'ron after us now. And I was in no shape to fight, so we were probably going to have to rely on our wits to get us out.

We were all doomed.

Chapter Fourteen

We barreled down the city streets, ducking between carts and pedestrians and generally upsetting anyone we came in contact with. If we wanted to get out of town without being noticed, this was not the way to do it. After a few blocks, one of the smaller girls wove her way to the front of the pack and motioned for us to follow her.

"I've been here longer than anyone else. I know the quickest way to the gates!"

Tamara motioned for the rest of the girls to follow, and we all did as we were told. I ran through the streets of the capitol city of the Summer Court of the Fair Folk with half a dozen human refugees, dodging guard patrols and ducking into alleys when we had to, hauling ass for the gates whenever we could.

I felt like a year, but was probably more like half an hour, when the gates finally loomed into view. I waved all the girls into a nearby alley so we could catch our breath and plan for a second before trying to make our final escape.

As soon as we were far enough down the alley to be hidden from the street, I started stripping off armor, almost dropping to my knees when I tried to take the mail hauberk off. "Can one of y'all give me a hand with this thing?" I asked, gritting my teeth in pain.

The girl who put my shoulder back in place, Elle, and the girl who led us to the gates came over and tugged on my sleeves, pulling and yanking until the chain mail shirt was lying in a heap on the ground with the guard's tabard and helmet I'd stolen. I sat down on a nearby crate and tried to catch my breath. Sweat rolled down my face from the pain and exertion of getting out of armor with a bum shoulder.

"Why did you take your armor off?" Tamara asked. "We might still have to fight to get out of here."

"We probably will," I said, slipping into my shoulder holster. It had been tucked under my tabard, but now Bertha was just hanging out in the open for anyone to see. Oh well, it's not like I wasn't also wearing a friggin' *sword*, so anyone in line of sight of me would know I was ready to throw down.

"But if I'm dressed like the biggest guard they have, and obviously *not* a half-ogre, then there's no chance we get past the guards without a fight. A fight that I'm not sure I can win without killing a lot of people, which I'd rather avoid. So I'll try to pass myself off as a traveler instead, which gives us maybe a three percent chance of not having to fight our way out of the city. But that's two and a half percent more than we'd have with me in that armor. Not to mention the fact that it's heavy as shit and my shoulder is killing me."

"I've got some ibuprofen." Tamara reached into her pocket and handed me a couple of brown pills.

"Screw ibuprofen, I've got some Vicodin," Elle said. I raised an eyebrow at her. "Shut up, I get migraines. Take the stupid pills." She dug around in her purse for a minute, then tossed me a translucent orange pill bottle. I shook out two Vicodin and dry-swallowed them with the ibuprofen.

"Great, gimme a bottle of Jack Daniels and I'll be ready for the Guns N' Roses reunion tour," I said, getting to my feet. I cut a triangle out of the tabard and turned it inside out to form a makeshift sling. I put it over my head, then slipped my right arm into it. It still hurt, but the constant pounding was reduced to a dull throb once I got it immobilized somewhat. I drew Bertha, ejected the magazine of silver rounds, and slapped in the magazine of alternating white phosphorous and regular rounds. I left the silver round in the chamber, mostly because I couldn't pull the slide back without help. I cocked my girl and slid the safety on, thanking my stars that the Desert Eagle had an ambidextrous safety.

After a couple of minutes, when I was recovered enough from dealing with my armor and my shoulder, I wiped the sweat off my face with the remaining scraps of the guard uniform and stood up. "Let's roll. When we get to the gates, let me do the talking." I really hoped I managed to do some good talking because my fighting and shooting was going to be pretty subpar for a while.

There wasn't a ton of traffic leaving the city, but we tucked in behind a pair of big carts loaded with bags and crates. The guards gave the carts a quick look, then waved them on through. I started after, and the girls were right on my heels when the guards lowered their halberds, forming a barricade.

"Halt." A smaller unarmed fairy with a pointy beard and a mustache waxed into long curlicues strutted up to me. His head barely reached my elbow, and by the look on his face, I knew we were screwed. I've had issues my whole life with short people in authority hating me on sight, just for being huge. This looked like it was going to be another one of those days.

"Where exactly do you band of rabble think you're going?" the snotty little man said, pulling a sneer so extreme he looked like a refugee from a Billy Idol cover band.

Tamara stepped forward, her head bowed. "Pardon us, sir, we're just heading out to pick berries for our Master Pudge the Baker, sir." She put a groveling note into her voice that put a smile on the little fairy's face and made my eyes go wide.

This smart-assed little kid managed to suck it up and play meek and mild? The least I could do was follow her lead. I stood there, silent and as stupid-looking as I could manage. Most people would say it wasn't much of a stretch.

"What about this great oaf? He looks too dim to know a blueberry from nightshade." He was right, of course, but it didn't make me want to pop his head like a zit any less.

Tamara laughed, but kept her eyes downcast. "Oh, you're right, sir. Olaf doesn't pick berries; he just stands guard. Look at how big he is, and he's strong as a horse, too."

"Looks like his arm is hurt. How much guarding can he do like that?" the guard asked.

"Oh, he's still strong enough with his other hand to hurt somebody. See? Olaf, pick me up." She pointed to her belt, and I reached down with my left hand and hoisted her into the air without any effort at all. I set her down, keeping my right arm pressed tight against my chest to keep Bertha from falling out of my makeshift sling and raising questions I could only answer with a ton of bullets and bloodshed.

"Alright," the guard said. "I suppose you're fine. Go on through, but try to keep a small basket of berries for me...wait a moment."

And that's when it all went to shit. The second the guards realized that we were "going out to pick berries" without a single basket or bucket between the seven of us was the same time that a breathless castle guard rounded the corner half a block behind us and started shouting about prisoners and escaping, and all sorts of really unpleasant accusations. All of which were true, of course, but still unpleasant.

One guard hit the release on the portcullis, and the one nearest me reached for his sword. I drew Bertha and rapped the butt of the big pistol across his forehead, making his helmet ring like a bell and his knees buckle. I grabbed his halberd and jammed the blade into the door behind him, effectively locking his buddies in the guard tower for a few seconds at least.

Tamara kicked Waxed Mustache right in the sweets and followed that up with an elbow strike to the back of the head. She looked up at me and grinned. I raised an eyebrow.

"What?" she said, plastering an innocent look on her face. "A girl can't like UFC? Come on, redneck, Conor MacGregor's *hot*. And a badass."

"Well, Little Miss Badass, we better get the hell out of here before the rest of the guards get through that door." The rest of the girls had already swarmed the other guard and taken him down. He apparently hadn't wanted to draw his sword on a passel of little girls, and he got a quick lesson in girl power when they beat his ass for him. We all bolted back into the city, passing through the city square at a dead run.

We had half a dozen guards hot on our heels when I spotted a familiar sign hanging off to our right. "In here!" I shouted, then slammed open the door to the pub where I'd spent most of the day. The second the last girl was through the door, I slammed it shut and barred it with the board leaning on the wall.

I turned to the bartender, who stood behind the bar, still polishing a glass. For all I knew, it was the same glass he was polishing that morning when I walked in. I hustled over to the bar and leaned on it.

"We need a back way out," I said, looking around. No guards, at least. We had that much going for us for once.

"Don't have one," was the laconic reply.

"Every bar has a back way out," I argued.

"Not this one," he said, implacable.

"Come on," I pushed. "The guards will be here in minutes, and if they find us in here, it'll be a bigger mess than the last time I was here."

"Find that hard to believe. That chair cost me ten crowns. And I had to get a man in here to fix the table. Not to mention how hard it is to get blood out of hardwood floors."

I looked around. The floor was dotted everywhere I looked with bloodstains, beer stains, and stains of an origin I neither recognized nor wanted to think about. I pointed to the spot where I left the guard lying a few hours before. "You just threw sawdust on it. You didn't even try to get the stain up." Sure enough, there was a light sprinkling of sawdust over the spot, barely enough to even call a token effort.

"That's step one. It takes several treatments to return the floor to its previous luster." He said it with a straight face, I had to give him credit for that.

Tamara hopped up on the bar and then to her feet. A dagger materialized in her hands from somewhere, and I realized she must have taken it off of Waxed Mustache back at the gate. And why not? When you're going to be either sold into slavery or hanged for escaping the dungeon and assaulting the queen's guard, what's a little petty theft but the cherry on top?

"Show us to the back door, or I'll gut you like a fish." She glared down at the bartender, who set his glass and rag down at last.

Then he blurred into motion, and the next thing I knew, Tamara was lying on her back flat on the bar, and the barkeep was holding the knife at her throat. He stared down at her for a long moment with the same emotionless expression he'd worn ever since I first saw him some seven hours before, then he flipped the knife over in his hand and handed to her, hilt-first.

"Put that away before somebody gets hurt, child. I said there wasn't a back door, and there isn't. But there is a way out, although you won't like it."

"Is it better than being dead?" Tamara asked.

"Yes."

"Better than being sold into slavery to some Winter Court fae or other creature?"

"Yes."

"Better than being locked up in a dungeon?"

"Probably, but it's a near thing."

"We'll take out chances. Now lead us to it before the guards break down that door and Bubba turns every piece of furniture you own into kindling."

He stared at the girl again, then held out his hand. She took his hand and slid down off the bar. The bartender waved for us to follow him and went through a door on the far side of the bar. Tamara went first, then the rest of the girls. I brought up the rear, just in case our pursuers caught up to us before we were safely away.

We all clustered in a small storeroom behind the bar, piled high with kegs, empty and full, as well as dozens of liquor bottles, wine casks, and boxes of assorted dry goods. The bartender knelt in the center of the room and pressed with both hands on the floor. I heard a loud *click*, and a section of floor about two feet by four feet sprang up slightly. Our host pulled the planking up and exposed a hole leading into blackness underneath the bar. I leaned over the hole, and a stink wafted up that almost knocked me down.

"Holy shit, that stinks!" I exclaimed, stepping back.

"Good nose," our laconic guide said. "Them's the sewers. Follow the flow of the water and you'll come out on the other side of the city walls. Drops out into a drainage pond about a half mile south of the city. I wouldn't fill up a canteen out of that pond if I was you."

"I'll keep that in mind," I said, weighing the options of fighting our way through the entire city guard with one bad arm against wading through miles of sewer and probably not fighting anything worse than my own delicate sensibilities. Not having any delicate sensibilities, the choice was pretty easy.

"Get down the ladder, girls. The faster you get all the way down in it, the sooner you'll quit noticing the stink."

"Is that for real?" Elle asked.

"Nah, it's total bullshit," I replied. "But the sooner we all get down that ladder, the sooner we're the hell out of this city." She nodded and swung her legs out into the hole. She climbed down the ladder, and a few seconds later, we heard the slight splash of her dropping into the water.

"Oh my god, that's *disgusting!*" she called up to us. "It stinks *so* bad down here, I can't even! And it's super dark, too. Does anybody have a flashlight?"

"I don't think there's a flashlight within a thousand miles, or at least not in this dimension," I said. I turned to the barkeep. "Torches?"

He gave a little shrug and passed me a fistful of long candles and a few matches. "Be careful of fire. Sometimes the gas collects down there. Try not to get blowed up."

"I'll do my best." I passed the candles and matches to Tamara, who was the only girl remaining. All the rest were in the sewer already, remarking on the stench and speculating on what was bumping into their legs. I never knew there were that many words for poop, much less that a bunch of teenage girls would know them.

“Thanks,” I said to the bartender.

“That little scar-faced bastard took advantage of my cousin. Had his way with her and then walked away, leaving her with a son and no husband. And she wasn’t the first or last. He deserved to die for that, if nothing else. And I don’t like slavery.” He pulled his collar aside to show me a gnarled line of scar where he’d worn a collar at one time. I shook his hand and descended into the stink. It’s one thing to take a trip to Fairyland, but having to walk around in its sewers is another thing altogether. But there I was, ankle-deep in shit again.

Chapter Fifteen

IT WAS DARKER THAN THE INSIDE OF AN ELEPHANT'S ASSHOLE IN THE sewers of Tisa'ron, and smelled worse. The girls were troupers, though, and after a chain-reaction pukefest, they pulled their shirts up over their noses and trudged on through. Tamara and Elle managed to keep the candles lit by holding them high in the air, and I walked point with Bertha swinging in my left hand. I didn't have a lot of faith in my ability to actually hit anything farther away than my nose, but I also thought the big bang my girl made would be a pretty good deterrent for anything that might be lurking in the shadows. Or worse, the water. Because anything that could survive the stuff we were walking through was way tougher than me.

"Hey, Bubba?"

I looked down and one of the girls was looking up at me. She was about sixteen, with long brown, curly hair that kinda frizzed out of a ponytail. I could barely make out a smattering of freckles across her button nose, and I instantly felt all big-brothery towards her.

"Yeah, kid? What's up?"

"Maddie."

"Huh?"

"My name. It's Maddie. But that's not really important right now, I guess. Um...so I was wondering...I saw that other gun in your belt, and . . . well, my dad taught me how to shoot when I was pretty young, so..."

"You want to carry the backup piece?" I asked.

"Yeah, I do. I'll walk at the back, so if anything comes up behind us, I can at least have a chance of defending myself, and the others."

"I don't know, I mean, I'm sure your dad taught you well and all, but for a little gun, this one packs a pretty good punch, and I don't want—"

"If you say you don't want me to hurt myself, I'll take that pistol and shove it up your butt." I took another look at her and was surprised at the fierce expression on her face.

"Okay, what do you really know about guns?" I asked. I put Bertha in my right hand and reached behind my back for my backup pistol. I clumsily worked my Judge revolver from the paddle holster and brought it around in front of me. That rig was not designed for a left-handed draw, and I was lucky I didn't shoot my butt cheek off.

I held the pistol up to catch a little of the flickering light. "This is a Judge revolver," I started. "It can hold two different types of ammunition—"

She interrupted me again. It would be annoying as hell if she wasn't so impressive. "It holds forty-five long pistol bullets or four-ten shotgun shells. Most people use double-ought buckshot in the shotgun shells and call it 'the carjack gun,' but people who want a less lethal option load it with birdshot rounds. The revolver holds any combination of five rounds, and I'd expect you to alternate three shotgun shells with two bullets. Right?"

"That's pretty good, but for this trip I'm actually running five shotgun shells, all loaded with silver birdshot. Any idea why?"

She thought for a few seconds, then admitted, "I have no idea."

"Good. That shows you're not a complete wiseass. I thought there was slim chance I was investigating a mundane kidnapping, and I might need to shoot somebody and leave them alive. There aren't a whole lot of ways to do that with a Desert Eagle. A fifty-caliber bullet to the arm is going to blow that arm clean off, and whoever you shoot is probably dead. With birdshot, I can make somebody regret a lot of their decisions and still leave them alive to think on it. I went with silver shot because most things that aren't mundane really don't like silver. Of course fairies are the exception to that rule. They don't mind silver at all. But nothing *likes* getting shot, even if it doesn't kill it. And you're right, it'll give you a few more seconds than you'd have without it." I handed her the pistol, and she grinned up at me.

"Thank you," she said. "I didn't even have to talk about dad being an Olympic marksman." She grinned at me and dropped back to serve as rear guard. Elle went with her to make sure there was light at both ends of the group.

We trudged through the sewer for what felt like hours until we came to a big junction where a bunch of pipes came together into a circular pool. I held up my hand, and everybody stopped.

"Okay," I said, keeping my voice low. "If this was a horror movie, there would be a big friggin' monster in that pool. I'm not saying my life is a horror movie, but sometimes I think Wes Craven could write my biography without too much of a stretch. Now we have to go to each tunnel in turn to see which one is the outflow, and follow that one to get out of here. Yes, Tamara?"

Tamara had her hand raised and put it down when I called on her. I never felt more like a substitute teacher than that day. I was underprepared, surrounded by teenagers, and swimming in shit. Yep, definitely a substitute teacher kinda day.

Tamara cleared her throat. "I don't want to pretend to know more than you, Bubba, because you're the expert and all, but..."

"Spit it out, kid. I've got an ego the size of the Grand Canyon, but it's not big enough to not listen. Besides, I've never been to Fairyland before, and I'll be just happy as a clam if I never come back, so I don't know a damn thing more than you do. You need something beat to death, shot, stabbed, set on fire, or defenestrated? I'm the expert. You want to wade through poop while escaping the city guard in an overblown renaissance faire? I'll take all the help I can get."

The girl chuckled a little. "Well, I noticed looking at the pipes that one is larger than all the others, and it seems to be a little lower than the rest. And since the old saying is that you-know-what flows downhill…"

"Shit, Tam, it's okay. You can say shit," Elle said.

"Okay, shit flows downhill. And I'm pretty sure that it's all flowing to that pipe over there." She pointed to a pipe not quite exactly across the pool from us, but close. It did look like there was a little drop-off there, and that meant it couldn't be flowing into the junction. That was our way out.

"Good eye, Tamara. That's great. Now we just have to figure out how to get over there without disturbing anything that might be in the center of the pool. There's a little ledge that goes around the wall, I reckon so workmen can come down here and clear out blockages and things without getting as gross as we are. We should follow that to the outflow pipe and get the hell out of here as fast as we can."

"I'm all for that," Elle said. "It stinks down here, and I'm really starting to miss sunlight. Even the dungeon had windows."

"On the bright side, we stink so bad nobody will want to buy us for sex slaves," Maddie chimed in from the back of the pack.

"You kids sure are a bunch of damn Pollyannas," I muttered. "All right, here's the plan. I'm gonna stand here at the mouth of this tunnel. Maddie is going first to walk the ledge around to the exit tunnel. Once all y'all are over there, I'll follow. Now let's move."

Maddie joined me at the mouth of the tunnel, Elle right behind her with the candle. I helped them step up onto the ledge that encircled the junction about a foot out of the water, and one by one, the girls slipped around to the outbound pipe. When the last girl was over, I stepped up onto the ledge myself and pressed my back to the wall. I didn't have a candle, so the little light that was there streamed in from the grate overhead or the pair of candles on the far side.

I slid along the wall as close to soundlessly as somebody my size can get, with Bertha held in my left hand and my right strapped to my chest to try and relieve some of the stress on my throbbing shoulder. I got halfway across the room before everything went to shit. Or more to shit, since we started off in a sewer.

There was a slight splash in the center of the pool, followed by another, then another.

I really need that to not be some kind of fairy shit-monster. Just this once, let me be wrong about how awful something is going to turn out.

Of course my request to the universe went unheeded. Of course I was right about how incredibly terrible things could get, of course there was a friggin' giant alligator-man thing in the sewers. And of course I found it just when I thought I was going to get out of the sewer without having to shoot anything. Because if it were anything else, it just wouldn't be my life.

It rose up out of the pool slowly, like it understood how to make an entrance. It faced away from me at first, so all I saw was its huge back and shoulders. The thing was at least eight feet tall and covered in a green, scaly hide. And poop. It was also covered in sewage. It was vaguely man-shaped, but its head looked misshapen and squished. Then it turned around, and I saw that it looked like somebody had put an alligator head on Hulk Hogan and blown it all up by thirty percent. And it was pink. It was friggin' Pepto-Bismol pink, with splatters of nasty brown from the sewer.

I hate being right. Now I've got to fight a damn cross between an alligator, a bodybuilder, and My Little Pony. If I live through this, I am beating Puck's ass.

"Cover your ears and eyes, girls!" I shouted. I pointed Bertha at the gatorman and clicked off the safety. I didn't fire immediately. So far it hadn't done anything, just stood there glowering at me in all its toothy princess glory. It stood there for a few seconds, and I didn't move. Didn't breathe. Tried very hard not to do anything to antagonize the most ridiculous-looking monster I had ever seen.

And I didn't have to. I had half a dozen teenage girls with me, not a species known for restraint.

"It's pink!" Somebody said from the mouth of the tunnel.

"It should totally be wearing a tutu," said another girl. It was like they were determined to get me killed by the most embarrassing monster in history.

"I mean, it's cool and all," another girl said. "I mean, my cousin's gay and we still like him. It's the twenty-first century—monsters can wear pink and still be scary."

"Or not," came Maddie's voice, and the whole gaggle of teens cracked up. The fairy crocfather turned in their direction and began a charge, but I squeezed off three rounds from Bertha and got his attention right back to me. Hell, one of the bullets even hit the thing.

For all the good it did. Which was none at all. Two shots pinged off the walls of the sewer and ricocheted causing the girls to duck farther down the outflow pipe and me to crouch a little and hope I didn't die. The third hit the beastie in the big shoulder muscle, but it *thwack*-ed into the monster's scales and barely left a scratch.

Shit. Big, pink, and bulletproof is not how I like my monsters. I really prefer small, furry, and harmless. The pink part is fine. I mean, I'm not racist toward my monsters or anything. As far as monsters go, I'm very much a "you be you" kinda guy. I shoot them all. I'm an equal-opportunity ass-kicker.

Except this looked like a great chance for me to be an ass-kickee, a change in job description I wasn't real interested in. The croc fairy put its head down and charged me, and I made it a point not to be standing in the same spot when it impacted the wall. It hit the stone blocks with a wet thump and left a smear of poo on the stones as it slid down.

Is it going to be that easy? Did it just knock itself unconscious?

The monster groaned, got to its hands and knees, and shook its head.

Nope. Never that easy.

It struggled to its feet, then turned to face me. I was less than ten feet away, so when it opened its long gator mouth and roared at me, I got the sound full in the face. I could only kinda hear it, on account of just firing three rounds from Bertha in a small space and my head ringing like wedding bells in June. But I got a face full of fairy crocmonster breath, and my sweet Jebus, that stink made the sewer smell like rose petals, perfume, and barbecue all rolled up into one.

I have never smelled anything so foul in my life, before or since, and I shared a locker room with an entire football team. Nothing can destroy a bathroom like a defensive line, but this guy's mouth was worse than a porta-potty at a four-day music festival that passes out free fish tacos. I swear the funk bleached all the color out of my beard, crossed my eyes, and made my eyebrows run around to the back of my head.

"Jesus Christ, man, what the holy shit did you eat?" I hollered.

The monster clapped its mouth shut and looked at me. It cocked its head to the side like it knew what I was saying, so I decided to roll with it.

"I mean, damn, son. I know you live in a sewer, but for god's sake haven't you heard of dental floss? That is the funkiest breath I've ever run into, and my uncle Luther had halitosis that could knock a buzzard off a shitwagon at fifty yards. I'm glad you're big and strong and all, but you don't ever need to hit nothing, you just cough on somebody, and they'll drop dead right on the spot."

The monster cocked its head from side to side like it was a bulldog chewing on a bumblebee, not sure what that weird buzzing was, but damn sure that it wasn't having a good time with it. After a second or two of processing, I reckon it decided that I was either not funny or looked more like lunch than a standup comedian, and it opened its mouth to roar again.

I took one step closer, shoved Bertha right up to the end of that long alligator snout, and pulled the trigger twice. Two fifty-caliber rounds tore through the soft parts of the monster's mouth and blew holes the size of grapefruits in the back of its head. It spun sideways, smacked into the wall, and dropped facedown into pool of poop, now polluted with blood and gator brains.

"Next time, practice better oral hygiene you stinky bastard," I said, safetying Bertha and shoving her back into my sling. I walked over to the girls, who made a path for me to walk right to the front of the line.

"Let's get the hell out of here, ladies. It smells like ass down here."

Chapter Sixteen

Somehow we made it out of the sewers without further incident. I didn't even have to lift any kind of grate at the end, or crawl through some pipe made for hobbits, or anything like that. The worst thing we had to do was jump out of the pipe a couple of feet into a drainage pool and wade out. I sat on the grass, wet, stinky, and tired, but surrounded by half a dozen teenage girls who I had rescued from fates worse than death. My shoulder hurt like a sonofabitch, but nobody was currently being digested by a pink alligator dude. I called the day a win.

The poop pond was in a big field about a mile outside the city gates. There was one big-ass tree that I sat leaning against, checking ammunition and re-slinging my shoulder. Tamara and Elle helped with the shoulder, and I looked around to see if I could figure out where we were. I could see the spires of the castle, but the gates themselves were over a ridge off to the south. So we were headed in the right direction to meet up with Puck. All we had to do was walk for two days, avoid running into any search parties sent out by a pissed off Queen Titania, and convince a notoriously mercurial magical fairy prankster to change the terms of our deal in my favor and send at least the girls home, if not me too.

Yeah, it was going to be a long couple of days.

"Any of you girls know how to use a sword?" I asked.

"I took two years of Tae Kwon Do, but we never touched weapons," Elle replied.

"My parents are in the SCA," said an athletic-looking girl with short blonde hair.

"What's that?" I asked. "I went to an SEC school myself, but I've never heard of the SCA. Is that a new conference?"

"It's the Society for Creative Anachronism," the girl said, in that tone that only teenage girls possess, the one designed to make adults realize exactly how stupid they are without having to actually say "you're a moron."

"Is that like a renaissance faire?" I asked.

"On steroids," the girl said. "And way more historically accurate. I've been going to jousts and tourneys since I was four. I learned how to use a sword before I learned to ride a bike."

I looked at her and waved my left hand at Puck's sword where it lay on the grass beside me. "Well, I suppose that's good, since there's not a bike anywhere on this world. Take that sword and strap it on. If we get into trouble, I still want you to run like hell, but at least if you can't get away, you'll be able to defend yourself a little bit. But the dudes around here that carry swords use them all the time, and they aren't screwing around. Treat that sword just like you'd treat a gun—you don't draw it unless you intend to kill something.

"Is that how you feel about guns?" Tamara asked.

"Yeah, it is. It's what my daddy taught me when I was just a little boy."

She stared at me. "Okay, when I was *young*, how about that?" That got a laugh, but I went on. "I shoot a lot of things. Usually, they're like that alligator-slash-Care Bear in the sewer. They're things that want to kill me or somebody that can't help themselves. Critters like that, I'll drop 'em in a heartbeat.

"But I've killed creatures that are a whole lot closer to people, and sometimes that's hard. I killed a fairy since I've been here, and I regret the hell out of that. I didn't want to, and I sure as shit didn't like it, but he was going to kill me, so I pointed Bertha at him and I killed his ass. But it wasn't easy, and it won't be easy to get over. I'll see his face when I close my eyes for a long time. But I know what I did was right, and it was necessary, or you girls wouldn't be reveling in the glorious smell of drying fairy poop on a bright spring day. Y'all'd be in some slaver's wagon or ship headed off to who knows what kind of awfulness. That's what helps me sleep at night."

I looked back at the girl. "Sorry, didn't mean to get all deep on you. Another minute and the violins come out, and before you know it, we're in a damn Nicholas Sparks novel and my long-lost star-crossed love will step out from behind that tree over yonder. Then we'll all have a good cry and go home and drink too much merlot and drunk text all our exes at three in the morning."

"God, grownups really do that kind of crap?" Elle asked.

"I don't," I said. "I friggin' hate merlot. I drink whiskey." We had a good laugh, and then we got to our feet and started trudging through the woods in a generally northern direction. "Keep an eye out for a decent stream or something. We could all use some fresh water, and after we drink, I'd like to try to wash the worst of the poop off of us. But only after we drink."

"Maybe you're smarter than you look," Tamara said. "At least you didn't want to wash the crap off into our drinking water and then drink it."

"I might not be the smartest man in Fairyland, but I know better than to drink poop water," I replied.

We walked for a couple of hours until we finally found a creek deep enough to get into and wash off. I felt bad for putting sewage into what was a crystal-clear stream until we got into it, but I didn't feel bad enough not to get the stench off. Besides, fish poop in streams all the time, so how much worse could it be?

We all waded out of the creek a while later, cleaner, but dripping water from our everywheres, and started back northward, still hoping to find a road that would be easier to navigate than tromping through the woods. The sun was starting to set when I heard the jingle of horse's tack somewhere off to our left. We all ran toward the road but stopped a few yards back in the trees. I sent Maddie ahead to check things out, and she came back a few minutes later, breathless and grinning.

"We found the road!" she exclaimed in a loud whisper.

"Is anybody around?" I asked.

"Yeah, there's an old dude with a wagon full of barrels pulled off the road in a clearing just up ahead. He's kinda singing to himself and puttering around. It looks like he's setting up camp for the night." I looked up. It wasn't going to be dark for a while yet, but if there was a camping spot nearby, it made sense to stop now rather than risk being stuck in the dark trying to follow the road or set up camp in the woods later.

Something hit me then. "This old dude, what did he look like?"

"I dunno. Old. Kinda fat. He wore a vest, and he couldn't fasten it over his belly."

That sounded really familiar. "Did he have a long white beard?"

"Yeah, really long. Like that old band, ZZ something?"

"Top," I corrected absently. "And he had a wagon full of barrels?"

"Yeah, and maybe some other stuff in the back under some tarps, but it might have been empty. I didn't really look. He looked harmless, though."

"He's better than harmless, kiddo. He's the closest thing I've got to a friend over here. Let's go, if we're lucky, he'll have some extra food. At worst, he oughta have some beer."

We followed Maddie back to the road, and sure enough, there sat a familiar cart and a familiar round fairy with a long beard and a vest that hadn't buttoned in years. I stepped out of the woods right in front of him, and Oakroot almost dropped the pipe he was smoking in shock.

"How did your issue with Redfart turn out?" I asked, just like we'd only seen each other yesterday. Of course, we *had* only seen each other the day before, but a lot had happened in that time.

"Red...oh! Haha, yes, Redfart! That's a good one. The judge took less than a minute of listening to that prissy little shit to throw the case out and fine Redfern half a dozen gold crowns for wasting his time. Of course, Redfern didn't have that much money with him, so he's working off his debt to Titania by serving as a pack mule for thirty days and thirty nights."

"What does that mean, working off his debt as a pack mule?" I asked.

"It means she turned him into a mule and he has to do hard labor for thirty days, what do ye think it means?"

I just stared at him. "She can do that?"

"She's the Queen of the Summer Lands, lad. She can do anything she pleases."

My stomach did a little flip-flop at the thought of how pissed she would be at me when she figured out that I was the one who broke the girls out of jail and cost her a pile of slave money. I reminded myself that I really did not want her to catch up with me.

"But what are ye doing here, lad? Last I heard, ye had to fight the queen's cousin in single combat."

"I did. It didn't go well for the cousin. Then I beat up a guard, stole his uniform, broke into the castle, went into the dungeon, beat the shit out of everyone there, broke out all the prisoners to save these girls from being sold into slavery, beat up some gate guards, ran out of the city through the sewers, fought an alligator monster in the sewers—a pink alligator monster, by the way—then walked to here with a half-dozen hungry teenagers."

Oakroot stood the for a moment, gaping at me, then busted out with a laugh that threatened the structural integrity of his belt. "Oh my good lord, lad! You have had an adventure since coming to the lands of the Fae, haven't ye?"

"You could say that, I suppose. Come on out, girls, he's a friend," I called. Six ragged, still slightly damp human girls came out of the forest. One of them carried my pistol; another one carried Puck's sword. The others carried branches they'd picked up in the woods. They looked tired, hungry, and even after washing in a creek, it was pretty obvious none of them had bathed seriously in a few days. But there was a determined look in every eye. These girls were not going back to that dungeon without a fight.

"Come, sit, girls, sit. I don't have much food, and most of it's jerky and stew, the kind of things that last a while on the road, but what I have, I'll gladly share. I'll be in Lamoranth tomorrow afternoon, and since my old friend Redfern won't be needing any of the stores in his house, and since Titania awarded me any of his possessions that I wanted as compensation for having to deal with his foolishness, I can stock up there."

Oakroot handed me a small pack and pointed me toward a tiny pyramid of kindling. "Start the fire, lad. There's flint and tinder in the kit there." He turned back to his cart, dropping the tailgate and rummaging around in the back.

I stood there staring at the pouch in my hand, looking over at the "fire" every once in a while. Finally, I looked at the girl I'd given the sword to. "What's your name again?"

"It's Beth, and it's not again."

"What?"

"You never asked the first time, so I can't tell you my name again. But whatever. What do you need?"

"Did your D&D nerd parents teach you how to start a fire?"

"Did your jock education not teach you anything useful in the real world?"

"I can belch the alphabet and know how to spot the early symptoms of gonorrhea."

She looked at me for a second, a little wide-eyed. "I guess that's relevant. Fair enough. And yeah, my nerd parents taught me how to start a fire. Do you want to take back calling them nerds?"

"Can they argue for more than ten seconds about what's better, *Star Wars* or *Star Trek*?"

"Oh yeah, they can go for hours. What does that have to do with anything?"

"Just proves that I was right. They're huge nerds. Now start the fire."

"Why would I do anything for you after you insulted my parents?"

"One, I didn't insult your parents, I just pointed out the obvious. And two, you probably want the stew that Oakroot's going to make to be hot, so it won't taste like shoe leather. So you're doing yourself as much a favor as you're doing me."

"You're an asshole."

"Again, not an insult, just an observation. Now get going, Firestarter." She knelt by the kindling and opened the pouch. I figured I needed to watch somebody start a fire with rocks about as much as I needed to learn calculus at this point in my life, so I walked around to the back of the cart.

"What ya looking for, buddy?" I asked Oakroot, who was rummaging around in his Sack of Stashing Stuff.

He looked at me for a moment, then his eyes widened and he broke out into a wide grin. "Found it!" he crowed, pulling his arm out of the bag. His hand came out wrapped around the end of a smaller sack, and as he pulled, more and more sack came out of the other sack/magical portal. After long seconds of pulling, he finally reached the end of the other sack and pulled it completely out. He staggered once, and I stepped forward to make sure he didn't fall.

"Here, take this. And tell your girl to make sure the fire's big enough." When he handed it to me, I realized exactly what he had pulled out of the magical bag. I carried the biggest damn rack of ribs I'd ever seen over to where Beth stood looking critically at her fire, and put it down on the ground next to her. Even in a bag, it was an impressive slab of meat. Kinda like me.

"I think we're gonna need a bigger boat," I said. She stared at me, nothing even approaching recognition passed through her eyes. "Come on, kid. *Jaws*?"

"Oh, yeah. I saw that once. I'm not much into old movies. But that's a damn big chunk of meat."

"Just make the fire big enough to cook the ribs," I said, taking my old ass and my pop culture references off to sit down and tell someone to get off my lawn.

Chapter Seventeen

We slept through the night scattered around the clearing. A couple of the girls slept in the back of the wagon, a couple slept under it, and the smallest of the girls, a redhead named Allyson, spent the night sleeping on the bench up front. Oakroot and I took turns standing guard, but the sun rose without incident.

I came back from answering the call of nature to find Oakroot sitting on the bench seat of his wagon, grinning down me. His wagon, once loaded down with empty barrels and wine casks, was now loaded down with human females.

I looked up at him. "What in the hell are you doing, Oakroot?"

"Well, lad, I reckon ye have no idea how to get back to where the Goodfellow left ye, nor any chance of finding enough forage close to the road to be able to feed yourself and all these young mouths. So since I have a daughter close to this age, I thought it would be mighty unfeeling of me to let ye wander the countryside all alone. So ye will all be riding instead of walking. Do ye still have that mighty wee cannon tucked away somewhere?"

"Bertha? Yeah, she's always with me." I pulled the big pistol out of my sling. "But I doubt we'll need her help this trip since Scar's dead and most of his boys are scattered to the winds."

"Aye, I don't expect trouble. But that's how ye avoid it, don't ye know? Ye don't expect it, but make damned sure ye're prepared for it. Now climb on up here and let's get rolling. There's a hunk of jerky on the seat for ye. I want to make it to Lamoranth by midday so we can have a good meal on the sit-down instead of in the wagon."

I couldn't argue with his logic, especially since it was his cart, so I hauled myself up onto the seat beside him, and we rolled north toward Lamoranth and my meeting place with Puck.

The morning was pretty uneventful, as long as you ignore the torture of several hours' worth of "Hundred Bottles of Beer" screeched by teenage girls.

But even that loses its luster after a while, and eventually the girls drifted to silence and just watched the forest roll by on either side of us.

We pulled into Lamoranth just about half an hour after my stomach started to growl, and Oakroot parked the cart near the same cluster of tables in the center of the village where we'd first met Redfern. We all hopped down and stretched, and Beth and Tamara walked over to Oakroot to help him get the food ready.

I sat down at a picnic table and pulled Bertha out of my sling. I set the spare magazines out on the table, popped the mag from my girl, and ejected the round from the chamber. I counted up my ammunition and reloaded my magazines. I put the last few cold iron bullets in one magazine on top of the remaining white phosphorous rounds, then loaded the regular bullets into one clip, put the silver ones in another, and slapped the silver-loaded mag into the handle of the pistol. I chambered a round, safetied the pistol, and slid it into my sling. I slipped the spare magazines in my back jeans pocket instead of the shoulder holster pouches because my bound right arm made it very difficult to reach over underneath my right armpit.

Elle sat down next to me and held out the Judge, careful to keep her finger off the trigger and the barrel pointed at the ground. "You want this back?" she asked.

"Eventually, yes," I said. "But not yet. I can't really draw it left-handed the way the holster is made, and if you've made it this far without shooting me in the ass, you might as well hang on to it until we get back home."

"Thanks," she replied. "I haven't had to use it, but it does make me feel a little better knowing I have it. I thought I was going to have to empty it into that pink alligator-man-back in the sewers."

"Yeah, we got lucky on that one."

"We all got lucky when you came to rescue us. I don't want to know what those slavers would have done to us if you hadn't gotten there when you did."

I put on my best bashful face. "Aw shucks, ma'am. It weren't nothing. I just—"

The sound of horses approaching fast made me cut off, quick. I stood up on the table to get a better look down the road, but all I saw was a cloud of dust. "Y'all hide in the wagon," I yelled to the girls. Elle looked at me, startled, but ran to the wagon and jumped in back without a word of protest.

"Some of you can hide in Redfern's house," Oaktree said. He pointed to a neat little house facing the square. It has window boxes and a freshly painted door.

"How did I know his house would look perfect?" I grumbled. Allyson and Tamara were on that side of the clearing already, so they ran for the house. The other girls slipped into the back of the cart and pulled the tarp over themselves. I barely had time to hop off the table and pull out my pocketknife and sharpener before four city guards galloped into town, their horses in a lather and their armor gleaming. Each man carried a sword, shield, and two of them had bows slung over their shoulders and quivers on their saddles. These guys were ready to scrap, in a mix of chainmail and plate armor, way more serious stuff than the leather and chain the guardsmen in town wore. Didn't matter. If worst came to worst, Bertha would punch through plate mail like it was tissue paper.

One of the men had a plume on his helmet, and he rode straight into town and pulled his horse to a halt in front of me. He yanked the reins, and the horse reared, pawing at the air. I took an instant dislike to him, not just because he had a stupid-looking hat. Any man who needed to teach his horse to rear up on two legs not only wanted to show off, he also had no qualms about maybe hurting his animal to do it.

He looked down at me, his armor gleaming in the midday sun. The two riders with bows stopped at the edge of the village, drew their bows, and put arrows to the strings. One pointed his bow at me while the other aimed at the ground as he scanned the doors and rooftops. The last rider took up position on the other side of me, out of line of the archer if he missed, but in just the right spot to cut me off if I tried to run out of town in the opposite direction.

But I wasn't running anywhere. I wasn't even moving. Because I had a plan, and for once it didn't include punching or shooting everything in the vicinity.

"Stand up," the prissy little fairy with the plumed helmet commanded, glaring down at me. He had a prunish face, perpetually twisted into a scowl that either says "I hate you and everything like you," or "I'm really constipated and just want a really good poop." I'm never sure which.

"Why?" I asked.

"Because I am a lieutenant in the Queen's Guard and I command you to stand!" His plume shook as he shouted. It was kinda cute, actually. His face went all red and his feathers wiggled. It was kinda like one of those old troll erasers I used to have in school. I put them on the ends of pencils and spun the pencil between my hands to make its hair go all frizzy.

I let out a deep breath and stood up. I couldn't look him in the eye when I stood up, because of the horse, so I stepped up on the bench, then onto the table. Now we were eye to eye. I leaned an elbow on the horse's neck and scratched him behind the ears. The horse, not the bitchy lieutenant. Although maybe that would have improved his mood.

"What can I do for you, Mister Lieutenant?" I asked, keeping my voice overly mild. I was being irritating as hell, and I knew it. And I could see in his eyes that PlumeHead knew I knew it, and he knew I was doing it on purpose, but there wasn't a damn thing he could do about it. It was kinda great.

"You were seen fleeing the castle yesterday with six prisoners in tow. Where are they?"

"I don't know what you're talking about," I said.

"What?" His mustache started to quiver like his plume. I was starting to be afraid he was going to vibrate apart, but figured the comedy would be worth the mess.

"I've never been to a castle. I've lived here in Lamoranth my whole life. So I don't know what you're talking about." I looked him straight in the eye as I lied to him. It's a trick I learned in tenth grade, in Ms. Ferguson's biology class. Whenever she asked me what happened to all the frogs for dissection, I gave her the same blank stare and denial. It was years before I learned that most fried frog legs didn't have a formaldehyde aftertaste. They're a lot less chewy when they aren't embalmed, too.

"There were dozens of witnesses who saw you. Why are you lying?" He waggled his finger in my face, and I resisted the urge to snap it off and shove it in one ear and out the other.

Instead, I dug around in my left nostril with my pinky finger, found a big green hanger, and delicately deposited it on the tip of his wagging finger. He turned the finger back toward himself, and I reached out and smacked the back of his hand. His hand jerked forward, planting my huge booger right on the tip of his pointy little nose.

"Oops," I said. "Hey, you've got a little something on your nose. Do you need a hanky?"

He yelled at the other guards. "Search everything! Start with that wagon! You," he waved at the guard not carrying a bow, "find that fat beer merchant and interrogate him. Don't bother being gentle." PlumeHead reached for his sword, so I shoved him backward. He toppled out of his saddle and landed flat on his back. All the air rushed out of him in a *whoosh*, and he lay on his back in the dirt, wiggling his arms and legs like a turtle in a stupid hat.

I hopped down off the table and walked toward the nearest guard, who was off his horse and walking toward the nearest house. This was the one PlumeHead had sent after Oakroot, and I really didn't want anything to happen to the old dude just for helping me out. I might have stepped on PlumeHead's belly as I went past, further stomping him into the dirt and maybe mashing his breastplate a little flat.

"You should stop, pal," I said. The guard turned around a lot more nimbly than any dude in full armor should be able to, but he was a fairy, so there was friggin' magic involved.

I hate magic. Not a particularly helpful thought when you're standing in the middle of a fairy village with a fairy soldier drawing down on you in damn Fairyland, but that's where I was. He pulled his sword, I pulled Bertha, and I could see one of the archers turn to me with his bow drawn back. Things did not look good for our hero.

"ENOUGH!" Oakroot's voice cut through the air like a cannon shot. I turned to the sound, keeping the gun trained on the guy with the sword in front of me. Until I saw Oakroot, or at least I saw the fairy standing there in Oakroot's clothes, holding a white beard and wig in one hand.

"This has gone far enough. It was amusing for a time, but I will not risk injury or death to my guardsmen over a mere wager. Put away your weapons, all of you."

A wager? Like a bet? What the... My confusion didn't lessen an ounce when all of the soldiers sheathed their swords, dropped their bows, and knelt to the man who was apparently masquerading as Oakroot the Brewer. PlumeHead didn't kneel, though. He actually got up, took the helmet off, and peeled his face off, like Cameron Diaz in that godawful *Charlie's Angels* movie when she peeled off the LL Cool J face mid-skydive. Never mind, it was a terrible movie. Regardless, PlumeHead peeled his face off, and Puck stood there grinning at me like a teenage boy who'd just touched his first boob.

I looked from the soldiers to "Oakroot" to Puck, then back to "Oakroot," then back to the soldiers, then back to Puck again. I did this a few times, but all I did was get a little dizzy. It didn't make anything make any more sense.

"What in the holy shit is going on here?" I asked. I looked at "Oakroot." "I reckon you're important, so I probably shouldn't shoot you. But I don't think that applies to you, shithead." I swung Bertha over to Puck and pointed the barrel of the big pistol at him.

"Oh, be serious, human," Puck said, not the least bit nervous, or at least hiding it really well. "You could barely react well enough to shoot me when you're well, much less with your off hand. Put that toy away, and I'll tell you about our little game."

"Game?" I asked. "GAME?!? Okay, Goodfellow, I'm going to listen, but if I don't like what I hear, I'm going to start punching you, and I'm not going to stop until my hand hurts. Then I'm going to stomp a mudhole in your ass and walk it dry."

Puck just looked at me. "Of course you will, human. If thinking that makes you feel better, go right ahead. But you should probably sit down. And you can bring the girls out of wherever you've hidden them. They're in no danger. They never were, actually."

I sat on the picnic table. "Come on out, girls. This is the asshole who sent me to rescue you. Well, he didn't send me to rescue *you*. He sent me to rescue his girlfriend, some fairy chick who was supposed to be in the dungeon with you. But since you're all humans, I guess he had bad information."

"Well, actually..." The girl I knew as Allyson stepped forward. "I'm sorry, but I may have deceived you a bit." She reached under her chin and pulled off her face. In a cloud of sparkles, the diminutive redhead teenager disappeared to be replaced by a gorgeous brunette fairy woman with cascading curls, a smattering of glittering freckles, and a sheepish smile.

"My name is not Allyson," she said. "I am Princess Alethea, and I am—"

"My one true love," Puck said, dropping to one knee in front of the beautiful fairy. I didn't blame him. She was stunning, with a smile that could melt granite.

I looked around, then tugged on my beard, just to make sure. "Okay, I can't pull my face off. Can anybody else, or are we all who we say we are? And are we all the right species?"

Everyone laughed, then the whole group fell silent again as a glowing portal opened in the air beside "Oakroot," and Titania, the Queen of the Summerlands, stepped out.

Shit. I'm about to get my ass kicked by the Queen of the Fairies. I just hope she turns me into a good-looking frog.

Chapter Eighteen

THE WHOLE CLEARING FELL SILENT AS TITANIA LOOKED AROUND us, her royalty and gravitas settling on the day like a cloud. Everyone in the village joined Puck on the ground, dropping to one knee at the Queen of the Fae. Except me. I was grumpy, and I didn't feel like kneeling. Besides, if she was gonna turn me into a frog, she could damn well do it while I was standing up.

She walked over to me. Glided would have been a better word, since I never saw her feet actually touch the ground. But with the way the front of her gown was cut, I honestly didn't look at her feet that much. Or her face. Frankly, all my attention was focused somewhere between her bellybutton and her collarbone. There was a really pretty necklace there. I think.

"You don't kneel before your queen, human?" she asked, and I looked up. There was a smile on her face, but it didn't even get into the same zip code as her eyes. She wasn't amused, and I couldn't tell if she was pissed that I didn't kneel or pissed that I stared at her boobs. Probably didn't matter if I was going to spend the rest of my days sitting on a lily pad eating flies.

Screw it, it's not like I can get in any more *trouble.* "I don't have a queen. I don't think we were ever properly introduced. My name is Robert Brabham, but everybody calls me Bubba. I hunt monsters, and I put bullets in 'em. You might remember that from what happened with your asshole cousin." I held out my hand.

She didn't shake; she just stared at me. Then she laughed. And it was a real laugh, not like the smile she wore up until that second. This was a head back, belly shaking, come from the toenails laugh, and it made me feel like there was at least a three percent chance I wasn't about to be an amphibian.

When she stopped laughing, she reached out and shook my hand. "I like you, Bubba the Monster Hunter. You are brave. A little stupid, but very, very brave."

"I'll take that, Your Majesty. I've sure been called worse. Now can you tell me what the hell is going on here? Oakroot over there said something about a wager?"

"Oakroot? Oakroot the Brewmaster? I haven't seen that old codger in a century! How is he?" Titania asked.

"Why don't you ask him? He's standing right there. Or at least some dude is standing there that was wearing Oakroot's face until a couple minutes ago." I pointed to the imposter brewer, who I then noticed also wasn't kneeling.

"Darling," he nodded to Titania.

"Hello, dear," she replied, and Queen of the Summerlands or not, her voice got real damn frosty. She turned back to me. "Bubba, this is not Oakroot."

"I figured that out about two seconds after he peeled his face off," I said. "I'm human, not stupid."

"The two are not mutually exclusive, Bubba."

"Fair enough," I agreed. I mean, she's right. I've got C-Span. I know what kind of stupid humans can get up to. "But who is he?"

"Please allow me to introduce myself," the tall fairy said, stepping forward to stand beside Titania. He was dark to her light, all dark hair and trim beard with high cheekbones and brown eyes. He was thickly muscled and moved like a big cat, power poised to spring. This was not a guy I wanted to face in combat, no matter how many guns I had on me. If I had to take him out, I'd want to use something effective. Like a jet. Or half a dozen Navy Seals. Or two Marines. Something like that.

"Are you a man of wealth and taste?" I quipped. Blank stares all around. Note to self—teenage girls don't get *Jaws* references, and fairy monarchs don't get Rolling Stones references. I hope I never need to remember that.

"Excuse me?" he asked, a puzzled expression breaking the planes of his perfect face. He didn't even have an eyebrow hair out of place after wearing another dude's face for several days. *I hate magic.*

"Never mind, a silly joke," I said. Not worth it to try and explain rock n' roll to extra-dimensional beings. I've tried before. Never works.

"I am Oberon, King of the Summerlands and husband to Titania."

Shit. "Shit."

"Excuse me?"

"Sorry. Just surprised is all. So you're the king of the fairies, and you've been pretending to be Oakroot for the past few days?"

Oberon blushed a little. "Yes."

"Why?" I asked.

Titania smiled, and it was like the sun broke through the clouds. It's a good thing there were no cliffs nearby because if she'd said "jump," I'd have been halfway to the ground before I realized it was a bad idea. "He was cheating," she said, giving Oberon a nasty little grin.

"Cheating? Cheating at what?" I hadn't been that confused since eighth-grade algebra. And this time I didn't have Skeeter around to explain shit for me.

"We had a wager," Titania started. "Oberon and I made a wager on the security of my city and my dungeon. I bet him that no one could escape from my dungeons and get out of the city without being recaptured or killed, and he took the bet. We chose the greatest trickster and escape artist in all the Known Worlds to make the attempt, and promised not to intervene."

"And that trickster happens to be one Robin Goodfellow," I said, pointing at Puck. He stood and made a florid bow, complete with a doff of his imaginary hat.

"To encourage Puck's participation, we gave him a little incentive," Titania continued.

"You threw the woman he loves into the dungeon, then told him to break her out."

"We told him that if he could rescue her, they could wed," Oberon chimed in. Titania shot him a dirty look, and he shut right up.

"We gave Puck no guidance in how to perform his task and provided no assistance," Titania said. "Or at least we claimed to provide no assistance. Some of us seem to have forgotten that part of the agreement."

"Well, actually..." I started, but shut my mouth when Titania glared at me.

"No, go on, Bubba. How can you justify my husband's cheating?"

"He only helped me get to and from the city," I said. "Once we got to the gates, I was on my own. And we broke out on our own, unless Oberon was masquerading as a tavern owner?" I looked at the fairy king, but he shook his head. "Then he didn't actually cheat. He gave me a ride from point to point, but I did the breaking in and the breaking out. So he played it straight, Your Majesty. You just lost. Sorry."

Titania stepped up close to me and lowered her voice. "I. Don't. Lose. Human." She was almost tall enough to look me in the throat, but I was tired of this shit, tired of Fairyland, and really damned tired of people saying "human" like it was a synonym for monkey poop.

I leaned down and put my gigantic face right down almost nose to nose with the fairy queen's perfect little aquiline, aristocratic sniffer. "You. Lost. This. Time." I added a "Your Majesty" on the end just to mitigate my insolence a tiny bit.

She looked me dead in the eyes for a long time, so long I really needed to blink, but I had a little brother, so I grew up having staring contests over who got the last Pop-Tart. I never lost. After a ridiculously long time, she stepped back and blinked. "I have to revise my earlier opinion of you, Bubba. You are absolutely the bravest *and* stupidest human I have ever met."

"Oh, Your Majesty, I'm not even in the top one percent. One of these days, you can come over to Mount Bubba and I'll introduce you to my cousin Redmond. He once tried to take a mountain lion to his senior prom. It didn't end well for Redmond, or for the school gym."

"I have no idea what you are saying, Bubba, but I do have to respect you. Not many men could look into the eyes of the Queen of the Summerlands and not be swayed by her charms," Oberon said.

"Well, Obie, I gotta admit, it's been a while since I've seen a pair of charms as impressive as hers, but I'm taken. I've got a lady back home, and as soon as I get y'all to agree to send me and all these girls home, I'm gonna take her out for some of Nashville's best hot chicken and cold beer, and then take her home with me. I ain't messing that up for nothing, no matter how smokin' hot Titania is. No offense, Your Majesty."

"None taken," Titania replied. Oberon just grinned.

"Well, what's the deal? Who won the bet? Shit, I don't care who won the bet, can we just go home?" Tamara butted in. The girls had all gotten up off their knees and were sitting on one of the picnic tables around us. Puck and Princess Alethea were sitting on the grass in front of another bench, about as close as two people can be with clothes on.

I looked at Titania. She looked at me, then to Puck. "You both attest that Oberon only provided transportation to and from the city, and nothing once you were within my gates?" We both nodded. "Then it seems, my husband, that you have been victorious. This time."

Oberon grinned and sketched out a shallow bow. "As always, Your Majesty, I appreciate your grace, even in defeat."

"Don't push it, Oberon." Titania scowled at him. This was not a relationship I ever wanted to try to understand.

Oberon turned to Puck. "Robin Goodfellow."

Puck stood up. "Yes, my liege?" All hints of the mocking grin were gone; his face was totally serious for the first time since I'd seen him.

"You have been successful in the task I set before you, rescuing your lady fair from the deepest dungeon of Tisa'ron. As promised, you have our permission to wed, should the Princess Alethea so desire."

Puck turned to where the lovely little princess sat, a demure blush on her cheeks. He knelt in front of her and said, "My dearest princess, would you consent to make me, at long last and in all truth, an honest Puck?"

She squealed a little, wrapped her arms around the startled Goodfellow, and tackled him to the ground, smothering him in kisses.

I looked at Oberon. "I reckon that's a yes. Now how about sending us home?"

"Indeed," the fairy king agreed. He waved his hand, and a portal opened up in midair. I peered through, and damned if I couldn't see Fort Nashborough through the glowing ring. I stared at it for a second, then Amy came into view on the other side. I hadn't realized just how much I missed her until I wasn't in danger of being killed or turned into a frog right that second, then it hit me like a hammer.

Something must have shown on my face because Oberon leaned over to me. "I know exactly how that feels, my friend. And she is lovely. Take care of her."

"Oh you don't even know, Obie. I don't take care of her; she takes care of *me*. And together, we take care of the whole damn world. Or at least our little piece of it." I spoke louder, so the whole clearing could hear me. "Time to go, girls! And if you aren't from Tennessee, now's the time to speak up."

"Don't worry about that, Bubba. The portal is magic. They will all be returned to the exact spot where they left, and only two days will have passed, no matter how long they have been in Fairy," Titania said.

Oberon looked at her, and the queen shrugged. "What? I can't be a gracious loser?"

"Not usually," he muttered, but I noticed he smiled when he said it.

I watched all the girls go through the portal and vanish, then it was just me and the little pain in the ass that started it all, Tamara, standing there looking at Nashville. I held out my hand to Oberon. "Thanks, King. Your Majesty." I nodded to Titania, and she inclined her chin back at me.

I started to say something to Puck, but he seemed pretty distracted by all the kissing, so I just shook my head and waved Tamara toward the portal. She stepped through, and I turned to go.

At the last second, I turned back and looked at the King and Queen of the Summerlands. "Y'all ain't half bad, even if your royal cousin was a dick. If y'all ever need anything shot, stabbed, beat slap to death, set on fire, or defenestrated, y'all just...nah, screw that. Call somebody else, I'm going home." And with that, I stepped through the circle of magical light and appeared on the other side about six feet from where I left, and judging by the look of things, only about half an hour afterwards.

"Bubba? Where the hell are you, dammit? You know I hate it when you turn your comm off. I don't care if you're peeing in a corner, it won't offend me. This isn't funny, Bubba! You answer me right now, dammit!" The stream of bitching in my ear told me two things. First, I was home and all my tech worked again. And second, that Skeeter was still one hundred damn percent Skeeter.

"I'm here Skeeter. I wasn't taking a piss, but I'll have to explain the rest of it when we get home tomorrow. It's a long damn story."

"It better be a good one," my best friend and tech wizard replied in a huff.

"Oh, trust me, son. This is one for the ages."

Then I stepped out from behind the building to see Amy and Sergeant Yates standing over Tamara, who just stood in the middle of the Fort, shaking her head. I knew the feeling. These questions were not going to get answered tonight, and it was gonna be hard for anybody who wasn't there to believe the shit we went through. Literally, even.

That's when I looked down and saw Puck's sword hanging from the belt around my waist. Last time I saw that, it was in the hands of the girl with the ren faire parents. I felt around my waistband, and there was my Judge revolver, tucked nice and neat in its holster. I'd forgotten to get it back from Elle before she went through the portal, too. Then I realized that my shoulder didn't hurt. I took off the sling and rotated my arm a few times. Good as new.

I guess magic doesn't suck all the time after all. I shrugged my mystically repaired shoulder, holstered Bertha, and walked out to kiss my girlfriend.

Oh Bubba. Where Art Thou?

My sister has been asking me for years to put my family's story in a book.
This is some of them.
For Bonnie - be careful what you ask for, sis.

Chapter One

"I HATE COUNTRY MUSIC. I DON'T EVEN KNOW WHY WE WASTED the money to come to this thing," I said as we walked up Broadway back toward our hotel.

"Well, to be fair, we didn't pay for the tickets," Amy said, walking beside me. She was right. She almost always is, not that I'll ever tell her that. The tickets to the Ryman Auditorium Christmas Spectacular were a gift from the Nashville Police Department, a nice gesture of appreciation for our help in solving a disappearance a few months back.

"Good damn thing, too," I grumbled. "I mean, I reckon it was all fine, if you're twenty-three years old, stupid, and want to get laid."

"And you're only two of those things," Amy said with a laugh.

"I told y'all you should have come with me to Play," Skeeter said from the other side of Amy. "The drag show was fab-u-lous, and that cute little bartender was mixing me double margaritas all night and only charging me for singles. I do believe he was trying to get me drunk." Skeeter tripped over a crack in the sidewalk and almost took a header into a light pole. Amy caught his belt at the last second and kept my best friend, tech guru, and the current drunkest person in Tennessee from busting his gourd all over the sidewalk.

"I do believe he succeeded," Amy said with a laugh. "Now get your shit together before Bubba has to carry you to your room."

"Wouldn't be the first time," Skeeter slurred.

Amy looked at me with a question across her face, and I shrugged. "We did go to UGA, you know. Athens might be a little bit of a party town. Skeeter ain't never weighed more than a buck-seventy-five, so about four beers and he loses control of his feet."

"So he got too drunk to walk?" Amy asked.

"Nah, he loses control of his mouth at about three beers, so by the fourth he's usually got somebody pissed off enough to knock his ass out," I replied.

"Then after I'd beat their ass, we were usually asked to leave, which led to a good half dozen trips across campus with Skeeter out cold over my shoulder."

"There's a visual I hope I never have to see in real life." Amy shuddered a little at the thought.

"Me too," Skeeter said. "For such a big dude, Bubba's got bony shoulders. But what was so bad about the concert, Bubba? I thought there was supposed to be all kinds of big-deal country stars there."

"There were, not that I could tell you what any of them's names are. For all I know, every damn one of 'em was named Brett or Sean. It was like a douchebag convention, only with more guitars. I ain't smelled that much Axe body spray in my life," I said.

"The level of testosterone was pretty through the roof," Amy said.

"You might have been the one in the gay bar, Skeeter, but we were in the presence of the tightest damn blue jeans I'd ever seen."

"Damn, Bubba," Skeeter chuckled. "Now I'm a little bit jealous!"

"And I reckon the tight pants strangled what little bit of talent these dudes had, because couldn't nary a one of them do more than play three chords on their guitar or sing on key."

"But most of them had the booty shake down pat," Amy added.

"Yeah, it was more like watching damn *Solid Gold* than a country concert," I griped.

"So nobody sang about Mama, or trains, or getting drunk, or their woman leaving them?" Skeeter asked.

I thought for a second. "Nah, there was plenty of songs about getting drunk and a bunch about shaking your sugar shaker, whatever the hell that is, and to listen to these boys, you'd think country girls only ever wear Daisy Dukes and that every redneck drives a truck and has a bunch of guns."

"I don't want to say nothing, Bubba, but..." Skeeter saw the look on my face and let his little smartass comment die on the vine.

"Then don't. I have a truck for work, and I hunt monsters for a living. I need my guns." I glared at him.

"Don't worry, Bubba. If Obama hasn't tried to take your guns away yet, you're probably safe for a little while longer." He looked at Amy. "How did you like the show?"

"I thought it was fine," she said. "It's not really my kind of music anyway, so it didn't offend me like it did Bubba. And I thought the lights were pretty, so that was good. It was a little loud. Even with my earplugs in."

"You wore earplugs to a concert?" Skeeter asked. "God, you really are an adult."

"True, but I can still hear you, and I wouldn't be able to if I had left my earplugs at home. Anyway," Amy said in a way that let me know that the subject was closed, "it was very nice of the detectives to get us the tickets and nice of Father Joe to get us a couple of rooms at the Renaissance for the night." She gestured to our hotel, and we all stepped into the lobby.

"Yeah, it's nice to be somewhere away from home and not have something trying to kill us for a change," I said.

Skeeter and Amy both looked daggers at me, and I held up both hands. "What? What are y'all looking at me like that for?"

"You asshole," Amy said through clenched teeth.

"You totally jinxed it, Bubba. We spent the whole night with nothing nasty or magical coming out to kick our ass, and you had to go and tempt fate like that. I can't believe you are that big an idiot," Skeeter said.

"Skeeter, you've known me since middle school. You know *exactly* how big of an idiot I am. Wait a minute, that didn't come out right."

"And my point is made," Skeeter replied. Just then his cell phone rang, and he wobbled around for a minute slapping his own ass and crotch before he figured out which pocket had his phone in it.

"Cello?" Skeeter said into the phone. When he gets real drunk, he thinks he's JJ from *Good Times.* I try to explain to him that he didn't grow up in the projects, he grew up raised by a bunch of white people in Georgia, but he usually tells me to shut my cracker mouth, that he is dy-no-mite. It's never worth the fight.

But it was hilarious watching him try to act sober on the phone when he was absolutely shithouse drunk. He was all full of "yes, sir" and "no, sir" just like when we were sixteen and hauled into the principal's office for a misunderstanding about planting marijuana in the Future Farmers of America community garden. The misunderstanding was that I didn't understand how long it took weed to grow, so I forgot about it, and when we all came back to school after summer break, there were several pot plants flourishing in the rich Georgia soil. This was not considered nearly as fantastic by the administration as it was by the drama students.

Skeeter listened more than he talked, so it must have been somebody pretty damn important. Finally, he hung up and looked at me and Amy. "Well, my buzz is gone now."

"Who was it?" I asked.

"It was Bishop McTigue. We've got a gig."

"Joe's boss? Why didn't Joe call you?"

"Joe's having a little bit of a crisis of faith right now," Skeeter said, not quite looking me in the eye.

"What the hell do you mean, he's having a crisis of faith?" I asked. "Asked" might not be exactly the right word since I kinda blew his hair back with how loud I hollered at him. "He don't get to have any kind of damn crisis of faith. He's a friggin' Knight Templar!"

"Well, maybe crisis of faith isn't exactly the right word for it," Skeeter said. "It's more like he's negotiating his contract with the Church."

Damn, sounds like his weekend with his ex-girlfriend down in Florida went better than I thought. "Alright, so Joe's out of the picture for this one. What's the gig?"

"Well, if you're pissed off about the state of music, maybe this will make you feel better. You're going to Muscle Shoals."

"Yes!" I fist-pumped. I ain't ashamed of it. I was going to redneck Mecca, where some of the greatest pickers and singers in the world recorded. I was gonna be walking the same halls as Duane Allman, Keith Richards, Lynyrd Skynyrd, Bob Dylan, and Dr. Hook & The Medicine Show. Then I stopped.

"What am I hunting?" I asked.

"We ain't quite sure yet, but it seems to be just a haunting," Skeeter said.

"I don't do ghosts," I said. "I don't ever do ghosts. You know that."

"Why not?" Amy asked. "We deal with ghosts if need be. We have teams especially for that." The "we" in question there was DEMON, the Department of Extradimensional, Mystical, & Occult Nuisances, the super-secret government agency Amy worked for. No shit, it was way off the map. Black helicopters and everything.

"Well, of course y'all do," I replied. "Like you said, y'all got whole teams of ghostbusters and shit."

"They really don't like being called that," Amy informed me.

"Why not?" I asked. "I saw the remake. It wasn't bad. Not as good as the original, but not bad. Anyhow, y'all can deal with ghosts because you've got all kinds of super-tech ghost-blasty shit that deals with ectoplasm or ethereoplasm or whatever kind of shit ghosts are made of."

"Well, yeah," Amy said, like you'd be stupid to go in after them with anything else. "But we also have mediums to help them cross over, too."

"Well, I ain't got nothing that ain't at least an XXL, sweetie. There ain't been nothing medium on me since I was nine years old. And I shoot things. Or I beat the shit out of them. That's what I do."

"Except ghosts," Skeeter interjected. "Hard to shoot something that's incorporeal."

"I don't know what the hell that means, but I can't shoot shit that ain't got no body. My bullets just go right through it."

"That's exactly what…never mind," Amy said. "I see your point. So, what are you going to do?"

"Well, I reckon first thing in the morning I'm gonna get in the truck and head down to Muscle Shoals. Good news is it ain't but a couple hours from here."

"The bad news is they want you there by eight in the morning," Skeeter interjected.

I looked down at him. "How damn drunk *are* you? There ain't no way in hell I am getting in the truck at…a quarter 'til midnight, driving close to three hours to Ala-damn-bama, then getting up and meeting with…some asshole at eight in the morning!"

"Bishop McTigue said—" Skeeter started.

"Is Bishop McTigue here?" I asked.

"What?" Skeeter's eyes crossed a little as he tried to focus on me, and I made it a point to sway in the opposite direction of what he was swaying. I'm a dick sometimes, but he's my best friend, and if you can't screw with your friends when they drink, what's the point of living?

"Is the bishop standing right here? And is he going to send me directly to Hell if I'm late for this meeting?" I asked, waving my arms around to further prove the point that there was no bishop around.

"Well, no, he ain't here, but…"

"But nothing, Skeet. I have a beautiful woman, a hotel room with a jacuzzi tub that's actually big enough for me and somebody else to fit in, and a bottle of champagne on ice not fifty yards from where we are standing. If you think for a second that I am spending the night tonight anywhere but in the loving embrace of all those things, you are the single dumbest person to ever graduate from the University of Georgia. And you met a lot of the football team, so you know that's a high bar to clear."

Skeeter stood there for a few seconds trying to wrap his head around everything I'd just said and opened his mouth a couple times like a fish gasping for air, then his eyes rolled back into his head and he passed out, right there in the middle of the sidewalk.

I bent over, picked Skeeter up, tossed him over one shoulder, and started up the steps to our hotel. Amy just stared at me.

"What?" I asked. "Do I have a booger?"

"You got champagne?" She looked up at me with a sweet little smile, and I grinned down at her.

"You better believe. And I got Korbel, too. None of the cheap stuff for us, baby."

She shook her head at me, but grinned while she did it. "You got a lot to learn, Bubba Brabham, but damned if you aren't a pretty quick study."

We walked into the lobby, I dumped Skeeter onto an empty luggage cart, stuck his room key in his mouth, and me and Amy held hands on our way to the elevator.

Chapter Two

I PULLED INTO THE PARKING LOT OF CELEBRITY RECORDING STUDIOS in Muscle Shoals, Alabama, a little after noon. I got a little bit later start than I had originally hoped because in the middle of my morning shower, Amy stepped in there with me and volunteered to wash my back. I returned the favor, then we got on to washing some more interesting parts, and next thing I knew, we both needed another shower. So it was closer to ten than eight when I got on the road.

I stepped out of the truck and gave the building a once-over. It didn't look like the kind of place to spawn musical legends and create some of the greatest bluegrass recordings in history. It was just a low, one-story cinderblock building at the end of a poorly paved county road. The parking lot was huge for a building that probably couldn't hold fifty people at its fullest, with room for a couple dozen cars and five or six tour buses all to fit with plenty of room to maneuver. A tattered and faded green canvas awning flapped in the breeze over the front door where a cheap black-and-orange hardware store "CLOSED" sign was taped over the small window.

I opened the back door of the truck and flipped up the back seat. I popped the lid on one of the built-in cabinets under the seat and pulled out Bertha and her shoulder rig. I shrugged into the holster and slipped the big pistol into her home. I pulled out a magazine loaded with silver bullets and another full with cold iron rounds, and slid them into the mag holders under my right arm. A third spare magazine with alternating white phosphorous and silver rounds went into my back pocket, and I threw a baggy Dickie's work shirt on to hide the gun.

It didn't make me look less threatening. That ship sailed a long damn time ago, but at least now I didn't look like the giant psychotic *armed* leader of a biker gang. I tightened my ponytail, did a quick crumb check on my beard, and walked to the door.

It was locked. I looked around and confirmed that yes, there was another car in the lot. It wasn't much of a car, a beat-to-shit minivan riding on a donut, but it was there, and it didn't look like it was broken down, so that meant somebody was inside. I tried the handle again, but it hadn't miraculously unlocked itself in the last five seconds. I knocked, as softly as I could manage with a fist the size of a Honeybaked ham. Nothing. I knocked a little more firmly. I stood there for a good two minutes before I hauled off and banged on the door. Hard. From the other side, it probably sounded about like a horse trying to kick the door down because that's about how I was starting to feel—like a horse's ass.

Nothing. I stood there for another minute, then turned to go back to the truck. After three steps, I pressed the Bluetooth earpiece and said, "Goddammit, Skeeter, where are these bastards?"

A weak voice came back to me. "Do you have to yell?"

Oh yeah, Skeeter was dealing with a mother of a hangover. *Serves him right*, I thought. I was starting to get really grumpy since I'd left a sexy and very naked federal agent sprawled in the middle of a sea of sweaty sheets to drive to Ala-goddamn-bama and talk to some jackass about a gig I probably couldn't do anyway, since I don't do ghosts. And now this asshat wasn't even here.

"Hell yeah, I've gotta yell," I yelled. "Ain't nobody here, Skeeter. Where are these sonsabitches?"

"Bubba, what the hell are you talking about? Where are you and what the hell are you doing there?" Skeeter asked, his voice getting stronger as he shook off his lingering drunkenness and was able to focus a little better.

"You don't remember? Goddammit, Skeeter, I'm in Muscle friggin' Shoals because Bishop McTigue called and asked me to come down here and help out with a haunting, which I don't even do, but I came because he's Joe's boss and because it's Muscle Shoals, so, you know, Skynyrd, but now I'm standing out here freezing my nuts off in a parking lot in Alabama when I could be curled up around Amy in my room in Nashville, so you need to get this shit dealt with, and now!"

Skeeter was silent for a few seconds, then came back on the line. "Sorry, what was that? I was busy throwing up. Did you say anything I give a shit about?"

I sighed and looked down at my feet. "No, I reckon not."

"Good. I just messaged your contact at the studio. Somebody ought to be out to open the door in a minute. Now can I go back to bed? I feel like refried ass."

"Next time the cute bartender wants to hit on you, just get his number instead of taking all the free booze," I advised.

"That's not a bad idea," Skeeter agreed. "Hey! Guess what?"

"What?"

"I just found his phone number written on my hand!"

"Good deal. Now get some sleep so you won't be puking in a trashcan when you call him."

"That's a good idea. Later." Skeeter clicked off.

I walked back over to the door and tried the knob again. Still locked. I reared back to start pounding again, then heard a little mechanical *click* that told me someone had unlocked the door remotely. I was used to that sound—the underground poker room where I played cards once in a while used the same kind of security. Of course, they also had reinforced steel doors, a high-tech video surveillance system, a door guy named "Beef" that made me feel skinny, and a cocktail waitress with a Colt 1911 on her hip. I had a sneaking suspicion I was not walking into quite the same environment here.

I was right. I pushed open the door into a small office, all wood paneling and threadbare burnt orange carpet, with an unattended receptionist's desk and three rickety chairs along one wall. A little balding dude in jeans and a polo shirt stood by the desk and stuck out his hand when I walked in.

"Hey there, you must be Bubba," he said, walking forward with his hand out. That shit always made me nervous for some reason. Like, why you gotta be coming at a dude with your hand out like you're some kinda Robbie the Robot? Why can't you just walk up to somebody, then put your hand out like a normal person? Whatever, I shook his hand.

"Yeah, I'm Bubba. And you are…?"

"I'm Billy Ricks, owner and proprietor of Celebrity Studios. We're the home of the legends of music, making a big-city sound with small-town service."

"Nice sales pitch. But I thought y'all were closed."

He sagged a little bit and walked back to lean on the front of the desk. "We are. It's just hard to break the habit, you know?"

I didn't know a damn thing about whatever he was talking about, but I nodded like I did. "Sure, dude. I get it. Now, what about these ghosts?"

"Oh yeah. Um…we're haunted. And I wanted to know if you can make them go away." Sure, because that's enough information to go on. I'll just dance around naked in the hall yelling "Get out, spirits!" Shit, come to think of it, that had about as much hope of success as anything else I could think of.

"Could you be a little more specific about what kind of things people are experiencing? Are there cold spots, hot spots, do people hear mysterious footsteps? What exactly makes you think there are ghosts in the building?"

He looked up at me like I was a moron. I get that a lot. Sometimes it's because I say stupid shit, but sometimes it's just because people assume that giant ex-football players are stupid. I don't mind so much about the stupid shit part, but I don't like being profiled as a dumbass just because I'm too big for most doorways.

"I think there are ghosts here because when I'm here alone at night, I see dead people walking through the halls."

"Like, glowing, ethereal-looking dead people?"

"Yeah, dude. Ghosts. They walk through walls, appear randomly in the studio, and generally scare the shit out of me."

Yup, sounded like ghosts all right. "Okay, so what do you want me to do about it?"

It was almost funny, the way he turned red all the way to the top of his bald spot. "Do about it? I want you to get them the hell out of here! I ain't had a booking in eight months, and I can't sell nobody a haunted recording studio. That's why I called the Cardinal! That's why I've given so much damn money to the Church all these years! So when I need something spiritual, they take care of it. Well, now I've got a spiritual problem, and you gotta deal with it!"

"I think there's a difference between a problem with spirits and a spiritual problem, dude. One of those the Church takes care of pretty well, and the other one needs a Venkman." He looked confused. "You know, like Bill Murray in the movie? Oh, forget it. Look, man. I don't really know what good I can do for you. I hunt monsters. Werewolves, vampires, chalupas, that sort of thing."

"You hunt down Mexican food?" Now he looked *really* confused.

"Dammit, no. I meant chupacabra. I mean, I'll hunt down some Mexican food, too. I love me some arroz con pollo, and a good mole sauce over shredded chicken is my jam, but that ain't the point. The point is, I hunt down things that go bump in the night. Then I shoot them." I drew

Bertha for emphasis, and homeboy almost tripped over himself backing up. I reckon that's a natural response when a man that's six-and-a-half feet tall and over three-hundred pounds pulls a pistol that's almost a damn foot long and waves it front of your face.

"Calm down, jackass. I ain't gonna shoot you. I was just trying to say that I might not be the man for this job. I'll give it a shot, but I ain't making no promises. I've fought a whole lot badass monsters in my day, but I don't know what the hell I'm supposed to do about ghosts." I put Bertha away, and my host started to look a lot less like he was about to piss himself.

He took a real timid step forward. "But you'll try?"

"Yeah, I'll try. Now why don't you give me the nickel tour and tell me where all you've seen ghosts and what they've been doing. And did they ever get into any badass ghost jam sessions in here?"

He laughed a little. "Nah, nothing like that, although more than one of them has looked over the rack of guitars in the studio like they wished they could pick one up and go to town."

"I bet they would, some of the pickers that have been through here," I said, looking at the walls. The paneling was almost covered with signed photos of legendary artists, from the original Lynyrd Skynyrd boys to the Allman Brothers, from Mavis Staples to Clarence Carter, from Johnny Cash to the Cowboy Junkies. There were bluegrass giants like Earl Scruggs and Doc Watson, blues legends like B.B. King, Muddy Waters, and John Lee Hooker, and even some more recent folks like a very young Jason Isbell, a beardless Steve Earle, and Jack Black throwing the goat in a classic metal pose. If you were an incredible player, songwriter, or just wanted to be one, you recorded at Celebrity.

"So why are y'all closed?" I asked. "I thought this place would still be rocking out."

"Technology, man. All our gear is old, and a lot of our best engineers are dying off. Our session musicians all moved to L.A. or Nashville where they could find more steady work, and with so many people putting studios in their houses now, there just ain't the desire to come down and record stuff the old-fashioned way. So we've gotta shut things down. I've got an offer on the property, but it's contingent on me getting rid of the ghosts."

This old boy looked like somebody shot his dog, just thinking about closing the doors to his place. I could see he still had a lot of love for the business, even with what it was turning into. I actually felt bad for him, and that shit just don't happen to me.

"Fine, I'll do what I can. I ain't making no promises, but if I can't handle it, I know a dude up in Charlotte who's better with the whole demons and ghost stuff than I am. I'll call him in if it gets to be more than I can handle."

"Will you? That's fantastic! Thank you so much, Mister…uh…Bubba. What's our next move?"

"Well, first you're gonna give me the tour and show me where George Jones sat when he recorded here. Then we're gonna go get some lunch, and then you're gonna tell me some stories about my favorite musicians. Then tonight, I'll spend the night here and see what I can see, and if I can, I'll handle your ghost problem so you can sell this place and get on with your life."

"I appreciate it, Bubba. I don't want to sell, but I don't see a choice. And if I can't get rid of the ghosts…well, I just don't know what I'll do." Little dude looked like he was about to cry. I definitely needed to get the hell out of here before we started to get in touch with our feelings or some shit.

"Don't worry about it, bro. Now, you show me the board you mixed B.B. King on and let me worry about the monsters." We started down the hall toward the studio, and I coulda swore I saw something flicker ghostly blue out of the corner of my eye.

Chapter Three

THE TOUR WAS AMAZING, TO SAY THE LEAST. JUST WALKING AROUND in that room where so many legends of music played was more holy than going to church for me. I sat on a piano bench where Dr. John's butt once rested. I touched a mic that Johnny Cash sang into. I saw a cigarette burn in the carpet that came from Keith Richard's cigarette. Well, at least "cigarette" was what Billy admitted to.

And all through the tour he told me stories. Stories of late-night fried chicken runs for Gregg Allman, stories like finding one particularly loopy guitar player walking down the center line of the highway after eating a shitload of mushrooms and taking off all his clothes in the middle of a recording session and screaming about finding Jesus, stories about fistfights between Rock n' Roll Hall of Famers, and marathon drinking and writing sessions with unknown lyricists and composers all trying to channel the magic of the room into their own hits.

We finally walked back into the main control room and sat down behind the big mixing console. I ran my fingers across the knobs and faders, imagining for a second that I was a giant-sized Rick Rubin, or Mutt Lange, or even Jack White. I sat there for a minute, just drinking it all in, feeling the sanctity of the place just seeping into me.

"Feels almost holy, don't it?" Billy said from the chair beside me.

"Man, you don't even know. Growing up, we didn't have cable TV. It wasn't even a thing out where I lived, and the trees were too thick up on the mountain to get a satellite dish. This was back before they had them little ones that can strap onto the top of a big pine tree, this was back when they were six feet across and cost a shit-ton of money. Which we didn't have. We weren't ever hungry, but we were about the furthest thing from rich you can think of."

"Yeah, I grew up down here. You saw driving through town what kind of commerce we got," Billy replied. "My daddy was a farmer, and I didn't want no part of that life. I was a picker. Nothing great, just enough to get a gig now and again, but it was enough to get me hooked. And once the music gets its hooks in you, it don't ever let go."

"You ain't even wrong, man." We sat in silence, and my mind went back to a summer night when I was about thirteen, long before shit went south with Jason, before I blew out my knee playing ball, before I went on my first hunt. I was sitting out back of the house on a stump with a beer in my hand and a grin on my face you couldn't take off with steel wool and Comet cleanser.

There was a fire burning in an old 55-gallon drum that had a rectangle cut out at the bottom for an ash scoopin' port. Every so often, Pop or Grandpappy would get up, grab a shovel, and scoop some of the hot coals out of the bottom of that drum and sprinkle them underneath a half a pig we had skewered on a couple pieces of rebar spanning a fire pit made out of cinderblocks. The Brabham Fourth of July pig-pickin' and pickin' was the kind of event people came up the mountain from three counties to attend, and this was the first year I was old enough to stay up with the menfolk and tend the fire.

For most of us, tending the fire consisted of drinking beer and throwing the empties into the fire. For Grandpappy, Uncle Tom, Uncle Luther, and a few other old men that I had no real idea how we were kin, it was mostly a pickin' circle, where they passed around moonshine and various instruments and made music and told lies all night. There were cinderblocks, lawn chairs, tree stumps, and even one old tractor tire repurposed into seats for the weekend, and it was my favorite time of the year. It was better than Christmas, especially to a jaded preteen who found out that Santa Claus was bullshit years before and was disappointed to know that Krampus was very, very real.

Grandpappy finished up a rendition of "Orange Blossom Special" and passed the fiddle to Uncle Luther, who held out his other hand for the jar. He laid the fiddle across his knees and twisted the lid off that Mason jar, taking a deep slash of the clear liquid inside.

"Damn, Pete, that's smooth. What you put in there?" He turned to a man I only ever saw once a year, a mountain man named Pete who showed up at the pickin' with a peach crate full of quart jars and was always welcome to eat his fill. Men would pass by wherever Pete sat all weekend long, passing him folded banknotes and accepting a jar with a nod.

"I put some wild cherries in it. Cuts the bite a little bit but don't make it too sweet. And just a pinch of cinnamon in a gallon jug." Pete's voice had the gravel of a man who doesn't talk to other people too much, but when you got him going on about his liquor, he had the soul of a poet.

"Well, it sure is good, old son. Robbie, you want to play something with me?" Uncle Luther turned to me with a grin. "Or you too drunk off them two beers?"

Even at thirteen I was over six-feet tall and pushing hard at two-hundred pounds, so a couple of beers wasn't enough to make me drunk. It was enough to make me brave, so I grinned right back at Uncle Luther and said, "I'll pick with you, but I just started learning. Mama ain't taught me but one song, so if you can slow it down enough, I'm willing to try."

My whole life I'd only wanted two things—to hunt monsters like Pop and Grandpappy and to play with the men at the pig pickin'. This was my first chance to make one of those things come true, and I wasn't letting that chance slip away.

I got up to get my guitar, but Uncle Tom handed me his and said, "Just use this one, son. It's older than dirt, but it'll still ring."

I sat back down on the stump and settled the big old Alvarez across one knee. I had a pick in my pocket from my lesson earlier that afternoon with Mama, so I fished it out and got it positioned between my thumb and forefinger. I looked around at the circle of men and felt butterflies in my stomach all of a sudden.

"I ain't real good. Y'all might not want me—"

"What's the song, Robbie?" Luther said. His voice was gentle, but there was steel under it. I knew if I crossed him now, after he made the offer, there wouldn't ever be another one.

"Michael Row the Boat Ashore," I said. I hit a C chord on the guitar and started right in on the lyrics, thinking as hard as I could about getting the words and the chords right.

"Michael, row the boat ashore, hallelujah." I stumbled a little on the transition from C to F then back to C, but when all the men in the circle joined in on the "hallelujah," I felt something magic happen. Uncle Luther put his bow to the strings as I started in on the second line, and I could almost feel the salt spray on my face.

Mr. Gerald, the man that ran the furniture store in town, came in with his banjo on the second chorus, and half the men held back on the "hallelujah," giving it an echo that made it sound like there was thirty people singing together, instead of half a dozen men and one overgrown kid sitting out by a fire in the middle of the night.

For a couple of minutes, I wasn't Robbie, I wasn't Bubba, I wasn't Old Man Brabham's grandson, I wasn't anybody with any expectations, I was just a guy with a guitar and a song. And I belonged to something bigger than myself for the first time. I was part of the song, part of the music that tied the whole world together, and it was the best damn thing I ever felt. Then a couple years later, Mama left, and I leaned my guitar in a corner of my bedroom and picked up a gun. I never touched strings again and never knew how much I missed it until that moment in the control room.

I looked over at Billy and was surprised to feel my cheeks moist. I wiped away the tears I didn't even know I'd cried, and I just stared at him.

"We get that a lot," he said, a sad smile across his face. "I feel it, too. This place has made so much music, so many memories, touched so many lives. Hell, you probably grew up listening to records made in this very room."

"I'm sure I did," I said. "There's a lot faces on the walls that I've seen staring back at me from album covers my whole life."

"And now it's about to be gone," Billy said, running his hands across the mixer again. "I'm gonna miss it, but it's either let this place go or lose my house at this point, and I can't sleep at the studio forever." He gave a little chuckle. "Even though that's exactly what I'm asking you to do tonight."

"Well, let's get out to the parking lot, so I can start getting all my shit ready," I said, standing up. "I've got some gear in the car that oughta help me listen and look for ghosts and other supernatural shit."

"Like EMF detectors and infrared cameras and all that other stuff I see on the TV shows?" Billy asked, walking me to the front door.

"That and a Ouija board, a few candles, a Bible, and a shitload of holy water."

"What's all that stuff for?" he asked, his face turning a little pale and all the excitement rushing from him like water down a drain.

"Billy, let me be as clear as I know how to be. There's a lot of things out in the world that we don't understand. There's real ghosts, witches, vampires, werewolves, and other shit that I ain't even got words for. And a fair amount of those things don't like people all that much. Or they do like them, but they prefer them in bite-sized chunks. That's why there are people like me—'cause when something nasty brushes up against our world, you need somebody just as nasty to send them back to where they came from. Now come with me to my truck and help me unload the beef jerky and beer."

"You hunt ghosts and monsters with beer?"

"Son, if there's anything I can't do with a beer in my hand, it better involve a good-looking woman. Otherwise, I don't know that it's worth attempting in the first place."

It took us most of the afternoon to get all the equipment wired up to Skeeter's satisfaction. The first thing he made us do was set up an iPad in the main control room so we could video chat while we set up. I think most of that was just so he could tell me about it every time I put the wrong damn wire in the wrong damn place. After three hours of screwing around with delicate technology, I was convinced that I hated ghosts more than any other supernatural creature, and this is coming from a man who once had to wrestle a naked Bigfoot and only survived by almost pulling Sasquatch's wiener off with his bare hands.

But finally we were rigged up to Skeeter's satisfaction, and I sent Billy home to his trailer and his dog. I settled into the studio with a cot and a sleeping bag and set up the iPad on a drum throne next to my beer cooler. I drank about six beers watching *Daredevil* on the tablet and laid down to sleep about eleven-thirty, thinking I'd get a good night's sleep and review all the footage in the morning with Skeeter.

Of course, I only slept for about three hours before Hank Williams walked into the studio and woke me up. That's Hank Senior, not Bocephus or Hank III. The one that died in 1953. Yeah, that one.

Chapter Four

I SAT BOLT UPRIGHT, WHICH WAS A LOT LESS LIKE SNAPPING UP TO A sitting position like The Undertaker at *Wrestlemania*, and a lot more like a fat dude trying to sit up, flipping a cot over so he lands on the floor ass over teakettle with a cot on his head, then cussing a lot before finally giving up, throwing the cot across the room to knock over a cymbal with a gigantic crash, flinging the blanket to one side and sitting with his back up against a wall staring at the glowing form of a no-shit legend of country music.

"Damn, son, I ain't heard a racket like that since the time I got drunk with Ernest Tubb and Jimmy Short backstage at the Opry and Short fell all up in the drum kit. Knocked it to Hell and gone."

"Sorry, Hank, you surprised me a little bit. I wasn't expecting to recognize any of the ghosts I ran into tonight. I just figured they'd be old dead pickers and such."

"You trying to say I ain't a picker, boy?" Hank bowed up a little at me, and I had a moment of fanboy in my head. *Hank Williams wants to whoop my ass* before I settled that down.

"I ain't saying that at all, Hank. I'm just saying I expected nameless session guys or something like that. I didn't expect an honest-to-God legend."

The ghost appeared satisfied by that. I was glad. I didn't want to whoop Hank Williams' dead ass in a haunted music studio, but I figured if push came to shove, I was gonna be okay. It wasn't like he could actually lay hands on me, and even if he could, Hank was a skinny fella.

"Well, all right, boy. I reckon that's fine, then. But I ain't just a ghost. You oughta know that I am the bona fide Ghost of Music Past, here to show you how things used to be and how they can be again."

"Huh?" I looked at him, trying to figure out exactly what the hell he was talking about. I mean, I'd heard about ghosts going batshit crazy when they died, on account of not wanting to be dead and all, but this wasn't some kind of pissed off revenant shit, this was just weird.

"What do you mean, 'huh?'" The spirit asked, and for the first time I realize that I could kinda see *through* him. This was all uncharted territory for me. Like I told Billy before I sent him home for the night, I'm the guy people call in for monsters that need a can of whoop-ass opened up all over them. I'm not the "flights of angels sing thee to thy rest" kinda guy.

"I mean what the hell are you talking about? Ghost of Music Past? Is this some kind of redneck Christmas Carol or something?"

"Wait, ain't she done been here? Goddammit, they told me this woman would be late for her own damn funeral, but I figured she was already dead, what else would she be doing? She can't be late for this, right? Nope, wrong again!" He took off his hat, looked up at the ceiling and hollered, "BONNIE! Get your ass down here and tell this dumb hillbilly what's going on so I can get on with this shit!"

A redheaded woman with a kind smile and crystal green eyes walked through the wall of the studio and glared at Hank. "I'm coming, Hank. Jesus, keep your pants on! I got stuff to do, man, don't you understand that?"

"You are *dead*, woman. You ain't got shit to do except listen to music and play with them damn ghost dogs."

"Hey! My ghost weenie dogs are very important. Ain't that right, boo-boo?" She bent down and picked up a glowing dachshund from the floor. The little dog wriggled in her arms and licked her face. I reckon ghost dogs can lick ghost faces.

Hank cleared his throat, something that surprised me a little. I wouldn't expect ghosts to get phlegmy, but I reckon it was more for emphasis than anything else. "We're waiting."

The ghost woman shot Hank a look and pursed her lips. "Alright, keep your pants on." She set the dog down and turned to me. "I reckon you're Bubba?"

"I reckon," I said. "And you are?"

"I am the Spirit of Music," she said, holding her arms out in a grand gesture. Unfortunately for her, grand gestures are less grand when they're made by dead women wearing capri pants and a Mast General Store sweatshirt.

"And I am Bubba the Monster Hunter," I said. "Pleased to meet you. I'd get up and shake your hand, but I don't think you can shake hands anymore."

"Yeah, we can skip that part," she said. She spread her arms wide and took on a tremulous, wavering voice. "You will be visited by three ghosts this night to show you the power of music and the consequences of the events about to unfold here in this very studio."

"What kind of events?" I asked.

She scowled at me. "Look man, I just learned the words to this part last night, so how about you let me get through it before you start asking me stupid questions?"

"Why don't you just tell me what you want me to shoot without all the bullshit?"

"It's a whole ritual, man. I've got to tell you about all the ghosts, then the ghosts come and show you a bunch of stuff, and then you come back and have some sort of…what's the word?"

"Epiphany?" I suggested.

"Yeah, epiphany. You come back here, you have an epiphany, and then you go off on your own to save the day, motivated and transformed by all the important visions you've seen."

I cocked my head to Hank. "That all sounds good, but why don't we just stay here and drink?"

"Did you just quote Merle Haggard *to* Hank Williams?" the Spirit of Music asked.

"I did," I confirmed.

"I'll give you credit, son, that's pretty good," Hank said with a grin.

"Thanks."

This time it was the Spirit of Music who cleared her throat. I looked at her. "Are ghosts allergic or something?"

"What?" she asked.

"You and Hank both been hocking up loogies ever since you got here."

"I was clearing my throat to get your attention."

"Yeah, I've never understood that. Why not just say something like 'Hey Bubba, pay attention'?"

"It's just a thing, man. Don't overanalyze it. But now that I've got your attention, can we get on with it? We've got to get all this crap done tonight, and time's a-wastin'."

"Okay," I said. "Three ghosts. Got it. One of them is Hank Williams, the Ghost of Music Past. I reckon one of them will be the Ghost of Music Present and then the scary one, the Ghost of Music Yet to Come."

"Pretty much. I reckon you've read the book?" she asked.

"Nah, saw the cartoon and *Scrooged*. I like that movie."

"I do, too," the Spirit agreed.

"I ain't seen it," Hank chimed in.

"You pipe down," the Spirit said to him. "You were early, and it screwed up my whole karma, man. So you just sit there and be quiet."

"Whatever, Bonnie," Hank said.

"Bonnie?" I asked.

"That was my name in life. But now I am the Spirit of Music, and I have been tasked with protecting the soul of music against all threats." She did that whole wavy arms and spooky voice thing again. I wasn't real impressed.

"We can skip the theatrics. What's the threat this time? I do a lot better with something to punch or shoot."

"I can't tell you. You have to learn it on your journeys with the Ghosts."

"Then what are you here for?"

"I'm here to tell you that there's a threat to the existence of music, and you have been chosen as the Champion of the Boogie."

"Champion of the Boogie?" I asked.

"I just made that up. You like it?"

"It ain't the worst thing I've been called this week."

"Damn, son. It ain't but Monday."

"I've got a talent for pissing people off."

"I reckon. Anyhow, you will be visited by three Spirits this night, and they will show you different aspects of music and its impact on people's lives."

"How about I just say I'll fight whatever you want me to fight, and then I go back to sleep. Then tomorrow I'll get up in the morning, beat the shit out of whatever you want beat up, and we can all go home?"

"How about you just shut your mouth and listen to me while I tell you how this shit is gonna go. You are about to get on my last nerve, now." I'd never seen a pissed-off ghost before, but then, I didn't have a whole lot of experience with ghosts. That reminded me of something, and I started to reach into my pocket.

"You put a hand on that damn pocket watch and I will get all poltergeist on your behind," she said before my knuckles even brushed Aunt Marion's watch. "Everything you heard about it is true. It will control ghosts, but this shit it way too important for you to be messing with that. Now please, just sit there for another minute and listen to me."

I looked up, and she was looking at me with pleading eyes. Whatever she had to do meant a lot to her, so I decided to at least give her the benefit of the doubt. "Okay," I said. "Go on."

"Now when you have been visited by all three Spirits, you will be returned to this place, and tomorrow your battle will begin."

That much was nice at least. Usually I don't get any advance warning when I'm gonna have to shoot stuff or blow something up. "Okay, I got it."

"You sure?"

"What else is there? There's a bunch of ghosts, I'm gonna see some shit, then tomorrow I have to whoop somebody's ass. Just like most Tuesdays. Well, the ass-kicking. Not so much the ghosts. This is kinda new to me."

"Yeah, me too." She looked around and found Hank's ghost sitting on a stool in the corner of the studio trying to pick up a guitar. "Hank, you ready?"

"Just about," the ghost said, looking distracted. He stroked the neck of the guitar with fingers that passed right through it. "The only thing that sucks about Heaven is all the damn harp music. All those musicians and not a guitar anywhere."

I shuddered. "You sure you ain't in Hell, Hank?"

He smiled at me. "Some days I wonder, boy. Some days I really wonder. But I get to see what my boy is doing, and my grandkids. That girl Holly is making some fine music nowadays."

"Yeah, she is. I love that song of hers 'Waiting on June'," I said.

"Me too. That girl can write some music."

"Well, she might have a little genetic advantage."

"Thank you, son. I appreciate that. But I reckon if we don't get on with this show, Miss Bonnie over there is gonna whoop my spectral ass."

"You ain't wrong, Hank. Legend or not, you're here to do a job, and I'm here to see you get it done," the Spirit said.

"Yes, ma'am." Hank tipped his hat to her, then turned to me.

"All right, son. Let's start this all over. I am the Ghost of Music Past, and I'm here to show you how it used to be. Are you ready to ride?"

I looked up at the ethereal form of the once and forever King of Country Music, and I said, "Yes, sir. This might be the most surreal damn thing that's ever happened to me, and I've wrestled Bigfoot, hunted a chimichanga in Florida, and gambled with a leprechaun. But you lead, and I'll follow." Hank Williams waved his arm, and a glowing circle appeared in the air in front of us. He stepped through, and I followed, feeling like a weird cross between *Highway to Heaven* and a David Allan Coe song.

Chapter Five

WE STEPPED OUT OF THAT GLOWING CIRCLE OF LIGHT, AND I squinted against the sunlight glaring off age-bleached asphalt. I stood in the middle of a parking lot in front of a pale blue metal prefab building with "Bullock Creek Fire Department" on the side in white letters. Three white metal roll-up doors stood open, the doors looking like missing teeth in a baby-blue Muppet mouth.

The parking lot was full of pickups and firetrucks, and people milled around inside and out. Everybody greeted each other with hugs and handshakes, and a lot of "thank you for comings" bounced around. I smelled something delicious, so I followed my most delicate of senses around to the side of the building where three old men stood gathered around a huge cast iron three-legged pot, stirring it with what looked like a broken oar.

"What is that smell?" I asked. "It smells like Heaven, only spicier."

"Turkey stew," Hank said. "And no, you can't have any."

"Why not?" It smelled really good.

"We aren't really here, jackass. Besides, looks like it wouldn't hurt you to miss a meal." He pointed to my belly, which rumbled at the attention.

"Kiss my ass. I'm big-boned."

"Yeah, you got a huge bone in your gut?"

"Kiss my ass," I repeated. I walked over to the men and leaned in between them. Well, I planned on leaning between them, but one stepped sideways right when I tried it, so I ended up leaning right *though* him. I stood up quick, and the man shivered, rubbing his arms and looking around at something he couldn't see. Something that was probably me.

"Damn, Hank, that was weird."

"Yeah, you probably don't want to do that too often. You ain't a real ghost, so I don't know what will happen if you get stuck inside somebody."

"That can happen?"

"Yeah, man. Don't you watch movies? I love horror movies. They didn't have many good ones when I died."

"I don't watch many horror movies. It's kinda like watching training videos for me, I fall right asleep. Unless they get something right, then I get in touch with the director and threaten to whoop his ass for letting the secrets out."

"They ever care?"

"Not yet. That Whedon fella, though, he's alright. He promised to make all his shit funny so people won't believe it. But man, ever since he came up with that thing about vampires turning to dust, I been really wishing it was true. It would make cleanup so much easier."

"That's not what happens?" Hank asked. I just stared at him. "Hey, I don't know, man. I ain't never seen a vampire. I didn't even believe in ghosts until all of a sudden I was one."

I thought for a second, then nodded. "That makes sense, I reckon. No, vampires don't turn to dust. They don't really turn to anything. They just leak blood all over the place and make a damn mess. Did you know you can't get blood out of hardwood floors? It gets down in the cracks and just messes everything up."

"I did know that, as a matter of fact, but we ain't here to talk about me."

I looked at Hank Williams' ghost for a long second, then decided not to push him on it. However he learned that you can't get blood out of hardwoods was a long time ago, probably in a honky tonk that hasn't existed for fifty years, and besides, I didn't want him to get pissed off and leave me in Bullock Creek, wherever the hell that is.

"Okay, Hank," I said. "Why are we here? I don't hear no music, so what's this got to do with music past?"

"Be patient, son. Just be patient."

Hank waved his hand, and the images before me sped up, like he put the whole shindig on fast forward. People came out with styrofoam bowls on trays, and men filled them up with the savory stew. More trays, more stew. All along, people kept tossing more stuff into the big stewpot, keeping a never-ending stream of what I figured out was turkey stew going all morning. I saw dozens of people go into the fire station through the side door, be gone about long enough to eat lunch, and then come back out grinning. As the day progressed, a van pulled up at the opposite end of the building and half a dozen men started to unload sound equipment and instruments.

I walked inside, where a flurry of activity took place. Folding tables were broken down or moved aside to clear out the center of the building, and cakes and pies were laid out in a big spread by a small kitchen. Concessions were set up by the kitchen window, and a white-haired woman with sparkling blue eyes and smile took a little metal money box and sat by the door. The second she sat down, time slowed back down to its normal pace, and I noticed that the bay doors were closed, and through the door at the end of the building, I saw black sky and stars. Neat trick, that whole speeding up time thing. I coulda used that in statistics class back at UGA.

A strawberry blonde woman that looked kinda familiar walked into the building, and the woman gave her a big hug. A shortish man followed her, his mullet resplendent in blond curls. He wore jeans and a plaid western-style dress shirt, and the woman was in jeans and a green blouse. He turned to shake the hand of a trim man with a beard and long hair by the door, and I saw "BUBBA" on the back of his tooled leather belt. I was very much among my people.

A little brown-haired girl hid behind her mama's legs until she saw the older woman, then she ran out to hug her and took a seat right next to her, obviously overseeing the proper use of the cash box.

"How y'all doing?" the older woman asked.

"We're fine. Tired, but fine. She's getting bigger," the redheaded woman said. "Four pounds now. The doctors said maybe another month and she can come home if she gains enough weight."

"That's what they told me yesterday. She's going to be fine."

I turned to Hank. "Preemie?"

"You ain't as dumb as you look, Bubba."

"Nobody's as dumb as I look, Hank."

He laughed at that. "You obviously didn't spend any time in honky tonks in the fifties, son. There was some old boys there that made you look like a rocket scientist. But anyway, yeah, the white-haired woman, her name's Frances. The other woman is her daughter. She just had a little girl about six weeks ago. She was real premature, and they didn't know if she was gonna make it."

"But she's getting better?"

"Yeah, she's getting better. She'll probably be okay."

"So what are we doing here? Is there something I need to shoot?" I looked around, but most of what I saw was country people milling around, talking to their neighbors, looking at the stuff on the cake table, pouring a little something out of a flask into a styrofoam cup of soda—normal stuff.

"You ain't got it yet, boy? You ain't supposed to shoot nothing tonight. You are just supposed to watch. Watch, and learn, and maybe enjoy a little good picking." He waved over to the end of the building where the band was tuning up.

A man stepped up to the microphone in the middle of the band and tapped it a couple times. People quieted down and he leaned forward. "I'd like to thank y'all for showing up today and tonight. We really appreciate how our community comes together to help one another, and there ain't no better way to do that than with music. We appreciate Clyde and the boys coming out here to play this benefit square dance for us, and don't forget to come back next month when we'll actually pay them!" The crowd laughed and clapped, and a round little man with a mandolin balanced on his belly sketched a little bow.

I turned to Hank. "These boys are playing for free?"

He nodded. "Yep. It's a tradition in these parts. These ol' boys will play a benefit dance whenever anybody needs help. They've done it when somebody in the community has cancer, somebody's house burns down, somebody's got too many medical bills for one reason or another—any time people need help out here, folks rally around the fire department and help out. They do just like they did today. They hold a turkey shoot and cook stew in the morning, then have a square dance at night. Then about two weeks later, they have what they call a makeup concert, where the band gets to keep all the door, instead of just a piece like a normal event. That way they get paid back for playing for free."

"Sounds like a pretty good system, long as people come back to the makeup dances," I said, nodding.

The man at the mic went on. "Now y'all all know why we're here. Bonnie and Wayne just had a little girl, and she was real early. She didn't weigh but about two-and-a-half pounds when she was born, and she's been in intensive care up in Charlotte ever since then. She's doing real good, and Bonnie just told me she oughta be home in a few more weeks, but y'all know how expensive it is to go in the hospital, so we're here to come up with some money to help these folks out with their expenses.

"We've got a lot of cake walks and raffles for later on tonight, but for right now, let's get some dancing going on!" He waved a hand back at the men behind him, and walked off the "stage," really just a big piece of carpet somebody laid down at the front of the room.

The little mandolin man stepped forward and spoke into the mic. "Hey y'all. How's everybody doing tonight?"

The crowd cheered and clapped, and the man grinned back at them from under a big floppy hat with buttons and pins all over it. "Good, good. Well, we're the Back Creek Boys, now let's get it going."

Then he tore into that mandolin and whooped it like it owed him money. He kicked off an old bluegrass classic, "Rollin' in My Sweet Baby's Arms," and he tore it down. His fingers moved like lightning, and people were tapping toes and clapping along, and before you knew it, a brown-haired girl got out in the middle of the floor and started clogging. She didn't have any fancy shoes, just feet that had to move. A half-dozen other folks got out there dancing with her, and by the time a bald man with a western shirt and a bolo tie stepped up and called the first square dance, that tin building was full of people all grinning and dancing and just generally having a good time.

Over all of it, sitting by the door collecting money and welcoming people, that white-haired woman with the blue eyes smiled as she looked out at the crowd. She reached over and hugged the little brown-haired girl beside her, and with her other hand patted the red-haired woman on the leg.

I stood there for a long time, just watching this community step forward and take care of their own. After an hour or so, Hank put his hand on my shoulder.

"Time to go," he said. "You've seen what you needed to see."

"How is she now?" I asked.

"Which one?"

"The baby? Did the baby turn out okay?"

"Well, why don't we go find out?" Hank asked right back. He waved his hand, and that glowy circle appeared in the air again.

"Why can't anybody in my life just take a damn bus?" I asked as I followed the Ghost of Music Past through the magical circle to our next destination.

Chapter Six

WE STEPPED THROUGH THE GLOWY THING INTO WHAT I IMMEDIATELY recognized as my kind of place—a bar. Well, maybe not a bar exactly, but someplace that served beer, and that was close enough for me. I started walking toward my own version of an oak-topped polished nirvana with taps reading out chapter and verse of the Holy Scriptures of Stella Artois, Sweetwater 420, OMB Copper, Miller Lite, and even a throwback to the original First Place Beer—Pabst Blue Ribbon. I was hauling ass toward those taps like a dying man using up his last dregs of energy to get to an oasis in the desert, but of course Hank got in front of me and cut me off.

"You know you can't drink, right?" He looked at me like I was stupid. I might be ignorant in a lot of ways, but I'm not stupid.

"I know there's beer, and there's me, and if there's one person in the history of music that I wouldn't expect to lecture me on the evils of drink, it'd be Hank damn Williams. Well, and Jimi Hendrix. And Janis. And probably Jim Morrison. I reckon Keith Richards, too. Shit, I reckon there ain't nobody except maybe Amy Grant or Steven Curtis Chapman that I *would* expect to tell me not to drink. So what's your damn problem?"

He kept looking at me like I was stupid. I was starting to get hot, I'll admit. Then he answered me, and I realized that maybe I am just a little bit stupid some days. "We ain't really here, jackass. We're outside the events that we're observing; we can't participate."

"Oh."

"Yeah," he said. "Now just stand here and watch."

So I did. I watched as the bar—really an old movie theatre with all the seats ripped out and a stage built at one end—started to fill up with people. It was a nice place; the concession area was bigger than most, and it held the bar that was determined to sit there and tease me, half a dozen cafe tables with them tall chairs that can't make up their minds whether they're chairs or barstools, a bunch of band poster with autographs scribbled all over them, and twenty or thirty people wandering around greeting each other and hugging, or shaking hands and slapping backs.

I looked through the open door into the theatre, just to see what folks were working with in this joint, and was pleasantly surprised. The walls had a fresh coat of deep purple paint on 'em with acoustical paneling spaced out all over to break up the sound in the room. The movie seats were gone, but there were chairs arranged in rows in front of the stage, which was a little thing, about twenty feet on a side with stacks of speakers on the floor beside it and two racks of lights overhead.

A bluegrass band was setting up on the stage. Not the same band from the last vision, this one was a group of young folks, maybe just out of college, with scruffy beards and ironic t-shirts. But they handled their instruments with care and took time to tune their shit, which was more than I can say for a bunch of people I've seen recently.

I heard a noise behind me and turned as Hank cleared his throat.

"Everybody's got allergy problems lately. I don't understand it," I said.

Hank gestured over to the door, where a gorgeous little blonde girl walked in with an equally attractive brunette and a forty-ish redhead who was obviously their mother, just judging by the way she never took her eyes off her girls, unless it was to look around and make sure nobody was going to mess with her girls. A short blonde woman in her forties walked beside her, and every once in a while they'd lean close to each other and laugh like old best friends. Something about the woman tickled in my head, but it was the brunette that I recognized right off.

"Hey!" I exclaimed. "I know that girl. She was the one running the cash box at the square dance with that older woman."

"Yep," Hank confirmed. "That's her, and the old woman was her granny. That woman was a force of damn nature, let me tell you. We got into it one time about six months ago over whether or not I was allowed to play guitar on Sunday. She told me right damn quick that Sunday was the Lord's day, and there wasn't to be no music played. I reminded her that we were in Heaven, and since we were in the Lord's living room, practically, it was probably alright. She didn't agree with me and told me so in no uncertain terms."

I chuckled, thinking back to the sharp blue eyes I'd seen looking over that cash box. "Heh heh. What did you do?"

"I put my damn guitar away. I ain't no idiot. I'm dead and in Heaven, unless I'm carting morons around through time, I can give her one day a week."

"So what's up with this chick?"

"It's not the brunette you're here to see, it's the little sister," Hank said, pointing at the blonde.

I looked back at the girl he indicated, a tiny little thing who looked to be in her early twenties, if that. She had angel-blonde hair halfway down her back, and a pale green t-shirt paired with one of those big swirly hippie skirts that kids wear at the music festivals. The skirt was light purple with some blue stripes, and I could see her Granny's blue eyes sparkle from halfway across the room.

"Looks like she turned out alright. Last time we heard anything about her, she was in the NICU," I said.

"Yep," Hank replied. "She got better, and she got bigger. She'll always be a little girl, but she's healthy now."

"So what am I here to see, Hank?"

"Keep watching," the specter said.

I did, and I watched the girl walk over to one of the tables with her mother, sister, and the friend. They sat down for a few minutes to talk, then all of a sudden, I could hear the girl's voice just like I was standing next to her.

"I know that guy," she said. "We went to school together. I'm gonna go talk to him." Without another word or a backward glance, she hopped down off her little chair/stool thing and walked across the lobby to where a boy maybe a year or two older than her stood talking to a friend of his. She walked right up to him and started talking, and I could see from across the room that he was instantly crazy about her. The second he turned to her, the band started up with a cover of "Blue Sky" by the Allman Brothers, forcing them to lean in close to one another to talk. Neither one of them seemed bothered by this.

"They knew each other, huh?" I asked Hank.

"Yeah, he might have noticed her once or twice in passing."

"Looks like he did a lot of noticing her," I replied.

"Yeah, but it took her half a dozen years to notice anybody noticing. Now shut up and pay attention."

I turned back to the pair, but as I turned my head, the room spun around and everything changed. All of a sudden I was standing in a big room with fifty or sixty people in suits sitting in folding chairs arranged with one aisle down the middle.

The same boy stood at the front of the room, his hair pulled back in a ponytail, looking sharp in a tuxedo, standing next to a fat guy dressed all in black, also sporting a ponytail. They both smiled as they looked at me, and I waved a little before I realized they were looking past me.

I turned around, and the girl from the concert started down a flight of stairs into the room with a string trio playing "Falling Slowly" by The Frames as she walked. I watched her descend the steps, looking even more beautiful in a long white dress with her blonde curls piled high on her head. Looking around at the crowd, I saw the redheaded mom sitting front and center, with a gaggle of happy family members around her.

The little blonde woman walked down the aisle, and almost walked right through me, but I stepped aside at the last minute. Okay, Hank might have pulled me aside, but I got out of the way regardless. We stood there watching the pair look at each other with eyes full of love while their family and friends drank it all in, then watched for a little while longer while they all danced and drank the night away. Just as Hank turned and opened up his glowing hole in the air again, I heard the familiar sounds of "Rolling in My Sweet Baby's Arms."

I followed Hank through the circle back to the studio, wincing at the loud "POP" in the air as he closed the portal to yesterday.

"Okay, I get it," I said once we were back in Muscle Shoals in what I assumed was my normal time. "Music was a part of this little girl's whole life, from the minute she was born to the day she got married. Dude, music is a part of most everybody's life like that. Hell, I can remember the first time I got up in front of the church and sang in the children's choir."

"Shit, son, how big were you when you were a kid? The congregation must have thought somebody was bringing a ringer into the kiddy choir!"

"I was a big kid, yeah. Let it go," I grumbled. I stomped across the studio and sat down in a chair. There was an old flat-top Gibson leaning on a stand next to me. I picked it up and strummed out a rough chord, turning the knobs on the head of the guitar to bring it back in tune. The steel strings felt hard under my fingertips, but I managed a couple quick chords before putting it down.

"You ain't never gonna be no Clapton, son, but that don't mean you can't pick a little," Hank said, smiling at me.

"I ain't played in years, man," I replied, thinking back on the day I shut my guitar case for good, when I finally decided my Mama wasn't coming home again.

"That don't mean nothing. It's like anything else. The callouses might fade away, but your hands'll remember where they're supposed to go."

"I reckon." I reached over and stroked the neck of the guitar. "This is a pretty one. I've always liked blue guitars."

"Yeah, me too. I used to want one back in the day. Never got around to getting one. My old Martin always did just fine by me."

"I think Neil Young has that guitar now," I said.

"Yeah, he's got one of mine. He plays real good," the ghost said. He looked at me, really *looked* at me, and said, "I don't know if you can do this, son. I don't know if we even got time to show you everything you need to know *to* do this, but I know I done my part, and now it's time for me to go."

He walked over, shook my hand, then he turned away. He didn't wave his hand for a glowing circle in the air, didn't leave to some great chorus of angels singing "Jambalaya," he just opened the door to the studio and walked out. I sat there, staring at the great man's back as he walked down that long hallway. After a minute or two of walking down a seemingly never-ending hallway, he just vanished into the mist. I stood up, walked across the room, and just about had a damn heart attack when I turned back around.

Standing in front of me, resplendent in purple crushed velvet, huge brown eyes staring up at me from underneath a purple top hat covered in purple fur, was the Purple One himself—Prince.

Chapter Seven

I STOOD THERE, STARING AT THE DIMINUTIVE MAN IN HEAD-TO-TOE purple long past the point of awkward. He didn't say anything, just waved his hand in the air, opening up a portal of his own, this one bathed in lavender light. He gestured for the opening, and I stepped forward, then paused.

"Just to clarify, you're the Ghost of Music Present, right?"

"Yes." The voice was just like I imagined it, soft, almost to the point of being delicate, but precise.

He looked up at me. "You coming, or are you just going to stand there gaping at me all night?"

I ducked my head a little and stepped through the hole in midair. There was no sensation of travel, no flashing lights as I passed through the wormhole, I just lifted one foot from Alabama, and put it down again somewhere else.

I didn't know exactly where I was in the world, but I knew exactly where I was, nonetheless. The smell of lemon-scented cleanser is universal to hospitals, and the confused moaning from behind some of the doors lining the tiled hallway told me in seconds that I was in a nursing home, and not one of the high-rent ones where everybody smiles in all the pictures and orders filet mignon for dinner from room service.

This was a run-down, squeaky floors and overworked nurses kind of facility. The lights overhead flickered a little, but I couldn't tell if that was from disrepair or the fact that a ghost and an astral-projected giant redneck just teleported into the middle of the building. That's the kind of thing that will blow a fuse or two if you're not careful.

I looked down at The Purple One. "Where we headed, boss?"

Again with the no talking thing, he just walked off down the hall, the heels of his purple patent leather alligator skin boots *click-clicking* across the tile. I shrugged and followed. What else was I gonna do? He stopped outside a room about two-thirds of the way down the hall on the right and gestured for me to go in. I looked at the closed door for a second, then just took a deep breath and stepped through it.

It's a weird feeling the first time you walk through a closed door. I'd been thrown through a few, and even ran through a couple, but passing through a solid door without opening it and without violence involved was a new experience for me. I didn't feel anything, but I saw the inside of the pieces of wood as they passed through me, or I passed through them, or whatever. It was pretty damn strange, and that's coming from a fella who counts a Georgia snake-man as a friend.

I stepped into your standard hospital/nursing home room that hasn't been redecorated since the nineties. There was one window with a hospital bed a few feet from it. A pitiful little cactus sat on the windowsill soaking up the meager sunlight coming through, and there were two chairs, armless things that made my ass hurt just looking at them. A TV blared the new *Let's Make a Deal* at a volume loud enough to wake the dead, reminding me quickly just how stupid that show has always been.

In the bed was the shell of what had once been a big man. He was still tall, but his skin hung loose, like he was sunk in on himself. His skin had a little yellow tinge to it, like he was permanently jaundiced, and his nose was covered in the spider web of broken blood vessels that told of a life spent with a bottle nearby.

The old man's eyes were vacant, staring at the TV but not registering what was happening on the screen. It was a good thing, too, because Wayne Brady was talking to some skinny Asian woman dressed like a banana, and there was a lot of jumping up and down and shrieking. I shook my head and grunted, and the old man looked right at me.

"I ain't ready yet," he rasped. I stared at him, my mouth falling open again.

"You can see me?" I asked.

"I'm prob'ly more dead than alive, son. I see you better than I see my granddaughter when she comes to visit. Now get on out of here, I told you I ain't ready."

"I'm not here to take you anywhere, sir, I'm just here to...well, to be honest, I ain't real sure why I'm here. But I know I ain't here to take you off."

"Then why are you...I reckon you just said that, didn't you?" The man's mouth wasn't moving in time with his words, and I looked over at Prince. He raised an eyebrow at me and shrugged. Chatty was not a word I'd be using to describe him anytime soon.

"How are we talking?" I asked the man.

"I reckon it's my spirit talking to yours, or something like that. I don't know, boy, I ain't never done this before, either. But why don't you sit down? You're making me nervous just standing there like a giant moron."

I sat down in one of the chairs, trying to figure out how to sit on it without falling straight through to the floor, but it wasn't a problem.

"You won't fall," Prince said, once I figured that out on my own. I gave him a look that told him what I thought of his timing, and he laughed, a little mocking, lilting thing that made me regret, just a little, paying for the deluxe edition of the Purple Rain remaster when it came out a few years back. He looked back at me and kept talking. "Sorry, didn't mean to be rude. You expect to be able to sit on the chair in this form, so you can. Just like you expect to be able to walk through walls, so you can."

"So you're saying if I didn't believe I could walk through walls, I woulda busted my face on the door?"

"Yes," he agreed. "And that would have been pretty funny, so I was going to win either way. You would be in the room, or I'd have a good laugh. So I let you go for it. And it worked out, didn't it?"

"I never thought I'd say this, but you're a little bit of a dick, Prince."

He laughed, and this time there was no mocking to it, just an honest laugh. "I've been called worse, my friend. I've certainly been called worse." He turned to the man in the bed. "It's an honor to finally meet you."

"You coulda come by any time," the old man said. "I liked your music."

"Thank you, that means a lot," Prince replied. "I have enjoyed yours as well. You are a talent the likes of which the world may never see again."

The old man laughed. "I'm flattered. You're wrong, but I'm flattered. There'll be somebody else better than me. Probably already is, at least half a dozen of them. We just ain't heard 'em yet."

I held up a hand. "I'm sorry, sir," I said with some deference to the old dude. "But who are you? I'm afraid I don't recognize you."

He laughed again. "I wouldn't expect you to, son. My name is Buford Scatlin. I used to pick a little."

I knew the name. Everybody knew the name. His given name might have been Buford, but the world new him as Professor. They called him that when he started picking solo back in the late 40s after coming back from the war in France. He used to be a trim man, with almost freakishly long fingers, but big, the kind of man that people step sideways when he comes down the sidewalk. Not like me, who makes people run for cover and hide behind cars when I walk towards them.

They called him Professor Fiddle because he wore these little wire-rimmed glasses that always made him look like he was squinting or thinking hard about something, and because he revolutionized the way people thought about bluegrass fiddle. He taught people a whole new style of playing, with short strokes of the bow sounding almost like picking a guitar. I remembered listening to his albums with Grandpappy when I was real young, and Grandpappy telling me about seeing The Professor play the Opry with Earl Scruggs and Doc Watson.

I stepped closer to the bed and held out my hand. "He's right, sir. It is an honor. My Grandpappy used to tell me a story of seeing you play the Opry with Earl Scruggs and Doc Watson. He said he'd never seen more musical talent on the stage at the same time in his life."

The old man looked in my general direction and gave me a smile. "Well, son, you tell your Grandpap thank you for me. I reckon I'm the only one of that trio still drawing breath, and I'm getting a lot closer to seeing Arthel and Earl again that I reckon I want to, even if I do miss their company something fierce."

"I would love to tell him, sir, but he passed some years back."

"I'm sorry to hear that, son. Was he sick?"

"No sir," I replied, remembering the night Grandpappy died, and the wolves that killed him. I swallowed hard. "It was…a work accident."

"Well, shit, boy, I sure am sorry to hear that. Well, I reckon I'll probably see him before you will, then. I'll tell him you said hey." He smiled up at me, and I saw the resignation in his eyes. He was dying, and he knew it.

"What do you have, if you don't mind me asking," I said.

"What I have, son, is a terminal case of ninety-five years old. I have lived the kind of life most men dream of. I have played in front of thousands of people, made gold records, traveled on tour buses with the legends of music, and now it's getting close to time to move on. As the man said, I have wined and dined with kings and queens, and I have slept in alleys and dined on pork and beans. But those days are gone, and it's about time for me to take my last curtain call, I reckon."

I stood in the middle of a nameless nursing home in Nowhere, USA, with a music legend quoting Dusty Rhodes at me while Prince's ghost stood in the corner in a purple fuzzy fedora smiling at the scene. In all the weird shit I have lived through, this one might take the cake.

"Why are you here, though?' I asked. "I mean, no offense, sir, but this place is kind of a…"

"Dump?" The Professor said with a smile. "No, it's fine. I ran out of money a few years ago. Doc and Earl had better people running their finances than I did, and Doc, in particular, always lived a modest life. He always said there wasn't any place he'd rather live or die than the mountains of Carolina, so that's what he did. Me, I liked the shiny cars and the big houses and the pretty girls, and them things don't come cheap. I never figured I'd live this damn long, so I didn't make nothing in the way of plans for my old age." He smiled again, and again it was like a ghost smile overlaid on his face. His body didn't really move, but somehow his essence was able to talk to me like he was already a ghost.

"So you're here? Damn, that don't seem right."

"Boy, let me tell you something about dying. When it comes down to it, there ain't but two ways to go—fast or slow. I reckon if you go fast, you pretty much just wake up dead one morning or something like that." I looked over at Prince, who didn't give any indication that he was listening. He just sat there like a stone, but the tightness in his jaw and the little hint of moisture in one eye told me he heard every word and was thinking about his own passing, much too soon and much too sudden.

"But when you go out slow, every day is like laying ties to the railroad tracks. The train's coming for you, but it only moves a couple feet every day, and it started a mile off. So you do everything you can do to slow down that ol' locomotive, but you know no matter what you do, before too long, it's gonna be right up on you. And when it gets there, it don't much matter if you're in a penthouse or a shithouse, you want to be anywhere but in front of that damn train. So yeah, this place ain't much. But ain't no place going to be any better, so you might as well just lay there and hope the nurse who comes in to wipe your ass is pretty."

I stood there for a minute, just looking at this legend of music, lying in his dingy hospital bed alone, wishing I could do something for him. "Is there anything I can do?" I finally asked.

"I don't know why His Royal Purpleness over there brought you to see me, son. So I don't know what he, or whoever he works for, wants you to do. But I reckon if there's anything I would want you to do, I'd just say keep the music alive, boy. There's so much out there nowadays to interfere, but if you want to do anything for me, because I've done something good for you sometime, work hard to keep the music alive."

I stepped forward and reached out a hand. He clasped it, not with his physical hand, but with that ghostly overlay of his spirit. I looked down at this legend in his last days and said, "I will, sir. I promise."

"Thank you, son. I'll look for your Grandpappy when I cross over. I'll tell him you said hey."

"If you don't mind, sir?" I looked in his eyes, surprised to find him blurry.

"What is it, boy?"

"Tell my brother and my dad that I'm sorry. They'll know what for." One big fat tear rolled down my cheek, and I knocked it away with the back of my hand.

"I will, son. I will. Now I reckon your buddy has somewhere else he wants you to go." He nodded, and I turned around.

Prince stood by another one of those glowing purple circles. I let go of the old man's hand and stepped through the doorway of lavender light, glad this time that my guide didn't have much to say.

Chapter Eight

I STEPPED OUT OF THE CIRCLE INTO A HALF-EMPTY DIVE BAR advertising PBR specials and "mystery shots" for $2. The beer taps were all domestic, and the liquor quality topped out at Maker's Mark. No Gentleman Jack or Johnny Walker Blue Label here; this was a joint where people went to get drunk as shit and maybe hear a little bit of music.

And a little bit of music was all anybody could hear in this dump, too. The acoustics were for absolute shit, and the sound system was a pair of plastic JBL speakers with built-in amplifiers stuck on folding stands at the corners of the "stage." The band was on a couple of little risers that were basically sheets of plywood nailed to some two-by-fours laid on end. There might have been six inches of elevation, but not more.

The decor was a mix between *Roadhouse* and T.G.I.Friday's, with a bunch of old movie posters, a couple of pool tables with beer lights over them, and a couple dozen stools arranged around the long bar. Most of them wobbled because one or more of the legs had been broken at some point, probably over some dipshit's head, but it didn't matter much since most people were doing that whole "sit with one butt cheek on the stool and one foot on the ground" thing that folks do in a bar where they might have to fight or duck with not much notice.

On the "stage" was a man with a guitar. He was a big man, in his fifties, with close-cropped hair and the build of a man who's known some days of hard work in his life. His guitar had the look of one that had been banged around in the back of a van on the way to more than one gig, with a strap fraying at the edges and the finish wearing off the edges of the sound hole from getting slapped with a pick for years. I could tell he was a player because I could see his callouses from a dozen feet away, and he tuned by ear, not using any kind of electronic tuner. I was never good enough to hear it. I always had to use a little electronic tuner my mama gave me.

He finished tuning and stepped up to the battered mic on a straight stand. He adjusted the stand to his height, and it slipped back down. He twisted it again, and it slipped again. Rather than try again, he just reached down to one of the barstools and pulled it up to him. He sat down, lowered the mic, and leaned into it.

"Hey y'all, welcome to the Dawg. My name is Dave Abbott, and I appreciate all y'all coming out here to see me tonight. And if you ain't here to see me, then I hope I don't run you off before you finish your beer." He chuckled a little, then played a little riff on the guitar, and the second his fingers touched the strings, I could tell that this man wasn't just a player, he was a damn *master*.

Those big ol' fingers that looked like battered link sausages moved up and down the neck of that guitar like crickets jumping in a bait tube. He noodled the strings, just messing around, picking out the opening to the *Green Acres* theme song, then jumping into "Dueling Banjos," then hopping into "Steam-Powered Aeroplane." I turned to Prince to see what he thought of this dude, but the Purple One just reached up with two fingers and pushed my lower jaw up to close my mouth for me.

"Damn, dude, that boy can *play*!" I said. Prince just nodded.

"I mean, he's better than most of the people I see on TV or hear on the radio." Prince just nodded again.

I watched a little while longer as he covered some bluegrass classic, then ripped into some old blues tunes, like "Red House" and "One Way Out," then played some original tunes, and damned if the songs he wrote weren't as killer as his playing. Every once in a while, I would look over at Prince, and every time, he just met my eye and nodded.

After about forty-five minutes, the singer/songwriter/musical genius leaned into his mic and said, "Y'all go ahead and get another beer. I gotta go pee, and I'll be back in a few after I wet my own whistle."

The half a dozen people who were paying attention clapped, but the other ten people in the bar were seriously dedicated to their mission of getting as absolutely shithoused as they could. He stepped down off the stage, set his guitar on a stand, and walked through the sparse crowd to the bathroom at the back of the building. He was in there for a couple of minutes, then came out drying his hands on his jeans and walked back up to the bar.

He leaned on the smooth dark oak and motioned the bartender over. I stepped in closer to be able to hear their conversation, figuring if I couldn't be seen or communicate with anybody, I might as well have a better idea what's going on around me at least.

"I'm sorry I couldn't get more people in here, Johnny," the man said as the bartender passed him a Jack Daniels on the rocks and set a Rolling Rock in the bottle beside it.

"Don't worry about, Dave. It's hard to get anybody out on a Tuesday."

"I know," the singer replied. "But sometimes it just feels like people don't want to come out any night anymore. It's always been hard, but it seems like it's been harder and harder the past couple years."

"You ain't wrong, old son," the man slinging beers agreed. "We used to be able to put three dozen people in here every night, no matter what else was going on in town. Now it's all we can do to get twenty people for a decent touring act. And that really hurts the locals like you, who might not have as big a name."

"I know that's right, brother. I quit the touring thing a few years ago because I couldn't afford to keep taking all that time off from my day job. Now I reckon I only play out two or three times a month when I used to do four nights a week, about every week."

"And ain't none of us getting any younger, either," the bartender said, holding up his own green glass bottle. The two men clinked their Rolling Rocks together, then the bartender's head whipped to one side.

"Hey, cut that shit out!" he yelled, and I turned. My Spidey-senses went on full alert, but it was nothing supernatural. That was good because it meant that nobody was likely to get eviscerated and eaten in the middle of the bar, but it was also bad because it meant that I probably couldn't do a damn thing about it.

A skinny man in his mid-twenties was holding up his hands with a classic "Who Me?" look on his face. Next to him was a brown-haired girl with a furious look on her face.

"Touch me again, you son of a bitch!" she hollered up at the man.

"Oh, come on, honey, he was just showing his appreciation," a dark-haired guy with a baseball hat turned around backwards, khaki shorts, flip-flops, and a polo shirt said to the girl.

"Yeah, baby, that's all," the guy she yelled at lowered his hands and moved closer to the girl. He had a little piece of a beard, but only on his chin, with enough crap in his hair to make it onto *Project Runway.* He also wore the uniform or the

Southern Twenty-Something Douchebro—khaki shorts, dress shirt untucked, baseball cap, and flip-flops. I've stared down vampires and fought trolls, but there ain't no way in the world I'd walk around a dive bar in flip-flops. Some of the shit running around on those floors will straight up kill your ass.

"Showing appreciation does not include putting your hands on my ass, you dick," the girl said. She was dressed to go out, in a little spaghetti strap top with shorts and sandals. Nothing about her outfit screamed "grab my ass," and she was letting Douchebro know it in no uncertain terms.

Out of the corner of my eye, I saw Dave move toward the back of the bar where the pool tables, and the altercation, were. He still clutched his Rolling Rock bottle, but I noticed that it was empty, and he had the neck in his clenched fist like he knew how to use it as a weapon in addition to refreshment.

"Is there a problem here, son?" Dave asked, and his voice was low, but serious. I recognized the voice. I used it myself to calm shit down when I didn't feel like beating some dumb bastard's ass but needed him to understand that I not only could, but I would at the slightest provocation.

"Nah, Grampa, there ain't no problem. You can go back to drinking your Ensure. Me and my new friend here are just having a discussion." He grinned down at the girl, who was at least half a foot shorter than him. "Ain't that right, sweetheart?"

"No, it's not, asshole, and if you call me sweetheart again, I'm going to kick you right in the balls." She turned and took a step back toward the rest of the bar, but the kid reached out and grabbed her arm.

That turned out to be a bad idea. The girl swung around and laid a slap across that boy's face that sounded like a .22 pistol shot and left five distinct finger marks across his face. He let go of her arm in shock, and the girl stepped up to his face.

"Don't you ever lay hands on me, you son of a bitch!" she shouted.

"You bitch!" the boy shouted, raising his own hand.

Dave stepped in then, putting one big hand on the boy's chest and walking him backwards to the nearest wall. "You are about to make a very big mistake, son. Now you can walk out the front door with a hurt cheek and your pride beat to shit. But if you push this, you're going to end up thrown out the front door on your ass, with a whole lot more beat than your pride. Do you understand me?"

The boy spit in Dave's face. "Screw you, old man! That bitch deserved it, walking around here dressed like some whore. So you stay the hell out of it or I'll whoop your ass, too." He shoved Dave back and then came at the older man, his right hand coming around in a huge haymaker.

Dave threw an arm up to block the boy's punch, then stepped to one side, grabbed the back of the boy's head, and slammed him face-first into a nearby pool table. The kid's nose broke with a loud *crunch*, and a fountain of blood joined the multitude of stains on the table's felt. The kid slid to the floor, out cold, and Dave turned to the girl.

"Are you okay?" he asked, his voice now tender.

"Yeah, I'm fine," she said. "He's a dick. I probably shouldn't have—"

Dave cut her off. "Held back? Yeah, probably not. He deserved worse than you gave him, so don't feel bad about that for a second. You sure you're okay?"

"Yeah, I'm fine."

"Good. But you were right to slap him. You don't have to take that kind of shit off anybody. There ain't nothing wrong with the way you're dressed. Screw that dude."

She smiled up at him, the gentle giant. "Nah, I wouldn't screw him. He probably has a tiny dick." They both laughed, and she went back to her friend who was waiting at the bar.

Dave turned and looked at Douchebro's buddy, who was kneeling next to his unconscious friend. "Get him out of here. And the next time you or your pal decides to put your hands on somebody without their consent, remember the beating he just got."

Dave walked back to the front of the bar and looked around. The place was empty. Even the devoted drunks bailed once the confrontation in the back turned violent. Dave picked up the pickle jar labeled "TIPS" in blue magic marker and shook it in the general vicinity of the bartender.

"Four dollars and some change," he announced. "And one kid who hates me forever because I embarrassed him."

"But one that thinks you're the white knight to end all white knights," the bartender replied.

"Yeah," Dave said. "Guess I ain't quitting the day job this week, though." He picked up his guitar and started packing it away.

I turned to Prince, who stood in front of another glowing purple portal. “I don’t know what I’m supposed to take away from that, man. Can you give me a hint?”

“Maybe it’s like a song,” Prince said. “It means something different to everyone who hears it because everyone hears with different ears.”

“That don’t make any more damn sense than anything else,” I said.

“Then there’s only one thing to do,” said the suddenly verbose ghostly guitar god. “Keep moving forward.”

So I stepped through the portal and did just that.

Chapter Nine

WE STEPPED OUT OF THE AIR INTO A CHILLY NIGHT OUTSIDE what looked like an old movie theatre. A line of people snaked around the building, all bundled up like it was twenty degrees out instead of sixty. I was a little chilly, but part of that was only wearing a pair of jeans and an Allan Brothers t-shirt, and part of it was the fact that I'd had goosebumps ever since meeting the ghost of Hank friggin' Williams, and walking through thin air with Prince as my escort wasn't helping matters none.

I looked around, trying to figure out what the Ghost wanted me to see here while still trying to figure out what he wanted me to take away from our last stop, and my eyes lit on a brown-haired boy with a trim beard and ponytail walking down the line with a pretty blonde girl next to him. I'd seen them before—it was the boy and girl I'd watched meet and get married when Hank was taking me through the Past. He was walking, holding up two fingers in the universal symbol for somebody either looking to buy tickets or looking to sell them. I wasn't sure which, but whenever I saw him stop and talk to somebody, they'd speak for a couple seconds, then one of them would shake his head, and the kid would move on.

They got right in front of me and stopped, staring up at the marquee. "JOHN HIATT & JASON ISBELL—ONE NIGHT ONLY—SOLD OUT" was one the battered triangle jutting out from the front of the building in mismatched red plastic letter.

"Sorry, babe," the kid said. "I should have gotten the tickets earlier. I knew it was gonna sell out."

"Don't worry about it," the girl replied. "They were way too expensive. Let's just go get something to eat and go home."

"Okay, but I really wanted to see the two of them together. And it's been forever since we've been to a concert."

"I know, babe," the girl said, reaching out and twining her fingers in the guy's. "But it's fine. We'll see them at Merlefest, or somewhere we don't have pay TicketBastard an arm and a leg." They turned and walked across the street, and I stared at Prince.

"Well, that was subtle as a damn hand grenade, Eddie Vedder," I said. "I get it, ticket prices are stupid high, and it ain't like the money goes to the artists. It's all going to some asshole in a suit thanks to a shitload of surcharges and stupid fees."

Prince didn't say nothing, just turned around and wiggled his fingers in the air. Another purple portal opened up, and we stepped through.

And stepped into a swanky-ass office with about two dozen platinum records lining the walls. The carpet was so white I was scared to take a step, even though my ghost feet couldn't possibly track in any mud. The office was as long as a damn basketball court is wide, and at the far end, there was a massive metal and wood abomination of a desk with a sawed-off little bald-headed man who looked more like an insurance adjuster than a record exec. The words "PARAGON RECORDS" hung in huge letters on the wall behind the desk, and I figured this joker was probably some kind of corporate suit because he didn't look like any musician I'd ever seen. Even symphony oboe players were cooler than this schmuck.

He wore a brown suit, a brown tie, a white shirt (No stripes. Not for this dude), and thick plastic-rimmed glasses that reminded me of Tommy Cornest in sixth grade when he tried to pants me in P.E. I was already training with Pop by eleven, so I didn't know if whatever had a hold of my britches was friend or foe, so I spun around and caught Tommy right above the nose with a huge right hand. His plastic glasses split right down the middle. So did Tommy's nose. I got a couple days detention, but so did Tommy for trying to pull my pants down.

But as fascinating as the nebbishy-looking turdmuncher behind the desk was, he had nothing on the nasty bastard next to him. Every muscle in my body tensed up when my eyes lit on the demon by the desk. He was your average, run-of-the-mill, just about what you'd expect demon, standing there with red skin, yellow eyes, cloven hooves, a spiky tail, and black horns curling up off his head like a cross between a person and an evil antelope.

I charged him. I couldn't help it, and part of me figured that I wouldn't do anything but run right through him, so I put my head down and went after him like I was back in college chasing quarterbacks all over Augusta on a

Saturday afternoon. I barreled toward that skinny fucker, all three-hundred-and-fifty pounds of redneck fury hell-bent on turning him into nothing more than a smear of demon guts on the wall so I could go back to sleep and forget about all this ghost bullshit.

And then he looked up at me, grinned, and I knew I was about to be screwed, glued, and tattooed. Apparently demons can touch things in the spirit world, which makes sense now that I think about it. I mean, after all, if you can't lay hands on a spirit, how can you torture the souls of the damned?

Well, I learned the hard way that demons can indeed lay hands on people in the spirit world, and they're strong as hell besides. This fella didn't look like a whole lot, about six feet tall and skinny as a rail—maybe a buck-fifty, buck-sixty, tops. But he grabbed me by the throat and the belt and hoisted me straight up over his head like I was a damn toddler looking for an airplane ride from his favorite uncle.

Except I'm nowhere near a toddler, and this asshole wasn't my favorite anything. He flung me into the air, and right about the time I expected him to let me go and send me through the ceiling, he hung on and pitched me at the wall like I was a damn lawn dart.

I went sailing right through the wall, of course, and found myself outside the record company's office. In mid-air. Fifteen damn floors up. But I thought about as I flew across the sky, my momentum increased by the demon's toss, and decided that since ghosts usually floated, if I was a ghost, I could float, too. So I just floated myself around, pointed my head back in the direction of the wall I'd just flown through, and drifted back there. I was almost to the building when Prince stepped through the plate glass window.

He held up a hand, and I floated to a stop in front of him. "That probably wouldn't be a good idea," His Purpleness said.

"I don't reckon I give a single damn if it's a good idea or not, Prince, there's a damn demon in there, and he's screwing with that dude!"

"Is he?"

"Is he what? A demon? I don't reckon it's Halloween, so unless there's some monster I ain't never heard of that likes to run around in red long johns and stick antlers on its head, that bastard in there is a demon."

"Oh, there's no question that's a demon, my overwrought, overlarge friend. The question is whether or not he's 'screwing with that dude.'"

I almost fell out of the sky, I was so flabbergasted by what Prince was saying. I'm not sure what would have happened if I would have eventually stopped falling, if I would've fallen and hit the ground, or just fallen through the earth, but I didn't want to find out, so I decided not to fall and floated back eye-to-eye with him. Which meant that my toes were like a foot lower than his, but whatever.

"What do you mean, he might not be screwing with that guy?"

"How do we know that the human isn't a willing participant to the partnership?"

"Yeah, dude, plenty of people think they know what kind of deal they're making until it comes time to pay the bill."

"And plenty of people know exactly what kind of deal they're making and don't care, valuing short-term fame and fortune over eternal life and love," the dead rocker replied.

"I guess you would know, having seen it a lot closer than me," I said.

"You don't even want to know some of the conversations I've had at parties, my friend."

"Well, I reckon we oughta figure it out," I said, drifting back toward the building and passing through the wall.

The demon looked over at me and grinned. "Back for more, hillbilly?"

I held up both hands like I was surrendering. I was also putting my hands up in case I needed to block a punch or three. "No," I said. "These ghosts been dragging me around all night, wanting to show me shit. I reckon there's something they want me to see here, so go on about your business. I won't interfere."

"That's a good idea, meatsack. You stay out of my way, and I won't make you eat your gallbladder. Nobody likes the taste of raw gallbladder."

He turned back to the record company man and pointed to the papers on the desk. "Now this contract with TicketsRUs will add a four-dollar facility maintenance fee to every ticket purchased."

"But we don't do any real maintenance on the facilities," the nebbish said, surprising me by showing a shred of soul.

"I don't care," the demon said. "It's a split between you and the vendor every time they purchase something. Most of these simpletons only go to one or two concerts a year, and they don't go back to the same venues, so they have no idea if the facility is being maintained or not." The demon and the record exec shared a good laugh, and the demon gave me a wide grin, baring his fangs.

"You know," the demon said, "the boss is very pleased with your progress. We're just a few steps away from controlling every step in the chain, from studio production, to distribution, to performance. A few more deals like this, and we'll get rid of live concerts altogether. Then all music will be consumed digitally, and we can control the music, and then we control whatever message we want to bury under the Auto-Tuned backbeats!"

"So…" the bald man said with a nervous grin, "the boss downstairs has noticed all the hard work I've been doing up here?"

"He has," the demon agreed. "He has indeed. He told me just last week that he's grooming you for a spot in his personal retinue when you come to work for us directly. But don't worry," the demon said quickly, holding up both hands, palms out, "you've got plenty more work here on Earth. We've got a couple of other people in your business to bring around to our way of thinking, and then we can start looking forward to internal advancement opportunities."

I looked at Prince. "Hell is full of middle managers?"

"Did you ever have a doubt, Bubba-baby?"

"I reckon not. I mean, I ain't never had what you might call a 'real job,' but I always figured that all that corporate double-speak was just modern-day Enochian."

"You got it, my supersize friend," Prince said. "Are you finally starting to pick up what I been laying down?"

"Yeah, I get it, but why did you suddenly start speaking in jive?"

"I watched *Luke Cage* while you were scrapping with the demon. I'm feeling all New Harlem Renaissance up in this mofo."

"You watched a whole season of a TV show during that fight?" Yeah, *that* was the part of my night I had trouble believing.

"Time moves differently in the spirit world, baby. Shall we go?" He waved his hand again, and I stepped through another glowing circle. Demons cutting deals with record executives—how much stranger could my night get?"

Chapter Ten

I DIDN'T HAVE TO WAIT LONG FOR THAT ANSWER. NO SOONER HAD Prince deposited me back in the studio, opened a brand new hole in the air, and stepped through with a little bow "goodbye" and a host of, I shit you not, white doves flying around him, but my next visitor arrived.

And what a friggin' entrance. Where my last two ghosts had stepped through a glowing portal in the sky, this one popped onto the scene in a flash of light, a thunder of pyro, and an Auto-Tuned shriek of pure, perfectly pitched adrenalized audio. I tried to look at the spectacle, but the light was so bright and so abrupt that all I got was a hint of a person standing backlit by a cacophony of colors before I had to close my eyes against the sensory overload. It helped a little, but I still had the afterimage of a human in a hoodie standing in silhouette against a wall of fireworks.

The noise died down a little, and I blinked my eyes to clear the stars from my vision. "What the ever-loving hell was that?" I asked.

"I am the Ghost of Music Yet to Come," came a lifeless, robotic voice. "I am music perfected. In my world, there are no missed notes. There are no skipped choruses. There are no lags in pitch. There are no off-key vocals. I am the Ghost of Music Polished."

"Sounds like you are the Ghost of a Pile of Shit," I said, wiping my eyes with the back of my hand. The room was slowly dimming down from a big ball of overlit glow, and I could see the ghost standing there, head bowed and hands folded in front of his crotch like a boy band just about to break out in the beginning of a shitty concert. He was a little dude, barely five-and-a-half feet tall, and that was counting the patent leather platform boots. He wore skinny leather pants, a belt with a rhinestone-studded Captain America shield, and a sparkly sweatshirt with the hood up, concealing his face.

"You are obviously not a Belieber," the ghost said, raising his face to show me a featureless white mask.

"I don't even know what that is, unless you've got a cold. If your nose is stopped up, then I get it. But I didn't think ghosts got allergies."

"A Belieber is one of the legion of Justin Bieber fans throughout the world. True Beliebers have embraced the musical revolution that is coming. True Beliebers have already prepared themselves for the coming musicopalypse."

"True Beliebers sound like a bag full of dumbass, and you ain't a whole lot different. Now what do you have to show me, Ghost of Music Yet to Suck?"

The ghost's voice went even more robotic, if that was possible, shifting to something between Robbie the Robot and Peter Frampton. "Resistance is futile, music fan. Your kind will be—"

"I swear on Johnny Cash's grave, if you say 'assimilated,' I will whoop your ass all the way back to the great beyond and figure this shit out for myself."

The ghost cocked its head to one side, kinda like a surprised pug, then said one word. "Assimilated."

I was honor-bound to do it. The Guy Code clearly states that if you say you're going to whoop somebody's ass if they do something, then they look you right in the eye and do that very thing, you are obliged to whoop their ass until your whole damn arm gets tired.

So I did. I put my head down and bull-rushed the little ghost, planning to smear him across the studio wall like a junebug on my truck windshield. But shit never seems to work out like I want it to, especially not in Alabama. Like most everything else bad about the state, I blame Nick Saban.

I got within a couple feet of the ghost, and all of a sudden he went from Terrible Music Fan #3 in this horror movie to Jet friggin' Li. He jumped straight up, full-on *Matrix* shit, pressed his hands to the ceiling, and flipped over backwards three times in midair, landing like a cat, only more graceful, on his feet behind me.

Of course, I had to peel my face out of the acoustical foam to see that he was still on his feet because I couldn't check my charge near in time and smacked face-first into the wall of the studio. I pushed off the wall, leaving a giant Bubba-shaped impression in the egg crate foam on the wall, and turned back to the little shithead.

"Okay, fine, we'll do this the slow, painful way. As opposed to the fast, painful way I had planned," I said as I stomped toward the ghost. Did I mention Jet Li? Yeah, those comparisons didn't end with him jumping all the way over my head. This time he didn't try to run, just stood there watching me approach, and when I got close, commenced to whooping my ass in a ridiculously efficient fashion.

I didn't even manage to get a punch off before I caught three quick kicks. One to each knee, then a spinning reverse thrust kick right in the gut. I dropped down, and the little bastard nailed me with three more quick side kicks to the face, followed by a jumping roundhouse kick to the temple that spun me all the way around and dropped me to my knees. I put my hands up to my head, and he rained kicks on my ribs. I dropped my elbows to protect my sides, and half a dozen quick punches landed on the back of my skull in about four seconds.

As far as ghosts went, this son of a bitch was *solid*. I had nothing. I couldn't even get to my feet without getting kicked in the head three or four times. Good for me my head is hard as Georgia granite, so after I got used to the sting, I could still mostly function. I shook off a couple of good shots to the face, then I just went all Frankenstein on his ass. I reached out and grabbed the front of that hoodie, hefted the little dude up over my head, and flung him across the studio, intending to bounce him off some acoustical foam this time.

Except ghosts are assholes. Magical assholes, too. Instead of taking his lumps like a human, or any other monster, really, this dick decided to just pass right through the wall without hurting himself at all. Apparently, ghosts get to decide when they want to be solid, like when they want to kick somebody in the head, and when they want to be all intangible, like when that somebody tries to throw them into a wall. Like I said, assholes.

So he flew right through the wall, which was kinda what I intended, only without the busted paneling and plaster dust that I had planned on. Then he floated back into the studio and flew over to stand right in front of me, hands on his hips like some kind of tiny Power Ranger.

"Want some more, asshole?"

"I'm the asshole?" the ghost asked, and the Auto-Tune was missing from its voice this time. "You try to solve every damn problem in the world with your fists or your guns, and *I'm* the asshole? Jesus wept, Bubba, when are you going to realize that not everything can be dealt with by beating the crap out of it or shooting it?"

"I know that!" I protested. "Some things you gotta set on fire." The ghost didn't look amused. Well, really, it didn't look anything, on account of that faceless mask, but I could tell by his posture that my joke was not going to be considered funny by any stretch.

"You might be the most colossally dense human being I have ever encountered, and I have been around for a very long time."

"Well, if you're gonna do something, might as well go all the way," I countered. "I mean, if you're gonna be stupid, go whole hog. Go full on Dan Quayle or Kanye stupid. No point in just being third-string stupid."

"Oh, don't worry. You are the Super Bowl MVP of stupid. Did you really think you could beat up a ghost? I'm a *ghost*. With all the crap that means. I walk through walls, pop out of dark places yelling 'boo!' and I cannot, ever, get my ass kicked. Dipshit." He muttered that last bit, but I still heard it.

"Now are we done? With the fighting, I mean. I've still got some shit to show you."

"Yeah, I reckon. I'm sorry, I just needed to blow off some steam."

"It's alright. Like I said, it ain't like you could hurt me unless I let you," he said, then reached up behind his head and dropped his hood. Long, golden yellow hair cascaded out around his shoulders, and I thought, *Great, I just got my ass beat by one of the Hanson brothers.*

Then he took off the mask, and I had to quickly reconsider my pronouns. This wasn't a little dude standing in front of me, having just beat my ass from pillar to post. This was a girl, about thirty years old, with brilliant blue eyes, a pixie smile, and long blonde hair.

"Hey," I said, realization hitting me. "I know you. You're that girl…"

"Kinda," the ghost said, walking over to a chair and folding both legs under her as she sat down. I never understood how girls do that, sit cross-legged almost anywhere. If I tried that, I'd break my fool neck. I just sat in the chair opposite her like a normal person. I gestured for her to go on, and she spoke again.

"I'm using her form because it's one you're used to seeing. She's not dead; I'm just the essence of the music in her. And even that's not dead, but it will be if you don't pay attention to what I'm showing you tonight and figure out what to do about it soon."

"No pressure," I grumbled.

"You've had it pretty easy this year," the ghost shot back. "You took care of your brother last fall, but everything you've gone after this year has been kinda small potatoes in comparison. Well, it's time to get back in the game, Bubba-boy. The Spirit of Music needs you."

"What am I supposed to do?" I asked. "I mean, look, this whole trip through musical memory lane has been cool, even if they weren't my memories, but I don't have any more of a clue what I'm supposed to do than I did when I left Nashville last night."

"Well, that's my job," she said. She stood up and held out a hand. "Are you ready to see what's in store for music if you fail?"

I wasn't sure I was. This whole night was a damn confusing ride, and I didn't know if I wanted to see any more. But if it gave me some clarity on what all these ghosts wanted me to do, I figured it was worth it.

I got up and took her hand, looking down at her bright blonde head. "I reckon I'm ready to go if you are."

She started to wave her hand in the air, but I reached out and stopped her. "We don't have to use the pyro to get there, do we? That shit gives me a headache."

"No," she said. "We can even skip the strobes, just this once." She opened a portal in the air, this one rimmed with blue-green light.

I took a deep breath and stepped through, wondering what I was going to see on the other side that told me how to save music from the music industry.

Chapter Eleven

I STEPPED OUT ONTO A BARREN FIELD WITH PILES OF UNRAKED leaves and a weather-beaten stage at one end. The whole place was deserted, but it was an enormous field, easily the size of a mid-sized college football stadium. I closed my eyes and could almost feel the energy of tens of thousands of people covering the grass, all jamming to blues, or bluegrass, or some kind of weed-infused jam band.

I walked toward the stage, and as I got right up to the front of it, I stepped on something hard under the carpet of brown leaves. I knelt down and brushed the leaves aside, feeling them crinkle under my touch and fall away to dust. Buried under years' worth of fallen leaves and grass clippings was a wooden rectangle, paint faded away to almost nothing, but still recognizable, if just barely. I looked at the sign laying there in the grass and rocked back to sit on my heels.

"GrooveFest?" I asked, turning the ghost. "This is where Groovefest used to happen? Man, I've heard about that festival for years but never made it out here. *Everybody* played here—Steve Earle, Doc, Earl, Emmylou, Bela Fleck, Nickel Creek…everybody who was anybody in bluegrass or Americana music played here. What happened to this joint?" I looked around again, and there was nothing to see. No chairs, no crowds, no musicians waiting in the wings—nothing.

"It shut down," the ghost said. "Too many artists got swept up in exclusive performance contracts and could only play in SuperSound venues, or SonicWorld concert halls, or some other joints that their record labels were in bed with, and the festival scene dried up because they couldn't book diverse acts. The big venue management companies started their own festivals and stocked them with their headliners, and that ran the little guys into the ground."

"That sucks," I said. "This whole place was built out of musicians coming together to honor one of their own fallen friends."

"I know," she said. "This place saw some amazing collaborations over the years. Doc Watson and Earl Scruggs playing together in their 80s."

"A New Grass Revival Reunion," I said.

"Pete Seeger playing with his grandson in The Mammals," she added.

"John Paul Jones wandering on stage to pick with Chris Thile," I said. "And now it's gone."

"Now it's gone," she agreed.

"Shit," I said.

"I couldn't have said it better," the ghost said with a nod.

I walked up the stairs to the side of the stage and looked out, staring over an expanse easily twice the size of the field at UGA, where I played college ball. I pictured it in my mind's eye all full of people, men and women of all ages scattered into the reserved seats down front. Moms and dads, suburban yuppies settled in right next to mountain men and farm women, every one of them saving up for months to take a family music vacation. Then back behind that, I could almost see the general admission lawn with blankets and bag chairs and little mini-campsites set up as far as the eye could see.

"Yep, it looked about like that," came the ghost's voice from beside me.

"I didn't hear you come up," I said.

"Ghost, remember?" She grinned up at me.

I let out a sigh. "What's next?"

"If you're ready to find out, we can go," the girl said, waving her hand. A hole opened up in the air, but there wasn't any golden or purple light around this one. It was just a gray, featureless hole in the air, with all the color sucked out of it. Kinda like this place. I took a deep breath and stepped through.

Right into a cemetery. "Hey, isn't this supposed to be the last thing I see before I wake up and go buy a turkey for Tiny Tim?"

The ghost smiled up at me and took my hand. "Yeah, but in that story the Ghost of the Future didn't talk, and it's a lot harder to make fun of you when I don't talk, so I like this way better."

She led me through the tombstones, and I read the names as I passed. It was a friggin' Who's Who of music legends, all recently passed on. I saw BB King, Lemmy Kilmeister, David Bowie, Prince, Johnny Cash with June Carter Cash right next to him, Doc Watson just a couple of stones down from his boy Merle, finally reunited after the father of the flat pickers passed on. I ran my fingers across the top of Stevie Ray Vaughan's headstone, Natalie and Nat King Cole's, Glenn Frey's guitar-shaped monument, and then a string of rocks commemorating legends like Hank, Merle, and Waylon.

I didn't even notice when I left the cemetery of musical geniuses and ended up walking through a real country graveyard. There were probably twelve rows of markers, about nine across, behind a white clapboard church with a gleaming white cross atop an old steeple. If anything in the world ever screamed "country church," this was the place. I walked through the rows of Smiths, Barnhills, and Rathfields for a few long minutes before something started drawing me to a back corner of the cemetery. I walked up and down the rows until something in my gut told me I was in the right place, and I stopped in front of a plot with no stone, just a small commemorative marker the funeral home left behind.

I looked down at the little gray metal square holding a handwritten card, proclaiming this the final resting place of one George Buford Scatlin, of Pine Lick, West Virginia, born February 8, 1929, died November 2, 2016. There was no stone, no monument marking the resting place of one of the greatest fiddle players of all time, just a little chunk of tin and paper that would probably be destroyed the first time the groundskeeper rolled by on his big old riding Snapper mower.

I knelt down beside the almost unmarked grave and cried, right there in the grass. I cried for the kind old man dying alone in a nursing home without anyone knowing who he really was or what he had meant to so many people. I cried for all the people I'd lost in my life that I hadn't let know what they meant to me before it was too late, and I cried for the soul of the world, a little bit darker without the magical music of Professor Fiddle. I ran out of tears after a bit, but I still stayed there on my knees feeling the dark red clay seep into the knees of my pants, thinking that I could hear, faint as an old train whistle buried underneath the cold November wind, the strains of "Orange Blossom Special" dancing along the mountaintops.

I looked up at the little ghost and said, "Why did you bring me here? Why show me this? I know he's dying. I mean, shit, we all get old, if we're lucky enough, but why did I need to see *this*?"

"I can't tell you what to take from it, Bubba. I can just tell you that bullets and fists don't solve every problem."

"Shit, you think I don't know that? That's why I carry swords and fire." I managed a laugh, trying not to blow snot-bubbles when I did. I don't know why the old man's grave hit me so hard. Maybe it was the lack of a mark. To many damn hunters I know ended up in a hole in the woods somewhere instead of all laid out in a nice cemetery, but even they got some kind of marker, even if it was just a little cairn of stones with a bullet on top of it. But Buford didn't get any of that. He just got tossed in a hole somewhere the grass will get mowed, but not even a rock to mark his passing. It hit me wrong, somehow. This man dedicated his life to bringing joy to people; he deserved a more fitting tribute.

I stood up and looked at the little ghost. "I reckon you've got one more thing to show me?"

She gave me a look with a question mark on the end of it.

"This shit always comes in threes, right? There's three of y'all, each showing me three things?"

"You're almost right, there's actually a couple more things, but brace yourself—this next one ain't pretty." She snapped her fingers, and I was sitting in my truck. Not bad, as far as transitions go, but the view was a little wrong. Then I understood—I was sitting in the passenger seat. Just as I started to slide over behind the wheel, the driver's door opened, and I got into the truck.

Well, it was kinda me. It was me if my balls got cut off and the entire offensive line of the Pittsburgh Steelers held me down and shaved me. I looked over at the man sliding his fat ass in behind the wheel and was absolutely horrified at what I saw there. I wore a blue dress shirt, a pair of khakis, and a sport coat. That wasn't the worst thing in the world, I'd worn crap like that before when I was impersonating an FBI Agent going to a funeral.

No, something terrified me even more than the lack of beard, which exposed all the failings in my chin that I started hiding in high school, as soon as I could grow a beard. The absolute worst part, the thing that almost sent me screaming into the void, was my haircut.

I had a haircut. And not one of these "cut a couple inches off the end of the ponytail" haircuts that I get every few months when I start to sit on my hair. No, this was a "I have a real job, where people give a shit what I look like" haircut. Couple that with the clothes, the shave, and the shoes, which were a pair of penny loafers, and it all added up to Bubba having a legitimate job, with a boss that wasn't, you know, the Pope.

I watched myself as "I" reached up and pulled out a laminated ID card tucked underneath the sun visor. There was a picture of me on it, smiling like a moron and wearing an even worse necktie. "Rothsteen Security" was written across the top, above my picture, and below it said "Supervisor" in big red letters. I wasn't just a Rent-A-Cop, I was a Rent-A-Cop middle manager.

I sat there, my mouth hanging open as this Bizarro Bubba closed the truck door, put on his seatbelt, and cranked up the truck. I felt the familiar rumble under my seat, then Opposite Me leaned forward and flicked on the radio. Instead of XM Outlaw Country, or a Sturgill Simpson CD, or even some Chris Stapleton blaring out of the speakers, there was a steady *thump-thump-thump* of a hip-hop beat with some redneck rapping over top of it.

I spun around in my seat. "Bro country? What kind of friggin' horror movie is this where you think I'm ever gonna let damn Luke Bryan on the radio in my truck? That shit can't stand, little Casper-ette. This shit cannot stand."

"This ain't the worst, Bubba. You think this is bad, let's return to the original scene of the crime." She snapped her fingers one more time, and she wasn't lying—we were back at the place where I first started bitching about the state of music today and how it wasn't like it used to be. We were standing on the sidewalk out front of the most holy place in the history of country music—the Ryman Auditorium.

"This can't be good," I muttered. "Of course, ain't nothing you've shown me yet been good, so why should anything change now?"

"Well, I ain't here to show you the sidewalk, so let's get on inside," my escort said, walking up the steps and passing through the door like it wasn't even there.

I stood for a second, hung up once again on why she didn't fall through the steps, until she stuck her head and shoulders through the door and said, "Come on, dumbass, it's about to start!"

I did as I was told. My default position on about everything might be "contrary," but she was the one driving the bus, so I had to hope she knew where we were going. I walked up the stone steps and passed through those hallowed doors one more time. It seemed fitting, I thought as I passed through the wood. After all, I was walking back from the Ryman Christmas Concert when I started bitching about all this.

The ushers were passing out programs that read "2020 Country Music Hall of Fame Induction Ceremony," and my blood ran cold. I didn't think I wanted to see who was on the list, but I had to. I knew it was going to be brutal, but it got nothing but worse when Jeff Foxworthy came out to emcee.

After ten minutes of him trotting out his tired "you might be a redneck" schtick, I was about ready to puke in the aisles, but then he dropped the real bombshell on me.

"Please join me tonight in honoring the latest round of inductees into the Country Music Hall of Fame," Foxworthy said from the stage. The crowd applauded politely.

"Luke Bryan!" The crowd clapped like mindless drones.

"Florida Georgia Line!" One asshole actually screamed like he cared, and the drones clapped even more.

"Jake Owen!" Even more applause, and I think I saw one woman fan herself a little.

"And last, but certainly not least, here to kick things off, our first inductee of the night, joined on stage by Ludacris—Jason Aldean!" The crowd sprang to its feet, screaming and jumping up and down.

"The fact that there is a group in which Jason Aldean is considered not 'the least' is damn depressing," I said to the ghost.

"You don't like mixing rap and country?" she asked.

"I like hip-hop. I like old-school Nas, I like old Biggie, and I like a lot of Jay-Z. But no, I don't like hicking up rap with country licks, and I don't like rapping up country with hip-hop choruses. It's like dropping a Charlie Parker solo in the middle of "Night on Bald Mountain." I just can't hang." I was walking down the aisle to the stage, looking around for anything I could do to stop the shitshow that was about to hit the stage. My incorporeal hands wouldn't unplug the amps, no matter how much I tried. I even tried to trip Aldean as he walked to the stage, but he just passed right through me.

Then I saw him. I caught sight of the same sonofabitch I saw in the Paragon Records office. "I shoulda known," I muttered. "This shit stinks to high Heaven of demon." He was standing off to one side of the stage, grinning to beat the band at the Hell he had wrought. He saw me from across the way and smiled, giving me a little bow and a wave, then gesturing to the stage as if to say, "Look what I did."

I couldn't hold back anymore. All the anger I'd felt this whole time about old Buford dying alone and penniless, about the festival site shutting down, about *my damn haircut.* All those things all bubbled up inside me, and with a demon grinning at me from across the stage, I screamed, and the world turned white around me.

Chapter Twelve

I SAT BOLT UPRIGHT, FLIPPING OVER THE COT I WAS LAYING ON AND smacking my nose on the floor. I pushed myself up to my feet and ran out the front of the studio, not even bothering to make sure I had on shoes. I was all the way to my truck before I noticed I was still fully dressed. I hadn't undressed when I laid down, thinking something weird might happen in the middle of the night. In my wildest damn dreams, I never expected to end up as the star in a remake of *Scrooged*, only set in Muscle Shoals.

I yanked open the back door of my truck, wracking my brain for what kind of weapon I could use on a record executive who's in cahoots with a demon. Or just wondering if I had enough quicklime to keep the body from stinking when I threw it down the nearest abandoned well. That's the great thing about the rural South—there's almost always a burned-out farmhouse within a couple miles where you can find an abandoned well to toss the bodies in if you know how to look for it.

I stuck my head into the crew cab of the truck and staggered back like I'd been hit in the face with a damn frying pan. To tell you the truth, that's about what I felt like, only without the bloody nose. I blinked, wiped the last of the sleep out of my eyes, and looked back in the truck. Then I closed the door, wiped my eyes again, and opened the door. It was still there.

Laying on the back seat of my truck, still covered in the dust from the corner of my room, was a beat to shit old guitar case. There was a cracked red vinyl sticker of the Rolling Stones lips, another one of a tie-dyed Allman Brother mushroom, and a blue-and-white rectangle that just said "My Name Is" with "Robbie" scribbled under it in red Sharpie.

I looked around, but there weren't any ghosts to be seen. Except for all the ones hanging out in that damn guitar case, I reckon. I even got down on my hands and knees and looked under the truck, but there wasn't anything there. Just my truck, right where I parked it the afternoon before, still locked up 'til I clicked the little button thingy on my keys, but in the back seat was a guitar case I hadn't touched since the day my mama walked out the door.

The last time I played that guitar was at a school talent show. I didn't win, but I didn't embarrass myself, either, and that was the sticker still hanging on by two decades' worth of dry-rotted adhesive and dust bunnies, right there on the neck of that case. I started to reach for the case, then pulled my hand back.

I looked around. "How the hell did y'all do that?" I called out.

Nobody answered.

"I'm talking to you, Hank!" I hollered louder this time.

Nothing.

"Goddammit, you little purple ghost, how did you even *find* this damn thing?" I shouted.

Nobody said a word. Nothing from Prince, nothing from Hank, nothing from the strange little blonde girl, and nothing at all from the Spirit of Music.

"Well, that the hell am I supposed to do with this?" I asked the world.

The world didn't answer. The world is an asshole sometimes.

I leaned into the truck and looked the case over. I still didn't touch it, but I got so damn close to it I think we were married in three states. It was my guitar case, all right. No damn question about that. I finally stretched out one finger, the pinky finger on my left hand, just in case it got bit off, or disintegrated, or something. I figured I could live without my pinky, or my ring finger, but I need my trigger finger and my communication finger was too much. My pinky was pretty much only good for picking stubborn boogers and hitting the "delete" key when I screwed up typing something. But I didn't need the left one for that, either, so I figured I was good.

I tapped the case with my pinky, and nothing happened. Well, I felt the fake leather surface, and it sounded like somebody tapping on a wood guitar case. I knocked on it harder, still using my left hand in case there was some kind of weird ghost hand-rotting disease. I needed to keep my right hand. I never got good at shooting lefty, and Bertha is an unforgiving mistress.

Nothing happened. I picked it up, and it felt just like it did when I was a kid. Lighter because I was bigger, but it was just my old guitar case. I pulled it out of the truck and walked around to the back. I dropped the tailgate and laid the case crosswise along my newly created redneck table. I flipped the latches on the case and raised the lid.

My guitar wasn't there. There was a guitar there, but it wasn't the battered old Sears & Roebuck guitar that I learned on. What was nestled in my old battered case was a brilliant blue Gibson acoustic with mother of pearl inlays on the fretboard and a black leather neck strap laid across it in the case. I'd never seen that guitar before, except in my dreams. This was the guitar I always wanted when I was a kid and used to play, and now it was right in front of me, laying in my old case.

There was a piece of paper folded up and tucked behind the strings. I pulled it out and unfolded it, seeing my mama's handwriting for the first time in a couple decades. I took a deep breath, pushed down all the anger, and guilt, and feelings of betrayal that came every time I thought about my mama, and started to read.

"Robbie," she wrote. "I know you won't understand what is happening, but my leaving has nothing to do with you. It doesn't even have anything to do with your daddy, although his refusal to abandon the life of a Hunter has set things in motion that he doesn't know, and I can't tell him. Just please know that I love you and Jason more than life itself, and I hope that someday I'll be able to come home and be with my most precious boys again. Until that day, please play this guitar and think of me. I had some money tucked away for a rainy day. Well, it's pouring now, but I wanted to leave this for my darling boy to remember me by before I had to go. Please try to think of me fondly, when you think of me. Love, Mom."

I didn't know I was crying until I saw a tear splash onto the body of the guitar. I picked it up, slid the strap over my head and one shoulder, and settled the body against my belly. I expected it to ride high on me since I was a lot skinnier when Mama left, but somehow the strap was adjusted just right for me. I looked down in the case and grabbed a pick, giving the strings a little strum to see how out of tune the thing was.

It was beautiful. It sounded like it had just been set up by a damn master luthier, and the strings felt light under my fingers, not stiff and tight like I'd expect from a guitar sitting for twenty years played by hands that ain't held an instrument in almost that long. I looked around the room, trying to see if this was another ghosty trick, but it looked to be around eight in the morning, and all I could see around me told me this was real, it was really my guitar that my mama had left for me when she left. And now it looked like she didn't just leave because she was pissed off at me and my pop. I pushed all that aside for another time, most likely a time with a lot more liquor and self-recrimination.

I put the guitar back in the case and cleared up my sleeping area. I needed a plan if I was going to take down a demon sticking his nose into the affairs of a small recording studio in Alabama.

I had the beginnings of a plan starting to formulate when Billy walked into the studio about an hour later. He looked about like I felt, with bags under his eyes and the kind of look a man wears on his face when he's about to lose his life's work. But at least he brought coffee and doughnuts.

I reached for a cup in the tray he was holding, and he turned it away, presenting a different cup to me. "Unless you like a little Irish coffee for your pick-me-up, you want to drink the other one."

"I don't mind a little dram no more than the next fella," I said, "but it might be for the best if I stay clear-headed today."

"Did you see any ghosts?" he asked.

"Yeah," I replied. Billy started, like he didn't think I was going to find anything.

"Yeah," I continued. "This place is haunted as shit. I don't know what you could possibly do to get this place clean of spirits, but whatever that is, it's going to take a lot of time. If I was you, I'd take the place off the market until I could get some exorcists in here and send the spirits packing."

Billy sighed and sat down on the bench sitting in front of the upright piano a few feet away. "I wish that was an option, Bubba, I really do. I hate the thought of shutting down Celebrity Studios as much as you do, or worse, seeing it turn into some kind of computerized hit factory like every damn place else these days. But a man's gotta eat, and I can't keep pouring money into this place if nobody can record here because of the ghosts. So I've got a man from New York coming in today at noon to make me an offer on the place, ghosts and all. He says he ain't superstitious. If it's any kind of decent offer, I've got to take it, Bubba. I got kids, man, and they deserve to be able to go to college."

"I understand," I said, understanding more than I really wanted to. "Well, at least let me try to get some things going around here to bring the spirits some kind of peace before you sell. If this old boy ain't superstitious, he probably won't do anything to lay anybody to rest, either."

"That seems fair," Billy said. "I don't want nobody to suffer because of me, even if they are dead. I'm gonna go to my office and get the books in order so I've got something to show this man when he gets here." He turned and walked to the door.

I called out to him just before his hand touched the doorknob. "Hey Billy?"

"Yeah?" He turned around.

"How'd you find this dude? I thought you said the offer you had on the property was contingent on getting rid of the ghosts."

"It was," he said. "But this morning around six-thirty, some dude called me out of the blue and made an offer, and he didn't seem like he gave a shit if there were ghosts or not. I even mentioned the fact that the place is haunted, but he didn't care."

Yeah, I didn't figure he did. Especially not if he was a skinny little bastard with expensive suits and horns growing out of his head. "Fair enough," I said, and Billy continued on his way out of the room. I looked around the room and said, "Okay, ghosts, I might need just a little bit of help, but I think I've got a plan. Y'all gather your dead asses around here and let's get to work."

I felt a chill in the air, and even though I couldn't see them, I knew my posse had arrived.

Chapter Thirteen

ME AND MY ETHEREAL ROADIES HAD EVERYTHING SET UP BY THE time the record company asshole showed up with his pet lawyer in tow. I remembered them both from my trips through the world on the wings of a ghost, but even without that, it was easy to tell who was the demon. He was the one with thousand-dollar wingtips. Without my ghost guide to pull the scales from my eyes, all I could see was his human suit, but every inch of him screamed "dick."

He wore his long brown hair pulled back in a shiny ponytail, and he was perfectly groomed from head to toe. His suit fit like a glove, with charcoal pinstripes and pleats in his pants so sharp you could shave with them. A black dress shirt lay beneath his red silk tie, and his pocket square almost glowed on his chest. A narrow goatee protruded from his chin, taking after his boss's signature look, and his dark eyes showed flecks of demonic yellow when he smiled. And he smiled a lot, showing off perfect teeth and perfectly angled cheekbones.

He must have used up a lot of demonic juice crafting a human guise to absolute perfection, but I guess if he could bring about the downfall of the entire country music industry, the rewards would far outstrip the costs. His brilliant appearance made his partner look all the more bland, wearing the same boring brown suit I saw him in during my dream walking. The little guy stepped forward and shook Billy's hand.

"Good morning, gentlemen," he said, and his nasally voice grated on me instantly. I could totally see how this guy probably got his ass beat every day in middle school. And not even by jocks like me. This was the guy that the other nerds beat up. "My name is Edwin Vaxred, and I am here on behalf of Paragon Records. As I said on the telephone this morning, we are looking to bring more of our production in-house so that we can more closely control the quality of the recordings we are putting into the market."

"Good to meet you, Mr. Vaxrel. I'm Billy Ricks, and I own Celebrity Recording Studios."

"Who's your friend?" the demon asked, giving me a smile that made every hair on my arms stand up. I wasn't sure this dude remembered me from the dreams, but he sure as shit knew there was more to me than he expected.

"I'm Robert Brabham," I said, stepping forward and shaking hands with Vaxrel and the demon. The demon's hand was cold, like shaking hands with a block of ice, but I didn't let on. I might have made sure to have a rosary that Uncle Father Joe gave me wrapped around my wrist with the crucifix buried in my palm when we shook, too.

Burning demon flesh does *not* smell like pot roast. It smells more like rotted pot roast braised with sulfur and elephant shit. But the look on the demon's face when that crucifix burned itself into his palm was worth a little stink. He didn't pull away, there was no way he was going to give that much ground, but he looked me right in the eye, and I could read his intentions there as plain as if they were written on his forehead in Sharpie.

"You know me, human?" he asked, and his voice was no longer the smooth human tone that he used when he walked into the room. This was the rasp of a demon that's spent eons screaming at human souls, the voice of a torturer, the voice of a monster.

"Yeah, I know you, horn-boy. And I'm here to tell you that you ain't getting this studio. I've got a counteroffer on the table to buy this place, and you're shit out of luck."

"I don't think so, mortal. My verbal contract with Mr. Ricks is very, very, binding, and he can't sell the studio to anyone else without giving me a chance to match the offer."

I turned to Billy. "What the hell did you agree to with this dude? All you did was talk to him once."

"I don't remember, man. He woke me up when he called, and all I remember is he said he was from New York, and he wanted to buy the place. I told him to come on down here, and we'd see if we could work something out."

"And I mentioned an opportunity clause to match any offers you received in the meantime, did I not?" Vaxrel prodded.

"Yeah, maybe…" Bully's voice trailed off as he looked from me, to the lawyer, to the demon, and back again. "I don't know, man. Like I said, I got kids, man."

"Shit, Billy…" I turned to the demon. "I want a shot at it."

"And I want a pony, human, but that's my job—to keep you flesh-toting morons from getting what you want. You want to buy this place, you need to offer me something worthwhile to walk away."

I wracked my brain and couldn't think of anything a demon would want more than chance at destroying country music and ripping out a good chunk of the heart of the South. I paced a little, trying to get a good idea to drop out of my noggin, but nothing was coming.

"If you don't have anything to sweeten the pot, mortal, then I think it's time for Mr. Ricks here to sign some papers. After all, what could you even offer me that's worth more than the soul of an entire region?"

"What about the soul of a Templar Knight?" I asked, half a second before the thought was even fully formed.

The demon's head snapped up, and the grin vanished from his face. "What?"

"You want quantity or quality, pal? I'm an official Monster Hunter of the Holy Roman Catholic Church. I'm as close to a Templar Knight as it gets nowadays. That oughta be worth something, right?" I wasn't being exactly truthful. I was the official Hunter for the region, but Joe was the actual Templar. I wasn't much for supervision, so I kinda told Church leadership to kiss my ass too many times to be a full-on Knight myself. But I was the closest thing to a Templar they were gonna find in Muscle Shoals, Alabama, that morning, least as far as they knew. That's the good thing about only being kinda Knight-adjacent—I can still lie like a son of a bitch when I need to.

"You've got a deal, human. You give me your soul, and you can buy the studio." The demon stuck out his hand to shake on it, but I held both of mine in the air.

"Slow down there, Speed Racer," I said. "You want my soul, you gotta do it old school. You're gonna have to win it."

The demon's eyes narrowed. "Win it?"

"You ever heard the song 'The Devil Went Down to Georgia'?" I asked.

"You want to play me for it? And whoever plays the best song wins?"

"The whole shooting match," I confirmed. "My soul, the studio, the whole mess. You in?"

He looked thoughtful for a long moment, then started to shake his head. I could feel the moment slipping away, almost see the deliveries of new computerized Auto-Tune equipment pulling up to the studio doors. I did the only thing I could think of, I reached deep into my negotiating toolbox, and I started to cluck.

"What are you doing?" the demon asked.

"I'm - cluck - not doing - cluck - anything," I said. "Do you - cluck - hear a chicken - cluck - in here anywhere?"

"What?" the demon looked baffled.

"Well - cluck - I can't imagine that a real - cluck - demon would be - cluck - afraid of a human. So you - cluck - must really be - cluck - a chicken."

His face went about eight shades of red, and he glared at me, yellow eyes shining through his human mask. "You're on, redneck. And you shall know torment the likes of which you've never seen once I get you into the pits."

"I doubt that," I said. "One, I don't plan to lose. And two, Skeeter once made me watch three seasons of *Gilmore Girls* over one unholy weekend a few years back. Let me tell you, there literally wasn't enough alcohol in Georgia to make that pain go away."

"Well, then, Bubba, it is, as you humans say, *on*."

"As we humans say," I said, "come get some."

The demon stepped into the middle of the studio and waved his hands in the air. Four more copies of himself appeared out of thin air and took up positions all around the studio. One strapped on a big Fender fretless bass, one grabbed a telecaster from a rack, another sat behind the drums, and the last one stood behind a keyboard. The demon himself magicked a Gibson Jet Black Les Paul out of thin air, and they lit into a song like nothing I'd ever heard. It started off with a simple blues riff, then shifted into a little poppy thing, then transitioned into old-school rock n' roll shifting slowly into a metal guitar solo that almost made me cry, it was so technically perfect.

They played a good eight-minute song, bounding and dancing notes around the room like they were skipping rocks across a creek. Not a one of them ever missed a note. Everything they played was so technically perfect, it was like watching a master class in how to play musical instruments. They played until I was sitting there breathless, then the lead demon spun that black Les Paul up into the air over his head and brought it crashing down to splinters on the floor in front of him.

He waved his hands in the air again, and the other demons vanished, their essences flowing back into him like smoke. He took a little bow, then grinned at me. "I believe that is what you call a mic drop."

"That was pretty good, pal. But now let me show you what music really feels like."

I walked to the middle of the room and picked up my old guitar case. I flipped open the latches and pulled out that blue guitar. I ran my fingers over the strings and nestled the guitar against my body. I ran my hand up and down the neck and let myself drift back in time, back to when we all lived together—me, Pop, Jase, and Mama. I put the pick to the strings and plucked out a few notes, turning the pegs to make sure she was as in tune as I could get her.

I looked up at the demon, and I started to sing.

"Amazing Grace, how sweet the sound,

Tha-at saved a wretch like me.

I once was lost, but now, I'm found.

Was blind, but now I see."

My fingers slipped, and my voice cracked, and the demon just sat there grinning.

"You know, son, just because it worked out okay in a song, doesn't mean you should actually *put* your soul on the line in a musical battle against a creature born of magic who carries around his own backup band. But don't worry, after the first thousand years or so, you hardly even feel the whips."

I just smiled back at him and said, "Thanks, I knew I was forgetting something." I looked up at the booth window. "Y'all ready?"

A light flipped on in the previously pitch dark control room, and I watched Skeeter, Joe, Amy, and the one person I never thought I'd see again in my life walk out the door, then they all trooped into the studio and picked up instruments. Amy sat down behind the drum kit, twirling the sticks to calm her nerves. I knew she hadn't sat behind a kit since she was a teenager and her daddy taught her how to play. Her dad left her his drum kit when he passed, and it sits in her garage now. It's all set up, and she'll polish it once in a while, but I've never seen her even touch a stick.

Joe picked up a Fender Stratocaster, knocked it into tune in seconds, and let fly with a little blues riff that would have made Jimi Hendrix smile. Skeeter picked up a battered old P-bass and plucked a couple chords. I remembered him playing bass in the jazz band in school. Like there weren't enough reasons for people to beat him up. He was black, gay, and skinny as hell, then he went and joined the jazz band on top of it. Even with me to back him up, I wonder how he survived.

Then a dark-haired woman I hadn't seen in over a year and thought I never would again walked in, looked at me for a quick second, and walked over to an old Hammond B-3 sitting in the corner. She blew the dust off the keys, fired up the Leslie amp sitting next to it, and sat down.

I smiled back up at the demon and said, "I forgot my band. How silly of me." Then I nodded to Amy, and she counted us in. This time, when we ripped into the first verse of "Amazing Grace," it wasn't a dirge, it was a praise song, shouting to the heavens about the love we found in God, no matter what we had done in our lives.

We moved into the second verse, and Mama leaned forward and started to harmonize with me. We sang together for the first time in better than twenty years, and it started to feel like all the old wounds we'd caused each other were finally getting cleaned out and healed.

"'Twas grace that taught my heart to fear.
And grace my fears relieved.
How precious did that grace appear
The hour I first believed."

The demon looked a lot less sure of himself as we moved into the third verse. I dropped out of the rhythm guitar and concentrated on just singing, just pouring out every bit of emotion I'd ever felt in a church, or at a concert, which are about the same damn thing to me most of the time, and I felt my heart swell with emotion as I sang.

"When we've been there ten thousand years
Bright shining as the sun
We've no less days to sing God's praise
Then when we first begun."

I stood up for the last verse, and everybody stopped playing and stepped up to surround me. Even Billy pushed his chair off the wall and stood with us in a semicircle, singing a cappella gospel and flinging it right in the face of the demon and his lawyer, telling them without ever using the words that they could go back to Hell because we had God and music on our side. Mama stepped forward and took my hand in hers. I didn't look at her. I couldn't. But I could sing with her, and with the rest of my family, one last verse.

"Amazing grace, how sweet the sound
That saved a wretch like me.

I once was lost, but now I'm found.
Was blind, but now I see."

Those final notes hung in the air, and the demon hung his head. He just nodded once and started for the door.

I picked up the microphone in front of me, stand and all, and tossed it to land at his feet. "*That's* a mic drop, bitch."

Epilogue

WE STOOD IN THE MIDDLE OF THE ROOM, LAUGHING AND DRINKING beers that Billy pulled from a little fridge in the control room. There was a lot of hugs, and a fair amount of back-slapping, and finally after a few minutes, I walked over to where my mother sat on the piano bench. I held out a beer to her, but she shook her head.

"I never was much for beer, Robbie."

"I know," I said. "I just didn't know how else to come talk to you."

"You could have just walked up and said, 'Hey Mama'."

"That's way too easy," I replied, and we both smiled.

We sat there in silence for a moment, then she said, "I see you found the guitar I left you."

"Yeah, I found it today. I ain't opened that case since the day you left, but it was in the back of my truck this morning when I went out looking for a gun."

"Did you pack it?" Mama asked.

"No, but that kinda thing happens to me a lot. I reckon Hank Williams put it there last night."

"It says a lot about the time I spent with your father that I'm just not going to ask about that," she said.

"Yeah, I reckon it does."

Silence fell between us again, then Mama asked, "Now what?"

"What do you mean, now what?"

"Now what happens here? From what I heard, you now have the right to buy a recording studio in Alabama."

"Well, technically I do, but I think I'm gonna let the Catholic Church buy it instead and turn it into a museum of southern music. I talked to Joe, and he said they can use it to raise money for old pickers that don't have good insurance to cover their end-of-life expenses. 'Cause some of those old boys didn't get good record contracts, or haven't sold much in a long time, and they're pretty broke now."

"That sounds like a good idea, son."

"I'm glad you came, Mama. I wasn't sure when Skeeter told me about it..."

"I was in the car with Skeeter, Robbie. 'Not sure' is an understatement."

"Well, I mighta said some things that were less than kind."

"I could understand that," she replied.

"But what I don't understand is how were you there in the first place," I said.

"How was I at Skeeter's?" Mama replied.

"Yeah."

"I was looking for you. We didn't part on good terms last year, and..."

You know that feeling when you're talking to somebody and they trail off, and you know that there's another shoe, and it's about to drop right on your damn head? Yeah, I had that feeling right then.

Mama looked at me and said, "Son, I know I walked out on you and your daddy a long time ago without any explanation, but there was a whole lot more going on than I could tell you then, and I'm probably going to cause all kinds of trouble telling you now, but here goes—"

That *thud* off in the distance? That was a shoe. And it sounded like it was going to be a big one.

My mother looked at me, then the air around her *shimmered* with lavender light and white sparkles, and when the light faded, she looked almost exactly the same. Except her features were a little more angular, her hair had more luster, and her ears were very, very pointy. Like *Lord of the Rings* pointy.

Like, "my mother is an elf" pointy.

"Robbie, I need your help." My elf-mom looked at me with tears welling in the corners of her eyes. "I know I don't deserve it, but it's a matter of life and death. And not just for me, but for your sister, too."

A sister? Well, shit.

Afterword

THIS IS MORE OF A SUGGESTED LISTENING LIST THAN AN AFTERWORD, but if you catch me in a bar sometime and want to know, I'll tell you the true-life stories about the sights Bubba saw in his travels. At least half of them are true stories, and way too many people in this story are built loosely around my family members.

But this much I do believe to be true - there are still people out there making amazing music, and here are a few of them you might have heard of, and some you might not have. Either way, if you give them a listen, or a few nickels, then awesome.

Check these folks out -
David Childers
Jonesalee
Doubting Thomas Band
Sturgill Simpson
The Waybacks (Merlefest Album Hour recordings)
Chris Thile
Nickel Creek
Doc & Merle Watson
The Avett Brothers
The Overmountain Men
Jason Isbell
Reckless Kelly (live "Break My Heart Tonight")
Laura Love ("Amazing Grace" on *Octoroon*)

And take every chance you get to support local musicians and the places that produce live music.

About the Author

John G. Hartness is a teller of tales, a righter of wrong, defender of ladies' virtues, and some people call him Maurice, for he speaks of the pompatus of love. He is also the best-selling author of EPIC-Award-winning series The Black Knight Chronicles from Bell Bridge Books, a comedic urban fantasy series that answers the eternal question "Why aren't there more fat vampires?" In July of 2016. John was honored with the Manly Wade Wellman Award by the NC Speculative Fiction Foundation for Best Novel by a North Carolina writer in 2015 for the first Quincy Harker novella, Raising Hell.

In 2016, John teamed up with a pair of other publishing industry ne'er-do-wells and founded Falstaff Books, a publishing company dedicated to pushing the boundaries of literature and entertainment.

In his copious free time John enjoys long walks on the beach, rescuing kittens from trees and getting caught in the rain. An avid Magic: the Gathering player, John is strong in his nerd-fu and has sometimes been referred to as "the Kevin Smith of Charlotte, NC." And not just for his girth.

Want to know what's new
And coming soon from
Falstaff Books?

Try This Free Ebook Sampler
http://bit.ly/falstaffsampler

Follow the link.
Download the file.
Transfer to your e-reader, phone, tablet,
watch, computer, whatever.
Enjoy.

www.ingramcontent.com/pod-product-compliance
Lightning Source LLC
Chambersburg PA
CBHW030548310726
48979CB00010B/2080/J

* 9 7 8 1 9 4 6 9 2 6 2 6 5 *